THE GOOD DEAD

AL SIM

Published by Underground Voices
www.undergroundvoices.com
Editor contact: Cetywa Powell
Proof reader: Abbie Waters

Cover Design: Harrison Sim
Photography: Martín Montaño-Pilch
Artwork: Olivia Sim

ISBN: 978-0-9988923-1-3

Printed in the United States of America.

THE GOOD DEAD

Part I:
This Could Be Bad

Chapter 1

I wish I still had the map my uncle made for me. Even done in his shaky hand as he approached death his work was beautiful. Or at least to my eyes. Maybe no one else would agree. But I saw something more than just roads and arroyos and hills in the contours of those lines scrawled in red ink across the white hospital stationary. Something vivid and startling. Life was impressed into them. Like petroglyphs on the rock of a canyon wall.

But that map is long gone. And so is the day when I held it in my hand as I bumped across the dirt roads in the backcountry. I have a strong memory of being bent over that map after stopping where a road split off from the one I was on. I had lost my place in my uncle's depiction of the terrain and wanted to reorient myself before I continued on.

That was when I heard a motor approaching from over a rise up ahead. I had been following a fresh set of tire tracks. So I already knew someone else was out there. Whoever went before me would have to come out again and in the backcountry there are never many ways you can go. The way out is often to retrace your way in. So I half-expected to encounter whoever made those fresh tracks.

But when I heard that other vehicle I became wary. And I couldn't say why. This was back in the days before it was easy to get yourself killed out along the border by stumbling into the wrong people. Back then you just kept to yourself and kept moving and no one felt the need to eliminate all witnesses.

My apprehension grew stronger when a truck appeared traveling fast. But high speed driving is common on those back roads. Men delight in doing stupid things like bouncing over dirt ruts battering their trucks into pieces. So the speed didn't trouble me.

What did was the man at the wheel. A big young Anglo sitting tall behind the glass in a 1950s-vintage turquoise-colored Ford pickup. Wide bony face. Big hands. Pale brown hair parted low on his left. Large pale blue eyes. Pink skin a little sunburnt. His pale blue eyes flickered over at me and back to the road again. Like a big lizard.

And then he was gone. All that was left of him was the sound of his truck banging away behind me down the only road in and out. I listened to him go and tried to decide what it was that I knew about that Anglo. Something in his being so clean-scrubbed and upright. And so very bone-chillingly White.

Then it came to me. As I watched his dust cloud blow away across those empty scrublands. Even just that glance as he raced past was enough to tell. That dude was full-bore Mormon. Completely stamped out in the mold of Brigham Young. He could not have looked more LDS if he wore his magical underwear on his head.

I had no trouble finding the canyon. My father's grave was another matter.

My uncle's map showed a path along the streambed. But the bottom of the canyon was choked with debris. The only path was twenty or thirty feet up the side of the canyon where it wound over and around and among the many boulders and outcroppings. Narrow and rough and slow. Probably cut by javelina and deer pushing in there to forage. Maybe widened a little by the occasional hunter following after them.

Why everything was so different from what my uncle's map depicted became apparent when I stood up on the rim and saw the track of a boulder that had tumbled a hundred yards down the streambed crushing small trees and gouging up the earth. A flood had torn through there.

Everything was different now.

The sole cottonwood of any size, my uncle's primary landmark, had become part of the debris that filled the streambed. The old giant must have withered and died before the roaring waters knocked it over. I could see a huge gray trunk down among the boulders and shattered branches jammed where the flood had pushed them.

From the fallen cottonwood I determined the general vicinity of where my father's grave should be. But there was no pile of rocks to mark his remains. A high bank of yellowish earth and rounded stones that my uncle noted on his map as standing above the grave was nowhere to be seen. When the flood came it took all that away.

When I saw that bank was gone I gave up on finding the grave. After a few minutes of looking around at the place where I believed my father had once been interred I began picking my way down the streambed. Eventually I expected to find this route too challenging and climb back up to that narrow path along the canyon wall. But for now I wanted something different.

When I reached the downed cottonwood I took my time among the logs and boulders. And pictured that old giant standing upright spreading its branches and leaves over my father and uncle. Wondering what those two brothers talked about to distract themselves while they sat in the big tree's welcome shade. How scared they must have been. Hiding from the law out here in the middle of nowhere.

It was among those logs and boulders where the old cottonwood had broken apart that I found the bones. A long one that I guessed must be a leg bone. Along with four ribs and three vertebrae. When I realized what I was looking at I began searching for a skull. If I had found a human skull then I would have assumed those were my father's bones laying tossed around among the boulders. Looking very much to the glancing eye like broken tree limbs.

But if a skull was there it eluded me.

❖ ❖ ❖

A woman said my father and his brother beat her and raped her and stole all her money. It did not matter that she had no witnesses. And only a few minor injuries that could have been self-inflicted. Or that she could not say for certain how much money she had lost and her purse was still stuffed with cash. Or that my father and my uncle had been working with five other men when she said they attacked her and defiled her.

Of course none of that mattered. How could it when she was rich and white and they were poor and brown? The money owned the law so the law did what the money ordered. Following a hurried assessment of their options my father and my uncle decided to disappear while they hoped and prayed this woman's lies would fall apart. Back at that time in Doña Pero just to be caught could be fatal. Bad things often happened to a man between his capture and his trial. If justice was ever served she was often served too late.

But out in that canyon where they went to hide, a bad thing found them anyway. A rattlesnake bit my father while he was sleeping. Although it wasn't the snake bite that killed him. It was because my father got spooked. And because of that he gave up. He stopped eating and drinking and in two days he was dead. My uncle spent a few hours staring at his brother's dead body in disbelief. Then he buried the corpse as best he could with his bare hands. Mostly he just piled on rocks so the coyotes would have to work to dig him up. Then he went into town and to the sheriff's office and turned himself in.

But while he was out hiding with my father the crazy rich Anglo woman had decided it was three Indians who attacked her. So the police didn't want my uncle anymore. He told them what had happened to my father and they said in a few days, when they weren't busy chasing phantasmagorical Indians, they would call him and he could show them where my father was buried. At which time they would deal with the body. If the coyotes hadn't dealt with it first. In which case they would deal with whatever was left.

Chapter 2

At first I thought the footprints were mine. That I had already crossed this portion of the canyon during my failed search for my father's grave. But then I saw they were too big. And that the soles of the shoes didn't match the ones I was wearing.

Whoever made them crossed the streambed and came back again. They led down from the path that skirted along the wall of the canyon up above the tumult left below by the havoc-wreaking flood. Then they returned back up to the path and presumably out of the canyon.

While I examined them I kept remembering my brief encounter with the tall young Anglo who drove that old turquoise Ford. It played in my mind like a film loop. He had to be the one who made these footprints. Given that I had only seen one fresh set of tire tracks out on the road.

So what the hell was he doing here? It seemed he had a destination. He went somewhere and then he came back. And drove away like a demon was chasing him. Now all that speed seemed suspicious.

My scrutiny of the Anglo's actions was short-lived. Not because I had so little to scrutinize. I could have obsessively pushed those scant facts around in my head for several hours. Instead what wiped away my thoughts of the Mormon was a powerful feeling that my life was about to be transformed. Into something entirely unanticipated. And wholly unwanted. For an instance I saw with paralyzing clarity how my life was about to unfold. That I would not, as I had begun the day believing, soon arrive in California. Or pursue the half-naked women I had hoped to find there. I saw that all I had hoped my future would hold was about to vanish. Like a mirage. As I entered a desperate world full of hard men and harder living.

And what did I do when this feeling came to me? And in the moments after when it was gone but the memory of it remained fresh? Did I beat it out of there as fast as my young feet would carry me? As sound reason and just caution would dictate?

Oh no. Of course not. How much of a story would I have to tell then?

What I did was follow those footprints back among the shadows thrown by the looming boulders. Like a puppet worked by God with no will of my own. All control over my actions ceded to the call of a higher power. Perhaps it was my own will to follow that path. And the power of my will was so great at that moment that it seemed to come from beyond me. As if I was both the puppet and the master. But that was not how it felt. My experience was that I had no choice whether I would walk the path that opened before me. The path had opened and taken control.

All of the will and power seemed to reside in the path itself.

My uncle was a patient man. But he waited impatiently to hear from the sheriff's office. The days came and went and they never called. So finally my uncle called them. And spoke to someone who was useless. Then he went over there and talked to someone else who maybe could do something.

But still nothing happened.

So when a few months had passed with no action from the law my uncle decided to retrieve my father's remains on his own. He wanted my father reburied at our local church, in consecrated ground. But when he mentioned his plan to the parish priest the reverend father would not have it. He said the law must be involved. So my uncle returned again to the sheriff's office. And again they did nothing.

After more than a year of sporadically confronting the inaction and apathy of the law my uncle saw there was no sense in persisting. He had a wife and three kids of his own and with my father's death now me, my mother, and my little sister all to care for. He could not spare the time it took to beg indifferent officials to act when it was abundantly clear they would not. So reluctantly, with a heavy heart, he stopped trying.

It was almost another year before he returned to my father's grave. He went without the law or anyone else to accompany him. My sister and I were too little and my mother refused. She was terribly disturbed by the thought of her dead husband's grave all by itself out in the middle of some lost canyon in the lonely desert. She had nightmares about it. Every month or so she would wake up in the middle of the night screaming his name and crying out about the Devil.

So off my uncle went all by himself. He found the canyon and my father's grave with no difficulty. He was relieved to see that the coyotes hadn't dug his brother up. And this time, without the law chasing after him, he found the little canyon pretty and peaceful. My uncle told us later that it wasn't until he stood there beside that rude grave in the quiet of that isolated and desolate place that he finally surrendered ever bringing his brother home. Once he was back there it seemed that was where his brother belonged. And that to disturb his resting place would be the real sin. So my uncle piled on some more stones and put some wildflowers on top and made a cross with two branches he tied together with his bandana.

When I was about ten we saw a grave like that on TV. In an old black-and-white Western.

My uncle began to cry.

❖   ❖   ❖

Finding that kid scared the hell out of me. I screamed and jumped back.

12

Which did nothing to disturb him. The boy remained exactly as he was. Sitting with his back against the flat side of a boulder. For a second I wondered if he was dead. Then saw that he was breathing. While I stood there watching him breathe sweat coated my skin. Even that hot dry desert air could not suck up all the perspiration pouring off of me.

"You scared me," I said.

No response.

"What are you doing back here?"

Nothing. I took a moment or two to do some breathing of my own.

"Are you all right?"

He blinked. But that was all I got.

Now the wicking sweat left me chilled. I shivered for a few seconds before it passed. And welcomed the return of the baking heat. To shiver in the heat of the desert is an unnatural and disturbing experience. It makes death seem much too close.

When the chill left me my head cleared. And I saw the boy more clearly too. Details of his appearance that had escaped my notice. That he was Anglo or maybe part Anglo and part Spanish. Blond hair but with color to his skin. No more than ten years old. Wide set brown eyes that stared ahead and seemed to see nothing. I looked where they were pointed and there was just another boulder. Not unlike the one he was leaning against. And nothing remarkable on it or about it.

I offered him some water. A moment later I offered again. The second time he frowned. I held the water in front of his face. He frowned at the water. Then looked up at me. At first his eyes did not seem to register my presence. Then I saw when he pulled me into focus.

He reached out and took the water. He looked at it before he drank. Then he sighed and drank some more.

That was fine for now. For now that was great. No rush.

Then he looked up at me.

"Will you make him stop?" the boy said.

Chapter 3

My mother said she would die too if we dragged her out to my father's grave. That her fear of that horrible place would knock her dead. And how she had wailed about him in the middle of the night left my sister so traumatized she wanted nothing to do with any idea of our lost father. She was too young to remember him alive. To her he was always a ghost.

The wall of fear those two erected kept my aunt and cousins from wanting to join us. Which left me and my uncle as the only ones who wanted to go.

I remember looking out the back window of the old Chrysler my mother owned as we pulled away, watching the distance begin to stretch out behind us, knowing I must return. That it was very important for me to come back. I did not think about my father at that moment. Just that I was tied forever to this place I was leaving.

We settled into our new home up north and the years began to accumulate. All of them much the same. Just scraping by. Never enough money to pay all the bills. When I was no longer small I left school and began working. Doing what I could to help out. Which was never enough to turn things our way.

I don't remember when I realized that my mother was trying to forget her dead husband. Maybe it was before we moved. Maybe it was after. And I don't remember when I began mentioning him in order to keep her from forgetting. To poke a stick at the flame that died slowly within her.

But I remember when she snuffed that flame out. And put him in the past. When she buried him in her heart.

That was when she began seeing her handsome jackass. The one she met at the hospital just two days before my uncle died. They shared a ride in the elevator and that was all the time he needed.

15

When my uncle passed this interloper pretended to console her.

But so much worse was watching my mother pretend to be consoled.

He tried to ignore the ache in his belly. But when it hit, the pain was written on his face. His features taut and the gleam of sweat across his forehead. My aunt chased him to the hospital and the doctors told him he might have stomach cancer. And that he would have to stay for tests and maybe surgery. He seemed stunned for about a day. Then he began making plans for all the things he wanted to do when they let him go home. Things he wanted done if the cancer was going to take him.

And first on that list was to finally make our journey to pay our respects to my father. Summer had just ended and Fall was upon us so we planned to go on Día de los Muertos. The Day of the Dead.

"Before I'm dead too," he said to me. "We need to go there."

But his illness turned out to be worse than the doctors suspected and it took him quickly. He never left the hospital. They operated but it was too late. In just a couple weeks he was gone.

On the very last day of his life my uncle struggled through his pain to draw his map of the place where my father was at rest. His shaking hands made that a long and laborious process. But he took his time and was careful. He gave me a good map. And the directions he wrote with it were clear.

Then we buried my uncle. And none of us were any good for some time after that. There were tensions among us survivors. But the one thing we could all agree on was the love and respect we felt for my uncle.

"He was one of the good ones," we all said.

And after we said it we were always quiet. Thinking of him did that to us.

After all these years it still does that to me.

❖　　❖　　❖

The jackass was indeed handsome. There was no denying it. And as if that wasn't enough he had money. Which in our world was like possessing magical powers. He bought the affections of all the others and cut me off from my own family. Isolated me within my cell of disapproval. A few lousy trinkets and they all leapt into his pockets like trained rats.

Then she agreed to marry him. And they announced the wedding would be in Los Angeles. And not only that but we would be moving there. Because my future stepfather had some very promising business interests with his brothers and cousins out in the City of Angels.

I remember very clearly how he turned to me wearing his phony smile.

"Swimming pools," the jackass said. "Girls in bikinis."

Then the jackass winked at me.

"Doesn't that sound good Andy?"

He was the only one who ever called me that. If he ever noticed how much I hated it he never let on. But I think he knew. I am almost certain that he did. Which of course means the prick did it on purpose.

I hated him even more for making me want California. For putting those nearly naked women in my head.

Plans were made for our relocation. By then I had bought my uncle's truck from my aunt and was determined to bring it with me.

My mother wanted it gone.

"Leave that old piece of junk here," she said. "I don't want to look at it anymore."

I insisted that if the truck was staying put so would I. And what was more I announced some plans

17

of my own. That I would not follow along with them straight out to LA. I would make a detour first, down south across the long miles to where my father was buried. Only after I had seen his grave and paid my respects would I quit the land where my father and his father and I myself were all born.

Then and only then would I turn west. And meet them in California.

How my mother screamed at me. Even for her it was excessive. My aunt tried to calm her and failed.

Only the handsome man could accomplish that.

"Let him go," the jackass said. "It is right that he should pay his respects."

He gave me a cold look when he said this. I knew the jackass could care less whether I did the right thing by my father. He just wanted to be rid of me for the trip west. Not to endure my sullen and disagreeable presence. To be free of my curt and rude responses to any question or command. To not see the hostile expression on my sour face. And who could blame him? I was a teenage boy after all. Who is better at being sullen and disagreeable than a teenage boy? Especially one who is nursing a legitimate grievance. Nothing stiffens the spine like a gripe with a strong moral core.

So the day came when we departed. I grudgingly helped load my stepfather's truck and my mother's car. Then I stood with my aunt and cousins and watched my mother and sister and the jackass drive away. I was the only one who did not wave goodbye. Just couldn't bring myself to do it. Not even to raise my hand and hold it there for a second. Not even that.

When they were gone I kissed and hugged my aunt and she wept a bit on my shoulder before I climbed into my uncle's old truck. Which even though the title had my name on it I still thought of as belonging to him. And then I drove away to the south where my people were from and went down Route 19 and followed my uncle's directions and his map off into the desert.

Chapter 4

The officer I spoke with on the phone told me to wait. That someone would be there soon to take my statement. I went and stood at the front of the emergency room. Where I looked out through the tinted glass for a patrol car to appear in the parking lot.

And soon enough one did. I watched the driver climb out and come lumbering across the pavement. He was shaped and moved like a small bear. Big-boned and tall with a round belly and sloping shoulders. Moving toward me slumped over in a rolling gait. When he got closer I saw his face was heavily pockmarked. And that he had hooded eyes and a fleshy nose. And that he wore his scraggly mustache drooping down around his sullen mouth.

Despair and disappointment and disgust. That was what I felt. In those first moments while I watched him. Because the situation desperately required a hero. And instead here came a fat man who was ugly and look corrupted.

This one did not look like a hero. Not even like an unlikely hero.

This one looked like a bad guy.

Shit, I thought. This could be bad.

He stopped inside the glass doors and stood looking around. I walked over and introduced myself. Doing my best to pretend I did not hate his guts at first sight. I had the advantage of those moments spent watching him. Time to have my visceral reaction and reject it. Time to tell myself you cannot judge a book by its cover.

But I wasn't looking at the cover. I was reading the first few paragraphs. Written in his body language. From which I had already guessed this book was headed for a rotten ending.

But I willed that first impression to come and go all at once. Chose to ignore what that inner voice said while it still whispered inside of me. Human nature makes us do so when we want something from a new acquaintance. The naked truth realized in that first piercing glimpse, the one that reveals the very soul of a man, is quickly supplanted by a false perception of what we hope to find instead.

We make do with what God gives us.

And God gave me Josef Armijo.

I wanted him to be a capable upstanding lawman who would hunt down the bad guy. So my initial intuitive revulsion was pushed aside and my rational mind reinvented this Deputy Sheriff in the image it preferred. It is simply amazing what lies we tell ourselves to create the illusion of comfort in this discomforting world. To deny the truth when we find it unacceptable.

Especially when we are young. I was not naïve when I met Armijo. I had seen enough of the world and how it operates to be wary of those who pull the levers. But I was still given to youthful self-deception. And the role I wanted Armijo to play was one the fat man played well. After many long years spent honing his skills. He knew how to impress and seduce with his strength and his power.

And if anything about Armijo bespoke power and commanded respect it was his deep rumbling voice. The sounds a man makes can do much to change what we think of how he appears. Especially when we are willing and eager to have our impressions improved. So when Armijo asked me in that voice what happened out in the desert—

I wanted to tell him everything. About my uncle and my father. About my search for my father's grave. About how I was supposed to be on my way to California.

But I knew he didn't care about all that.

❖　　❖　　❖

21

I should have started with the Mormon. Right up front. Point the lawman's eyes in the right direction. But when I told Armijo what happened I started with myself—

"I was out on State Road 506."

But the fat man raised a hand and stopped me.

"What were you doing out there?" Armijo said.

A question I no longer wanted to answer. Despite a moment before wanting to volunteer everything. I turned away from Armijo while I considered how to respond. I looked out through the glass wall at my uncle's truck parked and waiting. Two spaces away from Armijo's patrol car. I should be behind the wheel on my way to Los Angeles. And whatever there was for me in a life beside the ocean.

I turned back to Armijo. What I said wasn't a lie. Just not all of the truth. I hoped not all of the truth would be enough. That we could leave out the part about my father being buried in that remote canyon. And how when he died the law didn't care. So maybe the law could go right on not caring. And we could forget about the bones I found scattered among the boulders and broken tree limbs. If those were my father's remains I did not want them disturbed any more than nature had already. And that she could have her hand in how she would disturb them in the future. A lawman might head out there to look at those bones. And then those bones wouldn't stay there. Who knows where the law might take them? I couldn't imagine they would go anywhere those bones wanted to be.

"My father died out there," I said.

And hoped that was enough. While I expected Armijo to be surprised by this. But he displayed no reaction. He just stared out at me from under those hoods over his eyes.

That's not all of it, those wary eyes said.

The cold unfeeling eyes of the law. Maybe Armijo thought my father was an illegal who didn't

22

survive crossing the border. Or worse maybe a drug mule. I didn't want him to think those things. But I didn't want to give him anything else to think either.

"It's a long story," I said.

Then waited to see if Armijo wanted to hear that long story. He said nothing. But he also didn't blink. He just kept staring.

And that almost made me start blabbering. But I managed to keep my head and get things back on track—

"I saw someone out there. Before I found the boy."

Armijo frowned. While I told him about the young Anglo hurtling past out on the back roads in that turquoise Ford pickup Armijo frowned deeper and leaned forward. He stopped me and asked some questions about the Anglo and the truck.

The question that killed me was this one—

"Did you get a plate number?" Armijo said.

You would think by the second time I saw that damned truck, getting the plates would have occurred to me. But twice I had a chance and twice I blew it. Maybe it was the color. Somehow, on that particular truck that particular shade of turquoise kind of felt like a thumb in the eye. Whatever it was I didn't even notice what state the plates were from.

I hated myself while I shook my head at Armijo.

"No," I said. "That was really stupid of me."

Armijo shrugged.

"It happens," he said. "Don't beat yourself up."

I was affected by those words of kindness. Or which at least I perceived to be kind. They made me almost like the man.

Armijo asked me if there was anything else. I told him about seeing the truck and its driver a second time. And that he went west after he left the restaurant. On the road just to the south.

When I was done Armijo told me to come with him. He talked to a nurse in reception and she let him step behind the desk and use the telephone. Judging by what he said, he called the sheriff's station. I heard him pass along my description of the young Anglo and his truck and where he had last been seen and in what direction he was headed.

If I had gotten the plate number that would have been passed along too. And become part of the main case records. Not that I knew this at the time.

After Armijo hung up he gestured for me to follow. We went along a hallway flanked with rooms and when Armijo found the one he wanted we stopped and he told me to wait. He went into the room and I heard him speaking with another man. From what the other man said I gathered he was a doctor. And that also in the room with them was the boy.

Who said nothing. Although I thought I heard him cough once.

An orderly appeared pushing a cart loaded with chairs. He nodded hello and I did the same; then the orderly ignored me while I watched him place six chairs along the wall opposite the room Armijo had entered. The orderly and I nodded at each other again before he left. I watched him push his cart out of sight down the hall then sat down on one of his chairs.

Where I fought a strong urge to leave. To go back along the hall and past the reception desk and out through the glass doors to my uncle's waiting truck and then to drive far away. But not to California. Where I would go instead I didn't know. But a voice inside of me said not to go anywhere they could find me. And that I should leave right away and as fast as I could. Or as fast as was possible without drawing attention.

But I was a good kid. I did as I was told and stayed put. And told myself not to worry. That nothing bad would happen to me. I had done nothing wrong. What I had done was a good thing.

And they don't punish you for doing good things.

Chapter 5

I wasn't alone for very long. A few minutes at the most. Then a crowd began to gather in the hall outside the boy's room. Mostly law enforcement. Among the civilians was the boy's mother. There was one guy who appeared to be a reporter. Esperanza and her Tía Rosa were the only ones who sat with me on the chairs the orderly had put there. Everyone else stood around and got in the way of the medical personnel who kept coming and going.

During a quiet moment little Essie turned to look at me. I could feel her eyes on my face. When I turned to look at her she smiled. That smile was so wounded and trusting. I almost lost it. After what that day had already brought, her smile almost wrecked me.

Behind her Rosa spoke—

"Excuse me?" Rosa said.

I had trouble pulling my eyes away from Esperanza. I managed to smile back at the little girl before I responded to her aunt.

"Yes?"

"Are you related to Señora Morris?"

I must have looked confused. Rosa added—

"Elden's mother?"

For a moment I probably looked even more confused. When I made sense of her questions I shook my head.

"No."

Rosa and I watched each other. Esperanza sat between us, beside her aunt, with three empty chairs between her and me. She kept turning back and forth as her eyes went from one face to the other.

"The little boy?" I said.

Now Essie's eyes stayed on me.

"¿Sí?" Rosa said.

I frowned. I made the mistake of glancing at Esperanza and again I almost broke down and cried.

"I found him," I said.

Essie was staring at me now. I could feel her eyes burning into me.

"Is he all right?" Rosa said.

I knew the boy definitely wasn't all right. But had no idea how bad he really was. What I did know was that this little girl didn't need to hear anything worse than she had already.

"I think so," I said. "The doctors..."

I turned to the open doorway.

"I think so," I said again.

Then I kept my eyes turned away. I sat back in my chair with my hands on my thighs and stared across the hallway at the opposite wall. Essie watched me. Waiting for more.

Eventually she gave up.

Before they left Esperanza came and stood beside me. Where she said in her grave little voice—

"Thank you for finding my friend."

We peered into each other's eyes. The strength I saw in her made my own return. I nodded once.

"You're welcome," I said.

Then she took her aunt's hand and they left.

❖   ❖   ❖

Will you make him stop?

Those were the only words the boy ever spoke in my presence. Hearing them made me furious. Rage like I have never known before or since.

I don't know how long it was before I could think straight again. A minute. Five minutes. Maybe ten or even twenty. Time was elastic in those moments I spent with the boy back among the boulders.

When my mind returned to rational thought I persuaded him to stand up. And saw that the seat of his pants had been bloodied. I needed a moment then to stop feeling ill.

A few steps proved he couldn't walk. So I carried the injured child from the canyon where my father died and propped his limp form up in the cab of my uncle's truck. I worried that jostling and lurching over the rough roads would cause him terrible pain. But if it did he showed no reaction. He continued to stare ahead unseeingly as we made our way out of the backcountry.

❖   ❖   ❖

We were on the edge of town when I saw that turquoise Ford again. Parked away from the other vehicles outside a restaurant. The rage that boiled my blood out at the canyon came back and boiled it some more. My skin went hot and cold and I gripped the steering wheel like I was trying to strangle it.

Then the front door of the restaurant swung open and the tall young Anglo came loping out. He had his head down. The sun glinted on the keys in his hand. He raised his head and my heart lurched up into my throat expecting he would see me. And more to the point that he would see the boy seated next to me. I wondered if he had a gun and now he would panic and kill both of us before he took off. But the Anglo blinked and squinted against the sun and showed no surprise or recognition. He did not even seem aware of our presence going past him along the road. Then he lowered his head back down and the keys glinted in his hand again. In a few more long steps he would arrive at his truck.

That was when the boy slid down beside me and vomited across the bench seat of my uncle's old pickup. I don't know if he had seen the Anglo and this was his reaction. Or if what had happened to him finally took its toll and made him ill. Either way I was left with a decision to make. Would I turn my attention to the man I knew had attacked the boy? Because I was certain it was the driver of that turquoise Ford. Or would I get the poor sick child the care he needed?

Despite what I felt, it was an easy decision to make. I made it in an instant. But that instant remains one of the longest in my life. Because I so very much wanted to kill that tall loping Anglo. I could feel his sickness in my bones. I was young but I had lived through enough in this world to know evil by what evil does. Things had happened to me and around me that took away my innocence. And when I saw what this evil had done to that boy I hungered to wreak vengeance.

And at that moment I had the element of surprise. I could veer into that parking lot and maybe hit the Anglo with my truck. If that failed there was a tire iron under the seat. He might get the better of me. He might kill me and get away. Maybe he would snatch the boy again. But I felt strongly that the advantage was mine. And that I could stop him from repeating what he had done. He was young enough that this boy might be his first. If I stopped him now this boy would also be his last.

All that flashed through my mind while I went past him. I watched him stab a key into the door lock and swing the door open and duck inside. Then I put my eyes back on the road and did my best to ignore the turquoise Ford. But there it was in my mirrors. Where my eyes kept going.

Then it occurred to me I should see where he went. So I slowed and watched him swing out of the parking lot and turn south, headed away from me, back in the direction I just came from. Back toward the canyon where he had dumped the boy. I wondered if he had changed his mind about what he had done and was going back. Maybe to save the boy. More likely to kill him.

But then he slowed and turned right past the buildings that stood beyond the restaurant. He was going west away from there. Away from what he had done. *Good*, I thought. *Let him run.* I will tell the law

29

where he went and they will catch him in that turquoise Ford. Let him think he can slip away. While he is believing that the noose will tighten.

With that thought I put the Anglo behind me and set my focus ahead.

To where I wanted to believe they could put this boy back together.

❖   ❖   ❖

The crowd was gone and I was alone. I had lost track of Armijo. While I waited for him to show himself and wondered if he would, that urge to get out of there came at me again. I was a second away from acting on it when the fat man came lumbering up the hall.

He thanked me for waiting. Then said they needed me to stick around. How long exactly he couldn't be sure. Probably not more than a few days. He told me there were two reasons why they needed my help. First, depending on what their investigation revealed, they might have some more questions. To fill in the details of what happened. So they could be sure of an airtight case and a solid conviction. They didn't want this creep to get off on a technicality. Or out on appeal.

But that wasn't the main reason Armijo gave me for staying. His second reason was the one that kept me there. The first one was just the setup.

He peered into my eyes when he said—

"We want you to identify this man when we catch him."

That was how Armijo put it. *When* they caught him. Not *if*. Which was like red meat to me. The law catching that sick bastard.

Armijo kept his eyes on mine.

"Will you do that for us?" he said.

Of course I would do that. I would go looking for the guy myself if they would let me. Make me a deputy and give me a gun and put me in the posse.

Just like that old western with the grave in it that made my uncle cry. They formed up a posse and went riding after the bandit who put their friend in the ground.

But no posse riding for me. Instead the Sheriff's Department put me up in a dingy room at a crappy motel on the edge of town. I followed Armijo out there from the hospital. We went back the way I came. Past that restaurant where I saw the Anglo drive away in his turquoise Ford. As we went by the place I honked my horn and pointed it out to Armijo. He put a hand out his window and waved once.

I got it covered, that wave said.

I wanted to believe in that wave.

I very much hoped that wave told the truth.

Part II:
Loud as a Bomb

Chapter 6

Matthew Walker was reshelving DVDs near the back of the Megahits video store on the upper concourse of the Rolling Green Mall outside Walker City, Pennsylvania, when he heard his name shouted from across the room. He jerked his head up and spun around toward the front of the store. His supervisor, a slight and carrot-haired sickly looking man, glared from behind the counter. He held up a telephone handset.

Matt hadn't noticed the phone was ringing. Even though the store was empty and quiet. Was that how he had failed in his duties? But the supervisor was working the counter. And whoever was at the counter was supposed to take any calls. Did he really want Matt to cover the phones while reshelving? That was a new and innovatively stupid approach to assigning responsibilities.

"It's for you," the supervisor said.

Matt frowned. No one had ever called him here. Not that anyone called him anyplace else. Receiving phone calls had become an uncommon experience. He decided it must be from his other job. Maybe the dinner shift manager asking him to cover for someone.

Then the supervisor said—

"It's your father."

Matt stood up straighter.

"My father."

"That's what I said."

Matt started toward the front. The supervisor remained holding the handset. Matt wanted to tell him he could put the line on hold. Then maybe if today Matt could have just one tiny little shred of good luck the supervisor would find something to do somewhere else instead of hovering nearby. Allowing Matt some privacy while he took the call. But the supervisor was bad with technology and hated being reminded of it. So Matt held his tongue while the supervisor waited impatiently.

"You should get a cell phone," the supervisor said.

Matt felt his jaw tighten. He wanted to ask if one call in six months was too great a drain on company resources. And if he could get a raise to pay for a phone. Then he remembered that Megahits had entered bankruptcy. Which was another sore point he wanted to avoid with the supervisor. The response he offered became—

"Yes sir."

When he stepped behind the counter the supervisor glowered as he extended the handset.

"Thanks," Matt said.

The supervisor snorted.

Matt turned away. He lowered his head and put the handset to his ear. Then held his breath for a second before saying—

"Dad?"

"Whatcha doin' tonight?"

This was not a question Matt could have anticipated.

"Nothing?"

"How about a nice big steak at The Belfast."

The Belfast Tavern had been the Walker family's favorite restaurant. Back when they still dined out now and then. In the greater portion of his life that Matt regarded as being normal.

"Don't mess with me like that," Matt said.

"I got tonight off. You wanna do this?"

Matt didn't have to share what he was thinking.

"A couple steaks ain't gonna break us," Frank said.

❖ ❖ ❖

Matt and his father were utilitarian cooks. When they had the time to cook which wasn't often. As Matt retraced his steps to the back of the store he tried to remember his last really good meal. Then stopped trying when he decided it must have been before his mother died. He suffered through the rest of his shift and the drive home and getting changed for dinner with the taste and scent of what he anticipated on his tongue and in his nostrils. When he climbed into his father's truck he was almost drooling.

Halfway there the rain began. Matt watched the icy drops pelt the windshield and pictured how their arrival at The Belfast would unfold. John Kenny, the owner and manager, would greet Frank by name. Then call Matt "lad" while saying something complimentary to cover for not remembering his name. Next their host would comment that he hadn't seen them in a while. Which depending on his mood might give his father an opening to recount more of their recent family history than Matt cared to revisit. Then depending on how much his father chose to share in response to that first question John Kenny might ask if Helen would be joining them.

Matt was certain his mother would be mentioned by name. Like his brother Jack the first time they arrived without him. And his sister Gloria the first time she was absent.

The rain was falling hard when they pulled into the parking lot. Fat stinging drops even colder than Matt imagined. They hurried toward the pool of light at the door.

When they stepped inside John Kenny called out—

"Frank! Good to see you."
Prediction number one fulfilled.
"How ya been, John."
"Fair enough. You?"

34

"Still standing."

A gruff laugh. John Kenny grinned and nodded at Matt.

"You're looking well, lad."

Two down. Two to go.

"Thank you, sir."

John Kenny turned back to Frank. Matt braced himself for a question that might start his father talking. Something like—

Haven't seen you in a while. Been keeping yourself busy?

But John Kenny wore a closed expression Matt hadn't seen before. A look that said the owner and manager of The Belfast Tavern wanted to limit this exchange. Matt thought their host might jump straight to—

Will Helen be joining you tonight?

He resigned himself to getting it over with. He told himself it was like a tooth that needed to be pulled. A burst of pain and the worst would be over.

But with a quick gesture at father and son all John Kenny said was—

"Right this way gentlemen."

Matt was slow to start after his father. He had to double his step to catch up.

He wanted to ask why his mother had not been mentioned. He knew his question would sound agitated and belligerent. Like an accusation. Even more so if he pointed out that John Kenny had asked after Matt's siblings when they were gone but not the woman who gave birth to them now that she was gone. But he still wanted to ask.

What he didn't know was that was the wrong time to ask. During business hours John Kenny would have lied. He even had his lie prepared just in case. A joke that after 30 years in the trade he had finally learned to stop being so damn nosy. A quip he never used because of course no one ever did ask. Like Matt, everyone who noticed held their tongue over this change in the conduct of the owner and manager of The Belfast Tavern. Not wanting to start their big dinner out by making trouble.

To get the truth Matt should have asked when the place was closed. At the end of the night when John Kenny sipped a glass of whiskey at his empty bar. If Matt had made his way past the locked doors and taken a seat beside the owner he might not have had to ask. Because John Kenny would very likely have said—

I'm sorry, lad. For my behavior before. Will you tell me now me what happened to your mother?

After hearing the sad news John Kenny would have offered his sincere and heartfelt condolences. And allowed a respectful moment of silence to pass between them.

Then John Kenny might have explained himself. Sharing with the youngest Walker boy whose name he could never remember that after Long Valley Fabricators closed—not right away, maybe a month or two later—that was when the wave began to roll in through his doors. He had already seen the drop in business. That he could ride through without too much hardship. There were other customers whose fortunes were at that same time improving. And they liked to spend well.

It was what came later that unsettled him. When his usual queries to his regulars about whomever happened to be absent from that evening's party were met with front-line accounts from the local epidemic of misery and dysfunction. After too many customers fell apart at the mention of a spouse or a child who did not accompany them, after provoking too many stories of lives spiraling downward, John Kenny stopped asking. He avoided personal subjects and kept his conversation light and general.

Especially when old regulars reappeared following a long absence. As Frank and Matt had done tonight. And especially with anyone who worked at Long Valley Fab. As Frank Walker had done for almost the entirety of his adult life. And most especially when one half of a couple arrived without the other. Like Frank Walker coming in without Helen.

If the missing spouse was dead that was bad enough. But John Kenny had learned that when it came to causing scenes divorce could be very much worse. The bereaved were generally consolable and inclined to behave themselves. But the divorced were too often like banshees who only wanted to howl and wail out their grief.

❖　　❖　　❖

John Kenny seated the Walkers at the back of the main dining room, in a booth that could accommodate a few more family members if any arrived. That was how he had settled on handling these situations. Don't mention those who were absent but leave room for them. He was willing to spare a few seats if that meant keeping the peace.

He said something to Frank then turned and left. Matt wondered what he had missed then decided it didn't matter. He watched John Kenny depart and wanted his anger to follow.

It refused.

"He didn't ask about Mom," Matt said.

Then told himself he should have kept his mouth shut.

His father responded a moment later—

"What?"

Matt felt feverish. He shook his head.

"Nothing."

Frank nodded and looked away. He seemed to be somewhere else. Matt was happy to leave his father wherever he had gone.

Matt looked around the big room and didn't notice what he was looking at. When his mood began

37

to settle he found himself feeling grateful that John Kenny hadn't asked about his mother. Because that meant his father didn't have to explain once again that she had died. And they didn't have to endure the awkwardness that always followed.

Matt didn't want his mother to be forgotten. Not even by someone like John Kenny who only saw her once or twice a year and only for a few minutes at a time. But Matt also didn't want to keep revisiting that she was gone.

A plate clattered loudly on the far side of the room. Matt turned toward the sound and watched a busboy bend to recover what he had dropped. When a woman's voice spoke his father's name Matt felt feverish again. He looked up to see Mrs. Kenny holding a tray bearing dinner salads and ice water and a basket of bread with a dish of butter. She chattered while she delivered what she had brought. Then put the back of one hand against a generous hip and with the other held the tray down at her side while she took their order.

When their business was done Mrs. Kenny fussed over the Walker men for a minute or two. When she left them they felt both better and worse. A woman's presence was sorely missing in their bachelor lives.

Chapter 7

A loud voice entered. Loud enough and demanding enough to turn heads. The source was one of eight middle aged men, all dressed in business suits, that John Kenny escorted to the center of the room. Which one was so loud was made clear when the others took their seats at a large round table and the loud one remained standing, gesticulating as he spoke. He was a big man and powerfully built. Matt guessed he might have played football when he was young. Now those muscles were receding under fat.

"Jesus Christ," Frank said. "I should have known."

Despite his volume, what he said was unclear. The timbre of his voice and the room's acoustics and the sounds made by the staff and the other diners conspired to obscure his meaning. All Matt could make out was "and then I said" and "you wouldn' buh-lieve". After he delivered what must have been his punchline, the others with him laughed—most of them politely, only one with real enthusiasm—while the loud one took his seat.

"You know that guy?" Matt said.

"I checked him in this afternoon."

Frank worked at the local Sleep Rite motel.

"He asked for a good steak and I sent him here. So I guess that makes this my fault."

The loud one was talking again. Matt noticed that one of the men with him did not appear to like what the big man said.

"Guess what he does," Frank said. "Why he's here."

"Nothing that guy does could be any good."

"He goes around the country buying machinery from factories that have been shut down. Then sells it in China."

Matt felt sick. Frank pointed his fork at the man dominating the table loaded with men who didn't care to be dominated.

"He got all of LVF and the two subcontractors that supplied us. Some last minute swindle that cut out the other bidders. Next he's off to Ohio where some other company went bankrupt. He's real excited about that one. Three times the size of Long Valley."

Matt had stopped breathing. He refilled his lungs while he watched the big man put his head back and laugh.

"Sounds like you talked to him for a while."

"I said almost nothing. And I had to call him sir."

"Instead of you fucking bastard."

"Right after which I would punch that clown in the mouth. Then call my boss and tell him I quit."

"What's he doing at Sleep Rite? And he should get a new suit. He's popping out of that one."

"Too busy making money and doesn't like to spend it."

"Asshole."

"As big an asshole as I've ever met. May God spare me from ever meeting any bigger."

The loudmouth was coughing into his napkin. Matt hoped he would choke.

"I know this isn't exactly true," Frank said. "That things are more complicated. But when I look at a guy like him, I can't help thinking—that's where everything good went. To those bastards. They gobbled it all up and now they're just sitting on it. They don't give a shit that the rest of us are all down the toilet."

The loudmouth put his napkin on the table. He said something and then grinned when the guy beside him laughed.

"Maybe it's not more complicated," Matt said. "Maybe it's exactly that simple."

He looked at his father. Frank was watching the big man. Matt saw how his father had aged. He looked weary and almost gaunt. Then Frank shrugged and shook his head and returned his attention to his salad.

Matt turned back to the big man. At this distance he could just make out how the collar of the man's shirt cut into his neck. And felt white rage that the loudmouth was literally growing fat in this world that was gutting the Walkers. Matt wanted to take the steak knife from his place setting and stalk across the room and plunge the blade deep into that bloated throat.

❖   ❖   ❖

The big room filled up and slowly drowned out the loudmouth. Matt and Frank could comfortably ignore him when their sizzling T-bones arrived. Then the two hungry men were lost in red meat perfection, barely speaking while they devoured, communicating instead with gestures and grunts.

When only the bones remained on their plates they sat back and smiled. Life still had its good moments. Frank blinked and his eyes were damp.

"Son, this means a lot to me."

"Me too."

"I love you. You know that."

"Of course. I love you too."

"Your mother loved you, just like I do, with all her heart."

"I know. Me too. I love you guys too."

Matt did not care to parse the tense on that last verb. To separate his parents into the living and the dead. So he did not.

Frank swallowed hard and nodded. He lifted his ice water and drained it. When he had returned the glass to the table he stared at it.

"It was always very important to both of us that you go to college."

He raised his eyes from his glass and peered at his son.

41

"Very important," Frank said.

Matt nodded.

"I know. It's important to me too."

But it wasn't. Which Matt only realized as he spoke. He said what he did to please his father. College seemed too impossible. He had pushed it so far out of his mind that he didn't know if it still mattered to him personally. He stared into his father's eyes and was alarmed to discover that other than their relationship he could not say with certainty what did matter to him anymore. Nothing else in his life seemed to have any purpose or meaning.

Which was going to make it difficult to talk about college. Since apparently that was what they came here to discuss. Matt had been waiting to find out the purpose of this dinner since he got the call back at Megahits.

A busboy interrupted them. They sat stiff-backed while the small Hispanic man's hands darted rapidly over the table clearing their plates and sweeping up the mess. He left them with two fresh glasses of ice water. On his heels came Mrs. Kenny. She folded her hand back onto her plentiful hip and cajoled them into sharing a slice of chocolate cake with two decafs.

When she left Frank said—

"I have some ideas on how we might swing college."

Matt waited. Frank raised his water and drank. Then forced a smile and showed it to his son.

"Anyway I'm working on it."

"What kind of ideas?" Matt said.

Frank shook his head. He raised a hand and waved the question away.

"It's nothing solid yet."

Matt blinked. His eyes narrowed. A frown came and went. He blinked again and sat back against the bench seat.

Frank looked away across the room.

"I still need to sort things out," Frank said.

42

Matt stared across the table and tried to accept what had just been said. And more importantly what was not said. To not say what he was thinking was not like his father. Frank had never been evasive or vague with his youngest son. Instead he had always been remarkably direct. Talking openly about things other parents hid from their children.

Like that his oldest boy Jack went into the Army to avoid jail after stealing a car. And while over in Korea stole a jeep and went joyriding with a buddy and some whores. Then rolled the jeep and got himself killed.

Or that given how his middle child Gloria behaved they would all be lucky if she didn't get pregnant. That Helen was snooping on their daughter to see if she was still getting her period. Because if she wasn't she might not tell them until it was too late for an abortion. And that when she disappeared it was because she ran off with a trucker she met at the diner where she worked.

This history of candor left Matt unprepared for not being told what was going on. Part of him wanted to probe for an explanation. To seek out what his father was hiding. But the other part of him wanted nothing to do with it. If for once his father didn't want to say best just leave it alone.

Frank forced another smile at his son.

"But anyway I'm on it."

He looked away across the room. Matt watched his father's eyes search for something they would never find. Not in this room or anywhere else. He knew what Frank was looking for was a way out of this mess. This life they had been reduced to since he lost his job and Helen died.

The chocolate cake came and went. All that remained were a few crumbs and a smear of icing

43

along the plate. Then their coffee was almost gone and the check was waiting on the table.

"I need to get away," Frank said. "Go do some fishing."

Matt nodded at his father.

"That sounds great."

Frank folded his hands together and looked down at them.

"When do you want to go?" Matt said.

"Soon. I'm not sure yet."

Frank watched a waitress go by. Matt turned and watched her too. She was a well-built girl and the two lonely men stared. When she was gone, Frank and Matt looked at each other.

"I can probably get some time off," Matt said.

He was surprised by the pain that appeared on his father's face. Frank's next words were even more unexpected than what he said before—

"I need to go by myself."

Frank Walker had never gone away alone since he returned from the Navy long before Matt was born. He looked away and sighed.

"I probably should have done that after your mother died."

Matt managed to nod. Frank looked at his coffee cup. He used his finger tips to turn the glass slowly in its saucer.

"I need to sort things out," Frank said. "Make some plans."

Matt had no idea what kind of plans his father could make. Which made the possibilities seem troubling.

He decided that meant it was his turn to force a smile.

"Whatever you need to do," Matt said.

He pushed his smile wider. And then he lied. What Matt said next could not have been more untrue at that moment—

"I understand."

Chapter 8

Matt was working his other job when his father left. The one waiting tables at The Ol' Back Porch. On a Friday night that was busier than most. He was taking the order of an elderly African American couple when the ache began. In the center of his chest over his heart. A sensation that told him something was wrong not with his physical health but outside of his own person. That something severely terrible and horribly unwanted was about to happen in his young life. A premonition of disaster.

He did nothing to reveal what he was experiencing. Matt began working at The Ol' Back Porch just after the national chain was first sued by black people who felt unwelcome in the dining room, either to work or to eat. Management was doing their utmost to avoid any more legal defeats. Including oft-repeated instructions to the waitstaff to give African Americans the best possible service.

So Matt behaved as the good employee he was and put his personal concerns aside. He choked down his pain and his emotions and kept a smile plastered on his face. It helped him endure his suffering that the couple he was waiting on were nice people he had served before. He liked them and did not want to ruin their evening out.

When his shift was over and Matt went home something told him to check his father's fishing tackle. He found that Frank had left most of it behind. Which meant he wasn't planning on doing any real fishing. When Matt realized he did not know where his father had gone the pain in his chest returned and became worse.

Later, looking back, Matt could not recall the next day, a Saturday. He could remember working a few hours at Megahits on Sunday, then driving to The Ol' Back Porch and the first couple hours of his shift there. At the end of the night he was in the kitchen talking to his friend Pablo when his eyes glazed over and he sat down in the middle of the floor. A second later he slumped over unconscious. Pablo ran for the manager. By the time they returned Matt was sitting up again.

He insisted he was fine. The manager debated calling an ambulance. Matt insisted he didn't need one. His shift was almost over so the manager sent him home. Matt drove slowly, with traffic rushing past him along the interstate, and fell asleep on the living room sofa, still in his work clothes, with the lights on.

❖　　❖　　❖

Three strokes boom boom boom each loud as a bomb. The first stroke woke Matt up, the second put him on his feet, and the third sent him to the door. He pulled the door open and two state troopers stood before him in the hallway. Dressed in the big hats and tall boots of their particular sect within the law enforcement profession.

"Matthew Walker?" said the one on the left.

He was the older of the two, about Frank's age. Matt nodded once.

"May we come in?" the trooper said.

Matt nodded again and turned away from the door. The troopers followed him into the living room. He heard the door close behind them. He turned around and the older one said—

"You might want to—"

Matt sat on the couch. The state trooper paused.

"Okay," he said.

He looked directly at Matt. Who couldn't help noticing that the trooper's hat was truly huge.

"There's been an accident," the trooper said.

Matt knew what was coming. He felt as if he was watching a movie he had seen before. The

46

younger state trooper cleared his throat and folded his hands behind his back. The older one swallowed and Matt watched the man's pronounced Adam's apple bob up and down.

"Your father was involved," the older trooper said.

Matt felt bad for this man. What a terrible thing to have to do. To deliver such terrible news.

"Okay," Matt said.

The trooper struggled for a moment before he finally managed to form the words and get them out—

"Mr. Walker. I'm afraid your father is dead."

Finally. There it was.

Matt's eyes lost focus. Then they slid closed. For the instant his eyes were shut he felt he could drift off to sleep. And maybe beyond. Maybe he could just float away after his father and his mother. Follow them into the beyond.

Then his eyes were open again. He was staring at a point between the two policemen. Who stood incongruously before him in that sad anonymous apartment. With those grim expressions on their earnest faces. The enormity of their hats and boots struck Matt as astoundingly preposterous.

He almost laughed. He wanted to laugh. Maybe then this damn joke would be over and done with.

Instead he sighed. And felt like his soul was slipping out of him.

"Are you all right?" the older trooper said.

Matt gave the question some thought before he nodded.

He realized his mouth was hanging open. He closed it and swallowed.

The two troopers exchanged glances. The older one nodded at Matt.

"We're sorry to have to bring you this news," the older one said.

Matt nodded again. And discovered his mouth hanging open again. This time he closed it firmly and frowned while he swallowed.

The troopers looked at each other again. Again they turned back to Matt.

"Did you need us to call anyone?" the older trooper said.

Matt shook his head. This time he left his mouth open. He became aware he was breathing heavily. And that the policemen were concerned about him. He looked up at them and made himself smile. Which twisted into a grimace. Instead of improving his appearance this attempt to put his visitors at ease only convinced them they were right to be concerned.

"Thanks," Matt said. "I'm all right."

The troopers watched him and frowned.

"You sure?" the older one said. "We could take you to the hospital. If you're not feeling well."

Mention of the hospital and how he was feeling made Matt remember his episode of unconsciousness back at The Ol' Back Porch. Which happened earlier this very evening. But seemed to have occurred several years ago. Maybe the hospital wasn't a bad idea. Then he remembered going there to watch his mother die and decided the hospital was actually a very bad idea.

He made that same awful grimace-smile.

"I'm fine," Matt said. "Really."

The troopers looked at each other.

A moment later they were gone.

Matt remained on the couch. Beneath his blank and staring eyes his mouth hung wide open. His eyes only moved and his mouth only closed when they became painfully dry. As he blinked and swallowed and wanted a glass of water and wondered if he would ever find the energy to rise off the couch and move to the kitchen or anywhere else in this desolate world,

Matt noticed that the departure of the state troopers and particularly the absence of their enormous hats and boots had left the sad anonymous apartment feeling enormously empty.

Part III:
Catch That Falling Boy

Chapter 9

Esperanza was a mere six months old when her parents put their only child in the care of her maternal grandmother and went up into the mountains to tend an ailing relative. An aged paternal great-uncle who refused to come down from his little hut high up in a remote meadow where he had been born and was determined to die but was taking forever to get around to it. Hermán and Adelita would clean up his mess and make sure he had enough food and firewood to last through the next visit from the family members who took turns caring for that stubborn old fool.

On their way and while they were with him everything went as it always did. They wound their way up along the twisting mountain roads to find the ancient one waiting impatiently. He grumbled his disapproval at how they went about caring for him. Then turned weepy and grasping when it came time for them to leave. Hermán and Adelita had to peel off his clutching hands and push him away to climb back into their little Chevy hatchback.

"Te ruego que," the old man said. "Por favor. No les vayan tan temprano. Quédense aquí un poco más."

I'm begging you. Please. Don't go so soon. Stay a little longer.

But they knew a little longer was always followed by a little longer more. So they smiled and shook their heads and got in their car and started home.

❖   ❖   ❖

If only for that once they had done what he asked. And lingered with the old man for even just a few minutes before departing. Taken a moment to savor the mountain air. Enjoyed a taste of the clear sharp spring water to which the old man gave credit for his advanced age. And let the events of the world unfold for a little while without their active involvement. Even if they had delayed for merely a few seconds. How different things would have been.

But they went forward to their waiting fate. On a particularly tight curve of that winding mountain road. Where a half-ton Ford pickup came around the bend too fast. And over in their lane. There wasn't anything Hermán could do. Everything the brakes and steering wheel could accomplish were insufficient to save them. The truck knocked their little Chevy off the road and sent it tumbling down into a deep and stony ravine.

The driver of the truck fled the scene. Leaving no witnesses to say what had happened. The official report from the Doña Pero County Coroner's Office, which at the time consisted of one very old Anglo who was nearly blind, concluded that the deceased were both knocked unconscious by the collision and remained so while they died in the fire that consumed them.

Which was a lie. That failed in its objective of sparing those who survived the good young Armijos. By the ways of such things the truth was soon known. Word of how they died spread quickly from the deputies who climbed down into that ravine. From one mouth to another everyone who ever knew Hermán and Adelita came to know they perished while clutching each other as best their cramped conditions would allow. And that they had most likely been fully conscious and aware of their impending fate when the spilled gasoline ignited.

❖   ❖   ❖

That truth took a heavy toll as it jumped from mouth to ear. And hit no one harder than it did Halfbreed Henry Pennycoat. He tried to hide from it by crawling inside of many bottles.

But after a few months of especially hard drinking during which that truth only grew larger and more demanding, he went back up on that mountain road to the curve where you could see the scorched and dented hatchback still rusting down below. There was nowhere to park all the way off the road, so Henry left his truck with two tires still on the blacktop and two on the gravel, the keys still in the ignition and the engine still on. He finished the fifth of whiskey he had cracked open in his driveway, stepped out of the cab, got a running start, and leapt in after Hermán and Adelita.

His truck had run out of gas by the time it was reported parked there. When the sheriff's men went looking for Henry to return his truck and write him a ticket, something they had done more than once before, they found the scrawling tear-stained note he had left behind on his kitchen table confessing his role in the deaths of the young Armijos.

In those months while Halfbreed Henry worked up his courage to end it all, little Esperanza stayed with her maternal grandmother. But the suicide of Henry Pennycoat and the news of what he had done dealt a great double blow to Domencia Gaspar. Even the village priest had long ago given him up as a lost cause.

Now her old love had done two devastating things. First he had let his dissolute ways bring about the deaths of her youngest daughter, whom she cherished dearly; and her dutiful son-in-law, whom she had grown quite fond of; and in so doing had orphaned her little granddaughter, who was her dearest treasure in all the world. But as if all that was not terrible enough, he had then committed the grave sin of murdering himself. A sin for which there could be no forgiveness since it could not be confessed.

Three days after Henry Pennycoat took his life, old Domencia Gaspar had a stroke that left her paralyzed and unable to speak. Which sent the little orphan Esperanza away from her maternal Abuela. And into the household of her oldest paternal Tío.

Josef Armijo was a man who liked to surround himself with women. This was a pleasure routinely denied him by the manly nature of his work and by having mostly brothers and only sons. He had more than once expressed his wish for a daughter, or two, instead of all those boys.

So he was pleased to have his little niece come live with him. But of course the work of caring for the infant did not fall to Josef. His wife was not so pleased at first by this addition to her workload. Although she did not share this with anyone. Least of all her husband.

But soon Rosa Armijo was utterly besotted with sweet little Essie.

The child had a smile that could snap hearts like they were crackers.

Chapter 10

Most of her memories from that time were of her uncle. What little she saw of him when he wasn't out doing his job. How when he was home he was in a hurry to get back out again. Eating on his feet in the kitchen while talking on the telephone. Sitting out in his patrol car while he finished dinner so he could talk on the radio. She did not remember what he said or the sound of his voice. Just the ringing of the telephone and the crackle of the car radio.

In only one memory was sound important. When she heard him come home in the middle of the night while she lay awake praying that Elden was still alive. She listened to her uncle's heavy footsteps move through the house and was overwhelmed with love and reverence and gratitude for her strong Tío Josef working so hard to find her friend.

But in her most vivid memory of the events around the abduction she was alone. Even though she was out in public. At the store in the center of the village. The same store that Señora Morris sent Elden to on the afternoon when he vanished.

This memory had sound at first. Muted voices coming from inside the store while she moved up onto the wooden porch. The creaking of the steps and the floorboards beneath her feet. Then the voices and her footsteps were gone when she saw the big print blaring across the top of the newspaper in the stand beside the entrance—

MORRIS BOY STILL MISSING

She read it again. And then again. And still again. Esperanza read those words many times before she lowered her eyes to the first paragraph beneath the headline. Where she only read a few sentences more. Enough to see her friend's first name joined to his last. And to feel the stab into her chest that came when she absorbed the words "believed to be kidnapped."

She did not understand how something she already knew could hurt again. And stranger still hurt even more. Just because she read it printed in the newspaper. Nothing had changed but somehow everything was worse.

Years later she did not understand how the hurt could remain so intense.

As if it had only happened yesterday.

❖   ❖   ❖

The first thing she could recall about the abduction was coming into the kitchen after school to find her aunt Rosa holding Señora Morris while the poor mother wailed like her heart was being torn from her chest.

Mr. Morris took to the road with a shotgun. Where he terrified strangers he met out in the backcountry. A red-faced red-eyed red-bearded giant dressed like a lumberjack waving a shotgun over his head while shouting curses and threats. There were reports that on one occasion he fired his gun and barely missed a man who lived in the next county and was only out hunting rabbits.

One evening he appeared at the Armijo house, worked up into a frenzy over something he had seen or thought he saw in his fevered state. He and Josef stood out in the driveway together. Esperanza watched her uncle listen to their big neighbor release a thundering tirade. When Mr. Morris had stopped yelling and throwing his arms around Joe Armijo reached up a hand to the distraught father's enormous shoulder.

She didn't remember the words he used. Or even hearing them spoken. But she knew that her uncle told Mr. Morris he was only making things worse. That he should stay home and stay out of the way and let the lawmen do their jobs. Before he shot someone and wound up in jail. Then Joe put both hands on the big man's shoulders and stood with him while Mr. Morris covered his face with his hands.

The last thing he said before he left were the only words Esperanza could recall clearly from what she heard the two men say. After he had finished wiping his red face with his hands Mr. Morris stared down at Deputy Sheriff Josef Armijo and raised a single finger when he said—

"We only have the one, Joe. Just the one."

The white hallway was full of noise and confusion. They sat on hard chairs watching people come and go. Her uncle was among the lawmen in their tan uniforms. The doctors and nurses were all in white. One nurse kept striding past and wore shoes that squeaked.

Years later when she was ready to talk about Elden again Rosa told her they didn't see him while he was at the hospital. The doctors wouldn't permit it. So they sat and waited for more than an hour before they were told he could not have any visitors. And then they left.

In her aunt's car she stared out the window watching telephone poles march past and decided the pain she felt must be nothing compared to his. A drop of water beside an ocean. That he must be in more pain than she could ever comprehend. Like trying to take in the enormity of the night sky full of stars.

Chapter 11

It was early in the evening. Dinner had just ended. Rosa was heading out the door to check on Señora Morris. Esperanza wanted to go with her.

Rosa told her no.

"Why not?" Esperanza said. "I'll be quiet."

"Because she won't want to upset you. And if she needs to cry, then she should cry."

Esperanza remembered Señora Morris howling like a wounded animal here in their kitchen. She didn't want to see her like that again.

"Oh," Esperanza said. "Okay."

While her aunt was gone Esperanza paced. She had homework waiting for her but she couldn't make herself do it. She couldn't make herself do the dishes either. She tried but instead she just kept walking back and forth.

Rosa wasn't gone very long. And when she returned, as Esperanza hoped, her aunt brought news about Elden. But it wasn't news she wanted to hear.

Rosa told her that Elden would not be coming home anytime soon. He would go from the hospital in town to a state facility where they could take better care of him. He would be there for at least a few weeks and maybe much longer. The doctors didn't know yet how long his recovery would take.

"Can I see him before he goes?" Esperanza said.

Rosa frowned and shook her head.

"He's leaving first thing tomorrow morning."

Esperanza resumed her pacing. Rosa watched the girl go back and forth. Esperanza stopped when she asked her next question—

"Can I go see him when he gets there?"

Rosa sighed and shook her head again.

"I don't know, Essie. I hope so. Maybe once he's feeling better. But it's up to the doctors. We'll have to wait and see."

Esperanza peered intently at her aunt.

"Did she tell you what happened to him?"

Rosa grimaced. She balled her hands up into fists.

"Ah baby," she said.

Rosa smiled at her niece. Or at least she tried to smile. But she couldn't completely break the grimace that still lurked underneath. She went to Essie and embraced her.

"Let's not think about that," Rosa said.

Esperanza clung to her aunt and wanted to weep. But the tears wouldn't come. Instead her heart raced like she had just run home full speed across the village.

She stepped back and frowned up at Rosa.

"Can I write to him?"

Rosa smiled and now there was no grimace hiding behind it.

"That's a wonderful idea."

She pointed at the table.

"Why don't you write to him now?"

"I have schoolwork."

"I think this is more important."

Esperanza nodded.

"Yes. I think so too."

She went for her paper and pencils and made herself ready to write. When she was seated before a blank sheet she looked at her aunt. Rosa stood before the sink. She had her head bowed. The dishes remained untouched.

"I better not ask him what happened," Esperanza said.

Rosa turned to her and frowned.

"No. It would be best not to."

❖   ❖   ❖

Rosa watched her niece for a few moments before she turned on the water and started the dishes. Esperanza bent over the table and spent the next hour on her letter. She told Elden what he had missed at school and about things she had seen in the hills that she thought would interest him. And some things other children had said that he might think were funny.

When her letter was done Esperanza asked her aunt for an envelope. She folded her letter neatly and placed it inside the envelope and took her letter over to see Señora Morris. Who smiled at Esperanza even though her eyes were red and wet. Esperanza asked Señora Morris where she should send her letter and wrote the address at the state hospital on the envelope.

She spent a long moment in a moist embrace from the Señora before she brought her letter home. She copied the address into one of her notebooks so she could write to her friend whenever she wanted. She asked her Tía Rosa for a stamp and carefully pasted it onto the envelope. Then she carried her letter out to the mailbox and put it inside and raised the red flag that told the mailman there was something for him to collect.

And then Esperanza began waiting impatiently for a reply.

Chapter 12

Late one morning word went around the school that an arrest had been made. Esperanza first heard the news passed between two teachers as she and her classmates went through the courtyard on their way to the library.

Later at lunch a boy said it was her Tío Josef who made the arrest.

Of course it was, she thought.

Her heart raced with excitement. On her way back to class she imagined Elden sitting up in a hospital bed smiling and laughing as he poured over her letter. For the rest of the day, every few minutes she would remember hearing about the arrest and the news from the boy at lunch and then imagine Elden fully restored to his previous self. Happily resuming what only waited for his return. She felt boundlessly confident that everything would again be as it once was and should be.

Back when her life had been perfect.

And all that would be hers again because of her Uncle Joe.

What a great man he was. How very much she owed to him.

After school she found her Tía Rosa and Señora Morris listening to the radio in the kitchen waiting for news on the arrest. A few minutes after she arrived home the announcer said the man in custody was "a Mexican national" but the Sheriff's Department hadn't released his name.

"What does that mean?" Esperanza said.

Rosa kept her eyes on the radio.

"That he's from Mexico."

Esperanza frowned at the little speaker inside the device up on the shelf.

"I thought he was Anglo."

She looked at Señora Morris and saw the Señora was watching her.

"Me too," the Señora said.

They both looked at Rosa.

"Tío said they were looking for an Anglo man," Esperanza said. "A young guy in a pickup truck."

Rosa shrugged and shook her head.

"I guess they were looking for the wrong man," Rosa said. "And now they found the right one."

All eyes went back to the radio. They waited for more news. But when the announcer came back on he only repeated what he had said before.

Their wait for the man of the house and of the hour proved to be in vain. As dinner was drawing near, the telephone rang and Josef told his wife he would not be joining them. Before Rosa had a chance to ask about the arrest her husband said goodbye and hung up.

The rest of the family ate dinner with the radio on. Whenever the boys grew too loud Rosa would shush them and nod at the little device up on the shelf.

"I don't want to miss anything," she said several times.

So they were ready and waiting when Josef was interviewed. Only briefly, just a few questions. He confirmed that the suspect was from Mexico. He confirmed they were not ready yet to release the suspect's name. And most importantly for his family gathered around the radio in the kitchen while they ate dinner without him, Deputy Sheriff Josef Armijo confirmed that he was the one who had executed the arrest.

The boys erupted. Rosa had to yell them down so she could hear the rest of what was said. When the interview ended a few moments later the boys erupted again and this time Rosa and Essie joined them. No one cheered louder or loved Josef Armijo more or felt more pride and gratitude for what he had done than his young orphaned niece. She wanted to run around the village screaming out her joy at the top of her lungs.

She was absolutely certain everything would be set right again.

Chapter 13

For a week after the letter arrived from the doctor at the state hospital saying that Elden Morris was not ready to engage in correspondence, Esperanza said nothing that was not in response to questions or statements addressed directly to her. She stopped participating in class at school. She did not socialize with the other children. She did not come home with news of her day to share with her Tía Rosa.

When those seven days had passed Esperanza slowly resumed her former habits. Gradually she again became the active girl she was before. But that is not to say she was exactly the same. There was a seriousness about her now, even when she was laughing or carrying on.

Esperanza saw Señora Morris approaching their house and almost called out. But then she saw how the Señora moved with her head down and her hands knotted together. Esperanza stopped in the lane and watched the Señora knock on their kitchen door and saw Rosa let her in.

She remained where she was for a moment longer before she continued home. Then found the two women seated at the kitchen table. Rosa sent her back outside to do her chores. Confirming that her aunt did not want her to hear what was being said. She went to change out of her school clothes. The women resumed talking. They spoke softly but their voices carried through the still house.

Esperanza stopped and listened to what was being said back in the kitchen. Señora Morris had learned there was still no change in her son's condition. He still only spoke when spoken to. And there was still a delay before he responded. He still showed no interest in anything. He still barely ate. He still sat and did nothing unless prompted and still displayed no desire to do anything other than sit and stare. He would not read the books he was given. This from a boy who had loved to read. When outside in his most active moments he wandered in slow circles. As best the doctors could determine he still had no memory of being abducted. Or for several weeks before.

All of which meant the doctors could not set a date for his return. The day when Elden could come home was still likely months away. The time he needed to remain in the doctors' care might even be one full year. After that there would be no more funding from the state to provide further treatment. He would be released from the hospital whatever his condition. But they recommended he stay with them while he showed no improvement.

When Señora Morris said—

"My son is lost to me."

The house became deathly silent. A chill went down Esperanza's spine. She had to creep along the floors not to be heard continuing to her room. Where she sat on her bed for several minutes. Then changed before creeping again to make her way outside.

She didn't hear anything more of what was said out in the kitchen. Just the sound of Rosa's voice as she tried to reassure Señora Morris.

The sun was markedly lower in the sky by the time she finished her chores. She was standing in the chicken yard staring up at a cloud passing overhead when Rosa called her in to do her homework. The sound of her aunt's voice made her startle and jump.

For days Esperanza felt hollow inside. She went around with her head and her heart and her soul all feeling empty.

❖　　❖　　❖

When the year of funding provided by state law for his treatment at the state hospital had elapsed, the boy named Elden Morris finally went home. And as Esperanza feared but had come to expect— although still could not accept and still hoped and prayed against—the boy who returned was not the one she had known and loved. In her first encounter with the altered Elden—which took place in the yard outside his house, the same place where they had first met five years before—Esperanza saw with horror that this Elden was another boy entirely. The only resemblance that remained was physical.

This boy would not look her in the eye. Not anyone else either. Not even his own mother. Even though he now rode her skirts like a boat tethered to a dock. Never straying from her side. And never volunteering a single word. Only speaking when spoken to and often not then. Again not even to his own mother. Direct questions went unanswered as often as not.

But great as these changes were there was another that overwhelmed them for the girl who had once been his closest friend. This new Elden did not remember her. She could see it in his eyes. There was no recognition at all. Not even the slightest hint. Their special relationship—which she had once believed would endure beyond even the grave—was gone. Completely and utterly vanished. Like a handful of ashes torn away by a violent wind.

All that remained of their past together were her own fading memories. And it was hard to hold onto those memories of the old Elden with this new one going about acting spooky right in front of her. In the first few weeks after his return the haunted presence of the new boy pushed the old one into a dreamscape. The former Elden became a vague ideal and the world they had shared a hazy fantasy.

And Esperanza was forced to a bitter conclusion—

Life is just not all that good.

For many weeks after Elden returned she reviewed that conclusion each and every day. And each and every time it stung her like a scorpion. And for a time each sting seemed just as potent as the last.

But that time passed. With enough repetitions she finally became inured. And to see herself as matured because she could endure it. No longer just a child like the others playing around her.

What a horridly sour step to take toward adulthood.

Chapter 14

She was across the yard watching Elden start up the half-flight of concrete steps that led into the schoolhouse. They were no longer in the same class. Elden had to repeat a grade when he resumed his education. So now they only saw each other out in the yard. Not that he wanted anything to do with her or anyone else. But she always watched him out there. So she saw how he went slowly and carefully up those steps. As if each one presented its own challenge. And she saw that he stopped when he reached the top.

And she saw when he began to shake.

Esperanza ran toward Elden without consciously deciding to. Her feet were pounding across the yard before she was aware he was tumbling backwards. Señor Ramos, the school's janitor, reached the steps just before she did. He dove forward and grabbed for the falling boy but only managed to jam his hand against the concrete.

Blood came out from the back of Elden's head and pooled on the bottom step. He was still shaking. Now that she was standing over him Esperanza could see how the seizure distorted his face. And when she saw she began to scream. A howling wail that made others cover their ears.

The last memory she had of her friend before he vanished was running away from him. They were on their way home from school when a problem between the two suddenly flared up and exploded. One moment they were talking and the next they were screaming. What they had quarreled over she couldn't recall. The years robbed her of the particulars about the thorn. All she could remember was the wound.

Esperanza cried as she ran ahead. Elden did not chase after her.

And that made it so much worse.

Her Tía Rosa was the one who explained to Esperanza what was going on.

"Poor little thing," Rosa said. "You have feelings for him."

She buried her face against her aunt while she wept again. Then looked up at Rosa and said—

"What should I do? Should I tell him?"

Rosa stroked Essie's black hair.

"No. I don't think so."

"Why not?"

Rosa sighed.

"A boy his age isn't ready."

"But I'm his age."

Which was all of ten years old.

"Are you a boy?" Rosa said.

Esperanza found herself amused despite her suffering. She smiled and shook her head.

"No."

"That makes all the difference."

"Why?"

"Because boys remain boys when girls start becoming women."

Esperanza blinked at her aunt.

"I'm becoming a woman?"

Rosa sighed and nodded.

"There's no helping it," she said.

❖   ❖   ❖

His fall left Elden Morris with a cracked skull, a serious concussion, and seizures almost daily. Señora Morris confided to Rosa that before his fall her son had a few seizures at the state hospital and one at home just after he returned. Now sometimes he had three in a single day.

Which meant that his living at home was no longer viable. The parish priest found a Catholic charity hospital in California that would care for him.

68

Along with a job for Señora Morris in their cafeteria. Which would let them sneak by while her husband looked for work. A month after Esperanza witnessed Elden fall outside their school the Morris family was gone.

The little square adobe house two doors over from the Armijos stood empty again. As it had before the Morris family came and went. When Esperanza passed that small empty house she felt rage at the devil who had stolen her friend. Too much fury to let in any of the grief buried beneath it.

A month after they moved Rosa wrote a letter to Señora Morris. Esperanza included her best wishes for Elden. And again she monitored the mailbox hoping for a reply. Although with nothing like her former vigilance. But the days and then weeks passed without a reply. At Christmas Rosa sent a card. But the Armijos never had word from the Morris family again. Eventually the parish priest learned and shared with Rosa that Mr. Morris had found a good job and then lost it and then took a bad job and drank heavily. He had spent a night in jail. His wife feared what would become of him.

That was the last anyone in the village knew of the Morris family. Who had come among them and lost their son and feared him dead but when they got him back alive his being alive was all that could be said in favor of his condition. That family was gone now, both gone from the village and gone from this earth. The remnants had left for California but those were mere scraps and entirely unrecognizable. Gone was the jolly disposition of Mr. Morris. He was just a sad drunk now. Gone was the sweet nervous energy of Señora Morris. She was a haunted shadow of what she had been.

Most of all, gone was Elden. That bright charming boy. Who had been full to the brim with the promise of life.

As the days went past and her memory of him faded, what reminded Esperanza the most of Elden

Morris was the badly mended hand of the school janitor. When Señor Ramos lunged for Elden and jammed his hand against the concrete steps he broke the bone between his ring finger and his wrist. Others did not notice when Señor Ramos rubbed his sore hand and winced against the pain. But Esperanza did. Sometimes their eyes met and a look would pass between them. A glance that expressed their common guilt at their shared failure.

They both still wanted to catch that falling boy.

Part IV:
Enter the Mexican

Chapter 15

This was back before the cell phone changed everything. Before everyone and their cousin could place or receive a call anywhere at any time. So I couldn't call anyone until I was alone in that motel room Armijo checked me into. And when that happened my mother was still on the road to LA. Which meant I couldn't reach her.

Not that I wanted to talk to my mother anyway. We were already mad at each other and I knew she would get even madder when she heard what had happened. Because I wouldn't be there to help her move in.

So when I picked up the phone I was glad to be calling my aunt. But my aunt was at work. Where her moody prick of a boss sometimes screamed at her for taking personal calls. And on that day of course he was in his screaming mood. Before I could tell my Tía where I was and what had happened she said she had to go and hung up.

That long empty afternoon kept stretching out and getting longer. I paced around the room and turned the TV on and off and then finally the hour came when my aunt should be at home. But when I called I got her old answering machine. Which let me say about three words before it cut me off and disconnected. When I called back I didn't even get the machine. Just endless ringing. Which is what happened every other time I tried. Which was maybe ten or twelve times that night.

I kept myself occupied between attempted calls by staring at the TV. But none of what flickered across the screen got past my eyeballs. My brain was all filled up with finding that poor kid and what had happened to him. And when I could take no more of that, my mind jumped ahead to the new life I was promised out in California. Which I hated to admit sounded better and better all the time.

Finally I turned the TV off and stared out the window at the broken glass glinting under the lights in the parking lot. I listened to a semi going up through its gears as it climbed onto the interstate that cut through town off to the north and felt unbearably and brutally alone. I ached with wanting to follow that truck away from there. But that slab of red meat tossed into my cage had come with an anchor. Not *if* they caught him. But *when*. There was no way I was leaving before that happened.

And then I was overwhelmed with missing my family. Even that jackass my mother was going to marry. Maybe the jackass was right. Swimming pools and bikini girls sounded like just what I needed.

I hoped the law would catch that damned Mormon quick.

What a fool I was. Waiting patiently in the baited trap.

When coyotes started up out in the desert behind the motel they seemed so close they should have been with me in my room. I got out of bed and went around back to have a look. Even though I knew how the sounds coyotes make can trick you like that. Of course they were far way. Far off and free and wild and on the run after something.

When I was back in my room I tried the number I had out in LA. Maybe my mother would be there by then. If they drove straight through. I remember my dialing hand shook. I don't know why but I remember that clearly. Watching my hand tremble as my fingers touched the keypad.

❖   ❖   ❖

I was up at dawn waiting for the clock to tell me I could try calling people again. When I decided that the clock could go to hell I still didn't get any answers. Not out in LA or at my aunt's place. I didn't try my aunt later when she should have been at work. If her boss was in his screaming mood again I might get her fired.

I went out for food and came back and tried LA one more time. Then decided enough was enough. I would wait it out. Eventually someone would call me. Either Armijo saying they had caught the bastard and needed me to come identify him. Or maybe my mother or my aunt asking where the hell I was and what was going on.

If either of them ever thought to check who had called them and maybe try calling back.

When the damn phone finally did ring I almost jumped out of my skin.

A man introduced himself as Deputy X. I didn't catch his name. I don't remember him mentioning the Doña Pero County Sheriff's Department or any other law enforcement agency. Just that he was a deputy. He asked if I was Andreas Delmorales. Then said they wouldn't be needing me anymore and I was free to go. Before I could respond he said goodbye and hung up.

That big piece of red meat had just been yanked away. The disappointment hurt. I wanted to point my finger at that Mormon bastard and have him know I was the one who brought him down.

But I was just a dumb kid. And an angry one now. So at first I didn't question it. And as much as I had wanted to help catch the bad guy I was sick to death of that stinking motel room and itching to find out what California could mean for me. So I cursed Armijo for not having the decency to call me himself and started packing.

Which took maybe five minutes. But when I was ready to go and had calmed down some I didn't like it. Now something didn't feel right. I stared out the front window at my uncle's truck waiting to take me away from there then dug out Armijo's number and stared at the phone. Then stopped halfway through dialing. Then started over and let the call go through.

A woman answered. She said the Deputy Sheriff was out of the office and asked if I wanted to leave a message. I said no and thanked her and hung up.

I still didn't like it. But decided maybe that was enough reason to get the hell out of Doña Pero. If they wanted me gone there was no reason to stay. What could I hope to accomplish by sticking around?

I locked the room and put my bag in the truck and walked over to the office. When I pulled the door open the clerk seemed to be waiting for me. Or at least waiting for someone. I passed the key across the desk and thanked him. He nodded and didn't say anything. When I said goodbye he mumbled something unintelligible.

His eyes never met mine. Another thing I didn't like.

I wasn't liking any of this.

The interstate was the best way out of town. If I wanted the fastest start to Los Angeles. And I intended to take the interstate when I left the motel. But then I slowed down going past that restaurant where I saw the Mormon. And did a U-turn through their parking lot. So I could follow after him on that road going west.

All these years later and I still don't know why I did that. I knew there was absolutely zero chance I would find him. For all I knew he could have already been found. They could have let me go because they had a better witness. Someone who actually saw him snatch the boy.

But there I was headed down that road chasing after him. Seeing him in that turquoise Ford pickup somewhere up ahead of me. And feeling in my gut that he was still out there.

Thinking about the Mormon kept me distracted. I didn't notice the two patrol cars coming up fast behind me until the first one moved over into the oncoming lane and appeared in my side mirror. A glance at my inside mirror showed the second one closing fast on my bumper.

The first one went past and moved over ahead of me. They had their flashers on but no sirens. For a second I thought they would both go flying past. But then the first one pumped his brakes and blasted his siren.

As I pulled over onto the shoulder I recognized Armijo behind me. And for a moment I felt elated. They needed me after all. Maybe there was a mix-up and I shouldn't have been told I could go. Maybe that witness they thought was better had turned out not to be so reliable. Or maybe they had just realized their mistake and changed their minds.

I cut my engine and pushed the door open and stepped out onto the pavement. The sun stung my eyes and I put up my hand as I started toward Armijo. Then he came out of his car and there was a flash of light as he raised his hand.

I went a few more steps before I realized what made that flash. Then spun around and saw the other deputy close behind me.

With his gun pointed at my chest.

Chapter 16

Armijo and his gun didn't scare me all that much. But the other deputy and his were a different matter. That one was scary even without a gun.

He had been among the lawmen at the hospital. Big and Spanish with some Apache blood judging by the broad face and thick cheekbones. Tall and muscular with wide imposing shoulders. And young. Only a few years older than me. Built hard and hard-looking.

The expression on his face said he very much wanted to shoot me. And that this desire had little or nothing to do with me in particular. He just wanted to shoot someone. And right now I was the one he happened to be pointing his gun at. Give him any excuse and I was a dead man.

So I worked very hard at not giving him that excuse. I moved slowly and did exactly as I was told. He still chose to yank hard on the handcuffs he snapped around my wrists. This being back before law enforcement switched to those plastic restraints.

He marched me over to the back door of Armijo's patrol car and spun me around. His face was close in front of mine. With my eyes cast down to demonstrate my compliant submission my gaze fell upon his upper lip. And I saw it was covered with fuzz that he must have considered a mustache. Since if he didn't there was no reason to leave that shit there.

Then he folded me into the car and slammed the door behind me. Armijo said something to him I didn't catch. Then the fat man got in behind the wheel and I caught a glimpse of his face in the rear view mirror.

And being a young man I had a stupid thought. The kind that young men have when they are feeling humiliated and struggling against it. I considered that wisp on the other one's lip and what

Armijo wore on his own face and took some bitter pleasure in knowing that even though I was younger than both of my captors I could grow a good thick black mustache if I so desired. A far better specimen than that delicate fluff the Hispano Apache had beneath his nose. Or that sorry moth-eaten-looking mess that drooped sadly around the mouth of the fat man.

All these years later I can still taste how it felt. The rage and the shame and the sharp bite of resentment that put that stupid thought in my empty head.

❖   ❖   ❖

Ten days at the county jail spent waiting to call and then calling. Ten days without word from anyone about anything. Each and every one of my calls going unanswered. Endless ringing echoing through my troubled sleep.

Then the eleventh day came and a guard stopped outside my cell. This was a surprise in and of itself. Then he said something that was a much greater surprise. Words that made my heart soar—

"There's someone here to see you."

Oh those words were magical!

I wanted so badly for that someone to be my mother. Despite all the anger I still felt toward her. And despite having no reason to believe she even knew where I was. But my aunt could have heard what happened to me. Somehow. Maybe. That seemed more likely than my mother showing up all the way from Los Angeles. I pictured my aunt waiting nervously while I followed the guard down the hall. I couldn't speak to ask him who my visitor might be. I was too overwrought.

Then we reached our destination and the guard unlocked a door and let me into a small room. And I found myself standing across a banged-up metal table from a man I had never seen before. Who addressed me in Spanish but introduced himself with the entirely Anglo name of Bill Jameson. Although judging by his brown skin and black hair and black eyes there was at least one señora in his family tree.

He was short and round and rumpled. Black plastic-framed glasses that were clouded with grease. He needed a shave when I met him and most other times too. The brown suit he wore was old and stained and too small around his middle. He smelled of stale sweat and cigarettes and just a hint of cheap whiskey. That last smell proved to be with him most always.

This was the attorney who would be presenting my defense.

There was a manila folder on the table. The lawyer flipped it open. Then put his eyes on his paperwork when he said—

"¿Habla inglés?"

I frowned. But my lawyer was still looking at his papers. So he didn't notice.

"Yes," I said.

He glanced up for a second. But his eyes were hungry for those papers. They couldn't stay away.

"So," he said. "Manuel."

I frowned again. But again he kept looking down and didn't notice.

"Excuse me?" I said.

He didn't seem to hear.

"Why don't you tell me what happened," he said. "In your own words."

I kept frowning while I stared at him. Eventually the lawyer looked up and saw my expression. He frowned back at me.

"Is there something wrong?" he said.

I sat forward in my chair and folded my arms on the table. I stared into his eyes swimming behind those greasy lenses when I said—

"What did you just call me?"

❖   ❖   ❖

78

Bill Jameson looked down at his paperwork. His eyes scanned across the pages and then stopped. He put a hand to his mouth and cleared his throat. Then looked up at me when he said—

"Manuel Ortiz."

He frowned when I shook my head. Then glanced down at his forms. When he looked at me again I shook my head again.

"That's not who I am," I said.

I pointed at his paperwork.

"You sure you got the right guy?"

He put his head down and skimmed through his papers.

"You were arrested for the abduction and assault of a minor."

He stopped and put his eyes on my face.

I had trouble making myself agree with what he said.

He prompted me—

"Yes?"

I frowned and swallowed.

"Either you were or you weren't," he said.

I sighed. Then I nodded.

His eyes went back to his paperwork.

"Then I got the right guy."

He stopped and peered at a form. A finger tapped the table. He didn't look at me when he said—

"So who are you then?"

"Andreas Delmorales."

"Mexican? Your English is good."

"I'm not Mexican. I was born right here. In Doña Pero County. I've never even been to Mexico."

He blinked at me.

"But you have a Mexican driver's license."

Heat went up my neck. I frowned again.

"What?"

The lawyer looked down at the form on top of his stacked papers. The sheet was white and the printing was black and the spaces were completed in a scrawl of blue ink. He tapped it with one finger while he answered me.

"That's what it says here."

I pushed away from the table and sat back in my chair. I shook my head.

"That's wrong. I'm *telling* you. I'm not Mexican."

He blinked again. His eyes were blurred behind those greasy lenses.

"Look," he said. "This is no time to play around."

"I know that."

"So explain the license to me."

"That's easy. It isn't mine."

"It has your picture on it."

That shut me up. What could I say to that? He watched me and waited. Then he said—

"I lied. There's no picture on it."

I scowled at him and pushed my breath out through my teeth.

"Why did you say that?"

"To see how you would react."

"And?"

He only blinked.

"It's not my license," I said.

"Can you prove it isn't yours?"

I wanted to hit him. Instead I swallowed and frowned and bit my lip. Then folded my arms across my chest and shook my head.

"How can I prove that? I mean—what kind of question is that?"

We stared at each other. Then I unfolded my arms and pointed at him. I jabbed my finger while I said—

"*You* prove that *you* don't have one."

"Prove that I don't have what."

"A Mexican driver's license! What else are we talking about?"

"I can't prove that."

"Of course you can't!"

80

"And I don't have to. I wasn't arrested with one in my wallet."

Which shut me up for a second time. I folded my arms back across my chest. Bill Jameson watched me for a moment.

Then he cleared his throat and gave his attention back to his paperwork.

❖　　❖　　❖

I left him alone with his forms for a few minutes. Watched him shift his papers around and listened to him breathe. Then I stretched my arm across the table and pointed at all those forms. I put my finger right under his nose. He couldn't miss it even through those dirty glasses.

"Armijo," I said. "He's the one who says he found that license."

I took my hand back and put it down.

"Am I right?"

The lawyer shuffled through his papers.

"Well?" I said.

He stopped shuffling and shrugged. He didn't look at me.

"Could be. I don't know."

"You don't know?"

"What's it matter who found it?"

"Whoever found it is who put it there."

"And how do we prove that? "

"It has to be fake. Or else they stole it. From some real Mexican."

I folded my arms across my chest. I thought I was being pretty smart.

Bill Jameson looked at me. A look that made me think I might be wrong.

Maybe I wasn't so smart.

"Have you ever been fingerprinted?" Bill said.

I frowned. Then I nodded.

"Yeah. When they arrested me."

"I mean before that."

81

I shook my head.

"No."

"Ever been arrested before?"

"No."

"You weren't in the Army?"

"No."

"Navy?"

"No. And not the Air Force either. Or the Marines."

I shook my head and smiled.

"But I was a Cub Scout for a couple weeks."

"Don't be that way."

"How should I be?"

"Are you sure you were never fingerprinted before?"

I threw my hands up in the air.

"Why do you keep going on about that?"

"Because your prints match the ones that the Mexican government has on record for Manuel Ortiz. And you match his description."

I felt sick. When I shook my head that only made me feel sicker.

Then I made my lawyer flinch when I yelled at him—

"This is *bullshit!*"

Chapter 17

We were quiet after my outburst. Then Bill Jameson sighed. He looked down at the table and after a moment he flipped his folder closed. He stared down at the folder for another moment before he raised his head and looked at me.

Then he shrugged. A round shrug from round shoulders.

"Bullshit or not," he said. "That's how it is."

I put both my hands flat on the table and leaned toward him.

"I didn't do this."

Bill blinked and said nothing. I watched him and waited.

Then I leaned forward a little more.

"I did a good thing. Why is this happening to me?"

Bill sighed again. Deeper this time. His head went back and his shoulders went up while he drew his breath in and his shoulders came down and his head dropped forward when he let his breath out. His eyes went down to his folder and he reached out a hand to tease at one corner of it.

Then he mumbled to himself—

"El que se mete a redentor, sale crucificado."

Try to help ungrateful people and you'll end up crucified.

I didn't know what that meant. It wasn't an expression I was familiar with. When Bill raised his eyes he must have seen my confusion. His eyebrows went up over his cloudy lenses and the black frames that held them. He spoke softly when he explained—

"No good deed goes unpunished."

❖   ❖   ❖

My lawyer got me supplies for writing letters. Along with my family's new address out in LA. Which was in my wallet. Which the Sheriff's Department was holding as evidence. I suppose since within that wallet the Mexican driver's license was supposedly discovered.

Why they let me have that address I don't know. But I suspect Armijo was making things up as he went along and hadn't thought that far ahead. Hadn't realized he should stop any efforts on my part to get someone to come help me. I think he saw a poor kid out on his own in a beat-to-shit old truck and figured no one would miss me if I disappeared.

He should have cut me completely off from the outside world. But maybe he couldn't do that. Maybe as second in command he didn't have enough reach. Or maybe he was just too shorthanded to cover all the bases. I have no idea how many players he had on his team.

I think he was a gambler. He rolled the dice and took his chances.

Meanwhile I wrote my letters and sent them out. And tried not to wait for a reply. But of course I did wait.

I waited through every single moment of every day.

❖ ❖ ❖

No good deed goes unpunished.

Those words haunted me. I wanted to punch Bill Jameson for putting them in my head. They felt like a curse. And cursed was how I felt. While lying awake in bed at night. While on the telephone listening to no one answer.

But despite feeling cursed I managed to do some rational thinking. To sort out some of my impressions and make sense of them. And one thing I became sure of was that the phone call which sent me on my way so I could be "caught" trying to "escape" hadn't come from the Sheriff's Department. I suspected instead it had come from the front desk of that wretched motel. And from that same clerk who acted shifty when I returned the key. The same one who had checked me in and seemed to know Armijo.

I had already told my lawyer about that call. He said he would get the phone records. If there was a call to my room from the Sheriff's Department that would lend some credence to my version of events.

Those records arrived with surprising haste. And showed what I expected. What I told Bill they showed before he could tell me. There was no record of any calls made to my room while I was staying there.

Now it was that shifty desk clerk I wanted to punch. Slam my fist right into his mumble mouth and scatter some of his teeth across the floor.

Armijo I wanted to kill.

Finally one day a guard said I had mail. I did my best not to get excited. Not to let my hopes run away with me. But those poor hopes of mine went running all over the countryside.

Those poor hopes were in for a bitter disappointment.

When the letter was placed in my hands I sat on my bunk in my cell for a long time just holding it. There was no need to bother with opening it. Because this was the same letter I had written and sent to my mother in Los Angeles. And now it was returned to me. Next to the address of the place where my family was supposed to have moved stamped on the envelope in bold red ink were these words—

NOT AT THIS ADDRESS

I read those words over many times.
How could my mother not be there?

85

The next time I called LA I got a message saying the number I had dialed was not in service. I thought maybe I had dialed wrong so I tried again and got the same message. Then I thought maybe I had written the number down wrong and tried changing some numbers around. I got some answers then but not from anyone who knew me.

I tried again the next day. Just the number I had written down this time. And got the same not-in-service message.

At the same time I wrote my mother I sent my aunt a letter too. A week after the letter to my mother came back I gave up on the one to my aunt. Maybe it never reached her. Maybe she had moved suddenly. Maybe she was evicted.

It drove me crazy when my aunt didn't answer when I rang her damn phone right off the wall.

I wanted to believe the letter to my aunt never arrived. But I was hitting too many dead ends not to suspect that they were related. That behind them all was a single cause. Some significant misfortune that had struck my entire family. The simultaneous disappearance of both my mother and my aunt felt connected. Not merely coincidental.

But of course I had no proof of this. And alone in a jail cell—although I was not in fact physically alone; but the man I was incarcerated with at the time only glowered at me with raw venomous hatred which I correctly interpreted as his reaction to the disgusting crimes I was accused of (my cellmate said as much in a low growl just before he was discharged, informing me that when we met again it would be in hell)—I knew my distressed mind was likely to see ever greater misfortune lurking behind any aspect of my existence that was unusual or suspect. Especially anything also inexplicable.

Although the cause of my family's effective disappearance was unknown, one result of their absence was certain and profound. For all practical purposes I was alone in the world.

Abruptly and very ill-timed, I was alone.

Part V:
Disbursed

Chapter 18

The mourners came mostly from the old crew at Long Valley Fab. A few were from the Motel Sweet and the Gas-N-Get where Frank found work after Long Valley closed. One of his old Navy buddies flew in from Chicago and another from Tampa. Matt had met these two once before, when he was a small child and his father hosted a reunion of his old comrades-in-arms.

These two aging veterans were both struck by the strong resemblance of Matt to young Frank back when the three of them were shipmates. Which made them choked-up and teary-eyed.

"He was a good man," one said. "A real good man."

"The best," the other said. "Just the best."

Matt shook their hands and nodded and had no idea what to say. So he said the only words he could manage—

"Yeah. Thanks."

Then this pained conversation died. The veterans looked lost and Matt felt himself sinking.

During the arrangements Matt made another failed attempt to locate his sister Glory. He reworked all the leads that were already cold when his mother died. Then he tried searching the Internet. But he could find no evidence in the outside world that his sister had ever existed.

Which left Matt as the only family member present at the funeral. He stood beside his father's open grave with his hands clutched tightly together behind his back and looked at the others gathered to pay their respects. They were mostly men of his father's generation. More than half of them Matt did not know. More than a few of these he had met before but he could not place them now because they had aged so markedly since losing their jobs at Long Valley. Matt looked at these men and wondered how they were faring in their reduced circumstances. Apparently not too well.

But mostly he wondered who he was now that he was alone.

Matt did not hear what was said about his father in the graveyard. He looked at the face of each person who spoke and saw the emotions being played out there. But the words being spoken were unintelligible to him.

He dreaded asking for time off. But he was scheduled to work at The Ol' Back Porch on the day of his father's funeral. When he got himself in front of his manager he said without ever looking at the man's face that his father had died. And just like that his schedule was cleared for three days. The only difficulty came when his manager referred to this as "bereavement leave." A phrase that made Matt's skin crawl and left him slightly nauseated.

His shifts at Megahits didn't present any direct conflict. He was scheduled to work the day before and the day after. He thought having the day after off might be a good idea. But he didn't want to discuss it with his boss, who was dull-witted and spiteful. He could imagine how the man's face would twitch while his little brain squirmed as he tried to compute the minimum he could get away with conceding to the death of this employee unit's family member.

Matt considered calling in sick the day after the funeral. But somehow going in seemed easier than picking up the phone. So he dragged himself into his car and off along the interstate to the mall and went through the repetitive motions of his job. He was numb, it was numbing work, it all worked out.

But halfway through his shift his numbness was interrupted. When a trench-coated man appeared beside him. In the horror section where Matt was robotically placing videos back up on the shelves.

"Matthew Walker?" the man said.

Matt frowned and stared. A moment later he nodded. The man handed over a business card. The card said the man was named Bob Breckenridge, his occupation was Senior Investigator, and he was employed by American Provident Mutual Life. Matt stared at the card while he tried to place the name of the firm. Just as he remembered seeing paperwork on his father's desk with that company's letterhead the man before him spoke—

"I'm an insurance investigator," the man said.

Matt nodded again. He was not really sure what that meant but was too surprised by the man's presence to ask for an explanation.

Then he noted that the card he was holding said Bob and not Robert. And that was what cut through the fog in his mind. He wondered if being Bob instead of Robert was intended to soften the man's image. Make him seem more warm and human.

And that made Matt suspect Bob Breckenridge was one of the enemy. When did a friend of the Walkers work in a business like insurance?

"What kind of insurance?" Matt said.

Bob Breckenridge peered at him.

"Life," Bob said.

He pointed at the card. Matt looked at it again. And again he saw the word Life at the end of the company name.

So he had asked a stupid question. He waited to feel embarrassed. But apparently at the moment embarrassment was beyond his capabilities.

"How did you find me here?" Matt said.

Bob shrugged and glanced around the store before he looked at Matt again.

"That's what I do," he said. "I find people."

He shrugged again.

"Among other things."

He gestured out the door, into the mall beyond Megahits.

"Can we go talk somewhere?"

"Not if I want to keep this stupid job."

Bob made a lopsided smile, sort of a like a sneer. Only sad.

"Do you?" he said.

"I need the money."

"I'll buy you lunch."

"Not hungry."

"Coffee?"

Matt looked at the DVD he still held in his other hand, the one not pinching the business card between thumb and index finger. He was about to put the DVD back on the display shelves when Bob Breckenridge asked if he was Matt Walker. The DVD was *Fearfest IV: The Ghouls Last Stand*. The cover showed a skeleton with long straggly hair holding a scythe in front of a graveyard before a big crescent moon in a cloud-shrouded sky.

Matt kept his eyes on this image while he answered Bob.

"Sure," Matt said. "I could use some more caffeine."

Matt told the manager that Bob was "an investigator" who wanted to ask him some questions. He hoped that the dimwit would think that meant Bob was a cop. And apparently it worked. The manager stared at the man in the trench coat with newfound respect and a little fear.

"Okay," the manager said.

Then he frowned at his own answer. Something wasn't right with it.

Oh yeah. He hadn't been a dick. So he dickishly added—

"But make it quick."

Matt nodded and followed Bob out into the upper concourse. Then Bob followed Matt down the escalator and into the Keefers Coffee Company near the main entrance. Where they stared at the menu board while they waited in line. They both ordered the most regular-sounding cup of joe posted up there. Bob drank his black. Matt put in some half-and-half.

They sat in the back, away from the big glass panels that separated the coffee shop—scratch that, their corporate web site refers to their outlets as "barista bars"—from the main concourse. Bob looked at his coffee so Matt looked at his. They had a quiet moment like that. Then Bob looked up, and Matt looked up, and Bob nodded at Matt.

"Look, kid, I'll tell you why I'm here," Bob said.

He paused and sighed.

"Whenever there's a death of an insured in a single-vehicle high-speed accident, especially after a recent change in the beneficiaries, the company sends me out. Really, to be honest—and I shouldn't be telling you this—it's just a formality. So the bean counters can cover their ass. I'm supposed to poke around and make sure your father didn't drive off the road on purpose. But even if he did, who would ever know? You can never prove someone did or didn't. So what's the point in sending me? Again, to cover their asses. Everyone just going through the motions."

Matt's strongest impression from this short speech was of how much Bob Breckenridge seemed to hate his job. Or at least this assignment in particular. But that impression did not stop Matt from seeing where this would go.

"Okay," Matt said.

Bob raised his hand and opened his mouth like he was about to say more, to expand on his theme of the futility of his task. But then he stopped and closed his mouth and put his hand back down. He took a deep breath. Matt waited to see if Bob would continue. But he remained silent. So Matt said what was on his mind at that particular moment—

"I didn't know my father had life insurance."

Bob nodded while he raised his hand and put two fingers up in the air.

"Two policies. Whole life and term."

He lowered his hand again and folded his arms across the table. He looked at his coffee and sighed and lifted the cup to his mouth and grimaced when he took a sip. Matt watched Bob and wondered what he meant by "whole life and term." He almost asked but decided he didn't really want to know. Not now at least. Maybe later. Maybe it would never matter.

"The change in beneficiaries," Matt said. "Was that because my mother died?"

Bob sighed and nodded.

"Yeah. Leaving you and your sister. Look, I have to say kid. I've been doing this awhile. And you can get pretty hardhearted. But I feel lousy intruding like this. I wish I could leave you alone."

He sighed again. He spread his hands and leaned forward.

"But I gotta do my job. Soon as I start acting like there's nothing to it—I'm toast. You understand?"

"Sure."

Matt didn't really. But what Bob meant became clear as they kept talking. Bob nodded at Matt before he continued.

"Okay," Bob said.

He paused and frowned and sighed before he went on. He lowered his voice when he said—

"Do you have any reason to believe that your father would take his own life?"

Chapter 19

Frank Walker died at the bottom of a long steep grade on the Vann Oldham Highway about halfway between Oldham and Walker City. He was driving his old pickup truck that was not equipped with shoulder belts let alone with air bags. He came down that long hill in the middle of the night with the accelerator pressed to the floor and went off the tarmac and down a shallow embankment and into a bridge abutment.

About a hundred yards away from the crash, on the road that crossed the bridge overhead, lived an old man who couldn't sleep. He was up watching television and heard the impact. He listened for sirens that never came. He told the local newspaper he would have put the sound out of his mind but his dog started barking and wouldn't stop. The dog was a young Husky the old man's daughter had given him for company and security at the house. Finally the old man followed his dog out onto the bridge with a flashlight and he saw Frank Walker's truck smashed up down below. He called for help on the cell phone his daughter gave him for emergencies.

"She thought I would be the one needing help," the old man said.

No disrespect to the good and venerable gentleman. But when he stood out on that lonesome bridge across the Vann Oldham Highway in the middle of the night bent over his cell phone with the wind tossing his white hair and ruffling the thick fur of the young Husky at his side and slowly pecked out 9-1-1 on that tiny clicking keyboard the man in the crushed truck down below was already beyond help. Help was too late for Frank Walker by the time the sound waves from the impact reached the recliner in the living room of the house nearby along that back road where the old man was watching television because he could not sleep.

❖   ❖   ❖

While Matt absorbed the shock of the investigator's question he saw that he should have seen it coming. As clearly as a freight train barreling at him with bells clanging and its whistle blowing. Starting from the first sentence of Bob's short speech.

But Matt hadn't and he wasn't prepared and now the question felt like a hot blade cutting through muscle and flesh to slice deep into his entrails. He had wondered briefly and bitterly when the news of his father's death first came if the crash had been intentional. He remembered his father's strange words and behavior over their dinner at The Belfast before he went off on his "fishing trip" and now Matt saw that "last meal" in a sinister light.

But then the authorities mentioned seizure and heart attack and stroke as possible causes of why a person might drive off the road at a high rate of speed. And Matt let those explanations push his ugly thoughts aside.

Now Matt heard the investigator's question echo inside his head—

Do you have any reason to believe that your father would take his own life?

Yes, Matt thought. *Absolutely.*

He frowned at Bob and shook his head.

"No," Matt said. "Absolutely not."

Bob blinked and nodded.

"No. Good. I didn't think so."

Bob sipped his coffee. Matt did the same. A frown came and went from both faces. Matt's coffee tasted like hot wet cardboard and stale graham crackers. Without the half-and-half he guessed Bob's cup tasted even worse.

"Did he seem depressed at all?" Bob said.

For a person who was incapable of depression, yeah. He had trouble sleeping even though he was exhausted; he often had no interest in food and had lost weight. I hardly ever saw him checking out chicks like he used to, and his sense of humor, which he always had before, slipped away sometimes. Sometimes he couldn't take any joy in anything.

"No, not really. I mean, you know... it was tough when my mother died. But he's a real fighter—I mean..."

Matt paused and swallowed.

"He always made the best of things, you know? He was always the one who got us all through the bad times."

Bob nodded. He took another sip. Matt did the same and regretted it. The coffee hadn't improved any. Bob put his cup down and looked at Matt.

"Anything else you want to tell me?" Bob said. "Anything at all."

Matt made a thoughtful face then slowly shook his head. Bob nodded.

"Good," he said.

They took more sips and Matt wondered why he kept doing that. Then Bob put a hand down on the table and smiled at Matt.

"Well I guess that's it kid. Thanks for your help. I'll let you get back to work."

Bob repeated the odd motions he had made earlier. Again he opened and closed his mouth while he lifted and dropped his hand. Then he took a deep breath. But this time he spoke when these actions were concluded—

"Look, kid—I'm really sorry about your dad. People say great things about him. It seems like he was a special guy."

Matt nodded.

"Yeah. He was. Thanks."

They threw away their half-finished coffees on the way out of Keefers. As Matt let his cup slip into the overflowing trash can he almost said to Bob that they could get a better cup at the Gas-N-Get on the interstate where his father used to work. But he decided that was a thought he wanted to keep for himself. They stopped out on the concourse and Bob turned toward Matt and seemed about to say goodbye. But Matt spoke first—

"Do people really kill themselves like that? Driving into things?"

Bob raised his eyebrows and nodded while he answered—

"Yeah. They do. All the time. It's about impossible to prove."

He turned away and looked across the concourse toward the fountain that splashed among the shoppers.

"Suicide by vehicle is one of those widespread secrets in our society," Bob said. "Like doctor-assisted suicide for the terminally ill. It's how people who want to behave responsibly toss in the towel. Doesn't make a big drama. Can't prove it's suicide. So the insurers have to pay."

Bob turned to Matt and stuck out his hand. They shook.

"Good to meet you, kid."

"You too."

Bob made his lopsided smile again. The one like a sad sneer.

"I wish it was under better circumstances."

Matt didn't know what to say to this. He was glad Bob didn't wait for a reply.

"Take care of yourself, kid," Bob said.

He nodded at Matt.

"But you're gonna be all right. I can tell."

With that Bob Breckenridge pushed his restless hands deep into the pockets of his trenchcoat, spun on his heel, and walked away. Matt watched the slump-shouldered insurance investigator stride past the splashing fountain and angle toward the main entrance and round a corner and disappear.

⋆   ⋆   ⋆

Matt remained where he was for a moment longer. His mind went blank and he felt abruptly exhausted. When his brain was working again he imagined trailing after Bob out of the mall and going somewhere other than home. Somewhere and anywhere new. Somewhere fresh and unsoiled.

But instead he returned to the escalator and let it ferry him back toward Megahits and the horror DVDs waiting to be reshelved. He still didn't have anything better to do and he still needed the money. The rent for that anonymous apartment overlooking the Vann Oldham Highway, with its unobscured view of the Gas-N-Get where his father used to work, was coming due and Matt would have to cover all of it on his own.

He considered where he could find a smaller and cheaper place and saw himself in one of those decaying walkups in the dying downtown of Walker City with drunks and addicts and lunatics as his neighbors. And that made him remember the nice warm home his family used to have and the good people he used to share it with. Which made him want to scream and thrash around wildly and maybe even pummel someone. If he had to pick a target the person he would choose to pummel would be his small-minded manager among the racks up at Megahits.

But Matt did nothing untoward. He remained still and quiet as the escalator slowly lofted him upward. And as he rose ponderously, Matt pictured himself driving his mother's old Toyota hatchback down that long grade out on the interstate into that very same bridge abutment where his father crashed and died. He wondered if the old man who lived nearby would come out to find him too after his Husky would not stop barking.

Then his ascent was concluded and he was moving under his own power again. His legs carried him back along the upper concourse into the video store and back among the racks where his hands carried the DVDs back onto the shelves. And while his hands moved and the plastic boxes went where they belonged, Matthew Walker wished with all his heart that he had never existed. To have never been so he could be free of all this pain.

Chapter 20

With vast resources at their disposal, a mammoth concern such as American Provident Mutual Life should have no trouble locating the beneficiaries of their policies when the time comes to release payment. But it is not in the interest of an insurance company to disburse funds. While they hold those funds they can manage those funds; and it is to their advantage to be the manager of the largest possible amount of funds. There is interest to be made and fees to be collected and perhaps markets to be manipulated by the sheer enormity of the portfolio.

All of which made American Provident Mutual Life content not to locate Gloria Walker. Who was last seen working as a cocktail waitress on the Las Vegas Strip. And maybe also doing a little stripping herself. One profession has been known to lead to the other.

So while the corporate behemoth of American Provident Mutual Life sat on its collective hands it was left to the small estate of Frank Walker to find his long-lost daughter. He had willed a few things to her specifically, mostly a small amount of jewelry from her mother's family. Not that those pieces were worth much. Their value was largely sentimental. But the lawyer for the estate was diligent in his responsibilities. He consulted with Matt who agreed with his recommendation to hire a detective agency to locate Gloria.

Three days later the detective agency reported that Gloria Walker had been killed six years before in an accident on U.S. Route 95 between Las Vegas and Indian Springs. She was single at the time of her death, having divorced her husband—the truck-driving man she met at the diner where she worked while still in high school—in Reno two years before. She had no children, from her ex-husband or any other relationship.

Little brother Matthew was officially the last Walker left.

❖   ❖   ❖

Matt learned how his sister exited this world over the telephone from the estate lawyer. The lawyer had asked Matt to come into his office but when finding a time that was good for both of them proved difficult, a weary Matt lost patience and pressed the lawyer to give him the news. When the call was over Matt looked at the clock and saw he had to get ready for a dinner shift at The Ol' Back Porch. He got in the shower and while the water soaked him every few moments he would gasp and a few paltry tears would follow. But his sobs always caught in his throat. Instead of feeling his grief pour out of him Matt only felt like he was choking.

He managed to keep his thoughts still and his emotions in check while he toweled off and dressed. But when he was rattling down the Vann Oldham Highway he took stock of his dead. Every other member of his family was now officially deceased. And only his mother did not die while driving. She was also the only Walker by marriage and not by blood.

Which presented to Matt a vehicular fatality pattern of his Walker-blooded family members. His brother accidentally crashed, his sister was accidentally crashed into, and his father intentionally crashed. To complete that pattern Matt would have to be driving when someone intentionally crashed into him. A victim of homicide by vehicle-on-vehicle. He could not imagine how this could come to pass. It seemed a seriously flawed way to commit murder. But that was the pattern that presented itself as his mother's little hatchback creaked and clattered along the interstate.

Then he found another aspect to consider—his brother died while driving a jeep, his sister while

101

driving a sedan, and his father while driving a pickup truck. Which implied he might be safe as long as he stayed out from behind the wheel of station wagons, SUVs, and trucks other than pickups. Since apparently each deceased had to add to the collection of vehicle types.

And with the conclusion of that bitter and meaningless analysis Matt's grief was set loose. After those strange and stupid ideas went worming through his head. Thoughts he knew were ridiculous. And he suspected might verge on being insane. He wiped at his tears and pulled off at the next exit. He stopped along the ramp and let himself bawl loud and long. He gasped hard and his throat no longer caught. His tears soaked the front of his shirt. He could see as the minutes went past and his emotions did not relent that he would be late to his shift at The Ol' Back Porch.

Maybe he would be fired if he was too late. And there was still rent to be paid. And other bills. The life insurance was not here yet. He didn't know when it would be. And he felt sick whenever he thought of it.

"Fuck!" Matt yelled.

He banged his fists against the steering wheel. Then he put the car in gear and continued down the ramp and went up the one opposite and rejoined the relentless traffic upon the interstate.

The death of Gloria Walker made her brother Matthew the sole beneficiary of half a million dollars in life insurance proceeds. At his next meeting with the estate lawyer Matt asked if anything would be left from the life insurance after his "family debts" were paid.

The lawyer adjusted his glasses and looked at Matt quizzically.

"Your *family* debts?" the lawyer said.

Matt nodded solemnly.

"From my mother. When she died. The hospital. The doctors. All of that. It was a lot. I don't know how much. But I know we were on some sort of payment plan. And there's the undertakers. For the two funerals. I don't know if they were ever paid. Maybe they were paid something. But maybe not all of it."

The lawyer consulted the paperwork spread across his desk top. A minute later he raised his eyebrows when he looked at Matt again.

"The funeral home was paid in full. For both services. The debts to the hospital and the doctors were in your father's name. The insurance proceeds go directly to you. Or not quite directly. We'll get to that in a moment. What matters in our current discussion is that your father's creditors can make no claim on those funds."

Matt felt his pulse quicken.

"What does that mean?" Matt said.

"It means that you are in no way indebted to your father's creditors. They cannot make claim against his children."

The lawyer paused for a moment.

"There is no legal concept of *family* debt. In the past—*long* past—you may have been obligated to pay your father's debts. But that has not been the case since... I can't remember exactly. But I think that stopped in the nineteenth century."

Matt stared. His mind was blank. The lawyer continued—

"Now about that other matter I just mentioned. Where the funds will go. Your father setup a trust for your education. The insurance proceeds will go into the trust. Any amount not spent on your education will remain in the trust..."

The lawyer had much more to say about the trust. A great many things about the exact structure and purpose of this legal arrangement. How it would keep the tax man from taking a big bite of the life insurance proceeds. But Matt did not hear all these things the lawyer said. All he could think about was that last dinner at The Belfast and things his father said then—

I have some ideas on how we might swing college.

Maybe one idea is better than the others.

Anyway I'm working on it.

The mystery of his father's uncharacteristic vagueness was now resolved. This trust and how he could fill it with life insurance proceeds were what Frank had been "working on." Sending Matt to college through the ultimate sacrifice. Which meant that when Frank said, many times over the years, how important it was to him for his youngest child to attend college, Matt had grossly underestimated exactly how important his father held it to be.

Chapter 21

The disbursement of the proceeds from the policies held by Frank Walker with American Provident Mutual Life proved to be a comedy of errors writ both large and small. First the field report filed by Bob Breckenridge, the trench-coat-clad investigator, was lost when a computer crashed at a data processing center outside of Milwaukee. For reasons not worth going into and entirely due to incompetence it was a number of days before the backup copy of the report was restored to the appropriate server and became available to the claims processor assigned to review it.

Unfortunately in the interim, that claims processor had fallen ill after eating tainted pork—caused by lax inspection following deregulation of the meat-processing industry—and was unconscious at a hospital in Connecticut. Due to corporate downsizing—driven entirely by the quarterly profit concerns of financial analysts at major Wall Street concerns—staffing was insufficient at American Provident Mutual Life to readily absorb the caseload left untended by the comatose processor.

When all these many mishaps had been finally resolved, and the report filed by Bob Breckenridge had been processed and the disbursement approved, for some reason buried under the long workflow that had finally reached its oft-delayed conclusion, instead of the wire transfer that had been authorized and approved in triplicate, a check was issued and mailed instead. One half of a million dollars was sent via the U.S. Postal Service. Who delivered it without incident. But when Matt presented this vast sum for deposit at his bank the staff on hand collectively almost fainted.

Eventually the situation was rectified. The funds were not deposited in Matt's checking account, since they were bound for his educational trust, but placed with Legant Global, a huge international investment firm selected by the estate lawyer. The lawyer had worked with their local branch office several times in the past on similar matters. Always with satisfactory results. He knew most of the staff there and had faith in their abilities and ethics.

❖   ❖   ❖

This new account at Legant Global was assigned to a rising star at the local branch office. This ambitious young man promptly forged the signatures of both Matt and the estate lawyer so he could place all of the trust money, along with monies from other accounts he was also abusing, into a hedge fund that was showing enormous returns.

Four days later the hedge fund collapsed. Hundreds of billions of dollars were vaporized in forty-five minutes of frenzied panic. Billionaires became millionaires and millionaires became broke. In the midst of this fiasco a trader at the hedge fund had a heart attack on the trading floor. His life was saved by a janitor who knew CPR.

As the arriving EMTs pulled a gurney across the trading floor, providing the video clip that would dominate the evening news, that young rising star from the local branch office of Legant Global boarded an airliner to Las Vegas. Where he checked into a casino hotel and hired a very expensive prostitute. The next day he hired another one. On the morning of the third day his dead body was found floating in the hotel swimming pool. The coroner would determine it was drowning that killed him but it was alcohol and painkillers that put him face-down in the pool.

This unseemly end triggered an investigation into his accounts. Within the hour his disastrous scheme involving the failed hedge fund was uncovered. Within another hour a lawyer with Legant Global had called the estate lawyer. Who immediately called Matt.

The contract between Matt's trust and Legant Global made the investment firm immune to any legal action. Matt unfortunately also learned shortly thereafter that both this lack of accountability and the actions of the now-deceased once-rising-star were at one time made largely impossible by laws designed to prevent exactly this kind of malfeasance. But those laws were repealed under deregulation of the financial markets.

❖   ❖   ❖

When these ugly facts about his short-lived fortune were made known to Matthew and he struggled to absorb this new shock, his mind focused on those seven days from when his money entered the account at Legant Global to when he was told it had vanished. For those seven brief days at the tender age of nineteen Matt Walker had felt himself rich. Before the money was in the investment account—safely he believed—Matt could not have complete faith in its existence. Even when he held that staggering check in his hand.

But once he received word that his money was at Legant he could consider what it meant. Seven days to contemplate how the money would change his life. Seven days of thinking maybe he would not only go to college but might even get a graduate degree. Or buy a house after he completed his bachelor's. Maybe he would meet a nice girl who would want to share that house. And they could raise up a few kids of their own. Kids that they would send to college. Maybe then it would feel like his mother and father had not lived and struggled and suffered and died all in vain.

Seven days of hope and promise. Seven days in which he began his recovery. From the awful nightmare of the years just past.

But now what Matt thought about was that seven lousy days of hope and happy daydreams were not what his father had in mind when he jammed his foot against the accelerator of his old truck at the top of that long grade out on the lonely interstate. Matt had moments of fevered rage when he wanted the former rising star who stole the money his father had died for to be miraculously resurrected. So that Matt could track that son of a bitch down and kill him again.

Part VI:
Laugh Like a Maniac

Chapter 22

In the prosecution of Manuel Ortiz, an excellent job was done of observing his constitutional right to a quick trial. While to an equal extent violating his accompanying right to a fair one. Despite Doña Pero County being two-thirds Spanish, the jurors were ten affluent Anglos and a pair of respectable Spanish businessmen. Not exactly a jury of his peers. Although since the man they were putting on trial was a fictional Mexican and not the American citizen selected to play his role, his purported peers all lived across the border. And were therefore not eligible to serve.

Those two Spanish gentlemen who served on the jury knew their standing in the community very much depended on how well they pleased the Anglos who held the real power. And always did exactly what was wanted of them. The older one napped through much of the proceedings. I can forgive him for being uninterested. Even I, whose fate was held in the balance, in theory if not in practice since the outcome was a foregone conclusion, found myself monumentally bored.

The younger of the two was elected jury foreman. Which probably meant the ten Anglos were all unwilling to assume the duties that position required. Or maybe whoever was pulling the strings of all these puppets wanted another prominent Spanish actor in the cast of players assembled to send me to hell.

I do not believe the jury foreman in the trial of Manuel Ortiz looked at me, the putative defendant, once throughout the entire proceedings. I am fairly certain of this because I spent considerable time looking at him. This very same man had owned the house my family rented when I was young. He would come by occasionally to see for himself how his tenants behaved with his property. Always dressed in a three-piece suit. No matter how hot the weather. And always impeccably groomed. With silver-framed eyeglasses and a very black mustache that was perfectly trimmed. This distinguished Spanish businessman made a strong impression on my young mind. And now here he was playing a minor role in my hastily orchestrated downfall.

And he would not even look at me. Not even once. Although I doubted he would remember having seen me before. We never spoke and he was never interested in the children milling about. And I was a child back then and a young man sat before him. But still. It was bedeviling to encounter this man of some consequence from my past in this context and receive no assistance from him in reclaiming my real self.

I complained about it to my lawyer. Who sighed at me. He pulled off his glasses and rubbed his eyes while he said—

"Do you really think that would help?"

He put his glasses back on and sighed again. His round shoulders went up and down. He stared out from behind his grease-filmed lenses.

"Do you really believe it would be to your advantage for that man to remember you?"

Bill was right of course. If the businessman remembered who I was then he would know I was not the Mexican the prosecution claimed. Which would mean I was being framed. And being the man he was in the position he held within the stratified community of Doña Pero, the last thing he would do is challenge those who were framing me. He might even play his role with more vigor. So I might in fact be better off forgotten by the jury foreman who had once been my family's landlord.

Not that he should have even been on the jury in the first place. Which never would have happened if I had a lawyer who actually practiced the law.

❖   ❖   ❖

There was considerable evidence, both actual and fabricated, against me. Or more accurately against Manuel Ortiz. That dirty Mexican. And my/his attorney mounted a defense so weak that it was all but a concession of guilt.

First and foremost there was no one to corroborate my version of events. There was only one person who could and he was not talking. Not about the crime and apparently about little else. The doctor who was treating Elden Morris said the boy spoke only in brief answers to the simplest of questions. And what he said was not always coherent.

Regarding what happened to him he said nothing. When asked about it he seemed confused or distracted. The doctor said his mind may have buried the details or even banished them all together. He could have no memories of those horrific events. His mind could even be turned into mush. He might be a living ghost for the rest of his days. It was still too early to tell.

I will admit that although I felt terrible for the boy I could not help resenting his silence. I saved his life. Couldn't he help me out in return? But maybe he did not want to be saved. Maybe that was why he remained silent. Perhaps he would have preferred that I left him out in the canyon.

So there went the only witness who could speak on my behalf.

How about someone who could testify to my correct identity?

That shouldn't be too hard.

But all the leads I could think of had gone cold. Or so my attorney said.

He told me he went north over a weekend and visited the address I gave him for my aunt. He said she was not there and the neighbors had not seen her in weeks or months and knew nothing of her whereabouts. I felt he might be lying when he said this. And had the same reaction when he shared other discouraging details of my hopeless case. Such as being unable to find any government records confirming I existed. No birth certificate or driver's license or social security registration in my name.

I couldn't believe all these things were true. But I was young and scared and very much alone. And very much wanted to trust the only person who appeared to be helping me. So I chose to believe what Bill Jameson said. Even though my gut told me he was lying.

So my attorney claimed he had very little to work with. And what little he did have he did not work very hard. Looking back I have to say that he presented what little he offered supporting the innocence of Manuel Ortiz almost as if he was apologizing for what the Mexican had done. And made no effort at all to prove that the man on trial was in fact someone else.

He was inebriated to some extent throughout the proceedings. Each and every day he smelled of whiskey and aftershave in various proportions. I wondered if sometimes he confused the two and the aftershave went down his throat and the whiskey on his face. One day he came in unshaven while incongruously reeking of scent and I almost asked him. There were spots of booze or perfume or both on his collar and shirt front.

But before I asked it occurred to me that my lawyer had applied aftershave to his stubbled face hoping it would mask the smell of his liquid breakfast. Which it did. For maybe an hour. But then his cheap perfume faded. And my lawyer smelled like the unshaven disheveled drunk that he was.

And even then I still wanted to trust him. I was so very young. Too young and too traumatized to fight on my own behalf. To demand another lawyer. To fire the one they gave me and present my own defense. I could not have done any worse than the man I let speak for me.

But there is no fool like a young fool.

And we are all fools. In one form or another.

In every moment in which we live.

Chapter 23

I lost my faith during the trial.

Not faith that there is a God. I have always believed there is. With the passing years I have come to accept that I am a man of faith. Or a kind of faith anyway. And to take comfort in this. Despite faith seeming to be a denial of reality. To be somewhat insane. No matter how much pain and suffering God has inflicted upon me and upon mankind and upon our world—I believe. I believe in a great force that shapes our universe. But not necessarily toward any end we would consider desirable. Or even be able to conceive of. Our wants and perceptions are beyond insignificant in the eye and mind of this Great Creator.

But I have wandered from the point I wished to make.

What I lost faith in during the trial was God's love for me. That fundamental Christian precept that I like so many others was raised with and reared on. And maybe even God's capacity for love—but that is another matter. During the trial I became convinced that God was delivering his wrath upon me in this through-the-looking-glass horror show because I had done some ignominious thing, some act of true evil— perhaps in a past life? I had not lived long enough or hard enough to sin in proportion commensurate with the punishment I was receiving and could see I was still yet to receive. But I must have committed some great moral crime to deserve such a twisted fate.

And to face such a fate with no help but that which came in the short round never-quite-sober form of a myopic Spanish attorney with an incongruously Anglo name. A man I saw too late was not my friend but my Judas. Who went sighing regretfully to his task of helping nail me to the cross.

Having only him at my side seemed to be adding insult to injury.

On the day of Armijo's testimony my crisis of faith almost overwhelmed me. As the courtroom filled up for the day's proceedings my head began to swim and my heart felt choked within my chest. I looked around at the people gathering to witness my fate decided and saw I could count the faces I had known before the trial on one hand. And none of them were faces I knew before I brought Elden Morris to the hospital.

Or were faces in which I could see any concern for my wellbeing. Bill Jameson came closest. But I still didn't know if he believed I was innocent. Or even if he believed I was not Manuel Ortiz. While all that really matters is he did absolutely nothing to prevent me from being convicted.

Then there was the man I had once almost thought of as a friend. Because I had begun to think of him as one. After we met and I got over instantly hating him. When he seemed to care about doing his job and I wanted to believe he was going to do it. Fat Armijo. Who would soon take the stand and tell outrageous lies about who I was and what I had done.

Seated beside him at that moment was the one I had come to think of as Señor Fuzzy Lip. The Hispano Apache who wanted to shoot me the day I was arrested. He sneered at me now. That was not friendly.

The last face that I had known before the trial convened belonged to that stern prick up in the jury box. The one who had once been my family's landlord. Now the foreman in my sham trial. The leader of the jury who would soon convict me.

That had become certain in my mind. That I had not a sliver of hope for acquittal. Not of even a single charge leveled against Manuel Ortiz.

Every single thing was lined up against me. I was a poor bastard indeed.

Is it any wonder I had a crisis of faith?

Who would not?

There was a cough in the back of the courtroom as Armijo settled into the witness stand. His hooded eyes went to the sound then returned to the front of the room. He laced his fingers together and perched his hands atop his fat belly which mounded up within his khaki uniform. I looked at the woven fingers of those small fat hands and remembered how they were soft and warm like freshly dead animals when you held one. He had a disgusting handshake. The type that made you feel soiled.

I stared at Armijo while he made my world wobble on its axis. As the fat man unraveled his great lie I began to wonder if what he said was actually true. If I really was a Mexican national named Manuel Ortiz. And really did abduct and molest Elden Morris. And that everything I knew as my life—my early childhood spent not far from here; my father's death and burial in that remote canyon; the sudden loss of my uncle; the family that waited for me out in Los Angeles; the young Anglo in the turquoise Ford pickup who had become my personal bogeyman— maybe all of those things were just the products of my sick mind. Aspects of a grand delusion created by my dementia.

Over his folded hands and his round gut he nodded like a sage at a question posed by the prosecutor. Then responded in his deep rumbling voice of unquestionable authority. A voice that filled the courtroom in more ways than one. A voice that filled my head and turned it into soup. Maybe what he was saying was God's only truth. How could things said in that mesmerizing voice not be true? Once or twice the fat man gestured in my direction. He did not seem to hate me. Maybe he was a good man after all.

Maybe I was the demon he said I was.

Even in his drunken state Bill Jameson could see I was not doing well. Maybe my eyes were bugging out as I stared at Armijo. And those bugging eyes made Bill worried I would do something unseemly. That I would interrupt the fat man. Make a spectacle of myself. Jump up and yell out ugly words. Do something not in my best interests. Those interests he was supposed to be protecting. Even though he had done all he could to let me know short of saying so outright and directly that my best interests had already been totally and thoroughly screwed well before the trial began.

Whatever went through Bill's mind at that moment it was his booze-laced breath that came into my nose as he leaned close and spoke into my ear—

"Antes que te cases, mira lo que haces."

Before you marry, consider what you're doing.

Or as the equivalent idiom in English puts it—

Look before you leap.

As I have mentioned before I was not much of a Spanish speaker at the time. A fact Bill stubbornly refused to accommodate. Maybe if he had used that latter phrase, good standard American English familiar to his client, maybe then I would have comprehended what he was telling me. And inferred what he was worried I might do. But his intended meaning was lost to me. I was not familiar with the *refrane* he whispered in my ear. I only heard my lawyer caution me against hasty marriage. Which struck me as entirely bizarre. And therefore thoroughly in keeping with the consistently surreal events I experienced in this strange twist my life had taken.

But while Bill failed to communicate what he wanted me to consider, he did succeed in making me forget about Armijo. And what the fat man was saying up on the witness stand. Which broke the hypnotic effect of his words and that deep rumbling voice and made me stop wondering if he was right and I was wrong. And stop suspecting I might be an insane sexual deviant with an entirely fabricated life history. Bill's bewildering Spanish broke the spell of that moment and the spell remained broken.

I do not like to consider what might have become of my mental health if I had been allowed to proceed further into the chasm of self-doubt that opened before me as Armijo gave his testimony. My experience then makes me wonder if sanity can be lost in an instant. If under sufficient strain and disorientation a mind can slip away in the course of a few seconds. And a soul cross over into that living hell of a fractured personality. My rational mind and what I have read tells me no. But my own experience tells me yes.

For having turned me away from that instant when my sanity was in peril I will always remain grateful to Bill Jameson. Even though he had no idea what he was doing for me with his indecipherable *refrane* I will always feel a debt to that sad drunken man. Despite his numerous and enormous failures on my behalf. And despite all and everything that would happen to me after.

Chapter 24

The jury deliberated briefly. An article in the local newspaper claimed they were out for twenty-five minutes. I would have sworn it was ten at the most. They were back so quickly I wanted to stand up and cry out—

This is my life we're talking about. At least go back in there and *pretend* that you give a shit.

But I didn't do that. Instead I sat there with everyone else and listened to my family's former landlord who was now the foreman of the jury stand before his seat within the jury box and read out in his high piercing voice the results of their deliberations upon the charges presented before them.

Not a soul present in that courtroom was surprised to hear the man called Manuel Ortiz pronounced guilty on all counts. And there were many counts to be gotten through. Each more heinous than the last. Kidnapping. Assault. Corruption of a minor. Sodomy. Just to hit the highlights. All of it horrible stuff. The kind of wicked things only the sickest and most vile animals would ever do.

Which of course meant the sentencing must be harsh. The punishment must fit the crime. Or in this case the crimes. Plural. Which should logically require multiple punishments. As would in fact actually occur. Prison would for a time be nothing but a series of reoccurring punishments.

I am delaying needlessly. And simultaneously getting ahead of myself.

Indulge me please. Recalling these events is still upsetting.

While the Spanish businessman who had been our landlord and was now the jury foreman recited the announcement of my doppelganger's guilt, I recalled an incident from when he was an occasional presence in my childhood. An afternoon when he

119

appeared unannounced, as was his habit, and accosted me in the front yard about a perceived injury to his landscaping. When he was gone again my father announced that was it, he was done, we were moving. He was not going to have his kids spoken to like that.

But we did not move. Instead my father was chased out of town by the words of that crazy rich Anglo lady, out into the desert to that canyon where he lost hope and died and was buried by my uncle.

So I was thinking about my dead father when our former landlord finished reading his announcement. And called out his last *guilty*.

My sentencing immediately followed. The judge was not lenient.

I was given thirty-five years. The first twenty without possibility of parole.

❖　　❖　　❖

When the judge rapped down his gavel my lawyer did not offer any protest. Or tell me we should appeal. Instead his boozy breath wafted these words in my direction—

"Cuando una puerta se cierra, cien se abren."
When one door closes, a hundred open.

This made me very disgusted with Bill Jameson. What a dose of rotten oil to pour in my ear at such a moment.

I could not even look at him.

Instead I looked at Armijo as the bailiff put me in cuffs and led me away. At least I believe it was the bailiff who cuffed me. I did not notice who it was. My mind was on the fat man. The one who did this to me. And looking at him I had a moment of clarity. I knew I would have the revenge of a better life than the one he had thrown me into. Like so much trash. Or a dead animal scraped up and tossed away off the road. The life he had made for me would not last. I would live beyond it.

And then his gaze finally met mine as I was pushed through the doorway and out of the courtroom where my fate had been decided. And I knew that in the life that would come after this one they were sending me to, when I was a free man again, I would have the great pleasure of seeing Armijo at his death. Not just that I would outlive him. But that I would be close at hand when he died and my eyes would gaze down upon his corpse.

A thought that made me laugh. A maniac's laugh. A laugh that was loud and cold and utterly lacked reason and mercy. A laugh that made the bailiff—or whoever it was who snapped the cuffs over my wrists and forced me from the courtroom—shove me along the hallway that led to the door that opened to the van that would take me back to my cell at the county prison where I would await my pending transfer to the state facility. Where for a time I would endure the hell being wished upon me by many who had come to see my trial. Or I should say upon the man they believed me to be.

But I didn't care. Not in the least. I didn't care about any of it. Armijo would be dead and I would be alive and I would spit on his fat dead body. That and that alone was what mattered to me as I was pushed down that hallway toward my waiting fate. At that pivotal moment in my life.

That was the idea I chose to hide myself behind.

Part VII:
The Making of the Boss

Chapter 25

Maybe they did not like her uncle. Maybe they thought he was a fat grasping bastard. Maybe they took one look at him and got their hackles up. He had that effect on some people. Or maybe they changed their minds because of his campaign. Maybe they didn't approve of his opportunistic jump into the Republican party. He was a Democrat when that suited his purposes but when his purposes changed—well watch out. A lack of loyalty and tradition that could not be tolerated. Or maybe it was all that bluster and bravado that put them off. Incessantly beating the drum about how he protected their children. Always reminding everyone of that sad episode with the Mexican and the Morris boy—that did not sit well with more than a few.

So many different reasons to dislike the man.

But none of that touched Esperanza. Even his biggest opponents, the most ardent supporters of the incumbent, they all admired his hard-working niece. When they saw her coming with a stack of flyers clutched in her little hands they would nod in her direction and say—

"La Soldadita."

The Soldier Girl.

Some tried to say it in jest. But they could not twist this flattering nickname into mockery. Because it suited her too well. And even the most flippant of these jokers could never completely hide their respect.

How could you not respect her? How could you gaze into that determined little face drawn tight as she handed you a campaign flyer which you could not refuse when she was the one passing them out even though you had thrown a dozen away already? How could you not adore her at that moment?

Even those who ardently supported the incumbent could not help but have respect for the resolve and determination and tenacity of La Soldadita. And to wish they had the likes of her on their side. This despite the deep sense of betrayal they felt. The current sheriff being the same man who made a deputy out of the not-yet-so-portly Armijo when he was still a young man. In their minds the incumbent now had Armijo's bloody dagger stuck deep between his ribs.

While the fat man's hand squirmed like a toad working the blade still deeper.

❖   ❖   ❖

One afternoon, in the thick of that first election season, Esperanza came upon a debate just underway at the grocery store in the heart of their village. Two Spanish men were arguing the merits of the opposing candidates for sheriff. The first words she heard between them made it clear on which points their debate would focus—

"He's an Anglo," the older man said.

This man was lean and dark and rawboned. With hair and mustache of black and gray and a few specks of white. He wore a sweat-stained cream-colored cowboy hat.

The younger man nodded. He was thicker built. With more muscle and less bone. Not quite as tall as the older man. Clean-shaven and round-faced and round-shouldered. His skin was a cinnamon brown. The red in it said he had Indian blood. As did his wide stately nose.

"Sure," this man said. "Of course he is."

He extended a hand toward the older man and said—

"But he's *our* Anglo. Look what he did to that department. It was a sewer when he took over. And

123

white as snow. If it wasn't for him, Armijo wouldn't even have a job there."

"That's all well and good. But now it's time for one of our own."

"And Armijo is one of our own?"

"Of course!"

"Just because his skin is brown."

"Don't talk nonsense."

"Well what are you saying then? If it's not his skin. What is it? His last name?"

"Yes. He's one of us."

"And for that we throw over a man who has stood with us. That's how we thank our friends?"

"Maybe he's *your* friend."

"If he's good to *our* people, how is he not *our* friend?"

The older man waved his hand through the air.

"Bah!" he said.

The younger man leaned forward.

"What makes you so sure Armijo will be good to us?"

"Because, you fool. Like I keep saying."

The older man raised a fist into the air, unfurled his index finger, and jabbed that finger forward on each of the three words he wanted to emphasize—

"*He*. Is *one*. Of *us*."

He kept his hand where it was for a moment, with that lone finger extended. Then withdrew his hand and tucked his thumbs into his belt and stood back on his heels. The way he stood and how he looked at the younger man said that to his mind he had won this argument. That everything was settled now.

The younger man shrugged.

"If you say so."

He spread his hands in the air.

"But so what if he is? Plenty of our own people have screwed us. And screwed us but good."

He raised a hand and leaned forward—

"They're screwing us right now!"

The older man shook his head. But when he spoke he did not deny what the younger man said. He only reframed his main point—

"I'll take my chances with our own."

"If you think he is out for anyone but himself you have another thing coming."

"Like I said. I'll take my chances."

"How do you know he won't have his fat thumb in every pie he can get his hands on?"

❖   ❖   ❖

The woman behind the counter cleared her throat. When the debaters turned her direction she nodded at Esperanza. The Armijo supporter smiled at Essie. Gold glinted on one of his teeth.

"La Soldadita," he said.

The woman behind the counter gestured at her.

"I see you have more flyers for us," the woman said.

Esperanza nodded. The woman gestured again.

"Give them here, sweetie."

The woman cut her eyes at the man who had just been attacking Armijo.

"I will make sure *everyone* gets a flyer," the woman said.

Esperanza watched the younger man frown and lower his eyes, then she moved to the counter and handed the woman behind it a stack of flyers. When she looked at the younger man again he was looking at her. Their eyes met and he smiled, then Essie turned away and silently escaped from the store. As she went out the door onto the wooden porch that fronted the street she heard the man who had criticized her uncle say this behind her—

125

"If there is one thing that could make me change my mind when I'm in the voting booth—there she goes."

It took a moment for Esperanza to understand these words. By then she was off the porch and out into the street, cutting across it toward another store where she would leave more flyers. When the meaning of what the man said sorted itself out, Essie stopped where she was in the middle of the road.

A man in a pickup truck stopped and yelled at her.

"That's nowhere to stand!" he said.

She jerked her head toward the man, stared at him for an instant, then ran to the other side of the street. In those few seconds spent hurrying across the pavement the devoted disciple became a messianic crusader. By the time she stepped up onto the sidewalk Esperanza believed that she had been ordained by God to put her uncle into office.

Because of what that one man said. As an offhand remark to ease the tension left in her wake. As a child will, because of only that, Esperanza was now convinced the fate of her uncle's campaign rested squarely on her own slight little shoulders. Most children would have been terrified at such a prospect. And there was something like terror within Esperanza.

But more than anything she was thrilled.

Maybe those supporters of the incumbent who wished for another like her on their own side were the ones who admired La Soldadita the most. Maybe they were in the best position to appreciate how hard Esperanza worked for her uncle. And more importantly what she accomplished. It wasn't the marching up and down streets and lanes or knocking on doors to hand out flyers. Or the long hours spent at the kitchen table stuffing mailers into envelopes. That stuff was easy. That was kid stuff. Any child could do that.

It was the speech she gave on her uncle's behalf that so impressed them. The first version of which she presented to her schoolmates. She stood before them out in the yard and implored her fellow students to tell their parents and grandparents and aunts and uncles and cousins and everyone they knew who could vote that they must cast their ballots for her uncle—if they wanted their children to be safe. She reminded them how Elden Morris had been snatched as he went about their village without concern and it was her uncle who brought his abductor to justice. That thanks to her uncle the Mexican was now locked away behind bars and could not snatch up any of them as he had done to poor Elden.

Invoking the specter of the Mexican did not come easily. Saying those things before others made her eyes tear and her voice quaver and her knees knock together. But she stood there wringing her hands and said the things her uncle told her she must say.

La Soldadita did not back down.

Her admirers on the other side dearly wished that she had.

More than a few believed that without her Armijo would have lost.

Chapter 26

Fireworks and gunshots. That was how the men close to her uncle chose to celebrate. Esperanza remembered the chaos they created as a wash of color and sound. Orange and red and blue and green splashed against the black heavens. The screech and howl of rockets zipping up and away. War whoops from men silhouetted with their heads back. Rifles and pistols in the air and the sharp retort when an unseen finger pulled a trigger.

Armijo himself spent the night in the kitchen among the women.

"Mis encantadoras damas," he said.

My lovely ladies.

"You know how to behave."

The women laughed and nodded their agreement.

Finally Josef went outside and told the men to stop shooting off their guns. Before a stray bullet falling back to earth struck and killed someone.

"How many times does that have to happen before you stupid bastards learn?" Josef yelled.

All the guns were put away.

The next day Esperanza was shocked to hear that the results of the election were not yet certain. That a recount was likely. The day after that she heard murmurings of misconduct. Allegations of vote fraud. Something about a ballot box that went missing and resurfaced in questionable circumstances.

Esperanza heard but she did not listen. Her mind was shut tight. Nothing anyone could say would make La Soldadita ever even suspect that her Tío would be involved in such appalling conduct. Or allow others to do so, most especially not on his behalf.

He was a man of iron who stood fast against all wickedness and corruption.

❖   ❖   ❖

The election brought Esperanza back into the world. When it was over she needed something to keep her there. Something new to banish the darkness that still opened inside of her whenever she remembered Elden. And to mute those whisperings going around about her uncle and how he cheated himself into office. And to help her forget that since the election her uncle and aunt had been short with each other. A chill had descended on the house when her Tío Josef ascended into office.

She found that something new one afternoon in the village library. When she opened an encyclopedia and on the page before her was something old. A photograph showed three bedrock mortars clustered together on a gray slab. Esperanza had seen holes like those on a rock up the hills. She and Elden had wondered together what they were and what could they mean.

Now she learned the answer. Also called *morteros* or *metates* these grinding holes were used by native peoples to reduce hard seeds or kernels into soft edible meal. Which meant Indians had lived up in those hills. Esperanza decided at her next opportunity she would return to that big flat rock she had seen up there and take another look at those holes.

Meanwhile she read some more on the subject. Going from the entry in the encyclopedia to a book on the prehistory of Native Americans. And found this detour so engrossing she forgot to do the work that brought her here. She went home without having completed any research for the social studies report on Mesopotamia that was due by the end of the week.

She didn't do any of that research on the next day either. Instead she went back up into the hills. Where after a few wrong turns she found the *morteros* she knew were waiting for her. Inspecting them she was thrilled to know their purpose and to imagine them in use. To picture these hills alive with the people who lived here before her people knew this land existed.

Crouched down on that slab peering into those ancient holes, Esperanza decided she would become an archeologist. And that she wouldn't wait to get started. She would teach herself everything she could on the subject. And these hills would be her laboratory.

❖   ❖   ❖

Rosa and Josef did not want their niece wandering alone through the hills. Life was not so free anymore for the children of Doña Pero. Things had changed since the tragedy with the Morris boy.

Esperanza snuck away when her aunt was too busy to stop her. Sometimes she vanished when Rosa simply had her back turned. When this disobedience began Rosa and Josef were united in their stern disapproval. But when it persisted Josef shrugged and surrendered. He knew a losing battle when he saw one. And had his hands full with work. He left his wife to sort it out.

Rosa considered her options. Then decided on her terms and conditions. Which resulted in Esperanza owning a large intimidating dog, a dependable wristwatch, a razor-edged hunting knife, and a pistol with a waist holster. So equipped and after some gun training with her uncle she was reluctantly permitted to go off into the hills. But only when approved by Rosa with a set time for her return. No more sneaking away.

She was tall for her twelve years. With her wolfish hound beside her; looking out from underneath the white *ranchera* hat she inherited from her maternal *abuela*, the grandmother who cared for her when she was an orphaned infant; with her canvas knapsack of tools and supplies strapped onto her shoulders; and with her knife and gun dangling from the wide brown belt draped across her hip—Esperanza cut a remarkable figure.

Which thoroughly cemented her reputation as a local character. Fortunately, where she lived, eccentrics were embraced and even celebrated. La Soldadita was admired and cherished and even revered by the people of her village.

Which in her rush toward knowledge and her future she failed to see.

❖   ❖   ❖

If anyone had told Esperanza she was beloved it would have shocked her. She had an entirely different impression.

She had noticed that people began watching her after the election. Before they only looked at her. Like they would look at anyone else. Maybe with a little more curiosity than they would at most others. She was known, after all. She had been the gifted child who went about the hills with her gifted friend. The two little naturalists. Twin hopes for the village's future. And then she became the one who lost her dear friend to the dirty Mexican. And after that, during the election, she became La Soldadita. So she had a history that invited curiosity. And had learned to expect how that shaped the reception she received.

But now people watched her as more than a curiosity. Now they watched as if she might do something that would affect them. Some, the same way they would stare at a rattlesnake. Others, like they would the caller during bingo. And by the way others watched Esperanza, they could not tell if they thought what she could do would be good for them or bad for them. She decided they watched as if they were waiting to find out.

And then there were those not content to only watch. To just wait and see. The ones who proactively tried to advance their agendas. And this Esperanza disliked the very most.

The worst offender was the woman who ran the village store. Before Josef Armijo announced his candidacy she had not been any more solicitous with Esperanza than with the other children. That changed during the election. And changed again when Armijo won. Now she lavished attention on his niece. And Esperanza felt a little sick every time. She tried to negotiate with Rosa for other chores. But more often than not she could help her aunt the most by running to the store and was too dutiful to refuse. So off to the store she went. And into the cloud of obsequiousness that the storekeeper swirled around her.

Within that cloud she thought she might suffocate.

Chapter 27

Her uncle did not share her distaste for the fawning public. She saw how he drank in the deference he was shown. And especially how his eyes glittered when men and women of position bent to kiss his ring.

Esperanza told herself he had earned it. That this respect was deserved. But she never became comfortable with that side of him. And that side of him only expanded as the years passed. Like his belly which grew fat with his time in office.

Those years made him more than just the sheriff. He became a prominent man in Doña Pero. Someone to be consulted with when anything important was being considered. A man of consequence. Someone who knew how to make things happen. And knew all the people who got things done.

Which meant his second time in the ring wasn't much of a fight. Since all of the power lined up behind him. He went unchallenged in the Republican primary and was the heavy favorite on election day. The leaders of the county Democrats tried and failed to persuade Armijo's former boss to run again. Instead they wound up with a retired transit cop from Brooklyn. No one had ever heard of him before and the locals couldn't understand his accent. The result was an old-fashioned blow-out.

The election night celebration was held at a hotel. Not like last time when it was at the Armijo residence. The men wore suits instead of blue jeans. The women wore fancy dresses and gaudy jewelry. There were no fireworks and no gunshots. Instead there were speeches. A whole lot of speeches.

Esperanza stood on the periphery watching the goings-on and decided she preferred the former chaos. Because it was more real. She didn't trust these smug people strutting around like they owned the world.

And she could see that Rosa didn't trust them either.

❖   ❖   ❖

Esperanza hoped that her uncle's second victory would lift the chill between Josef and Rosa. The first election changed things so maybe the second would change things back. She knew this reasoning was simplistic and superficial. But she needed to hope so she stuck with it.

And things did change. Only not for the better. Now instead of ignoring each other they snapped and snarled like angry dogs. The chill had been replaced by a smoldering fire. Esperanza did her best to pretend nothing was burning. That the smoke filling up her throat and nose did not exist. But eventually she began to choke.

One afternoon after school Esperanza found Rosa distressed to the point of distraction. She could not focus on the tasks before her. She would start one thing and then begin another only to drop that one and go back to the first.

Esperanza asked if anything was wrong.

"Your uncle," Rosa said.

She sighed and shook her head.

"Impossible."

While Esperanza waited for more she scrambled over how that thought could be completed. Had Josef done something Rosa found impossible to tolerate? Or did she mean that he could be an impossible man? Or had things between them become impossible? Did she find him impossible to be married to? And if that were so, how could such a thing have come to pass?

Despite everything the two of them were bedrock. Were they not?

Before Esperanza could speak Rosa shook her head again.

"I don't know," Rosa said.

Which did not help Essie at all.

"What don't you know?"

Rosa waved a hand while she shook her head some more.

"Forget it. I shouldn't talk about it."

She folded her hands together and smiled at Essie. Her smile was twisted up and unhappy and not much of a smile at all.

"These are my worries," Rosa said. "Not yours."

❖　　❖　　❖

Esperanza was relieved when Rosa halted their conversation. She was afraid to know what lay behind the conflict between her aunt and uncle. The adult world that battle was part of, lay ahead of her as an inevitability. She had seen enough of it already not to be in any rush to get there.

But here it was rushing at her. That night she lay awake suffering with the question that had stuck its talons into her head and would not let go—who was in the wrong? She had struggled to remain neutral for her own self-preservation. She was far too attached in both directions to assign blame either way without feeling her soul being torn apart.

But she could not see her aunt at fault. Rosa was kind and generous and above all she was fair. While her uncle was doggedly single-minded. Rosa saw everything. Josef saw only what was in front of him.

The guilt must be with her uncle.

But he was the great mountain in her small world. For although she saw less of him since he had become sheriff, and he showed her less consideration and attention than he had before—

And although she was beyond disappointed that what she believed would happen after her uncle arrested the Mexican never came to pass, and that the boy who had once been the very best part of her life still suffered, maybe worse than ever, and was now completely lost to her—

And although she did not understand how her uncle could tolerate, and even enjoy, there was no other way to put it, the ass-kissing he now received, or tolerate the pompous jackasses he circulated with—

Her Tío Josef remained the valiant hero of her personal mythology. The great doer of good deeds. The one who took her in when cruel fate left her parentless. And had vanquished the dirty Mexican for destroying her precious friend.

(As day requires night there had to be an antagonist in her morality play. To stand in balance against her personal Santo Tío Josef. Which is why each and every night when Esperanza knelt to her prayers she asked almighty God to damn El Diablo Mexicano to a fiery Hell.)

But if Josef was the cause of whatever so greatly troubled Rosa—

What then?

Her mind kept backing up and taking another journey down this same path. Only to arrive every time at the same dismaying end. Try as she might her mind could find no way around it. And even worse nowhere beyond it.

Somewhere past midnight sleep finally began to creep over her. Her eyes had drifted shut and her mind was stilled. Then her uncle's angry voice came muted through the house and snapped her eyes open. She lay in the dark and listened. But as always when they quarreled, which they only did behind the closed door of their bedroom, she could not make out what was being said. She stopped trying and just listened to the sounds of their voices.

And looked beyond their fighting to what could come of it. She felt stabbed in the heart when she asked herself what would become of her—

If Josef and Rosa were to divorce.

A thought that before this moment had been totally unthinkable. She saw that she might not be allowed to stay with Rosa. That she might be handed off to one of the other Armijo brothers, one who was still married and could offer a stable home. She had nothing against those men and women and their children who were her cousins.

But to live away from Rosa would mean devastation. For the first time in her life Esperanza felt like an orphan. Alone and vulnerable and heartbroken in the dark of her borrowed room.

Chapter 28

The next night at dinner Rosa shocked the entire family by announcing that she was taking a trip. This from a woman who never did anything for herself. She had decided that she wanted to see the Grand Canyon. And she was going to leave as soon as she was ready.

Josef was dumbfounded. He narrowed his eyes at his wife.

And then for the first time they fought out in the open.

"What for?" Josef said.

"Because I want to."

Josef put a hand on the table. His fingers began to drum.

"You never wanted to before."

"*Now* you care what I want?"

The drumming stopped. His hand cut through the air.

"Please. Don't start with all that."

Back down on the table. The drumming resumed.

Rosa said—

"I'm taking Esperanza."

The drumming stopped.

Josef scowled at his wife. Then at his niece. Then at his wife again.

"No. That's not happening. Who will cook for me?"

"Of course you think of your belly first. And only your own. No thought for how your sons will eat. I don't know and I don't care how you get your gut filled. For once that's your problem. Maybe it will teach you to eat less."

One of the boys snickered. Josef's eyes flashed at all of them.

"You think this is funny?"

Everyone was silent. Josef scowled again. He shook his head.

"This is not like you."

"Maybe you don't know what I'm like."

His smile was ugly.

"Oh I know what you're like all right."

"Apparently not. Because I will do this. No matter how much you insist it can't happen."

"Because it makes no sense! And why all of a sudden?"

"Why all of a sudden did you run for sheriff?"

Josef was rarely without something to say. At all times in the most difficult situations he was ready to speak. Whether to smooth things over or fire them up or shut them down. But on this occasion, in his own kitchen before his wife and his niece and his sons, he was rendered silent. He stared at Rosa with confusion and rage. He swallowed and frowned and shook his head. But no words shot forth from his usually loaded tongue.

Rosa raised her hand slowly to point at her husband. Her voice was cold and level and unyielding—

"I do not have to explain myself. Not to you of all people. I have earned the right to do what I want."

She lowered her hand and thrust her chin out at him.

"*You* certainly do whatever *you* want. When have you ever cared how that affected anyone else?"

For a very long moment they stared at each other.

Then Josef rose to his feet. He stood over the table peering down at his wife. His hand rose and he pointed at her. His lip curled up and one of his eyebrows jumped.

Then without saying anything he turned and left. No one spoke while they listened to his new departmental SUV back out of the drive and roar away.

❖   ❖   ❖

For thirty-six hours Josef shunned the entire household. He did not speak to any of them or eat with them or in any way engage with any one of them. He went about his business as if his family did not exist. Then on the morning when Esperanza and Rosa were getting ready to leave he sent a message to his wife through their youngest son Roberto—

"He wants me to go with you."

"Of course he does," Rosa said. "Because he always has to be the boss."

She shook her head.

"You're staying here."

"What do I tell him?"

"That I don't care what he wants."

Roberto's face showed how little he cared to deliver that response. He stood in the kitchen doorway with his hands shoved in his pockets.

Rosa and Essie were making food for the road. Rosa stopped what she was doing and sighed at her son.

"Tell him I said no men. I want time alone with Essie."

Roberto nodded.

"Okay," he said.

"Stay clear of him while I'm gone."

Roberto snorted.

"You don't have to tell me that."

He glanced at Esperanza. Their eyes met and she could see his fear. Then he stepped into the room and went over to his mother. He spoke quietly—

"I don't like this."

Rosa peered up at her son. She put a hand on his cheek.

"Don't worry," she said. "Everything's fine."

He stared down into his mother's eyes. Doubt clouded his face.

"If you say so," Roberto said.

❖ ❖ ❖

Rosa hunched over the wheel like a woman possessed. All her attention was out ahead of them. Down the road to where they were going. Esperanza kept her tongue. She could see this was not the time. She looked out the window at the passing roadside. She watched monsoon rains off in the distance, veils of gray draped down onto the desert.

But when the time came she was ready to pounce. An hour had passed since they left home. She watched Rosa take a deep breath and settle back into her seat. Then let her breath out in a long slow exhale.

She was like a cat at a mouse hole. Muscles coiled for the attack. Because although she was excited about their destination there was another canyon she wanted to see even more. The archeological marvel called Chaco. Which she had recently learned was on the UNESCO World Heritage List. She wasn't sure what that meant but she was certain it sounded impressive.

She thought now would be good moment to share this with her aunt.

She was wrong. Rosa hunched back over the wheel.

"We already discussed that, Essie. I told you there isn't time. Now please don't bother me with it again."

Esperanza took this rebuff like a punch to her stomach. Her guts ached and her eyes swam. She turned to her window and forced her vision to focus on the distant rains and wished she could go stand under them. When she dared to look at her aunt again she saw that her uncle was right about one thing—

This was not like Rosa.

Part VIII:
They Called Me Dead Man

Chapter 29

There are ways in which prison life is much like attending school. Of course with the important difference that at the end of the day you cannot go home. No final bell rings to announce your freedom. No yellow bus waits to ferry you away. And while you may remember your school years as a form of internment—as many do, and often deservedly so—let me assure you there is an immeasurable difference between schooling and actual imprisonment.

But there are similarities. And one in particular that I wish to discuss. Which would be seating at meal time. As in school if you are new and unsure of your place in the hierarchy and facing a full room you will find yourself wandering the cafeteria with tray in hand being rebuffed. The lower your social standing the more hostile the glares and rude gestures. In prison this is far more likely to escalate into violence. Which will be brief and ruthlessly effective to avoid drawing the guards' attention.

At my first meal in the state facility I spent what seemed a small eternity searching for a table where I was not refused. Which did not entirely surprise me following the treatment I had received back at the county jail. Finally I found a table where I was permitted to take a seat. At first I did not wonder why these men allowed me to join them. I was too relieved to be accepted anywhere. It seemed I had tried every other table in the room before finally chancing on this one. So I asked no questions of the men around me. I did not inquire why they alone did not consider me a pariah.

But after a few days and a number of meals with my new acquaintances, and after some things that were said to me by other inmates, the ones who would not let me eat among them—I pieced together whom I was dining with. And therefore why I was welcome among them. At this table of the damned. For like me—or like my alter ego, the Mexican named Manuel Ortiz—each of these men had been convicted of child molestation.

With this knowledge the ordeal of meal time took on a new dimension. Now I looked at the faces of the men around me and knew what they had done. Once or twice I wondered if, like myself, any of these others were innocent. But I knew most child molesters were never caught. That was something I had read in the newspapers when they reported on the abduction of Elden Morris. So the evidence against these men I ate with was most likely solid. Few men are framed for such acts as I was.

I hated being cast down among such human filth.

More days passed. With more glares and gestures and insults. But nothing worse than that. I wanted to believe this was how things would be for me here. That tense and ugly was as bad as it would get.

Then at breakfast one morning, maybe ten days after I arrived at the state prison, I was examining the faces of the men around me, more than a few of which I now noticed were scarred and disfigured, while I struggled to choke down the slop we were given to sustain us, feeling an unsettling mixture of contempt for these men because of the acts that brought them here, alarm and dismay at finding myself among them, and grudging admiration for their ability to endure this existence—when it occurred to me I would have to learn from them. Especially if I was wrong and things got worse. Which made me feel like I must imitate rats and cockroaches in order to survive.

I almost vomited onto my plate.

At that moment the men seated across from me rose and found other places at our table. Those on each side shifted away. I watched them all scurry and scramble and knew I had been wrong. Things very much would get worse.

Before me appeared a man I hadn't seen before. Spanish. Big and muscular. Over six feet and just under two hundred pounds. With no fat on his clean straight bones.

He stood there staring down at me and I forgot to breathe. Then he sat down directly across the table. He stared at me without speaking for most of a minute. I would guess. Maybe it was only a few seconds. His presence distorted time. My vision began to cloud before I remembered to take air into my lungs.

Then he spoke in the voice of a vengeful god—

"A day will come when you will wish that you were dead."

He resumed his silence and continued to stare. I forced my lungs open and closed. It was like working a stiff old set of bellows.

He leaned slightly closer when he spoke again—

"When that day comes. When you want death to release you. I will be the one who puts that wish for death into your head."

He raised a hand and tapped the center of his chest.

"Every moment when you are suffering. *I* made it happen."

He lowered his hand and leaned a little closer and stared into my eyes.

"*I* will be the cause of all your misery."

He stared. Someone at our table muffled a cough. I began to feel faint. I had forgotten to breathe again. Suck the air in. Push it back out.

He raised a hand and pointed at my face.

"And when that day comes. When you are praying for death. Maybe I will give it to you."

He put his hand down again.

"Or maybe I won't."

He nodded once. Slow and heavy. As befits the head that wears the crown.

"I will be the one who decides."

He remained with us for a few moments longer. Seated across the table and staring at me with his eyes full of death. Then he rose to his feet and leaned over me. After a moment he nodded again. Slow and heavy just as before.

"Enjoy your breakfast," he said.

Then he bent down and spat generously onto my food.

❖   ❖   ❖

The table of the damned was silent for how long I cannot say. Maybe it was fifteen seconds. Maybe it was fifteen minutes. During those moments I assumed the men around me had all been through the same torment that I had just experienced. Why I assumed that I also cannot say. Maybe because I did not want to think I had been singled out. Maybe I found a scant bit of desperate reassurance in believing these disgusting degenerates I was forced to associate with had already been where I found myself now. And they had survived. So then maybe I could too.

But that illusion was short-lived.

"*Man*," someone said. "Never seen Silvertone like that before."

All at once the witnesses were talking—

"What's that all about?"

"Gonna be ugly for the new guy."

"Like it isn't ugly for us?"

"Come on. He never acts like we even exist."

"Yeah, dumbfuck. Has he ever said anything to you? Let alone anything like that?"

145

"He always sends a messenger. Every time before."

"Exactly. So why do you even talk? Just shut up. This is different. If you can't see that you're even more of an idiot than I thought."

"I'm just sayin' we all got it bad."

A man pointed at me and said—

"Not as bad as him."

All eyes turned my direction. And then looked away. And now they all were silent. With blood pounding in my ears and spots swimming before my eyes I thought maybe the day my visitor had predicted would not be long in coming. That soon I would be panting after death. Wanting it like a lover.

Dreaming of it at night as I slept tossing in my stinking hard bunk.

Chapter 30

I was given twenty-four hours to suffer with what Silvertone said to me. To live each minute with his prediction that I would come to long for death. To know that mental torment alone and on its own terms. Without interference from any other form of suffering.

Then almost to the minute when those twenty-four hours had passed—

My personal hell commenced. I was beaten and violated on a daily basis. Made to ooze blood from every orifice. Bones were broken and broken again before they healed. I acquired a limp and was made partially deaf in my right ear and partly blinded in my right eye. Hospitalized four times. Almost died once from a ruptured spleen and another time from blood in my lungs.

Those days passed in a blur of blood and pain.

Then one day the assaults ended. Just as abruptly as they began.

Nine months had passed. In the time it takes for a woman to make a baby my old self died and a new one was born. Who I had been before was thoroughly and utterly destroyed. And when the assaults were over like that baby a mother pushes out into this world I was entirely new.

The person I had become was inured to pain and suffering. He had learned to take the long view on this life and of this world. To be thoughtful and patient. Like steel gains strength from the blows of the smith's hammer. A far more calculating and determined and resourceful person was made from the foolish young simpleton I had been.

❖ ❖ ❖

My salvation began with my real name being called out in the prison yard. Not one of my prison names. Not one of the Mexican's names. Not Manuel or Ortiz. Which is how the guards usually addressed me. When they did not call me Dead Man. Which was the name the inmates always used. The name I acquired on that day when Silvertone sat across from me in the cafeteria.

So when a voice called out—

"Andreas!"

I did not respond. Because I no longer knew myself by my own name. There were other inmates with that name. And it belonged to them now. Whoever called out that name had to want one of them.

But there was a man approaching me. A thick-muscled Spanish man. With large dark eyes under a wooly head of hair. And a square jaw with a thick black beard. He called out that name again—

"Andreas!"

I watched as he came and stood before me. He was grinning and shaking his wooly head. He spread his hands out at his sides.

"Andreas Delmorales as I live and breathe," the man said. "You were just a pup last time I laid eyes on you. What the hell are you doing in here?"

I said nothing. The stranger's head stopped moving and his grin melted away. Now he frowned at me. When he spoke again his voice was softer—

"And what the hell have they done to you?"

He looked me over then. And was clearly troubled by what he saw. I did not understand why he would care. I did not know him. And no one else inside the prison cared what was done to me. Certainly not the guards. Some of whom liked to take an occasional swipe at me. Or give me a kick. Or spit on me. None of the other prisoners demonstrated any concern for my welfare. Certainly not those vermin I dined with at the table of the damned. Who were glad to have me take the brunt of Silvertone's wrath. They said right to my face that things were better for them since I showed up.

So who was this stranger and why did he care about me? I was trying to frame those questions—working against the pain of a couple broken ribs, multiple lacerations, and something torn apart inside my guts—when this man told me what I wanted to know.

But first he offered his hand. Something no one had done since I went inside. The last time I had shaken anyone's hand was when I said goodbye to my drunken lawyer Bill Jameson at the end of our last consultation before my trial. Holding this stranger's hand troubled me. The experience of non-violent contact was odd and disturbing.

"You don't remember me?" the man said.

I shook my head and let go of his hand. I was relieved to be rid of it.

The man pointed at his chest.

"Tranquilino Rojas?" he said.

He smiled and square yellow teeth showed through his black beard.

"Everyone calls me Tranq."

He extended his hand toward me again and frowned when I stepped back. He paused for a moment after I moved away.

"Okay," he said.

And lowered his hand.

Then he smiled again.

"I was your neighbor," he said. "And we're cousins."

He raised his hand and waved it in the air.

"Way back there somewhere."

He used his hand to scratch at his wooly head. Then he dropped his hand back down at his side and squinted at me when he spoke.

"You really don't remember me? I lived right next door. Your old man, he was good to me. Your uncle too. When I got in a little trouble, they helped me out."

He spread his arms and grinned.

"Come on, amigo. You gotta remember old Tranq now!"

I stared at him. He lowered his hands and frowned.

"No?" he said.

I stared and blinked at this man who insisted he knew me. Then I glanced around the prison yard and saw that others were watching. Finally I turned back to the stranger and shook my head. And as I looked at this man again I realized that I could remember almost nothing of when I was a child. Way back when my father was still alive. That was ancient history that had slipped away. At the time I doubted I would ever get it back. For at that moment I believed I would be dead soon. And nothing that ever happened to me had mattered anyway. So why bother to remember it?

The man extended his hand toward me again. This time I did not step back. He noticed this and smiled. I saw the warmth in his expression and allowed myself to think that maybe the appearance of this man before me was a good thing. This stranger who sought me out. Maybe his arrival meant things could get better. I let that hope flicker and did not snuff it out.

Then the man said something that brought the past back to me—

"I had a red motorcycle," he said.

I could see him on it. His wooly hair was cut short. The beard was gone and his square jaw was prominent. He grinned atop his motorcycle and his wide mouth was full of the same square teeth. But they were white back then. White and gleaming in the sun.

Of course such a man on such a vehicle would make a lasting impression on a young boy.

His eyes searched my face.

"A red chopper, man. You have to remember that bike. I took you for a ride on it."

I nodded once.

"Yes."

He grinned.

"So you can speak."

I smiled a little bit. Then I nodded again.

"Yes. I can speak."

But speaking was painful. Those ribs that had been broken before and were now broken again did not like it when I talked. They did not care for my breathing much either. Now that they were stirred up I had to take short shallow breaths.

Tranquilino saw me wince. He frowned and leaned toward me.

"You're hurting," he said.

He looked down at my chest and then back up at my face.

"Your ribs?"

I nodded. He nodded back at me. Then our eyes met.

That was too much. I looked away.

Chapter 31

Beyond Tranquilino my eyes caught motion. A man was approaching us. Bronze-skinned with a shaved head and black tattoos along both arms and across his broad rounded shoulders and up onto his thick neck. One of Silvertone's lieutenants. Tranquilino saw how my expression changed when I recognized this man and turned to see what I was looking at. The man coming our way took his time doing it. When he stopped beside us he looked at me with cold indifference.

Then he turned to face Tranquilino.

"You're new," he said.

Tranquilino stared at this man for a moment before he answered.

"Yes and no. I've been here before."

"When was that?"

"Ten years ago."

"Ten years is a long time. Things have changed."

"That's something you can count on. That things will change."

Silvertone's man rocked his head toward me.

"What do you want with him?"

Tranquilino raised his black-bearded chin and narrowed his dark eyes.

"Who's asking?"

The messenger rolled his head away from me. Back toward the kingpin across the prison yard.

"Should I know who that is?" Tranquilino said.

"Silvertone," the messenger answered.

Tranquilino nodded slowly.

"Yeah. I heard of him," he said.

He frowned, glanced at me, then turned back to the messenger.

"He and I know some of the same people. I should talk to him."

The messenger turned to Silvertone and a gesture passed between them that I did not catch. I guess the messenger made a sign that meant something to the big man. Silvertone stared in our direction and a moment passed. Then he nodded once and looked away. The messenger turned to Tranquilino and rolled his head toward Silvertone again.

The two of them set off across the yard.

❖   ❖   ❖

While I watched my fate being decided on the far side of the prison yard I concluded this exchange could only go one of three ways:

1. Tranquilino could convince Silvertone that I was who I claimed to be and not a Mexican named Manuel Ortiz and most importantly not a child molester.

2. Silvertone could convince Tranquilino to stay out of it.

3. Tranquilino could place himself in open conflict with the most powerful man in the prison.

Even in my beleaguered state I knew how highly unlikely that last outcome would be. So my attention was focused on the first two possibilities. Waiting for any clues perceivable from across the yard. Any little signs in how the two men behaved and interacted. Would I be set free from my hell? And if so what would prison life be like without the daily torture? Or would things go on as they had? Would Tranquilino become one of Silvertone's men? And be my ally for only those few minutes after he introduced himself?

I watched as Silvertone said something and Tranquilino responded. My guess was the new man had been asked to substantiate his claim that they knew some people in common. A few more words went back and forth. Silvertone nodded. Maybe he was acknowledging that he knew the people

153

Tranquilino mentioned. And that Tranquilino had said enough to prove his connection.

Tranquilino appeared calm but respectful before the big man. When their initial exchange had passed he spoke for a few moments. I guessed he was now explaining how he knew me. Silvertone watched and listened intently. When Tranquilino was done speaking Silvertone said something that made Tranquilino shake his head. Then Tranquilino shook his head some more while he said something in response. Next Silvertone appeared to ask a few questions. He nodded again at something Tranquilino said. Then Silvertone turned to his messenger and apparently he delivered his verdict. The messenger went off and spoke to some others standing nearby. Two of them glanced in my direction.

Now Silvertone and Tranquilino seemed to be making small talk. Silvertone even smiled and laughed. The exchange ended with Silvertone offering his hand. The two men shook. I took that as a very good sign. Then fought to keep my expectations in check.

I knew just how badly disappointment would shatter me.

Tranquilino returned alone. He looked thoughtful as he made his way across the yard. Still calm but now he seemed distracted. Maybe in his mind he was reviewing what had just happened. He looked at me and smiled as he drew near. At that moment my legs almost gave out and dropped me into the dust. I realized I wasn't breathing. When I sucked in my breath one of my broken ribs felt like it was stabbing into my lung.

When Tranquilino arrived he put a hand on my shoulder. That steadied me. When only minutes before shaking his hand had made me anxious.

154

"No more trouble for you," he said. "It will all be cleared up. In a few days. He's going to check out what I told him. When he finds out I'm telling the truth it will all be over. Until then he'll put out the word to lay off. So you're good, my friend. Hear what I'm telling you. No more trouble."

I felt warm all over. I swallowed and my ribs ached. When I spoke my ribs burned with white pain.

"You vouched for me?" I said.

Tranquilino nodded. His hand was still on my shoulder. He squeezed his fingers into my muscles.

"You're damn right I did," he said. "Your people were good to me."

The pain made me not want to say anything more. But there was something I had to know. I grimaced and choked out my words—

"How did you recognize me?"

Tranquilino smiled and his thick eyebrows went up high above his dark eyes.

"Old Tranq never forgets a face," he said.

He grinned and shook his head.

"Never."

He gripped my shoulder tight again and raised his other hand and pointed a thick finger at my face.

"Lucky for you," he said.

He dropped the hand he was pointing with and released his grip on my shoulder.

"That's all right," he said. "You can thank me later."

I felt heat on my cheeks and forehead.

"Sorry," I said. "Thank you."

The pain made me wince.

"It's all right, kid," Tranquilino said. "The shape you're in I shouldn't be yanking your chain."

He put his hand back on my shoulder. That steadied me again.

I hoped he would leave it there.

For maybe the rest of my life.

Part IX:
Beyond the Lonely Bridge

Chapter 32

A few hours into his shift Matt stood with his order pad in hand, looking down into one of the booths and found a face he almost recognized looking back up at him. The face of a middle aged man with a military appearance. Then Matt saw the uniform the man was wearing and the big hat on the bench seat beside him and realized where he had seen this man before.

"I know you," Matt said.

The state trooper frowned at him.

"Yeah," the trooper said. "But how?"

"You came to my house. I mean my apartment."

The trooper squinted.

"Which is it?"

"My apartment."

Matt lowered his eyes and drew a blue circle on his gray pad.

"When my father died."

He looked at the trooper again.

"I remember now," the trooper said.

He nodded at Matt.

"How're you doing with that?"

"Lousy. It sucks."

"Yeah."

Matt tapped his pen on the pad, then poised it over the paper.

"What can I get you today?"

The addition of that last word made Matt feel stupid. Implying that he saw this man and took his order on an everyday basis. When they had only met the one time before. And in very significant circumstances. In a situation that could only happen to Matt once.

The state trooper ordered a grilled ham and cheese and a cup of coffee. Matt ferried the food order to the kitchen and returned with the policeman's coffee. There were other customers to be served and Matt was kept busy. He delivered the trooper's sandwich and check in passing with more orders on his tray and was in and out of the dining room while the trooper ate.

Matt finally caught a moment to speak with the trooper again as the man sat over his empty plate finishing his coffee.

"Tell me something," Matt said.

The policeman gave him a wary look.

"Okay."

"What do you think happened to my father?"

The state trooper stared at Matt for a long moment. Then he spent another moment lowering his coffee cup slowly down onto its saucer. And a third moment using his index finger to spin his cup one full rotation.

Then he looked back up at Matt.

"You want the truth?"

"Yes."

"It wasn't an accident."

The trooper stared. Matt looked away and watched an elderly man make his halting exit from the dining room. When he turned back the trooper was still staring at him.

"Let me ask you something," the trooper said. "Since we're being honest here. He leave you any money?"

Matt felt chilled. He nodded.

"Life insurance, right?" the trooper said.

Matt nodded again.

"And he had a reason for that, right? Maybe he wanted you to go to college. Am I in the ballpark?"

Matt felt he might faint. He nodded again. The trooper nodded back.

"Yeah. Well. He isn't the first."

The trooper looked down while he put his cup through another spin. Then he stared up at Matt again.

"Your father did what he thought was best. Leave it at that. Go make a good life for yourself. That's what he wanted. You want to honor your old man's memory? Go to school like he wanted."

He pointed at Matt.

"And don't look back."

The trooper picked up his hat.

"I can't," Matt said. "The money's gone."

The trooper stared. Then he scowled. He rose to his feet and his scowl cut deep lines beside his eyes. Matt took a step backwards. The trooper put his hat on over his scowl and scowled out from under the wide brim. When he spoke his voice was tight and commanding—

"What'd you do?" the trooper said. "Leave it in Vegas?"

Matt shook his head.

"It was stolen. And then lost."

Matt did the best he could to explain what had happened.

"Like that Madoff bastard?" the trooper said.

Matt nodded.

"Yeah. Something like that."

He shrugged and shook his head.

"I really don't understand this stuff."

"That's because they don't want us to understand."

Matt felt a little better that the trooper had included himself in those who did not understand.

That they were together in their ignorance. And then he felt that what the trooper said implied that the people at large were being exploited. Not just Matt alone. And that made him feel a little better too. Although he knew it should probably make him feel worse.

"No way to get it back," the trooper said.

This was a statement. Not a question. Matt shook his head.

"No."

"That's some bullshit."

"Yeah."

The trooper looked away and Matt thought he better get back to work. He was about to say so when the trooper pointed at him.

"Want my advice?"

"Yeah."

"Join the military. Serve your country. Then go to school."

He nodded once slowly at Matt and for an instant the rim of that big hat covered the trooper's eyes.

"You'll get your life back on track."

The trooper reached out a hand and patted Matt on the shoulder.

"You got my check?" the trooper said.

Matt pointed down at the table where the yellow slip of paper waited beside the remains of the trooper's lunch. The policeman snatched it up and strode from the dining room with his tall black boots squeaking.

Chapter 33

Matt stood frozen and watched the state trooper stride away. Then shook his head as if he was coming up out of water before he went back to work. While he took orders and delivered them he tried to imagine himself in the Navy like his father. But Matt kept hearing his father's voice saying how much he had hated the Navy in particular and military life in general. Repeating the stories Matt had heard a hundred times about the things that drove him crazy. And how he didn't want that for his son.

College was the only thing Frank Walker had wanted for his last best hope.

At the end of his shift Matt was alone in the employee bathroom washing his hands and dreading his return to the empty apartment down the interstate when he looked at his reflection in the mirror above the sink and saw his face as if for the first time in months. And was taken aback by how gray and exhausted he appeared.

"You look like shit," Matt said.

And then he asked his drawn face floating in the mirror—

"What the hell am I gonna do?"

But his reflection looked just as clueless as he felt.

On his way out Matt stopped at the register to collect his tips. The cashier was a plump young woman with a matronly bearing and a kind dimpled face. She gave Matt a broad smile when he approached.

"You got a big one tonight," she said.

She showed him a credit card receipt. Beneath the charges for a grilled ham and cheese with coffee, a meal that cost eight dollars and change, the state trooper had left a twenty dollar tip. Matt stared at the number. He couldn't wrap his mind around it. That tip was as big as the trooper's hat.

And Matt couldn't see how he had done anything to deserve it.

"Jesus," he said.

"You know him or something?"

"No. I mean... I met him once before. But that's it."

"Well I guess he likes you."

Matt shook his head at the receipt.

"Yeah," he said. "I guess so."

❖   ❖   ❖

Matt almost made it to the door. And almost didn't stop when a voice he didn't want to hear called out behind him—

"Matt! Good! You haven't left yet."

He frowned at the door. What was so great that waited for him beyond it?

He sighed and turned around. The manager was standing at the entrance of the dining room with his hands on his hips.

"Can you do me a solid?" the manager said.

Matt winced. He couldn't help it. It was just too painful when the bosses acted familiar. Especially when this one in particular tried to be hip—an ex-jock going pudgy, squarer-than-square and straighter-than-straight, an All-American whiter-than-white poster boy for the Republican Revolution.

Stop that shit, Matt wanted to say.

"Whatta you need?" was what came out of his mouth.

One of the Guatemalans hadn't shown up for his shift. The manager needed help back in the kitchen washing dishes.

"Time and a half," the manager said. "Help me out here bro."

Which almost clinched it. Matt was about to decline for that "bro" alone. Then he remembered that Pablo was working. During the time spent with his friend maybe he could talk over what was troubling him. And the extra money wouldn't hurt. What else would he do anyway? Return to that horridly empty apartment and stare at the walls? He had done far more than enough of that already.

"Sure," he said. "No problem."

The manager made a cheesy grin and smacked Matt on the shoulder.

"My man!" he said.

Matt winced again.

Back in the kitchen over the steaming sinks and dishwashing apparatus Matt told Pablo about his encounter with the state trooper. And what the policeman told him he should do with his life.

"No way!" Pablo said. "Faget dat sheet."

He shook his round head.

"Don' do eet."

Pablo had served in the Guatemalan Army. He told Matt how he hated it. Which more or less echoed what Matt's father had said about the American Navy. When Pablo was done Matt asked for his advice.

"¿Entonces qué?" Matt said. "¿Qué debería hacer?"

What then? What should I do?

Pablo stared up at his young friend. He sighed before he raised his hand and pointed toward the front of the building.

"Lárgate de aquí."

Get out of here.

He leaned toward Matt and shook his head.

"Este lugar no es para ti."

This place is no good for you.

The next morning Pablo's words echoed in his head. And Matt saw that his friend was right. This place *was* no good for him. It never had been. Clearly he should try his luck elsewhere.

Which maybe his parents should have done long ago. Because this place wasn't any good for them either. Back in front of a mirror again, this time in the bathroom of his lonely apartment, as he spread toothpaste across the bristles of his brush, he wondered how his life would have unfolded if his whole family had decamped Walker City and Walker County and the entire damned state of Pennsylvania back when they all still had a chance. Before the rest of them all died and left Matt alone in this stinking place.

While he brushed his teeth and looked at his reflection frowning back at him he considered where he should go. And had no idea. Absolutely nowhere came to mind. He only knew that Pablo was right. He had to be gone from this place that was no good for him.

Then he wondered if maybe Pablo was wrong about the military. Which would solve the problem of where to go. The armed forces would send him somewhere away from here. Which seemed the primary problem. And his father had never considered that Matt might find himself in circumstances such as these when he told his son stay out of the service. So maybe they were both wrong about that. Maybe the military was the best solution. Matt pulled his brush from his mouth and said with white foam appearing on his lips and starting down his chin—

"Wud da fug um uh gudda duh."

What the fuck am I gonna do.

Then he rinsed and spit and went off to Megahits.

Where God seemed to send him a message. Matt was restocking the shelves, back in the horror section again, when a young man with a fresh buzzcut and dressed in a crisp khaki uniform came storming through the entrance. A moment later a young woman appeared behind him. At first Matt did not realize the two were together. Then he noticed that the lovely young lady was following the heated young man. She was tall and lithe and looked part Native American, with a round flat face and long dark hair. She wore a sad and defeated expression. Finally she caught up with the military man, who was half-a-head shorter, and he immediately began to berate her. His voice was hard and blunt and his words were cruel. He called her stupid and lazy and other demeaning things and larded his abuse with profanities. When Matt made the mistake of staring openmouthed, the jarhead glared at him and Matt jerked his head away.

When they were gone Matt realized that in the armed services he would suffer under the authority of men like that one. And everything his father and Pablo had said about military life snapped into new focus. He saw then how such a life might even kill him.

"Fuck that," Matt said.

His manager called out from the front of the store—

"Excuse me?"

"Nothing, sir."

"Watch your mouth."

"Yes sir. Sorry."

Matt bent his head to his work while he contemplated how the manager said nothing about the obscenities that poured from the jarhead but jumped down Matt's throat after a solitary "fuck".

"The customer is always right," Matt said.

The manager called out again—

"What's that?"

"Nothing."

"You got something to say to me?"

"No sir."

Matt kept quiet while the rest of the DVDs went back up on the shelves.

And pondered anew where he should go. Now that the armed forces were definitively eliminated. And began to feel just a little bit excited. Maybe life had some possibilities left in it after all. Maybe things could actually be better if he got away from here. Maybe where he went didn't matter. Just so long as he left.

Maybe leaving was all that mattered.

Chapter 34

He started in a supermarket parking lot. Early in the morning while it was still empty. He found the spot where his mother's car had been waiting when he went there with his father in the middle of the night on their way home from the hospital. The same old worn out red Toyota he was driving now. The space was at the end of a row beside a scraggly dogwood.

Matt remembered seeing that sad little tree when he switched on the headlights before he drove home. His father met him in the driveway and in the blanketing darkness of that moonless cloud-shrouded night they silently unloaded the last groceries his mother would ever buy. In the kitchen they found the milk was warm and the frozen goods all defrosted.

He sat staring through the windshield at the withered little tree while he remembered when he first saw his mother at the hospital. And how she already looked half-dead propped up on pillows in her mechanical bed with tubes snaking into her arm. And how pained she looked to be troubling them while she recounted what had happened. How the last thing she remembered before waking up in the emergency room was exiting the supermarket with her cart full of groceries. Wondering why she suddenly felt so ill. Then the shock of vomiting blood onto the pavement beside her car.

What happened next came to them from another source. The man who was passing by on his way into the store when he saw Helen start to fall and dashed over. He caught her as she collapsed and placed her unconscious form in the back of his Volkswagen microbus and drove her to the hospital with his flashers on.

Frank had a heart-to-heart with the man who rescued his wife while they sat together in the waiting room. An aging hippie who had been a medic in

Vietnam and one of the Winter Soldiers on the National Mall. He had scars from fighting the war and scars from ending the war. A piece of shrapnel in his leg that sent him home. And a fused crack in his skull from the nightstick of a Chicago cop who wanted to stop what the hippie did when he got home.

He visited Helen once while she was hospitalized. For just a few moments. To check on how she was doing. Then he smiled and squeezed her hand as he said goodbye and was gone from their lives. Matt wondered what had become of her rescuer since.

And what had kept him in Walker City. A place where someone like him was less than welcome. Family? Friends? History? Inertia?

❖   ❖   ❖

Wondering what had kept the old hippie in Walker City made Matt wonder what would happen to him when he left. Would he find something better or something worse? He decided that right now something different was all that mattered. Then offered this for the old hippie—

God bless your soul. Wherever you are.

And restarted the engine of his dead mother's old worn out car and went across town to the hospital where she succumbed. He did not stop there. He only drove past and looked at the rows of windows on the third floor where her room had been. The people inside dealing with life and death did not need him wandering among them getting in the way with his grief. So he offered his respects from afar and moved on.

To the Walker City Cemetery. Where he wound among the graves on the rolling hills to the Walker family plot. Where his family had been coming to rest for more than two centuries. Their numbers had thinned in the later generations so there

167

were few recent graves among the old ones. Just three to be exact.

He went first to see his brother Jack. Where he stood with his hands folded together behind his back and his head bowed while he remembered what he could of his older brother. Which was not very much. In Matt's life Jack had mostly been gone. Out late at night, away all weekend. Finally off to Korea from where he returned in his present condition. Matt did not have any tears to shed for his only brother. He felt sorry for Jack and his short stupid life but no real grief would come. Just a hollow feeling inside.

At his parents' graves the tears would not stop. For most of an hour he was overcome with emotion. Thoughts of his parents and love for them and wanting to live in some way that would validate for how their lives came and went were mixed with moments of complete despair that anything like redemption was at all possible for himself and by extension for his family.

When he had recovered enough to move on he went to the graves of his paternal grandparents. Where he felt solemn but as with his brother did not weep. These two were the first in the long line of his dead stretching back across time whom Matt had never known. Both were lying here before he was born. As was his one paternal aunt, buried beside them. These three and his parents and Jack were the only members of the last three generations to be found here in the Walker family plot. The others had all scattered and died and been buried elsewhere. Matthew was the last one left alive and now he was leaving.

The last Walker would be gone from Walker City.

❖   ❖   ❖

There was one final stop to be made before he was done. Outside of town on the interstate. At the

168

foot of a long hill halfway to Oldham. No exit there, just a bridge where an isolated back road crossed over the highway. Matt parked on the northbound shoulder, dashed across the four lanes and the narrow median to the other side, scrambled down a steep embankment, and stood before one of the concrete bridge abutments. The one with gouges cut into the cement. He stood in that lonely and nameless and to anyone else meaningless spot on a highway no different from most others and listened to the faint sound of a dog barking high up above. Which he could only hear when the traffic did not roar up on the interstate and the wind did not moan through the hollow beneath the bridge.

Matt knew that barking dog was the Husky that rousted its owner on that night not so long ago. And led the old man who lived in the house on that back road that crossed the highway overhead out onto the bridge with a flashlight in his hand that he shone down onto the old wrecked pickup where Matthew stood now. There was no other house close enough from which the sound of a barking dog could be heard down here in this hidden spot. The house that belonged to that old man stood off by itself among fields and pastures along that back road.

Then the dog stopped barking. And the traffic stopped too. Now the wind moaned only faintly. In that quiet moment given to him Matt stood before the scarred concrete and offered blessings to his father. And asked for his father's blessings in return.

And for his forgiveness. For abandoning the goals his father had set for him. And for abandoning the place their family had called home for generations.

Then Matthew ran back up the slope and across the highway and ducked into his mother's old beaten car. For a moment he sat with his head turned to the left looking out through the side window across the four lanes toward the place where his father died.

Then he turned forward and started the engine and put the car in gear and drove away.

When he was gone the dog barked again beyond that lonely bridge.

Part X:
Allies and Uxoricides

Chapter 35

Silvertone did not offer an apology. A man like him only apologizes when he must. And especially so given the situation. A man in his position cannot apologize without risking that position. And therefore the power that comes with it. Which a man like him would never do.

But Silvertone did offer something more valuable. He offered his protection.

Which I wanted to refuse. Again it was Tranquilino who saved me—

"Have you lost your mind?" Tranquilino said.

It was two days after he brokered my commutation. We were back out in the yard. Tranquilino waved a hand at the bare dirt and the other inmates.

"Look around you. Do you know where you are? In case you have missed it—you are in prison. And do you know what kind of men some of these are? You should by now. Given what many of them have done to you. And those aren't the worst ones. The worst have been kept on a chain. How do you think you will get by in here on your own? Yes, they know you aren't what they thought."

He waved a hand in the air.

"Before. When you first came here."

Now he pointed at me.

"But to many of them that doesn't matter anyway. They are beasts and they will devour you. Silvertone is the one who can keep them under control. Without him they will be unleashed."

With one hand he pointed at his own broad chest. He waved the other hand beside his head.

"And don't think old Tranq is going to protect you."

He lowered his hands and waved them both palms down at the level of his waist. He looked at me and shook his wooly head.

"I don't owe your family that much."

He stopped waving his hands and folded his arms across his chest. He peered at me, then turned and looked away.

"I can only promise you one thing. If they kill you I will write to your family."

Those words sent Tranquilino's dark eyes cutting back my direction.

"Which reminds me. About your family."

He unfolded his arms and turned to face me.

"Where are they in all this?"

❖   ❖   ❖

Tranquilino listened patiently while I rambled on about my mother and the jackass and that we were moving to Los Angeles when I came down to visit my father's grave and how I saved the boy and wound up in prison. He waited until I ran out of breath before he interjected—

"Your father died?"

When I told Tranquilino that not only my father was dead but my uncle had died too, his face grew heavy. He made me tell him how they died.

"Those were good men," he said.

Then he asked about my mother. Why she was letting me rot in here. I explained that I couldn't reach my mother or my aunt by telephone or by mail. He shook his head at me.

"You're in a real jam, kid. A real goddamn jam-up."

He shook his head again.

"Shit," he said.

He puffed out his cheeks and let them deflate slowly. I watched him walk a few slow circles across the packed dirt. When he stopped he looked at me.

"Shit," he said again.

Then he raised a hand and pointed.

"All the more reason to take what Silvertone offers."

He stared at me with that thick finger hanging in the air.

"You need this," he said. "You have to see that."

I stared at my savior. Then slowly nodded my assent.

"Yes. I see that."

Tranquilino nodded.

"Good."

He stepped closer and patted my shoulder.

"You made the right call."

Again I watched him make the journey across the yard. This time traveling alone. I watched him speak with one of Silvertone's flunkies and then be escorted to the boss man. He glanced my direction when he related that I would most gratefully accept protection as compensation for the long months of torture and the many injuries unjustly inflicted upon my person.

With time I would fully understand the merits of this decision and become deeply thankful that Tranquilino pushed me toward it.

But at the time it only made me feel ill.

❖   ❖   ❖

I never learned why I was singled out. That was not something you could ask a man like Silvertone. The men I could ask didn't know. As best as I have been able to determine he wasn't connected to Elden Morris. Not a relative or a family friend or even an acquaintance.

Perhaps there was some detail in the particulars of my case that put me in his crosshairs. Maybe I reminded him of someone he didn't like. At the time I was only twenty years old. Still a boy in the eyes of many. Much younger than the other men imprisoned for crimes of perversion involving children. Maybe the man who once promised I would someday beg for death had an ugly history with young men who liked to do terrible things to small boys.

So it remains a mystery why I was chosen for special abuse. From among my peers at the table of the damned. Those debased human vermin I was forced to dine with during my purgatory.

Some of whom dared suggest once I was raised up from their depths that I should advance their wretched standing due to a previously unacknowledged bond. Simply because I had been unjustly cast among them they now felt I could be persuaded to become their champion. These same men had done absolutely nothing to assist me when I was being so brutally tortured, not even on the several occasions when I was nearly beaten to death. They had instead openly hoped that my death would be delayed indefinitely not out of any concern for my wellbeing but so that they could continue to enjoy relief while I absorbed the brunt of Silvertone's formidable wrath.

They would have me use my innocence to help them avoid the consequences of their guilt. Hideous horrid and horrendous. Two-legged beasts entirely undeserving of being called human. With the many years gone past I retain more ill feeling for them than for the men who beat and raped me. May God show no mercy on their disfigured souls. Let us now forever close the book on their abject existences. And when their judgment day comes let us rejoice in the writhings and wailings of their eternal damnation.

Chapter 36

Silvertone was not the only man of power among the prisoners. There were others of lesser status with influence obtained in the same manner. Leaders of smaller and weaker gangs. Men who might occasionally risk a challenge to the king but ultimately had to obey when he commanded. Or else face being inevitably annihilated.

But there was one man who existed on the same plane. If in a realm apart. This man did not have need of a gang. Because his power came from the only other possible source. Instead of being drawn up from the other prisoners it was extended down from the warden. And even from beyond the prison walls.

I met this man one afternoon not long after my salvation when a guard found me in the cafeteria having lunch with Tranquilino. All the guard would say was that someone wanted to see me. Which of course inspired me to imagine the worst as I followed along after the guard. Still struggling to master the rhythm of my prison-acquired limp. And still adjusting to the hearing damage in my right ear. And still disturbed by the loss of peripheral vision in my right eye.

But although I felt half-wrecked and could only assume this journey through the prison would end badly, since most news is bad news and especially so for an inmate, despite all this I was calm. Maybe my heart had more faith than my mind in the protective powers of Silvertone. Or maybe I just did not care anymore. Whatever the reason I felt almost cavalier as I stumbled along. Looking back now I feel that in some essential way I was older then, while still in my youth, than I am in my aging freedom all these years later.

❖   ❖   ❖

Eventually we entered a section of the prison that was new to me. Not only had I never entered there before, I was not aware these hallways and rooms even existed. The guard led me along those unfamiliar passageways to a room that was a small windowless box. The only inanimate contents of this room were a metal desk with nothing on it and two chairs. A single fluorescent light fixture was centered in the low drop ceiling. Like the hallway outside the floor was a pale linoleum.

But behind the desk, seated in the padded swivel chair, there was a man. I could only assume he was the one who had summoned me. Something in his deportment spoke of such authority. Although his presence was unimposing. Spanish, a little on the short side, with a square face and a square shoulders. Dressed in black slacks and a short-sleeved blue work shirt. Graying at the temples. Large probing eyes behind black-framed bifocal eyeglasses.

He rose as I entered and offered his hand. I reached across the bare desk and took it. His hand was rough and his grip was solid.

"Daniel Salazar," he said. "Pleased to meet you."

"Andreas Delmorales."

My host grinned and raised his chin just a little.

"Not Manuel Ortiz?" he said.

His question provided an answer. And asked another question. His words told me he knew of my recent history. And asked what if anything that had to do with why he called me here. While wrapping both inside a jest.

And offering a chance to show I knew how to play this. Which I did. Well before I was set up and sent away. Gallows humor is second nature to anyone who grows up poor with half a brain. Combined with the fatalism that is the Mesoamerican-Mayan-Aztec-Mexican legacy of my people and by the time you're

176

out of diapers it's like breathing. The words flowed out of me without thought or prompting and I listened with detachment along with my audience and even shared their mild curiosity at what I would say—

"I hear that poor bastard is in prison across the border. Driving without a license."

Not a very good joke. Even a somewhat bad one. But good enough for the circumstances. A joke that showed I was game.

The guard who brought me there snorted. Salazar's grin grew wider. He nodded a few times. While these men who were strangers to me did these small things I realized that my poor jest had, like Salazar's before mine, provided an exchange of information. I had confirmed that Salazar and the guard knew a key detail of my ordeal, that a Mexican driver's license was given as proof that I was someone else. And since prior knowledge of that detail was essential to the joke's success, I had told these men I was aware that I had been the subject of detailed discussion.

All this subtext flying around that little room.

Salazar gestured at the chair beside me. On my side of the desk the seating was metal and plastic. Hard unwelcoming surfaces. No swiveling cushion for the buttocks of the interviewee.

"Please," Salazar said.

I sat and was uncomfortable. My bad leg— which is my right one, just like my ear and my eye, all my damage loaded up making me lopsided—gave me considerable grief in the first year or so after my injuries. I adjusted my position and was uncomfortable still. I accepted that was how it would be.

The guard stood against the wall beside the door. Salazar frowned at him. The guard said—

"I hafta bring 'im back."

"Then could you wait in the hall?"

"Sure."

The guard stepped out. Salazar called after him—

"And could you close the door?"

The guard reappeared. This time when he left the door closed behind him.

During this exchange with the guard I had a moment to consider the man who called me here. Specifically to wonder who and what this man Salazar was. At the time I was unaware that he was an inmate like myself. He was not dressed like one. Nor was he dressed like a prison official. No suit and tie. Not even today's "work casual". Instead, if his name had been embroidered on his shirt pocket, what this man across the desk wore would have been typical for a tradesman. A repairer of household appliances. Or a car mechanic.

Although his shirt and slacks were crisply pressed and spotless.

"I assume you know why you're here," Salazar said.

He was confounded to learn that I did not.

"No one has told you who I am?"

I confirmed that they had not. Then added that no one had told me much of anything since until very recently everyone had considered me a dead man.

"Of course," he said. "That explains it."

Salazar then explained what he wanted me to do and why I should say yes. Which was to make cabinetry in his woodshop. And that I should do it not for the pay—because there wasn't any—but for the company I would keep. Because his shop was an intellectual and cultural refuge within the prison. He selected the most educated and refined men to work there.

Not being a complete idiot I accepted his offer on the spot.

But being something of an idiot when we were standing again I asked why he wanted me of all people. Why not select someone who already had the skills he needed? Or was at least a high school graduate? I stupidly confessed that I was both unskilled and uneducated.

Salazar narrowed his eyes while he said—

"Most of these ones in here are animals. I can't work with them."

Now that he had determined I was not an animal he wanted to try me out. My lack of education and experience, not to mention my recently acquired physical handicaps, were of no concern to him.

"To me you are raw wood," Salazar said.

He looked at my bad leg.

"With a few knots."

Then he raised his chin and studied my face.

"And I am familiar with shaping the raw material into the finished product. To finish a man you must educate him. We'll see what we can do about that."

He told me I would start out sweeping the floor. Which was the first task he gave every new man. And that within minutes some men had the broom taken from their hands and were shown the door.

"So watch how you sweep," he said. "Details are everything."

Chapter 37

Only later would I learn the truth about Daniel Salazar. Which I will share with you now. There is no need for you to remain in suspense. You may only grow irritated with your narrator.

In his former life Daniel Salazar had been a successful contractor. Building fancy custom houses for high-end clientele. A business he had built steadily over the years. As men are prone to do when success finally comes bringing the good money rolling in, with middle age upon him and death now darkly looming out at the horizon of his years, Salazar fell under the spell of a younger woman. He tossed aside his faithful wife who had given him a son and two daughters to be the slave of a local beauty pageant winner. A blue-eyed blond who was almost still a girl.

Her family disapproved of his age and his recent divorce and most of all his Spanish-ness. What they did not disapprove of was his money. They had none and he had plenty. His cash overcame all objections. He bought them off and they went slithering back into their hole.

All was well enough for the first few years of his second life. Her family even began to accept him. Or at least to grow accustomed to his presence. But like all successful men Salazar was kept busy. Which meant his attractive young wife spent much time alone. Or at least not in his company.

During the frenzy in the local media around his trial a woman who lived across the street from the Salazars stood out at the curb by the end of her driveway dressed in tennis clothes and said of the second Mrs. Salazar—

"You want to know what she was like? I'll tell you. She was a worthless little hotpants tramp with a thing for Latin guys."

The woman waved a hand across the street toward where the Salazars lived.

"That place was like Grand Central Station for former Menudo members."

So you see where this is going.

Word came to Salazar that his wife had been seen out on the town with a handsome young man. Just that one word was enough to convince him he had been cuckolded. He confronted his wife and she vehemently denied the accusations. She was loudly indignant and threatened to leave him.

He begged her to stay.

But his suspicions remained. Try as he might he could not subdue them. He neglected his business to spy on his wife. He caught her at nothing but was plagued with doubt.

Finally he hired a private detective. This investment returned absolutely no evidence that his wife was unfaithful. Which at the time Salazar considered money well spent. For it convinced him that his fears were the work of the Devil. He confessed to his priest and to his young wife how he had skulked around behind her back and even hired a detective and pleaded for her forgiveness and for the forgiveness of God.

His wife tearfully granted hers. The priest said God forgave him too.

There is no record of whether God or the priest wept.

One afternoon, following a hurried and tense business lunch at a greasy spoon, Daniel Salazar felt sick to his stomach. Pulling out of the parking lot he decided to go home instead of returning to the office. As he drove he began to feel better. He decided to continue home, have some Pepto-Bismol to settle his stomach, and if he seemed to be all right then he would go back to work. Things were busy. He couldn't really spare any time off.

He emptied his stomach in his driveway. Where his vomit splattered onto the tires of an unfamiliar red sports car. Then he crept into the house he had built for his young bride and up the staircase and along the hall to the doorway of their bedroom.

Where he observed his young wife with a man even younger than herself. Almost a boy. Salazar crept away again and waited for them to finish and for the young man to leave. While he waited he was sick again in one of the bathrooms downstairs.

When the red sports car was roaring away with the sated juvenile stud at the wheel Salazar took one of his hunting rifles into their bedroom and shot his wife. He put five bullets into her as she lay spent and dozing in their defiled marriage bed. Twice in the head and three times in the torso. He was still holding the gun when he called for an ambulance.

"I've just my shot my wife," he told the operator.

Then Salazar described in detail exactly what had happened and what he had done. Every word of his conversation with the emergency services dispatcher was recorded in excellent audio quality by a brand-new automatic system.

Which did not leave Salazar's defense attorney any room to debate his guilt. Instead the attorney focused on lessening his client's sentence. He hired another detective and this one easily uncovered ample proof that Salazar's wife had been carrying on not only with the youthful driver of the red sports car but with several other men as well. That she was in the habit of picking up men at bars, having sex with them for two or three weeks, then tossing them aside for a new playmate. And the neighbor in the tennis clothes was right, the young blond hotpants Mrs. Salazar preferred men of Spanish heritage.

This new detective also proved that his predecessor, the investigator hired by Salazar, had found much of the same evidence. But instead of taking what he found to Salazar he took it to the young wife. Because he wanted to put it to the young wife. Which he then did. Several times.

While a hidden camera took photographs.

❖   ❖   ❖

At his trial Daniel Salazar was confronted with those photographs.

He responded by weeping copiously.

On the witness stand he insisted that he had no memory of shooting his wife. He claimed that he only intended to scare her. And that the gun must have gone off accidentally. The prosecution of course had a romping field day with this claim of firing five "accidental" gunshots. Two in the head and three in the torso. Immediately after he caught his wife in bed with another man. His critics in the media began calling the defendant "Denial" Salazar.

Needless to say the jury did not believe him. Or Salazar would not have been seated behind that metal desk in that small room within the state prison where I went to be interviewed.

So I was hired. For the job that proved to be the most significant of my life. Even though I was paid nothing. No money at all. Not even after years of loyal and dedicated employment.

But the benefits were extraordinary. They greatly bettered my condition both during imprisonment and after my release. For which I remain grateful to the uxoricide Daniel Salazar.

Uxoricide (from Latin uxor meaning "wife") is murder of one's wife. It can refer to the act itself or the man who carries it out.

Wikipedia; May 9, 2013
http://en.wikipedia.org/wiki/Uxoricide

A term I learned while in his employment. Without which I might have remained ignorant and downtrodden. So for me it was a good thing the man killed his wife. Very bad for her. But very good for me and a whole lot of others who worked for him while in prison.

But those who benefitted most from Salazar's imprisonment were of course not among his fellow prisoners. The greatest beneficiaries were the men behind the scheme that put Salazar at the head of that cabinet-making shop.

Because, as I have mentioned, like slaves we were not paid. But unlike slaves we were supported by the state. Our labor came at no cost to the owners of our output. They did not have to buy us, feed us, clothe us, doctor us, build and maintain the walls that sheltered and contained us, or pay the guards that kept us from running away. All of those costs were born by the taxpayer. So for the capitalists who were behind this scheme we were better than slaves. Exactly because we required no capital.

If you needed cabinets and had the right connections we would make them for you at a very nice price. For the remuneration of the prison warden and his political associates. Their little operation was enormously profitable.

And of course it was also entirely illegal.

Chapter 38

Unless you have been imprisoned it may be difficult to grasp why working unpaid in a woodshop would be highly desirable. Here then are some of the many reasons that was so:

1. As I mentioned before, employment in the cabinet shop placed you among a better class of men. The conversation and behavior found in this setting were immensely superior.

2. Working for Salazar brought the protection of the warden. Which greatly reduced the risk of being assaulted or raped. (And since I also enjoyed the protection of Silvertone my safety was now all but guaranteed. Of course I had already paid for that upfront.)

3. Being sequestered in the shop during the working day reduced the risk of becoming collateral damage in a random act of violence.

4. It also reduced the risk of witnessing criminal acts perpetrated by your fellow prisoners. Which you would have to keep to yourself for your own safety. Making you an accessory to a crime.

5. There was the pleasure of losing yourself in productive work. Which is invaluable in passing time while incarcerated.

6. We were given superior food for our midday meal, an inducement negotiated by Salazar in his dealings with the warden.

7. He also obtained for us the privilege of changing from our prison jumpsuits into work clothes while we were in the shop. Which made it almost possible to pretend during our working day that we weren't even imprisoned. That we were provisionally free.

8. There were occasional trips outside the prison to obtain supplies. On these outings Salazar was accompanied by a few lucky inmates.

9. When certain guards chaperoned the restocking excursions they could be bribed into allowing a brief detour to a local whorehouse.

These were the benefits that chiefly satisfied my fellow workers. But for myself and some others there was another far more profitable opportunity that came from being one of Salazar's men—

10. Education. Which has rightly been called the true fruit of liberty. So in the shop we were able to steal some of liberty's fruit.

Education that came not just through the usual prison channels, which Salazar and his deputies helped the new recruits negotiate. The shop also provided an education of its own. Being in the company of men more learned than ourselves had an elevating effect. And we were mentored by those men as we sought to improve our minds.

I was exhorted to read. Anything and everything. I did as they instructed me and quickly learned exactly how right they were. In prison if you have any inclination to thought you must set your mind wandering in order not to lose it. And a mind can wander very far between the covers of a book. I became an obsessive reader. So much so that at times I had to be told to stop reading the newspapers we used as packing material in the woodshop and return my attention to the job at hand.

One day they couldn't get me to. I waved my coworkers off and took the local newspaper I had found to a worktable and bent over it while I finished an interview with the newly elected Doña Pero County Sheriff Josef Armijo.

This was a month or so after I joined the woodshop. Since then another position had become available and I had put in a good word for my friend Tranquilino. I like to think that helped because Salazar hired him.

Tranq came over to see what demanded my attention. We had discussed many things since he found me in the prison yard. But Armijo was not one of them.

"So you didn't know about that," he said.

I shook my head. Tranq pointed at me with a thick finger.

"He got there on your back, my friend. That bastard rode you like a burro. And he rode you hard."

Tranquilino explained how Armijo used my arrest and conviction to take his boss's job. That his election campaign was all about how he had vanquished the dirty Mexican and would keep Doña Pero safe from such evil.

When Tranquilino was done I spat out three words—

"That fat fuck!"

Tranquilino stared at me with his eyes wide. Then he put his wooly head back and laughed. He was still laughing when he grabbed my shoulder and wagged that thick finger before my face.

"You're gonna be all right, kid!" he said.

Then he held his hands against his belly and laughed deep and hard.

And I joined him. With a searing pain in my twisted-up stomach I stood beside my good friend Tranquilino Rojas and I laughed too. We laughed together in fits and starts. Laughter that swelled and ebbed and washed over us again. And despite the pain that it came with, I have never enjoyed laughing so much in my entire life.

When the laughing was done I felt like a new man. Standing there in the woodshop recovering from our laughing fit beside Tranquilino I felt I could take whatever life threw at me. Even if the worst was yet to come. I had survived what would break many men. Maybe even most.

And I would survive that fat fuck being sheriff.

"Fuck that Armijo," I said. "He can go to hell."

With that we laughed some more. Not so much as the first time. Neither of us had much more in us. We choked and sputtered this time around. But when we were done for that second time the bond between us was complete.

That was the day we became soul brothers.

Let it be said here and now, and for all time to come, and before all who may ever have occasion to care, that I, Andreas Delmorales, of sound mind and body, do unequivocally state and acknowledge that I owe my mortal life and very sanity to that wooly-headed black-bearded dark-eyed yellow-toothed beast of man, that thief and criminal and all-round hardened felon, my good and true friend Tranquilino Rojas. For all his faults and failings, despite all his sins before God, a better man I have never known. From him I received all that my life has been since that moment when he approached me in the prison yard. And to him I can offer only my eternal undying gratitude.

God bless your soul my dear Tranquilino.

If you hate yourself, prison becomes even more challenging. All those long slow hours spent in your own despised company can easily drive you mad. The real jail cell becomes your own skull. If you are the least bit inclined to contemplate your nature and your place in this world, then in prison the impossibility of ever escaping from who you are becomes undeniable—and can grow to be unbearable. It is that impossibility of escaping from who you are and what you have done that pushes so many inmates into other forms of evasion. Drugs. Violence. Racism.

But if you do not hate yourself that is a great asset during confinement. It is much more comfortable being stuck in such close quarters with someone you actually like. And far easier to find the energy to improve yourself. Since you already have a favorable opinion of the raw material.

I was one of the lucky ones. If such a thing can be said of someone denied his liberty. I did not hate myself. I had done nothing awful to put myself inside. I did not have a long trail of violence and degeneration stretched out behind me, like a snail leaving slime everywhere it goes. After my initial ordeal I found myself in a situation as best could be hoped for within prison walls. And with the assistance and support of the best men I met there, I assiduously set about improving myself.

The truth is that being an inmate actually aided my intellectual development. On the outside I had my family to help provide for. And likely I would soon have met a young woman and begun making a family of my own. But on the inside—for better or for worse, whether I liked it or not—I was removed from all such claims and ties.

I obtained my high school diploma a little over a year after my interview with Daniel Salazar. Then entered into college study and eventually obtained a bachelor's degree in journalism. With time a master's followed.

I was planning to write my way out of jail.

And in a manner of speaking that's exactly what I did.

Part XI: Canyonlands

Chapter 39

They arrived late in the afternoon. When they had parked and were on foot crossing the lot toward the rim, Rosa swiveled her head looking around them. She seemed to be searching for someone or something.

"What is it, Tía?" Essie said.

Rosa shook her head and didn't answer. They continued forward.

And then the canyon opened up before them.

They were not prepared for this. Although this is what they came to see.

"¡Santa María, Madre de Dios!" Rosa said.

Holy Mary, Mother of God!

They stood and stared. Side-by-side with their eyes wide. Looking first one way and then another. Unable to absorb all the colors playing across the cliffs. Stunned by a rainbow shimmering through the wall of rain standing off to the west.

Rosa hooked her arm through Esperanza's. For another moment they stood and gaped. Then off they went strolling along the rim. The views that kept being revealed at each bend in the path convinced them both that they did not want to be anywhere else on all of the earth.

"I can't believe it," Esperanza kept repeating.

"I know," Rosa would respond. "Me either."

This went on for fifteen or twenty minutes.

But then something managed to distract young Esperanza. To turn her attention away from one of the great wonders of the natural world.

A boy did this. What else could?

He was Anglo. A year or two older than Essie. Taller than average but not remarkably so. Short

190

brown hair and broad shoulders and a wide-open face. Good looking but in an understated way. Not the kind of pretty boy who makes silly girls swoon.

He was with his parents and did not try to pretend otherwise. As so many teenage boys do, especially the Anglo ones, and only succeed in making themselves seem ridiculous. He did not have headphones on and he was not ignoring the canyon. Like some of the other young Anglos Essie saw there. This boy was aware and engaged, both with his surroundings and his parents. He smiled at them and laughed at remarks made by his father and at one point he put his arm around his mother's shoulders.

And then Esperanza and this boy looked at each other and their eyes locked.

The world seemed to stop for Essie and she thought she might launch into the air and go tumbling into the canyon. The boy only looked away when his mother called to him. He blinked and turned from Esperanza and looked to where his mother pointed at something down below. When he had seen what she wanted him to, he smiled and nodded and turned back to Essie.

And they locked eyes again.

And Esperanza realized that she felt like she already knew him.

❖   ❖   ❖

Their gaze was broken by a swarm of Japanese tourists. A tour guide packed her group into the overlook and the cameras were incessant while the guide rattled away in Japanese. Esperanza searched through the crowd for the Anglo boy but could not find him. She felt drained when she realized he and his family were gone.

Rosa tugged on her hand and they started through the crowd. They had to dart this way and that to find a path through the milling Japanese. The cameras kept whirring and clicking. The tour guide kept talking.

Eventually they broke through the throng and continued on. Esperanza felt her heart jump when she saw the Anglo boy ahead. But he was too far away now. They couldn't lock eyes at this distance. And the boy and his family were moving too quickly. The father was taller than his son and moved fast on his long legs. The mother and the son hustled to keep up with him. The father stopped and smiled back at his family and said something. Essie wondered what it was. Apologizing for going too fast? Teasing them about being too slow?

At the next overlook Essie and Rosa arrived just as the boy and his parents turned around.

"If we come back," the father said. "We're renting a car."

He saw Esperanza was watching him and smiled at her and nodded.

"Hello," he said.

"Hello," Esperanza answered.

Her eyes went to the man's son. Who was looking directly at her. Their eyes met again but just for an instant. The boy looked to his father when the man spoke and Esperanza did the same. She was close to the boy now and her heart was pounding.

"What a magnificent place," the father said. "I really had no idea. Nothing you read or hear prepares you for this. And the tour group we're on wants us out of here already."

He sighed and shrugged and smiled at Esperanza and at Rosa.

"That's too bad," Rosa said.

The man waved a hand at the canyon.

"We feel like we just got here," he said.

His wife nodded beside him. He sighed again.

"Oh well. Live and learn."

He nodded and smiled at Rosa and Essie.

"You folks enjoy yourself."

"Thank you," Rosa said. "Have a safe trip."

The whole family smiled and nodded. The boy looked at Esperanza when he said—

"Goodbye."

❖   ❖   ❖

Esperanza could only smile. Her throat was too tight for any words to escape. But her eyes glowed at the boy as he spoke and went past her and then she was watching him walk away and feeling more and more despairing with every step that he took. The boy glanced back over his shoulder just as he and his parents disappeared around a bend in the trail and her heart ached when he slipped out of sight. She kept her eyes where he had gone and filled her lungs and sighed out her breath.

When she could find the will to move again she turned to her aunt. Rosa smiled at her and nodded after the Anglo boy and his family.

"I saw that," Rosa said. "You like him."

Essie frowned.

"But we didn't say a word to each other."

Rosa smiled and shook her head.

"That's not true. He said one word to you."

Esperanza felt sick with regret.

"And like an idiot I said nothing to him."

"Maybe not with your mouth."

Essie felt faint. She stared at her aunt.

"What?" Essie said.

Rosa smiled and raised a hand and pointed forked fingers at her eyes.

"Sometimes these do all the talking."

Esperanza saw the truth of what her aunt meant and her faintness passed. Now she felt drained and chilled in the breeze blowing past them and down into the canyon. She watched Rosa look to where the Anglo boy and his family had disappeared.

"You will see him again," Rosa said.

Esperanza shivered.

"How is that possible? He's already gone."

Rosa took Essie's hand.

"Only for now," Rosa said. "You must believe what I am telling you. That one you will see again."

Esperanza had never been more confused.

"How can you know that?"

"The same way I knew that you had to come here. So you could see him the first time."

"I don't understand. We came here because you wanted to."

"I wanted to because you had to."

"Please, Tía. What are you talking about?"

"What I'm talking about is your future."

Essie jolted. She shook her head.

"I don't understand."

Rosa smiled at Esperanza. She drew her niece close and embraced her and kissed her on the cheek. Esperanza felt her soul begin to hum and buzz when Rosa whispered in her ear—

"I saw your future in a dream. And that boy was with you."

Chapter 40

No one was surprised when Esperanza Armijo graduated from high school as the valedictorian of her class. They would have been surprised if she had not. And when it was announced that she would attend the state university on a full scholarship no one was surprised by that either. Even those among her classmates who had decided to dislike her, the ones she had offended who savored licking their wounds, even they agreed she earned her success. Everyone acknowledged that no one was smarter or worked harder. There were just a few who thought maybe she could be a bit less arrogant.

When autumn approached she packed up her things and went off to the city. Rosa drove her in and wept when she said goodbye. Esperanza had no tears to shed. She was far past ready to leave home and the village and what those places had come to mean. The only pain she felt was at leaving her aunt. But they would talk on the phone. And home was only an hour away. No reason to stand and cry outside her new dormitory.

La Soldadita was again on the march. This time the object of her conquest was academia. And she could not have been happier or more determined. She shed her old life like a dead skin and rejoiced in the radical difference of her new one.

And upon this stage there strode a shining star.

Leslie Davidson was tall and lean with a heart-shaped face. Her dark blue eyes were set far apart beneath thick black eyebrows. She had a wide straight mouth under a delicate nose and her cheekbones were dusted with freckles. It was a girlish face with a woman's poise and confidence.

For the first session of the introductory archaeology course Dr. Davidson dressed for the part.

Which meant that when Esperanza found the classroom standing, at the front of it was this striking and impressive woman wearing the classic safari-style khaki archeologist outfit Esperanza had only seen before in films and in photographs. The professor even strapped on a pith helmet before calling out—

"Good morning class!"

Everyone stopped what they were doing and looked at her.

Esperanza was the only one who answered—

"Good morning, professor."

Her strong voice stood alone in the lecture hall. She sat in the center of the front row and could feel eyes on the back of her head. She imagined everyone who stared at her thinking she was a suck-up. She didn't care much what these faceless students thought but was distracted enough that she didn't at first notice Dr. Davidson beaming at her. Then she didn't give a damn whether anyone disapproved. She beamed right back. And thought the professor looked fantastic in her khaki and her helmet.

❖   ❖   ❖

The helmet didn't last long. Five minutes into her lecture Dr. Davidson took it off and asked if anyone else felt the room was warm while she shook out her chestnut hair and pulled it back into a ponytail. Which Esperanza would learn was how the professor always wore it. A youthful hairdo to go with her girlish appearance.

In what seemed to be about another five minutes that first session was over. Esperanza was stunned when she heard the other students begin to pack up and saw that the clock said it was time to go. Despite already having taught herself everything that was covered during the lecture she had never been more enthralled.

As she was preparing to leave Dr. Davidson appeared before her.

"Are you sure you're in the right class?" the professor said.

Esperanza's heart sank. Was she being thrown out? Had she said something objectionable? She couldn't speak. She stood like an idiot with her notebook clutched to her breast.

"You seem very familiar with the material," the professor said.

Esperanza frowned.

"Um..."

Dr. Davidson reached out and touched her arm.

"Don't get me wrong. I'm glad to have you here."

The professor smiled.

"I just hope you're not bored."

Esperanza came back to life.

"Oh no! I loved it."

"Good! So we'll see you next time then."

"Yes ma'am."

By the end of that second class Dr. Davidson was calling on Esperanza by name. Her star student never missed a session, always arrived early, always participated eagerly—and most importantly always knew the material inside and out. Other students began coming to Esperanza with questions they weren't able or willing to share with the professor.

By the end of the second week Esperanza had been to Dr. Davidson's office four times. Soon others in the department began to recognize her. One day at the end of class, while gathering her things, she realized that Dr. Davidson had become her mentor. Knowing this made her feel that without really looking she had found her place in the world.

She wanted to step over to Dr. Davidson and tell her what she was thinking. But when she imagined herself doing so her stomach dropped. The next thing she knew she was out in the hall hurrying away.

At the end of her freshman year Esperanza was accepted into the archeology honors program. She took pride in this distinction but by the time it came to pass the accomplishment was a foregone conclusion. The surprise was being invited to participate in an expedition over the summer excavating Anasazi cliff dwellings in a remote canyon in southern Colorado.

She was the only undergraduate on the dig. And a mere rising sophomore at that. Which inspired some hostility among the half-dozen graduate students. But one-by-one they recanted. She saw things they missed and knew things they didn't and was quick at things they struggled with. On top of all that she could cook. In the second week of the program even the single holdout who still resented her was forced to admit Esperanza deserved to be there. And would be an asset on any dig. Which infused her experience with a delicious sense of triumph.

The setting alone was cause enough to celebrate. Clear sharp air laden with the scent of pines. A cold stream tumbling down the bottom of the sheer canyon. Mountain goats on the high cliffs. Puma tracks along the stream bed. Hawks spiraling against the brilliant blue sky.

But for Esperanza all this splendor was not entirely without cost. A price she paid in the middle of her time there when she took it all in and her heart leapt up into her throat and almost choked her when she was stung by how much Elden Morris would have loved this place. She had not suffered with the loss of him so sharply in all the years since he disappeared. For half an hour after her feet were unsteady and her hands trembled.

Thankfully that moment never returned. Not even a memory of it. Years passed before she recalled how the old pain hit her so hard and unexpected.

Making that moment a notable exception to the rule of her joy there. During those long glorious days in that wonderland. Work she absolutely loved. Breakfast and dinner beside a campfire. Fascinating conversation that went on around the embers beneath a great sweep of crystalline stars. Then the deep sleep of the work-weary until morning came anew.

If only that summer could have never ended. But the calendar never yields. The great turnings must be obeyed.

The greater world would have them back again.

Chapter 41

When the SUV had rattled far enough down the mountain to reenter the land of cell coverage Leslie pulled over and all the phones came out. Esperanza dialed a friend with whom she had plans to spend the night. Her friend didn't answer. She left a message and called home. No answer there either. When she heard Rosa's voice on the outgoing message she felt unexpectedly homesick. She waited for the beep and said she was on her way home and would see Rosa tomorrow morning as arranged at her friend's place. She dialed her friend again. Still no answer. She didn't leave a second message.

She put her phone away and when she looked up, she saw that Leslie had gotten out of the SUV. Leslie stood about ten feet away with her back toward Esperanza and her phone pressed to her ear. Esperanza was in the rear seat beside one of the grad students. A pale blond in her late twenties with a dreamy singsong way of talking. A professor sat up front. He was about fifty and bearded and bespectacled and he growled out his words like a melancholic bulldog. The two of them blathered away into their little handheld devices and their voices filled the cab.

Esperanza stepped outside and shut the voices in behind her. She angled away from Leslie and stood facing the green valley spread out before them. A river ran down the far side shimmering like molten glass. There was a steady wind that carried Leslie's voice away with it.

Esperanza stole glances at Leslie and tried to decide what she would say if the moment presented itself. Comment on the view? How lame was that? Thank Dr. Davidson for including her on the dig and for everything else she had done for Esperanza? That was what she wanted to say. But the words to express those things eluded her.

She had never felt so tongue-tied as she did around Leslie Davidson.

Esperanza felt foolish pretending to enjoy the view. She didn't want to get back in the SUV but she did anyway. She sat stiff and irritated in the enveloping chatter from the professor and the grad student wondering why she was so embarrassed.

She watched Leslie end her call. Leslie remained where she was and stood looking out across the valley. First for one moment and then another. Then she turned and started back toward the SUV. Walking with her head down. When she slipped in behind the wheel her eyes met Esperanza's in the rear view mirror.

Their eyes locked for an instant. Esperanza thought she saw alarm in Leslie's expression. Then her heart pounded as Leslie started the engine.

They agreed not to stop for meals and ate snacks in the car. The grad student made a few attempts at conversation. No one was interested in joining her. Leslie politely refused all offers to take over driving.

Esperanza watched the world slide past and her mind wandered. She relived moments from the dig and felt quietly heartbroken that it was over.

She saw how things would be when she returned home. At first everyone would make a fuss over her. All of her aunts and uncles and cousins who weren't living too far away would come to see her. There would be a big dinner with the boys and their wives and girlfriends and their children. Then everyone would return to their usual routines. And in a day or two she would be itching to get back to the city and back to school.

The one cousin who definitely wouldn't be there was the one she wanted to see most. Roberto, the youngest, who had joined the Army and been sent to Japan. She remembered how much she missed his quiet controlled presence when he left her alone with Rosa and Josef. Being the only one there with them had been harder than she anticipated.

And now she would be alone with them again. For only two weeks this time. But two weeks was long enough.

The ride seemed to last forever.

Then suddenly it was evening and they were approaching the city. Esperanza called her friend again and left a second message. They crossed over the river to drop the professor at his house. Then they deposited the grad student at her apartment building north of the campus.

Esperanza directed Leslie to the house her friend shared with three other students. Her friend's car was not in the driveway or at the curb out front. Esperanza hoped it was parked down the block or around the corner.

She thanked Leslie and said goodbye and got her bag out of the back. She walked to the door and tried the bell. Then remembered it was broken. She banged on the door. No answer. Not a sound from inside. She banged again. More silence.

Esperanza took out her phone as she turned toward the street. Then stopped when she saw Leslie waiting at the curb. Watching from behind the wheel of her SUV. Esperanza put her phone away and walked up to the passenger window. Leslie rolled it down and leaned over and said—

"Something told me I should wait."

"My friend isn't here."

"What do you want to do?"

Esperanza looked away down the block. As if the answer to Leslie's question might be coming along just now. When she turned back she shook her head.

"I don't know."

She frowned.

"I could call my aunt."

"She's how far away? About an hour?"

"Yeah."

"Why don't you spend the night at my place?"

Esperanza felt her pulse quicken.

"Are you sure?"

"Of course."

Esperanza didn't know why she hesitated. She looked down the block again.

"I can't just leave you here," Leslie said.

Esperanza started jabbering. She couldn't imagine why her friend wasn't home. It wasn't like her to just disappear like that. She was very responsible. She hoped nothing bad had happened. She was so grateful to Leslie for taking her in. She didn't know what she would do otherwise. Sure she would call her aunt but where would she wait while her aunt came to get her? Maybe at the library if it was open. But it probably wasn't. Everyone she knew in the city was out of town. Except for her friend. She really hoped nothing bad had happened. That just wasn't like her. And she wanted to say thank you for including her on the dig. Which had changed her life. It was the most amazing experience she ever had.

A horn blasted beside her and she jumped in her seat. For a few moments all she could do was sit and blink. When she recovered she wanted something to do. Something to keep her occupied and stop her from prattling.

She realized she should call Rosa with the change of plans. She took out her phone and hit speed dial just as they pulled to a stop in front of Leslie's casita. Esperanza became flustered and dropped her phone when she went to end the call. She heard Rosa's voice sounding like it was wrapped in tin foil coming up from the floor—

"Hello?"

She grabbed for the phone but when she put it to her ear Rosa was gone.

Then for no reason she could think of she decided to explain—

"I'll call her later."

But Leslie was already out of the SUV.

They got their bags and started inside. Esperanza wasn't sure what to expect. What she found was more masculine than she would have guessed. Focused on work with very few personal items.

Leslie insisted that Esperanza have first use of the shower. She melted under the steaming blast of hot water. Such magnificent luxury after the privations of the dig. Her nerves began to settle down.

She was out in the living room dressed but with a towel still wrapped around her head holding her phone about to call Rosa when the front door swung open. An Asian man walked in carrying two bottles of wine. Behind him was a Native American woman carrying two boxes of pizza.

The Asian man smiled at her.

"You must be Esperanza."

She managed to nod.

"I'm Carl. This is Nascha."

He pointed a bottle toward the bathroom. They could hear the rushing water.

"I take it Leslie is in the shower."

Esperanza got her voice working—

"Yes."

"She's expecting us. We'll make ourselves useful."

They went to the kitchen and Esperanza put her phone down. She busied herself with the towel and then her hairbrush. Just as she finished Leslie appeared in nothing but a towel. She swept into the kitchen and greeted her friends and smiled at Esperanza on her way to her bedroom.

Esperanza went to see if she could help. Nascha gave her plates to put on the table. Five minutes later Leslie was back and dressed. When they sat down to eat there was a wine glass at Esperanza's place. She was distracted for a moment and when she looked back the glass had wine in it.

She let it sit there for a moment. Then she took a sip. It was round velvet on her tongue and delicate smoke in the back of her mouth. She took another sip. When a few more had followed she had forgotten whatever had made her so nervous.

Now she felt like she belonged here more than anywhere.

This is the kind of life I want. To live on my own like this. And have friends like this. And drink wine like this.

She was smart enough to stop at two glasses. And to drink both of them slowly. The others were not. They finished the two bottles Carl brought and a third Leslie had on hand and part of a fourth. Then Carl and Nascha went off laughing into the night.

And left Esperanza alone with Leslie Davidson. She felt elated to be so close and no longer intimidated by this woman she so greatly admired. The wall between them had been broken down.

She believed they could now talk as friends.

Part XII:
Ten Million Dollars

Chapter 42

Before we turn to the writing that eventually gained my release we should backtrack to some earlier writing that also changed my life.

This writing was not done by me.

About a month after Tranquilino Rojas ended my daily torture a letter found me sitting idle in my jail cell. I had a book to read but couldn't concentrate on the events taking place within its pages. Maybe that's because a few of those pages had been missing and in them apparently significant events had taken place. Or maybe my mind was just elsewhere. Maybe I sensed what was coming.

Whatever the case I set the book down on my bunk and was staring out through the bars when the mail cart arrived outside my cell. I did not expect to receive any correspondence and felt foreboding when the inmate manning the cart told me I had a letter. I tried to push that feeling of doom aside and feel anticipation instead. I failed.

It wasn't the first piece of mail that I received while in prison. But it was the first one I remember clearly. And the first I was afraid to open. The letter that finally came from my aunt had a return address in Los Angeles. Which was not right. That address made me feel ill. If my aunt was in LA then where was my mother? Why had the letters I sent to her gone unanswered?

My cellmate at the time was a big slow-witted Texan. He did not receive any mail of his own. Never in the time that we cohabitated did a single piece arrive with his name on it. He looked at my letter like a starving man at a banquet. He swallowed and licked his lips and drawled—

"Ar-ren ya gonna oh-pen it?"

He always spoke like his mouth was stuck closed with molasses. I ignored him and stared for a few moments longer before I tore the envelope open.

And learned that my aunt had followed my mother to California. My letter had eventually reached her there. Apparently it was stuck in the wrong box and went to a former neighbor who let it gather dust for numerous months on end before mustering the energy to forward it.

My aunt had taken a job working for the jackass. You remember him, the asshole my mother was going to marry. Everything in my aunt's new life in Los Angeles was fine for the first three weeks.

Then my mother was killed in a pileup on the freeway.

I stopped reading. The Texan watched me with his mouth hanging open. When I felt he was about to speak I bent back over my aunt's letter.

The Texan shut his mouth.

My mother was on her cell phone arguing with the jackass when she plowed into the back of a bus.

I stopped reading and put the letter down. This time the Texan couldn't stand it. He rose to his feet and stood beside his bunk wringing his hands. Then he sat down again.

"Wuz id say?" the Texan asked.

I did not answer him. I stared across the cell for maybe a full minute. Then I took up the letter again and read on. I read about the funeral and how much the jackass grieved and was almost sick to my stomach.

Then I read my aunt's promise to do everything she could to get me out of prison. There was a legal clinic near where she lived. She said by the time I read her letter she would already have talked to them. And that she would talk to the jackass too. Maybe he knew somebody. Maybe he had some ideas. Despite my shock and grief it still stung that the jackass would be implored to set me free. If my aunt had kept her promise, then he had already been so implored when I held that letter in my hands.

I checked the date the letter was written. Over a month ago. Apparently mail was not promptly forwarded from the county jail to the state prison. Which meant abundant time had elapsed in which the imploring could have taken place. And for the visit to the legal clinic to have occurred.

And nothing had happened. Nothing at all. I was still stuck here in prison. With no word from anyone that steps were being taken to gain my release. Surely by now I should have heard something. If a lawyer was involved, even one only slightly more competent as the drunken Bill Jameson, then my family should know I was no longer in the county jail. A second letter should have been sent directly to the state prison.

I couldn't help suspecting the jackass was the problem.

Maybe he had persuaded my aunt to forsake me.

He could be very persuasive.

Especially with women.

❖   ❖   ❖

What had the argument been between the jackass and my mother? When she stopped paying attention to traffic and rear-ended that bus? I hope it was some hell of a fight to make her so mad that she crashed and died. You don't want your mother to die a violent death for some petty little spat. Even if you never got along all that well with her. And sometimes you thought she was a pretty rotten person.

In general my mother was lazy. And most of the time indecisive and weak. But she could put up a fight when she wanted to. When she set her mind to something. With the news of her death I realized I was counting on her to fight for me. My aunt would defer to people she believed knew better. She would take what they told her on faith. My mother would insist on having her way. She would not accept what she found unacceptable.

And my current position would be very unacceptable. Imprisoned as someone else? People had to know who we were! And for such unspeakable things! That he did not do! How could people think her son would do such a thing?

She would fight to clear my name in order to clear her own.

And now my mother was gone.

While I rotted where Armijo put me.

The Texan was beside himself. He sighed loudly several times while peering out between the bars. Watching the nothing that went on before him. While feeding off the tragedy he could feel had been announced by that letter.

"Muz be sum bad news," he eventually said.

I said nothing. He turned to look at me.

"Anythun ya wanna talk 'bout?" he said.

I gave him more of my silence. He sighed again before he resumed peering out between the bars. A minute or so passed. Then he sighed one more time and lay down on his bunk with his hands behind his head and fell asleep.

I was grateful and relieved to be left alone with my thoughts and feelings. Privacy is a priceless commodity inside of a prison. I sat on my bunk with the letter in my hands and admitted to myself that the news of my mother's death did not come as a complete surprise. I had suspected it. For no definite reason. It was something I felt in my heart.

I tried to remain strong. To not let this latest blow knock me over. But the letter from my aunt left me devastated. The bad news was very bad and the good news was hardly any good at all. What was the good news? Oh yes. That someone out there knew where I was and what had happened to me.

Other than that there was no good in it all.

❖　　❖　　❖

Tranquilino drew more hope from the letter than I did. After he was done offering his condolences for the loss of my mother he leveled his eyes at me and put both hands on my shoulders.

"Just you wait," he said. "Just you wait and see. Your tía will get you out of here. And then you will sue that bastard Armijo. And the county. And the state too."

He gripped my shoulders tight.

"Just don't forget old Tranq when you're sitting pretty."

He did not make me feel any better. I thanked him anyway. There was no cause to be impolite.

I wrote back to my aunt that same day.

Weeks and then months passed. I heard nothing.

Once again a letter to my aunt disappeared into the void.

The help she promised vanished with it.

Which left me to conclude that she had been dissuaded from assisting me.

And I put the blame for that squarely on the jackass.

What else was I to think?

Chapter 43

My goal was to author a scathing exposé that would depose Armijo and win me back my freedom. While I pursued those multiple degrees in journalism, I drafted innumerable versions. Each one longer and more thorough than the last. Based on the best research I could do from behind prison walls. And I relentlessly sought to have my work published or produced. But none of the newspapers or magazines or radio programs or television shows that I contacted ever expressed interest.

And looking back I can see why. My story was preposterous.

My story *is* preposterous.

Everyone who would talk to me said the same thing—I didn't have enough evidence to support my allegations. They were right, of course. But I wasn't in the best position to attain all the facts. Try as I might, from where I was, the smoking gun would always elude me. And I failed to persuade anyone on the outside to chase down the truth. I was just another hard luck story. And not the best one around. At least so I was told.

But luckily I did not only write to editors and producers and journalists. I also wrote to lawyers. And more importantly to law students.

Which proved to be the writing that finally set me free.

At first I wrote seeking legal representation. To be some attorney's piece of pro bono. That yielded only a few boilerplate rejection letters. Then I started writing to student organizations at law schools requesting help with my research. Which also met dead end after dead end.

Until I received a letter from a young woman named Daniella Magallanes. A recent graduate from one of the countless law schools I had contacted. Who was now an attorney at a small legal firm with an excellent reputation. She had read my letter while on the committee at her alma mater that reviewed such requests.

Now she offered to accept my case as her first pro bono assignment.

An offer I of course immediately accepted.

Well not precisely immediately. First I leapt around my cell carrying on like a crazy fool. Which woke my napping cellmate. Who was no longer the Texan. My cellmate at that time was a young Mexicano thug from Los Angeles who was not so interested in my affairs as the Texan had been. He did not care what news had so excited me. Instead he said he would kill me if I did not shut up and let him sleep. In years gone past I might have reminded my insolent companion who exactly he was speaking to—a man protected by the two most powerful inmates in the prison. But by this time my safety was not so certain. The situation had changed. Change being the only constant. And for me this change was certainly not for the better.

The power structure was in flux. And that is always a dangerous time.

There was noise at the state capital about outsourcing management of our facility. Transferring control to a corporation that ran prisons. The most significant potential victim of this disturbance was my benefactor. For the cabinet shop to continue in business some new illegal arrangement would be required. Many assumed that meant Salazar's days of influence had become numbered. The man himself seemed sanguine about his prospects. Those of us who worked for him took that as a sign that he already had a deal in the works. But only time would tell.

Meanwhile there had been an attempt on Silvertone's life. The power behind this failed jailhouse coup was rumored to extend all the way across the border. To the same drug cartel that employed my obnoxious cellmate. Another sign of the times was that he survived. In the past he would have been killed for this connection alone. But a deal was struck that kept this beast and Silvertone both alive.

The present state of instability and the danger it created of course added to my excitement at the prospect of being released. Which in turn helped fuel my leaping about and increased the amount of noise I made. And therefore the amount of anger I instigated in my hazardous companion.

I did as he requested and quieted down. In a few moments he was snoring.

I considered holding a pillow over his face.

A week later I sat in another small room at another banged-up metal table. Once again seated opposite a newly acquired lawyer. But this time instead of my legal representative being short and fat and male and let's admit it more than a little disgusting my new attorney was a beautiful young woman. Hauntingly so. With large dark woefully mesmerizing eyes. A man could fall into those eyes and be lost forever.

Are you happy? Like Tranquilino when he learned this? Well I wasn't. Years had passed since I had been that close to an attractive woman. The last thing I needed in my confined and deprived state was to be aroused by my lawyer while struggling to understand the important things that she said.

One of my colleagues in the woodshop had anticipated this very problem. He recommended a few tricks that proved invaluable. Visualizing things that revolted me. Pinching the tender flesh on the inside of my wrist.

Imagining myself dying inside of prison.

I managed to remain more-or-less focused. I won't pretend it was easy.

❖　　❖　　❖

If she ever suspected the struggle going on inside of me, Daniella Magallanes did not let it show. That was one of the many things that impressed me. The cool reserve with which she surveyed the world around her.

She began our work together with the following question—

Which did I want more: justice or freedom?

I had once believed the two were inseparable. In essence one and the same. That both would be achieved in a single decisive blow. But I was young and naïve when I assumed that was true. By the time Daniella Magallanes agreed to represent me I had been disabused of my idealism.

She confirmed that the first step in my legal battle would be to establish my true identity. That alone could prove my innocence and therefore achieve my release. But would not prove that crimes had been committed in my arrest and conviction. Justice can be grossly miscarried without criminal intent.

She also confirmed that my freedom would be gained most expeditiously by making a deal with the state prosecutors. That deal would be much easier to achieve, and could be more generous in its other terms, if the state did not have to admit any wrongdoing on the part of its employees. So to ensure my freedom I would have to consider sacrificing justice.

But ensuring justice would delay and possibly even sacrifice my freedom. If I did not agree to a deal then I would have to remain inside at least until I could convince a judge to consider my release on bond and possibly until my conviction was overturned. In the end both freedom and justice might never be achieved. There was always the possibility that the conviction would be allowed to stand.

But most perversely if I pursued justice first and foremost freedom might come without justice being served. Proving that my arrest and conviction were fraudulent, that a conspiracy had existed, would lead to my release, and to charges being filed. Hopefully against Armijo and his collaborators.

But not necessarily. The slippery fat man could slide away. Some poor patsy might get stuck taking the fall. Armijo was likely to attempt such a dodge and capable of pulling it off. Given all the time that had passed, how hard it would be to tie him explicitly to any crimes, and all the damage his fall could inflict on the important people he was allied with, his odds of eluding justice looked pretty good.

So when my new attorney asked me what I wanted most—

Justice or freedom?

I did not need to think long.

I chose freedom.

There could be other ways of achieving justice.

Chapter 44

It's amazing what a good lawyer can accomplish. One who actually works on your behalf. Obstacles that had defied me for years melted away before Daniella Magallanes like butter confronted with a hot flame.

I finally learned what happened to my family. My aunt and my sister and my three cousins. When my lawyer tried to track them down so they could stand up before the law and verify I was who I claimed to be.

My aunt was swept up in an INS raid the morning after she wrote to me. At the bakery where she worked for the jackass. To this day I still suspect that somehow he was to blame.

She was deported soon after her arrest. Unbeknownst to me she had been born in Jalisco and never married my uncle. Which was an incredibly stupid oversight on both their parts. By law they had probably become common-law husband and wife. But I am not certain.

Their three children were left behind. Being citizens. Born on American soil to an American father. My aunt asked the jackass to take care of them. And to take care of my sister too.

Of course he did not. My sister and my cousins were swallowed up by the foster care system. For the few years that remained of their childhoods they were shuttled from home to home. They lived like refugees in the land of their birth.

My sister and my cousins vanished after they left the foster care system.

My aunt's trail ended when she was deported back to Mexico.

❖   ❖   ❖

I had tried to reach other people that I knew. Teachers, coworkers, friends, neighbors. Begging for help. I wrote letters and left messages. But I never heard back from any of them. For some I had addresses and phone numbers that I suspected were no longer good. But not for all. It was clear no one I managed to contact wanted to get involved.

Daniella found almost all of them. And got most of them to help. I wonder how many who said they never received my letters or messages—and there were more than a few who claimed that was so—how many only became willing to help because they were intimidated by my ferocious attorney.

And how much implied force Daniella employed in persuading them. The little hints she might have dropped at what the law could be made to do. She was not above making veiled threats. Especially if someone angered her.

The Mexican documents used against me at the trial, the driver's license and other government forms, were all real in that they were officially issued. But also easily proved to be fraudulent. Individuals employed in the appropriate offices and departments had been bribed or possibly threatened.

Daniella had no trouble finding the American documents that Bill Jameson said didn't exist. Such as my actual driver's license. Bill told me the only one he could find for an Andreas Delmorales was in Colorado and the man was sixty-four. And my birth certificate. Bill said there had been a fire at the micro fiche storage facility and my records there were destroyed. My social security registration. Bill said there wasn't one.

And now there would be DNA evidence. The biggest mistake Armijo made was not destroying the clothing worn by Elden Morris. Eventually even a backwater sheriff like himself would become aware of how DNA could turn a case. Maybe by then he had forgotten those shredded and stained garments stored in the state-run facility. Or maybe his influence was never great enough to allow him access. Maybe that state-run facility always remained beyond the reach of his corruption.

Or maybe he was just so damn cocky he didn't care.

Maybe Armijo always liked to play with a little fire.

The DNA proved to be our knock-out punch. The judge who ruled on our appeal gave greatest prominence in his decision to the laboratory findings. In his conclusion he emphasized them again when he described the collected evidence as "overwhelming". The district attorney immediately announced there would not be a second prosecution of the man formerly convicted as Manuel Ortiz but now proven to be the very innocent Andreas Delmorales.

The DA also stated publicly that I was not, and never had been, a Mexican. Which was part of the settlement attained by my gifted young attorney. Call me a bigot but I did not want the world even suspecting I was a citizen of Mexico. Not after what I went through when I supposedly was one. Being framed and abused and tortured as a Mexican had succeeded at something that a young lifetime of living in the States had failed to do—

I had become a proud American. Or prouder of being American. Or just so damn glad not to be Mexican I finally embraced being American. Whatever the case I wanted nothing to do with Mexico. Not ever again.

During our negotiations Daniella met with the businessman who had been foreman of the jury at my trial. The one who had also been my family's landlord. He had done very well for himself during the long years since he read out the guilty verdict that sent me to prison. So he had even more to lose than I had imagined.

Daniella said his eyes practically rolled around inside his head after she told him who she represented. He suddenly remembered a prior commitment and ushered her out of there.

An hour later she received a call from his attorney. Who mentioned that he and his client had connections with people who could help. Men and women in prominent positions. He offered to reach out on our behalf.

We of course accepted this kind proposal.

A few days later we received a much more attractive offer from the state.

The final settlement contained many little particulars and assorted details not worth bothering ourselves with after all this time has passed. What matters most about the deal was that for the great wrong committed against me and the great suffering I endured the damages awarded to me was the sum of—

Ten million dollars.

Or should I say—

Ten! Million! Dollars!

❖   ❖   ❖

One million bucks for each year stolen from my life.

While I awaited trial in the county jail, and then for my first year or so in the state prison, I did almost nothing to seek justice. Of course for much of that time I was being beaten and raped on a daily basis. Then I spent many years writing letters and making phone calls. Before one of those letters was read by Daniella Magallanes. Who had to finish law

219

school and become a licensed attorney before she could represent me. Putting the case together took time. Then the appeal had to work its way through the system.

All of which added up to a decade spent imprisoned as someone I was not for crimes I did not commit.

And yes. I did bear a grudge. No amount of money could ever buy that off.

But once again my good friend Tranquilino was proved right—

He had said I would wind up "sitting pretty".

You sit very pretty indeed when you're free and rich.

Part XIII:
Cool North

Chapter 45

Matt slept in his car just past the New York border. When he woke up he found a gas station and bought a map. On the map he saw Lake Ontario. He had heard the great lake was cool and that was what he wanted. To escape the summer heat. So that was where he went. Up between the Finger Lakes to Sodus Bay. He started at Lake Bluff and worked his way east and north. He had lunch in Oswego but that was a college town and higher education was a sore subject. So he kept moving. He stopped in Sandy Pond and stuck his toes in the water and it was cold. Nice and cold and that was good. But something told him to keep going. So he did.

He approached Sackets Harbor from the south, on the old county highway, two narrow lanes of rough gray asphalt. The town is built around a little harbor at the mouth of Black River Bay. Matt turned off the county road and drove through the center of town, down the four blocks of restaurants and shops that form the main drag, past the little harbor full of little boats, and out onto the bluff a little west of the harbor, where there is a park on the site of a battlefield from the War of 1812. Where Matt stopped his car and got out of it. A cool breeze came off Lake Ontario. Across the water he watched sailboats glide between some of the Thousand Islands. He returned to his car, drove the quarter mile back into town, parked by the public dock, and walked up and down the little commercial strip, past the shops and strolling tourists. Then he went out on the docks and looked at the boats. That nice breeze was still coming in off the lake. Everything was cool.

When he was done looking at the boats he walked back up the strip and at each restaurant he passed he stopped and asked for work. He was hired to wash dishes at the third place he walked into, a seafood joint on the water named The Captain's Table. It had a big noisy kitchen with huge exhaust fans. So it wasn't too hot. He started working that night, next to a Mexican named Hector. Who looked puzzled at Matt's Spanish. And asked if he had lived in Central America. So Matt explained about Pablo and Luis and the other Guatemalans at The Ol' Back Porch back in Walker City. Which made Hector nod and smile. After that he seemed more comfortable working with the white kid who blew into town.

The kitchen was staffed entirely with men. Most of the bussers were also male. But the wait staff was mostly young women. Hector explained that the girls were college students at summer jobs. While he scrubbed pots and pans and loaded and unloaded the dishwasher, Matt looked around the kitchen at the cooks and watched the wait staff come and go and wondered if he was the youngest person working there. Everyone he saw looked and acted older. Or at least older than he felt in this new place and situation. Away from home for the first time in his life.

Not that he had a home anymore. That part made him feel old.

He was putting plates away when he saw the employee who had to be the youngest. She looked much younger than him. She wore the floor uniform, black pants and a white shirt, and spoke with the chef. She had a round flat face, big wide-set surprised-looking green eyes, a small straight nose, and a wide mouth. Her hair was dark brown and past her shoulders, with a slight wave and parted in the middle. She wasn't short or tall, about five-five. But

222

her figure said she was fourteen at the oldest. Small high breasts and narrow hips, a tiny butt, coltish legs.

She glanced his direction as she was leaving. Matt felt a little dizzy when the girl was gone. He bent over the sink scrubbing a frying pan and told himself she wasn't his type. That he wasn't a child molester.

He didn't see her again the rest of that shift or the next couple days. He slept in his car or on the beach and worked every night. He found a campground where he could sneak a shower. He would park down the road and walk in through a little patch of woods. He smiled and said hello to anyone he ran into and they all returned his greeting and assumed he was staying there.

So three days passed without seeing the girl who looked fourteen. Then Matt was putting away dishes again when she appeared on the other side of the shelves. He put plates in and she took one away.

"I'm Meredith," she said.

He noted the lacked of preamble. No greeting first. Cut to the introduction. Almost if he should already know who she was. He smiled but she did not. She only stared with those big green eyes.

"I'm Matt," he said. "Nice to meet you."

Her smile came then, flashing quickly across her face. Then she was gone. Matt spent the rest of the night feeling both displeased and excited whenever he remembered those big unblinking green eyes.

She was standing by the back door when he left at the end of his shift. The floor staff generally cleared out almost an hour before the kitchen scrubs, who had to stay and clean up the last of the night's mess. So seeing her there was a surprise.

"Nice night," Meredith said.

Again the lack of preamble. Matt looked around to see if she was right and felt like an idiot doing it. He saw the sky was clear and the stars were out and the sky glowed with a bright half-moon. But best of all that wonderful cool breeze was coming in off the water.

"Yeah," Matt said. "It is. It's really nice."

"Walk me home? It's not far."

Part of him wanted to say no. Maybe even most of him. But that wasn't the answer Matt gave.

"Sure," he said.

And wished he hadn't. He followed her across the shadowed parking lot behind the restaurant. His stomach flipped over a couple of times before they spoke again.

"Where are you from, Matt?" Meredith said.

"Pennsylvania. Walker City."

"Where do you go to school?"

Matt almost said he was out of school. But then he realized she meant college. He didn't want to answer that question. He wanted college to not even exist so he would never have to think about it again.

They weren't even out of the parking lot yet and he already felt cornered.

Meredith turned and smiled.

"It's a simple question," she said.

They kept going while Matt didn't answer. They came out of the parking lot and turned east on a side street, away from the water.

"I don't," Matt said. "I'm not in college."

"Are you starting in the fall?"

Matt was looking down at the sidewalk. He brought his head up and looked at the moonlit shadows ahead of them. Snarly shapes twisted away from the trees that lined the street.

"No," he said.

And expected his interrogation to continue. But the next words from Meredith were—

"I'm going to Brown."

He would see her do this again. With short probing questions she would lead a conversation

224

directly up to something—and then change the subject.

The new subject would always be her.

❖   ❖   ❖

Matt assumed Meredith meant that she was planning on going to Brown when she graduated from high school. But she sounded so definite about her plans that he thought maybe she was already accepted there. He wondered if she was a prodigy who had finished high school early.

"That's great," he said. "Congratulations."

And wondered if he was right to congratulate her. Maybe he guessed wrong and she wasn't admitted yet.

Maybe he should turn and run away.

"I'll be a senior next year," Meredith said.

Matt guessed maybe it was possible she was sixteen.

"That's great," he said.

And felt like an idiot for saying it.

"Everyone thinks I'm a freshman. You probably did too."

Matt kept quiet. They looked at each other and he shrugged.

"I didn't start early," she said. "I turned twenty-one last week."

For a moment her words did not make sense to Matt. They collided with what he assumed to be true of this odd girl and rolled around inside his rattled brain. When he sorted out that she had just told him she was older than he was, by several years, and was entering her last year of college, not her last year of high school, he almost said "that's great" again. Fortunately he stopped himself before those banal words once again came spilling forth. He did not need to feel any more like an idiot than he already did.

225

Although he felt like an idiot for saying nothing. They walked along in silence for another block, then turned down a narrow cracked sidewalk to the side entrance of a big old pile of a house. They stood under a yellow light as she unlocked the door. When she stepped inside she seemed to expect Matt to keep following her. So he did. Down a short hall at the end of which she unlocked another door. This one led into the room she was renting for the summer. She stepped inside and snapped on a light and after a moment again Matt followed her.

"Where are you staying?" she said.

It took him another moment to get his answer out.

"I'm living in my car."

"You could stay here with me."

Matt looked around the small room and felt queasy. There was only one bed. He told himself she meant he could sleep on the floor. He looked at the bed, then down at the carpet, then he looked at some posters she'd stuck up on the walls. And learned that she liked *The Grateful Dead*. Maybe that fit with what he already knew about her. And maybe it did not. When he finally looked at Meredith she pulled her blouse off over her head. No bothering with the buttons down the front. Just a swift slithering snakelike movement and her blouse was gone.

Chapter 46

Matt worried his inexperience would betray him. But Meredith was assertive in what she wanted and there was no moment in the action when he was required to be in charge of what they were doing. For that he was grateful. Although he found having sex with the strange young woman who was twenty-one and looked fourteen to be a disconcerting experience. Even somewhat disturbing. All of which conspired to keep Matthew tense and his manhood erect and prolong their coupling by delaying his moment of release. To Meredith's quite apparent gratification.

As unsettling as he found their comingling itself, for Matthew the most trying aspect of the experience followed afterwards, when they laid together spent and Meredith began to chatter in the dark. While she prattled on about things she was going to do in the marvelous life she was certain stretched out before her, Matthew realized that he would sleep beside her in the bed. Not on the floor as he had envisioned. And he could see that he would spend the rest of the summer with her, living out of this small room, and would have sex with her many times. It wasn't what he expected when he accompanied her home. And he wasn't sure that he liked it. But he knew that was what would happen. The certainty with which he knew how the summer would unfold was what troubled him most. He felt unable to choose a different path. Devoid of free will. And that depressed him.

Which made Meredith's chatter unbearable. He interrupted her to ask for the bathroom and after relieving himself stared at his reflection in the mirror trying to convince himself that when he left the bathroom he would also leave Meredith. Even if that meant living in his car the entire summer. When he returned to her room she was asleep and snoring lightly.

He stood looking down at her before he surrendered.

❖　　❖　　❖

Back in bed beside her Matt could not sleep. He lay awake staring at the ceiling and thought about the guys he knew in high school and what they would say about his present situation. If he told them he wasn't sure he wanted to ball this pretty girl for the rest of the summer, they would call him a fag and rag on him until he was raw. They had ragged on Matt and questioned his sexual orientation because he never had a girlfriend. None of the girls in his school seemed to like him. And he didn't much like any of them. But of course that meant nothing to the guys.

You don't have to like them, the guys always said.

And now he had lost his virginity with a girl he did not like. Which made Matt feel low and worthless. He had always told himself he was better than that. Better than the others and how they behaved. Willingly ruled by their appetites. Laying there in that bed painfully awake beside the sleeping Meredith he sank to the lowest point he had yet reached in his brief unhappy life. His depression grew deep and broad and profound.

Solace came to him in a most unexpected form.

Staring up at the ceiling in the dark of that small room Matthew went back in time. To before his troubles began. When his parents were still both alive. And the three of them took a trip together. Their last vacation as a family. A bus tour of the Southwest.

Matt had a vision of a lovely Hispanic girl he had seen there. She seemed to glow before him in the darkened room. Her presence filled him with peace. And with hope. And renewed his sense of self-worth.

When his mind began again to have conscious thoughts he told himself he should rise up out of this bed of sin and return to his car where he could sleep honorably. But the Hispanic girl shook her head at him. And without saying a word she told him to remain where he was. To forget his troubles and ease his worried mind. To rest and begin anew when the day was new.

❖   ❖   ❖

Matt worked beside Hector washing dishes at The Captain's Table for twelve nights in a row. After that twelfth shift had ended, while Matt was lying awake again beside the sleeping Meredith, one of the other waitresses, a tall talkative blond who had become loudly drunk at a party aboard a yacht docked near the restaurant, fell off the gangplank and shattered her ankle. Thus ending her employment at The Captain's Table. And allowing for a small bit of upward mobility among the remaining workers. A busboy was promoted to waiter. And Matt was promoted to busboy.

Leaving Hector to handle the dishes by himself for that shift. He didn't stand a chance. Matt dumped dirty plates and glasses and cutlery beside his former comrade-in-arms and felt like a creep for taking the better paying job which he believed should have gone to Hector. Who had been employed there far longer. And was sending money home to support his family back in Jalisco. While Matt was, as he put it, "just some yahoo kid on a bum's summer."

On their walk home Meredith was a perky thing. Chattering away about the good tips she had made on their busy night. And how she heard that the girl who broke her ankle was now dating one of the guys who owned the yacht. All of which grated on Matt's darkened nerves.

"I bet you're glad to be bussing," Meredith said. "You can use the extra money."

He didn't answer right away. He looked at her as they passed through a shadow and saw her little nose standing out in silhouette.

"So could Hector," Matt said.

Meredith smiled at him.

"Don't worry about *that*," she said. "They would never put a Mexican out on the floor."

Her tone was soothing and pleasant. There was no subtext in what she said. Matt looked at Meredith again as they emerged from another shadow into the glare of a streetlight and saw the impossibly smooth skin on that mask of a face and wondered what went on inside of this creature beside him. Hector getting passed over was exactly the kind of thing a Grateful Dead-loving do-goody Brown student is supposed to rail against. But not this one. At least apparently not when it meant her boyfriend's good fortune.

Then Matt remembered how on their break earlier that night Meredith took his hand and led him around a corner into the shadows and they had sex standing up against an outside wall of the restaurant just out of sight from where customers came and went. He felt ill recalling it. Now he watched the shadows slither around them as the trees moved in the wind and heard their steps thumping on the uneven cement sidewalk and reverberating from the old houses and felt closer to the ghosts that such a night evokes than he did to the girl beside him.

That was the first night they did not have sex when they got home. Matt went down the hall to the bathroom and when he returned Meredith was asleep. He stood next to the bed and watched her for a little while, then turned off the light and climbed in. He was surprised to find that he wanted her. But was also glad not to have her. He lay awake in the dark and studied that paradox.

The next day Hector's nephew was hired to wash dishes. Tito didn't speak any English and only stared uncomprehendingly when Matt spoke Spanish.

Which meant he had to work beside Hector or he couldn't work there at all. So if Hector was given the job bussing tables Tito would still be looking for a job. Matt told himself that meant he wasn't taking money from Hector's family and stopped feeling so guilty.

Chapter 47

One Friday as the summer waned Matt was bussing Meredith's station out on the deck. She had her back to him and was talking to a customer. A man in his thirties seated alone at a table for two. He was slim and had black hair. He wore black-framed glasses and a dark blue dress shirt that was almost purple. Matt worked his way around Meredith while she and this man kept talking. The man was laughing and smiling and Matt didn't like him at all.

Matt kept working while the other two kept talking. A rush had just ended and the deck was mostly empty. Matt listened but couldn't hear what was said. There was some wind that night and cars out on the road. He moved to clear another table and now he could see Meredith's face.

And what he saw stopped him. He stood beside the table covered with dishes waiting to be cleared and stared at his girlfriend. She didn't look any different from all the many times before he had seen her make that same face. But now she was doing her wide-eyed thing for another man.

She was still doing it when Matt turned away. He cleared the remaining tables on the deck without looking her way again. The two of them were still talking when Matt went inside. He saw the manager walking the floor and wanted to tell him Meredith was spending too much time socializing with one of the customers. But then everyone would know his troubles. So he kept this information to himself.

Matt was emptying a trash can when he saw the black-haired man step into a red Miata with California plates. He pictured this joker driving around the countryside in his little two-seater sports car making the ladies wherever he went. And hated him for it. Matt remained beside the dumpster and watched the man pull out of the lot and roll away. And had his first itch to go since he'd arrived in Sackets Harbor.

Meredith avoided him the rest of the night. And for the first time since he started working at The Captain's Table she was gone when he completed his shift. He waited around for a little while outside where they usually met, thinking she might still be inside. Maybe she was in the bathroom. But after a few minutes he knew she had already left. At first he felt a burst of complete freedom.

Then he felt completely alone when he realized where she was.

On the walk to her place he wondered how he would get into the house and into her room. Since he never had keys. The first problem was solved when he arrived as one of her neighbors was leaving. They grunted hellos at each other as Matt grabbed the swinging door. He found a note taped to the door of her room and wondered how she had expected him to get that far.

The note said she would be spending the night with a friend.

"The fuck you are," he said to the note.

The door to her room was unlocked. Matt was inside just long enough to pack up the few belongings he had left there.

Then he went looking for that red Miata. Sackets Harbor isn't very big and he didn't have to look for very long. He followed his nose and discovered the obnoxious little roadster parked at the old stone army barracks north of town. The barracks had been converted into condos and apparently the black-haired owner of the sports car in question was staying in one of them.

Matt sat in his car with his engine idling and decided it didn't matter. He had spent most of the summer with Meredith and still didn't know the girl.

And had never really liked her. Getting involved had been her idea. He knew he only stayed with her for the sex and for somewhere to sleep and shower. So why get worked up over this? In truth he had it coming.

Then he heard her laugh. From an open upstairs window. The sound was unmistakable. Far too big and too robust for the girl who made it. Matt liked her laugh. He decided then and there that her laugh was her best feature. Then he put his car back in drive and rolled away. His bald tires crunched pebbles against the fractured asphalt of the parking lot while her laughter continued behind him.

❖ ❖ ❖

The next day Meredith came swinging into work with a man's dress shirt draped over her shoulders. A dark blue dress shirt that was almost purple. It was quiet in the kitchen as she sauntered past giving him those big green eyes. The fans were turned off. The dishwasher wasn't running. No one was banging pots around. Outside Matt heard what he could have sworn was a Miata gunning its way out of the parking lot.

Neither of them said a word. It was all business from then on.

And then a day came when the dinner shift began and Meredith was not among the wait staff. Two more days and she still remained absent. At the end of his shift Matt went to the beach with one of the other busboys. They drank beer and smoked a joint and laughed at anything that came to mind. They especially laughed when his companion told Matt that Meredith and another waitress had quit together and gone to Europe for a few weeks before the summer ended and college began.

Matt liked an ocean between the continents he and Meredith occupied.

"Good for her," Matt said.

He took a long toke and said in a constricted voice with smoke curling out of his nose and mouth—

"Maybe Europe will improve her mind."

His companion laughed himself silly.

Matt and this other busboy that we will not bother giving a name spent what remained of the summer smoking the nameless one's dope and drinking Matt's beer and laughing at anything and everything. Then the summer was over and the other one left for his first year of college down in Boston.

After he was gone Matt learned that the nameless one had dated the other waitress who went with Meredith to Europe. A girl Matt remembered as short and buxom and vulgar. He found it disagreeable that the nameless one had failed to mention such a relevant fact as his liaison with Meredith's traveling companion. His silence felt like a betrayal. And made Matt decide he was glad to be rid of the nameless one and his weed.

The once-crowded docks were now mostly empty. One-by-one the shops that catered to the summer trade were closing down. A morning came when Matt snuck into the campground for a shower and there were signs up saying that in two weeks the gates would be locked and the water and power would be shut off. Despite all these indications that the time had come for him to go, Matt was still caught by surprise when what few remained of the summer hires were summarily dismissed from The Captain's Table.

After his last shift Matt parked at the beach and didn't sleep much. In the morning a chop was out on the water. He sat in his car watching the waves and felt like they were rolling right through his stomach.

He was lost. Nowhere to go. Nothing to do. No one to be with.

Not even a girl he didn't like.

He started his car and pointed it down the road. When he stopped for gas and breakfast he looked at his map. The one he bought the morning after he left home. He told himself he would catch 177 East and wander through the Adirondack Park to 87 South. Maybe he would stop in Saratoga Springs or at Lake George. He had heard of those places. While the weather remained agreeable he would wander down to New York City. Where maybe he could get himself killed. And if not he would continue south. Like the retirees he met at the campground, snowbirds they called themselves, he would migrate with the seasons. Maybe next year he would come back to Sackets Harbor.

That was one option. Instead at Adams Center he turned north on I-81. A sign told him that was the way to Montreal. He had never been to Canada. Visiting a whole new country seemed like an appropriate thing to do. When you had nothing else to do and thought your end might be welcome.

Maybe he would keep going into the cool north. Drive until it turned frozen. Find a nice patch of tundra and let himself freeze to death.

Part XIV:
New Faith Holy Gospel

Chapter 48

We had our last conversation as prisoners in the same place as the first one. In that corner of the yard I retreated to during those awful early days. When I was a bug and Silvertone was slowing pulling me apart. Where Tranquilino found me half dead when he came back inside.

We had made that corner ours. Others joined us there at times. But it never became theirs too. It remained ours alone. Which was never mentioned but universally understood. And never challenged. Not that anyone had cause to do so. I had picked a corner no one else wanted. And between us we had more than enough pull to discourage unnecessary conflicts.

Now that corner would belong to Tranquilino alone. I wondered if he would keep it. If he would have any reason to return there when I was gone. Since we went there to be together.

I thought about that while we stood beside each other and kept our thoughts private. The territorial implications of my impending departure.

❖   ❖   ❖

I was waiting for Tranq to speak first. Something was clearly on his mind. Something he had been keeping to himself for a few weeks now.

When he was ready to talk he said—

"Things have changed around here."

By which he meant the political shake-up. The weakening of Silvertone. The rise of the Mexican cartel. The uneasy truce between them. Which was showing signs of fracture. The impending switch to corporate management. That threatened to unseat

Salazar. Which had wound its way through the state capital and been signed into law. In another month this facility would be expected to turn a profit.

I continued to wait. Tranq had only mentioned this as preamble to whatever he actually wanted to say.

But first he mentioned this—

"There's a dead pool on Silvertone."

Which sent my eyes across the yard. To where the man held court. I watched him give orders to one of his lieutenants. You wouldn't know anything had changed since the first time I stood there with Tranquilino. I had watched Silvertone on that day too. When he began his transition from my persecutor to my protector.

"It's a good thing you're getting out," Tranq said. "His days are numbered. The cartel is too big for him."

"Do I still need him?"

"I don't know. Call it insurance."

"Insurance is good to have."

We watched Silvertone yawn and scratch his head. The lieutenant returned and said something. He gestured while he spoke.

Silvertone shook his head and looked displeased.

When Tranq sighed I knew we would soon arrive at the heart of the matter. When we would discuss what was bothering him. I watched him and waited. Another sigh followed. Then at last he got to it—

"This is a bad time to lose a friend."

Which I took the wrong way.

"What're you talking about? I'll still be your friend. You should know me better—"

"A friend on the outside can't watch your back."

Now I understood. And felt stupid.

"Don't get me wrong," Tranq said. "I'm happy for you. You know that."

He paused.

"But I can't pretend this doesn't affect me."

I didn't know what to say. So after a moment I said—

"I'm sorry."

Tranq smiled.

"Don't be sorry. Now you're making me sorry. Shit."

He put a hand on my shoulder and grinned at me.

"Some going away party, huh?"

We managed to laugh a little. Then he pointed at me. And grinned again. When I lost patience with him I said—

"What?"

"I give you five minutes."

I frowned at him. He kept grinning.

"Five minutes for what?"

"Five minutes till you two are all over each other."

I groaned and rolled my head. The other half of his imagined coupling was Daniella. He had been teasing me about her relentlessly. Ever since I made the mistake of confessing she was gorgeous.

He laughed for a long time at the faces I made.

The next morning the gates rolled back and I stepped outside.

A free man once again.

I had wanted my uncle's truck to be waiting for me. In my fantasies the map he made, the one that got me into this mess, was in the glove box. There would have been a particular satisfaction in that moment. To climb back behind the wheel and find that map again. Then drive away as if merely interrupted by all that had happened.

But the impound department had long ago lost track of that good old truck. What became of it and the map I will never know.

Daniella sent a taxi instead. She was in court or she would have picked me up herself. On the way out we drove past the empty yard. I watched our corner and remembered Tranq laughing. And felt heartsick wondering if I would ever see him again.

I owed that man my life. And my sanity. He had become my only family.

I very much wanted to believe we would be reunited.

And out here. Not in there.

Chapter 49

A man comes out of prison with a stink on him. Being cooped up with those animals puts a stench on your soul.

He will often try to rub that stink off. Even if he knows better. The most common methods for attempting this are wallowing among whores and drinking and drugging. Frequently applied simultaneously. Both only make the stench worse.

Which can drive a man back inside.

Or make him wipe the reek out forever by taking his own life. Especially when a man is the only one who can smell his own stink. That can make the scent even more unbearable. To be alone in it.

I was sorely tempted to try rubbing my stink off on Daniella. Who was—as the uncanny Tranquilino half-jokingly predicted—half in love with me. Or half in love with the romantic figure she considered me to be.

Daniella was born into a poor Spanish family not unlike my own. Which was the first reason why my story resonated with her. The second was that her grandfather had also been framed by a corrupt lawman and sent to prison.

Even after all that amazing woman did on my behalf—and she refused to fully share in the compensation, insisting on a modest fee—even after all that I was tempted to use her and discard her. Which shames me to this day.

But I found the strength not to. And still feel relieved that I did.

The last thing Daniella needed was to be involved with me. Given what I had planned. And nothing would dissuade me from those plans.

Not even that incomparable woman.

So how did I get rid of my stink?

I didn't. Because you can't. Eventually, if you are fortunate and can remain patient, the stink goes away on its own. If you manage to live that long. The wise ones know this and just endure their stink as best they can. Until one day it has mercifully vanished.

But I was unwise and terribly impatient. I could not manage to just wait. Even though I had been told that was the only way by men who knew. So I tried to rub off some of my stink. On a sweet and gentle divorcée I met in a bar. A few years my senior with a warm smile and a kind face.

She asked if we had met before. At the time I was either too inexperienced or too distracted by my other concerns not to hear that as a clichéd come on. Instead I worried she recognized me from the publicity surrounding the settlement of my appeal. I had managed to avoid being on television but my photograph had appeared on the Internet and in newspapers.

In hindsight I suspect she saw my image somewhere. More than once she searched my face as if trying to remember where she had seen me before.

In the time-honored tradition we went back to her apartment. And spent two days in her bed. I was almost a boy when I entered prison. In some ways I finally became a man while making love to that good woman.

Or maybe I should say a man who was much closer to normal.

Whatever the hell normal is.

Before I left I looked into her bathroom mirror and resolved not to do this again. The goals I had set for myself required anonymity.

She had noticed my limp and asked how I acquired it. I told her in an auto accident when I was a teenager. That led to her asking more about my life. Which required additional lies. The lying was painfully uncomfortable. But the lies were not the problem.

The problem was that my disability would stick with her. She would recall being with a man who had limped. Marking my passage through her life. Which was risky for both of us. She did not need to be dragged into my future. No one needed that. Even in the smallest degree. This would have to be my last intimate encounter for however long was required to accomplish what I had set out to do.

I slipped away while that nice woman who wanted only to please me was out at the supermarket. Buying ingredients for the dinner she planned for the two of us. I hope she cooked that good dinner without me. If not on that night then on another.

And shared it with someone who deserved her more than I did.

Chapter 50

I arrived in Denver with a full beard and mustache. Which I kept impeccably trimmed. A little drugstore hair dye gave my temples a distinguished touch of silver. A pair of prescription-less black-rimmed eyeglasses imparted a professorial air. Going about town I wore a somber suit and tie, or sports clothes in black and muted grays, or a nondescript workman's uniform. With the uniforms I added a cap.

But my limp felt like a signature I couldn't erase. The one thing most likely to remind someone of that guy who had been released from prison under a brief flurry of press coverage a few months before. The crudely groomed and untailored fellow who had shirked away from the cameras.

I tried putting lifts in my shoes to change the shape of my stride. Which not surprisingly only made my limp more pronounced. Not to mention more painful. I considered wearing a brace on my ankle, as if recently injured. But that would only draw further attention. Making the casual observer even more likely to remember me. So I was forced to live with my limp as a distinguishing trait.

Some risks you have to accept as a cost of pursuing your objective.

My objective was a janitor at an evangelical megachurch.

For years I assumed the Mormon had disappeared. That all the law ever had to go on was what I gave them. That those incompetent bastards never managed to find any clues of their own. I was convinced all the lawmen involved were too lazy and stupid like the bloated Armijo to pursue a real investigation. Or too bloodthirsty and deranged like his hooligan sidekick. So they just hung it on me and forgot about it.

Which left me stuck in prison staring at the same dead end. All I knew about the Mormon was what I had seen with my own two eyes. How to learn anything more was beyond me.

A comment from Tranquilino changed my perspective and my attitude—

"So the trail is cold," he said. "That doesn't mean there isn't one."

At first that just annoyed me. What he said felt like a rebuke. But as usual my good friend was right. There was no use in lamenting that the trail was cold. I had to start asking where that cold trail could be found.

Three days later the answer came to me. After mentally reconstructing the likely course of the investigation following the recovery of Elden Morris. I believed that at first my account of those events would be acted upon. Which meant my description of the Mormon might have been distributed to the surrounding legal jurisdictions.

I had to wait many long years before I could work that lead. Until Daniella was my lawyer and I could ask her to chase it down. I don't believe she ever suspected an ulterior motive behind my suggestion that the neighboring law enforcement agencies might be able to confirm that information about the actual perpetrator had been ignored. Maybe someone else had seen the man I described. And not being part of the Armijo cabal they would be beyond the reach of any cover up. They might even still have records of what they had been told by Doña Pero. And anything they had learned on their own.

It was a long shot. But when long shots are all you have...

Better become an active sniper.

❖   ❖   ❖

Shortly after arriving in Denver it came to my attention that New Faith Holy Gospel Church would in about a month close for a period of two weeks. I cannot answer for why they had neglected to post this information on their web site. Which would have allowed for more advance planning on my part.

Renovations were apparently required. Despite the age of the building being barely ten years. The groundbreaking occurred while I was on trial as Manuel Ortiz. But such is the quality of contemporary construction. Sloppily done with shoddy materials. They would be repainting, installing new flooring, replacing faulty windows and doors, repairing a persistent leak in the roof, and upgrading their lighting and sound systems. Maybe they should have just scrapped the thing and started over.

Two days before the church closed the janitor fell off a step ladder. While in the act of changing a light bulb. Something he had certainly done countless times before without incident. I watched the EMTs gurney him out to the ambulance and followed behind as they ferried him to the hospital. Where it was determined that he had fractured the scaphoid bone in his right wrist. I was watching when he departed wearing a cast that immobilized his thumb and extended past his elbow.

We received a log sheet from a small town police department in the next county over. A clerk there faxed it to Daniella's office. An officer from their department had seen a turquoise Ford pickup in the parking lot of a motel almost two hundred miles to the west and a little north of where I last saw such a truck. The policeman was off duty at the time. And not yet aware of the bulletin issued by the Doña Pero County Sherriff's Department. When it came to his attention later that day he returned to the motel. The truck was gone. Fortunately that establishment had a policy of recording each patron's license plate number and state of registration. The policeman obtained the name of the driver and the tags of the pickup from the desk clerk—

Kirtland F. Sorenson
Utah XMQ 817

Of course he was from Utah. And had a name that could not have been more Mormon. He might as well have been dubbed Moroni. The Kirtland Temple outside Cleveland being the first one built by the Latter Day Saints movement. And Sorenson being a prominent LDS family name. I later learned the F stood for Fenimore, another surname with Mormon roots. As a small boy his family took to calling him Fenny to distinguish him from a young uncle who was also named Kirtland.

When this log sheet came to light I also learned the specifics of what would have happened had I thought to catch the Mormon's tag number myself. As I mentioned back at the beginning of this saga the plate number would have gone into the primary case records. And been generally distributed among regional law enforcement. Pointing directly at Kirtland F. Sorenson. Placing him very prominently in the crosshairs. Which would have rendered all but impossible Armijo's improvisation. The one that put me in prison instead.

And I do believe it was an improvisation. That Armijo made it up as he went along. Learning the identity of this man who had played such a significant if unwitting role made me see that extemporization clearly. As if I needed a name and a background for this particular piece of the puzzle before I could snap it into place. Revealing the picture as a whole.

❖   ❖   ❖

No one in Denver knew him as Fenny. I suspect that old familial nickname was a thing of the past. Another thing lost when the Church disowned him. Here he was Kirt. Quiet unassuming Kirt Sorenson. Diligent floor scrubber and window washer at New Faith Holy Gospel.

He had been handsome in his youth. But the years had been unkind. He had aged excessively. He stood hunched over. His wide bony face was haggard. His large pale blue eyes looked caved in. Those big hands seemed to clutch a steering wheel like he was holding on for dear life.

I hope it was stress that ruined him. I hope he suffered every day.

Not especially prudent using his real name. But so far he had only been caught once. And officials of the Church had covered up that transgression. Before they sent him packing. He was already in exile when I first saw him. Cast out into the wilderness following some unpleasantness during the tour of missionary duty that is required of obedient young Mormon men.

I believe we can assume the nature of that unpleasantness.

Maybe he assumed the good luck that had favored him since would hold forever. And no one in a position to stop him would ever again become aware of his proclivities. The precautions he took were not all that extensive. And he employed the same procedures every time. He was a creature of habit. That made him predictable.

Which is kind of like sailing a small open boat across a wide ocean and crossing your fingers that no storms will ever find you.

We all know that storms are inevitable.

Chapter 51

The first Saturday I was in Denver he slipped away from me. Sorenson was gone early and back late. It took me a few days to procure the correct equipment. But after that, thanks to a GPS tracking device, I knew where his car was at all times.

The next weekend he spent Saturday driving a long circuitous route through three sections of the city. He focused his most time and attention on residential neighborhoods that could generally be described as lower middle class. The next Saturday he visited the same places but reversed the overall course of his route. The following Saturday he dropped one section of the city and only visited the remaining two. He visited the same two sections the weekend after that.

The next weekend he dropped another one. He spent his Saturday in one district of the city. He parked frequently. Maybe he got out and walked. I'm not sure. He limited himself to that section again the weekend after that. Parked in a few of the same places along with some new ones.

That Monday while he was at work I drove his last route. And parked where he had parked. The last spot I visited was after school had let out. I sat and watched a boy play with a dog out in a front yard near an intersection. No one else anywhere in sight. Sorenson had parked there for twenty minutes.

Maybe that boy had been playing with his dog then too.

Kirtland F. Sorenson was a clean-scrubbed young white man with a spotless legal record and a wealthy family. He wasn't exactly in his clan's good graces but Armijo wouldn't have known that. And even if he had many rich families hire expensive attorneys to dig their wayward sons out of such predicaments. It is likely the Sorensons would have done the same.

Which would have sent a capable litigator to Doña Pero. Mounting the defense against a case that looked weak. The victim seemed too damaged to serve as a witness. And even if he recovered enough to testify he might not remember enough to put Sorenson away. It would be the word of the victim against the word of the accused and the lawyers in the room would be doing their best to twist all those words.

Elden being the only witness to the actual crime. Without those crucial plate numbers the most my testimony could hope to prove was that someone who looked like Sorenson and drove a similar vehicle had been nearby. That was hardly enough to convict. And easy enough to undermine. Any decent lawyer could turn my testimony around and make me look like the criminal—

Tell us, Señor Delmorales. Why did you just happen to be out there? When my client supposedly drove past you. Out there in the middle of nowhere.

For his pain he was prescribed Vicodin. The prescription was called in to a drugstore near where he lived. I watched a taxi return him from the hospital back to the church so he could get his car. I was across the street when he stopped at the drugstore to pick up his painkillers.

That must have been a tough trip. Driving freshly casted with a broken wrist. I found it remarkable that none of his good Christian coworkers went with him to the hospital. Or drove him home. Or provided a ride to work the next day. Or the day after. Why he didn't just stay home for those last two days before the church went on hiatus I cannot say. Maybe he was just that conscientious and dedicated as an employee.

But apparently he was driving while on hydrocodone. Which he must have been told not to do.

I watched all of this unfold somewhat dumbfounded by my good fortune. It was as if events conspired to assist me.

If I was so inclined I could have seen the hand of God at work.

At the time of the trial DNA evidence was still novel and expensive. And all but unheard-of in a backwater like Doña Pero. Where as is common in such places, change often encounters a deep and hostile vein of suspicion. Which could be mined by the defense—

Don't let these eggheads make fools of you with their fancy-pants science.

Armijo would have known how building a case around DNA could backfire. He was nothing if not good on reading the tea leaves of public opinion.

And for him the real trial was in the court of public opinion. Particularly in that portion of the public whose opinion mattered most—the moneyed Anglos. If Sorenson walked, those rich Anglos could turn on everyone who had persecuted someone they might see as being one of their own. Bringing a quick end to Armijo's political ambitions.

Even in the best case scenario—with that new-fangled DNA evidence being admitted and proven overwhelming and accepted by both the court and the public; with Elden recovering his senses and remembering what happened and delivering testimony that was convincing and damning—even with all that the most Armijo could claim about his role was to have been a good cog in the machinery of justice. To have executed his office with thoroughness and dispatch. A solid player on a winning team.

That wouldn't get him what he wanted. He wanted more.

He wanted to be more.

His fractured wrist would have bought his next victim some time. Sorenson was careful and cautious. Not smart or inventive. He would have postponed his plans while his injury healed. And if that postponement disrupted his plans instead of merely delaying them, if circumstances changed and made his plans no longer viable, then he would have started over.

He was a plodding criminal. And since he plodded, the facts of his past made a clear pattern. If not the boy I watched romping with his mutt then some other boy. And if not so soon as Sorenson had intended then a little farther off into the future.

Being a creature of habit made catching up with him easy. But unless he was caught in the act of abducting another boy, proving he had committed any crimes could be impossible. And what if the law got to him too late? Then another boy would have suffered and died.

Or the lawmen might spook him. And Sorenson would go underground. I knew he had inherited some money when he was young. Before his family disowned him. I hadn't seen any indication that money was gone. It was more than enough to buy a new identity and vanish. Or to live out his life in some third world nation. Preferably one with no extradition to the United States. As a young missionary he had become fluent in Spanish. Maybe he still was. That would widen his field of possible sanctuaries.

So the law just seemed too risky. Too likely to fail.

❖   ❖   ❖

Convicting a poor young Hispanic was always easy. Even in a county that was mostly Hispanic. Since the money was mostly Anglo and would deliver an Anglo jury. And especially when you had that poor young Hispanic in your clutches. And could plant all sorts evidence over him.

But the Hispanics had most of the votes. And although they were used to having their young men arrested and sent to jail they would not appreciate it being done by one of their own. Even if they were convinced that the young man in question was actually guilty, their opinion of Armijo would not be improved by his role in the conviction. And if they thought the young man was not guilty then Armijo might as well have been Anglo. All he would have to get him elected was any Anglo money he could pry away from everyone else trying to get their hands on it.

That was where the fat man had his stroke of genius. Because Armijo knew that a large portion of his fellow Hispanics in Doña Pero did not identify exclusively or even foremost as Hispanics. They considered themselves Hispanic Americans. Many would get their backs up and insist on being called Spanish Americans.

You might be surprised how many Hispanics born and raised along our southwestern border consider themselves distinctly different from—and often superior to—their brethren down on the other side.

By transforming me into a Mexican, Armijo made me no longer one of them. He reinvented me as the Other. To both the Anglos *and* the Hispanics.

Making him a hero to both. Which brought him money and votes.

It was a bold and inspired gambit. I'll grant the fat man that.

253

❖   ❖   ❖

I did not retrace the rest of Sorenson's route. After I saw that boy. There wasn't anything more I could learn out there. I drove back to my motel feeling small. Ashamed of who I was when the day began.

One of the reasons I went to Denver was to stop Sorenson from doing any more harm. But that was second on my list. Mostly I wanted vengeance. Which I told myself was justice. I wanted it for Elden Morris and his family. Although I don't know if they wanted it for themselves. And I wanted it for myself. Since I had paid for something Sorenson did.

Sitting there in that car parked on that side street in that run down and worn out corner of Denver watching that boy play with his dog, my motivations became inverted. Stopping Sorenson became far more important. My desire for revenge almost disappeared.

Almost but not quite.

I am human. We humans want our blood.

I could have paid someone else to do it. I had plenty of criminal contacts.

But I was the one passing judgment.

I should be willing to do the dirty work.

Part XV:
Disapproved Heart

Chapter 52

Esperanza was awake when her phone rang. She had been awake all night. Sleep had not followed naturally after the events of the previous evening. She brought her eyes down from the ceiling where they had been staring for most of an hour and found her phone on top of her bag. The number from home was displayed on the tiny screen. It put a knot in her stomach. She had never called Rosa with the change of plans.

But it was too early for her aunt to be in the city. The sun had just come up. Rosa was probably calling to say she was leaving now. Or maybe that she would be a little late. And it was good Esperanza hadn't called. That meant she could tell her aunt to meet her somewhere else. Not here at Leslie's.

She tried to put on a bright voice—

"Hola Tía."

There was no reason to suspect the call was from anyone else. No one but Rosa ever called from that number. But it wasn't her aunt's voice that came back at her. Instead her little phone buzzed and rattled with the rumble of her Uncle Joe—

"Esperanza. It's me."

His next words were in Spanish. Which he used sparingly and infrequently. Most often when he wanted to emphasize the significance of what he said. Which at this moment he felt compelled to also state explicitly—

"Escucha. Este es importante."

Listen. This is important.

He paused to clear his throat. Esperanza's heart began to throb. Whatever he had to tell her couldn't be good. She had a flash thought that it was

255

Roberto. Killed in some horrible way over in Japan. One of those training accidents that make the news every now and then. But of all the things her uncle could have told her she was probably least ready for this—

"Tu tía. Ella no está bien."

Your aunt. She is not well.

Esperanza felt like ice had been dumped all over her. She began to tremble. A bitterness surged up inside of her—

Did everything have to go to hell all at once?

Josef finished in English—

"She's going to need you."

Her shaking stopped. La Soldadita understood completely what she had just been told. Her uncle did not have to share the horrid details. There would be a time and place for that conversation.

She also knew what was being asked of her. Which was not that she should tend to her aunt while she was home for the rest of the summer. But that she leave her life away at college and return to the old village. So that she could nurse her Tía Rosa. Who may be dying.

"It's that bad," Esperanza said.

Her uncle sighed and made her phone crackle.

"I'm afraid so."

For a moment they said nothing.

Then Josef rattled her phone again when he rumbled—

"So where are you?"

Esperanza explained where she was and how to get there. Any thought of meeting elsewhere had become unimportant. When they said their goodbyes and hung up, she sat still and quiet in the shadows cast by the rising sun across Leslie Davidson's living room. She felt as if all the great sorrows of her young life had been compressed and distilled into that one brief conversation that had just ended.

She put together her things and went to wait outside.

Josef Armijo sent his newest deputy to fetch his niece home. Which however minor a transgression was still an abuse of public resources. If Esperanza had not been painfully distracted she might have wondered at the legality of her transportation. Having been close enough to her uncle and his office to know there were laws against such things. And that once he had taken pains not to break those laws.

Her phone rang when they were halfway home. Esperanza let the call go to voice mail. She debated listening to the message and decided to wait. She didn't want to hear what her caller might have to say in front of the silent young deputy she had just met.

The house was teeming with family. Coming and going and waiting around. All of the boys who hadn't moved away and their wives and girlfriends and offspring. Cousins and aunts and uncles and nephews and nieces. Women in the kitchen. Men milling around. Children outside running in circles. Cars and trucks and SUVs pulling up and pulling away. In some seeming magic that kept the house always full but never quite overflowing.

Esperanza was stunned by Rosa's appearance. Despite imagining far worse. None of the horrors she conjured up in her head prepared her for the reality of her aunt wasting away. The amount of weight Rosa had lost since the start of the summer. The gray cast to her skin. The flat lifelessness of her hair.

Her eyes shining with pain. That was the most difficult thing to accept. It got inside of Esperanza and wormed around in her guts. She tried to put on some cheer but her smile kept falling apart. So her efforts fooled no one.

Most especially not her aunt.

"It's okay," Rosa said. "I know I look bad."

Esperanza had to excuse herself after that. She didn't want to blubber in front of her Tía. There were two babies sleeping in her room so she went out in the backyard. She wanted fresh air and to be away from the adults. She knew the children would ignore her. They wanted to be lost in their world.

But there was another adult already out there. A man from down the street was taking away the few chickens that Rosa still kept. The pigs and sheep and the horse and burros were already gone. With no children left to care for them they had been sold or given away. The man came over to offer his sympathies and Esperanza wanted to slap him. He was a kind man who meant well and there was no reason for her to be angry. Wanting to hit him made Esperanza hate herself.

After the man was gone and the chickens were gone, Esperanza felt that her own childhood had happened a long time ago.

❖   ❖   ❖

Her uncle found her out in the yard. They discussed Rosa's condition in hushed tones. Not so they wouldn't be heard. The noise made by the children made it hard for them to hear each other. They spoke quietly out of respect for the awful work God does when he is killing us.

Josef summarized what the doctors had told them—

"First they said cancer. Which was bad. Then they said ulcerative colitis. And that was good news. Because you don't die from that. Not directly anyway. Sometimes the surgery to fix it can kill you. But now they say cancer again. So we're back where we started. And that is not where we want to be."

Esperanza could not absorb this. She had believed that doctors knew when you had cancer. That it wasn't something they guessed at.

"They don't know what it is?" she said.

Josef shook his head.

"She goes in for more tests tomorrow. Then we have to wait for the results. Then maybe we'll know."

He grimaced and shook his head again.

"Right now we don't know a damn thing."

He jerked his chin toward the house and the bedroom were Rosa rested.

"Other than what you see. Which isn't good."

His dark eyes bored into Esperanza.

"I'm afraid it's bad, Essie. *Real* bad."

Chapter 53

In the morning Esperanza confronted her messages. There were three of them now. The first from the morning before during her ride home, another from that afternoon, and a third from last night. Esperanza listened to the first message and half the second then deleted all three.

In the kitchen she found half an inch of lukewarm coffee in the bottom of the pot and a dirty mug beside the sink. A glance out the window confirmed that her uncle's SUV was gone. The house belonged to her and Rosa. Now her role as caretaker would begin.

She dumped the coffee and rinsed the pot and started a fresh one. Rosa came shuffling out as the machine begin to spit and hiss. Esperanza knew to let her aunt steer their conversation. This first time alone after learning she might be dying what Rosa wanted to talk about would be important.

They were seated at the table over their coffee when she began—

"I was thinking about our trip."

Esperanza didn't have to be told which trip. There was only one. This was not among the topics she had anticipated. She wished it wasn't the one Rosa had chosen.

"You remember," Rosa said.

Esperanza nodded.

"Of course."

"You remember what I told you."

Esperanza drank her coffee.

"Do you?" Rosa said.

Esperanza put her cup down and frowned at it.

"I remember."

"Tell me what I said."

Esperanza looked at her aunt. The pain she saw scared her. But she did not turn away.

"Tell me," Rosa said.

"You told me that you saw my future in a dream."

"And who was in that dream?"

"The boy we saw."

Rosa nodded.

"That's right."

Esperanza put her eyes back down on her cup.

"You don't believe me," Rosa said.

She could not lie to her Tía. Lying did not come easily with anyone in any situation. But especially not with Rosa. And especially not now. So although she wanted to lie very much, the most she had ever wanted to lie, the closest she could come was to keep her mouth shut.

"You don't have to believe me," Rosa said. "Just promise me you won't forget."

Esperanza asked herself it that was a promise she could keep. A voice inside of her said very definitively that the answer was yes. Because standing on the rim of the Grand Canyon listening to her aunt whisper that impossible prophecy into her ear remained one of the most powerful—and easily the most haunting—experiences of her young life.

"I will not forget," Esperanza said.

Later when she was alone that answer would feel like partly a lie. Not untrue but not completely true. A more accurate response would have been—

I cannot forget.

Because the truth was that she wanted to forget. She wanted to pretend that disturbing incident at the canyon never happened. She wanted to banish it and all other events she couldn't absorb and couldn't process. If she had a choice she would have chosen to live the rest of her life in a world governed only by reason and logic and verifiable fact.

❖   ❖   ❖

After a few days the messages stopped. A few days more and Esperanza stopped expecting them. Then a week passed and one morning there were three. Spaced an hour or so apart. Esperanza was in the kitchen when her phone rang for a fourth time.

"Take a hint," Esperanza said.

"Who's bothering you?"

Esperanza jumped. Rosa was standing in the doorway.

Esperanza put her eyes back on her phone.

"No one," she said. "It's nothing."

Rosa frowned at her niece. Then got a glass of water and left with it.

"I'm going back to bed," she called out.

"Good, Tía."

"I don't need lunch."

"Okay."

"Let me know when you want to talk about what's bothering you."

Esperanza froze.

"Nothing's bothering me."

Rosa didn't answer. Esperanza listened to her aunt's shuffling footsteps. They stopped and the house was silent. Then Rosa coughed off in the bedroom and Esperanza resumed her chores.

About an hour had passed when there was a knock at the kitchen door. Esperanza was dusting in the living room. She assumed someone had come to visit Rosa. She glanced out the windows on her way to the kitchen and stopped when she recognized the SUV parked out front.

Another knock came and got her moving again. She muttered as she crossed the kitchen—

"I need this like a hole in the head."

Then pulled the door open and scowled at Leslie Davidson.

Leslie took a small step backwards.

"I'm sorry to intrude," she said.

Leslie blinked.

"We need to talk."

Esperanza raised her chin. She pursed her lips and sighed through her nose. Then stepped aside and gestured for Leslie to enter.

"Thank you," Leslie said.

"Mm hmm."

Esperanza pointed at the table.

"Wait here."

She made her way through the house and stopped outside Rosa's bedroom. She listened to her aunt's regular breathing.

Back in the kitchen she sat down across from Leslie.

"We need to be quiet. My aunt is sleeping."

"I didn't come here to make a scene."

"You mean like at your place? Because that was a scene alright."

"I'm sorry about that."

They stared at each other. Then Leslie lowered her eyes.

"I saw that you dropped my class."

"I dropped all of them."

Her eyes came up again. She looked stricken.

"Because of me?"

"No."

"Good. I mean—"

"I understand what you mean."

"Okay. I'm sorry."

"I'm taking care of my aunt."

Leslie's eyes went to the doorway and came back again.

"Is she ill?"

"Yes."

Her eyes opened wide.

"I'm very sorry to hear that."

"Thank you."

Leslie lowered her eyes again.

She put her hands on the table and began rubbing them together.

"I came here to apologize."

She cleared her throat.

"What I did was wrong. And terribly foolish."

She looked at Esperanza. Then blinked and put her eyes back down.

"I understand if things between us can never be the same. But I hope you won't—"

She paused. Then forced her eyes up.

"I hope you won't hate me."

She shook her head.

"I'm sorry, Essie. I swear I couldn't be any more sorry."

Leslie held Esperanza's eyes until her own filled with tears.

❖   ❖   ❖

Esperanza didn't want to watch Leslie cry. She excused herself and went to check on Rosa. Just to escape from the kitchen for a few moments.

She didn't expect to find her aunt awake.

"Who are you talking to?" Rosa said.

Esperanza crossed the room. She sat on the edge of the bed.

"A friend of mine."

"I don't recognize her voice."

"You don't know her."

"I'll come out and meet her."

"No, Tía. You should rest."

Rosa frowned.

"If that's what you want."

"Could you hear what we were saying?"

"No. But I sure tried."

Esperanza smiled. She put a hand on Rosa's arm.

"You were snooping."

"Of course I was. I want to know what's wrong with you."

"Who says anything's wrong?"

"You think you can hide that from me?"

Esperanza shook her head. Rosa studied her niece's expression.

264

"Do you think you can work it out?"

Esperanza pictured herself back in the kitchen. Angry and hurt and resenting the woman she had recently admired so very much. But also glad that Leslie cared enough to come here.

Esperanza shrugged. She shook her head.

"I don't know. Maybe."

"You're still angry."

"Yes. I am."

Rosa watched her niece for a moment. Then she nodded.

"Okay then."

She patted Esperanza's hand.

"You should get back to your guest."

Chapter 54

Esperanza was relieved that her guest wasn't still crying. Leslie remained seated at the table with her hands folded together. She smiled at Esperanza then looked at her hands. Esperanza sat back down across the table. She waited until Leslie brought her eyes up to meet hers. She didn't know what she would say. Only that she had to be brutally frank. Because that was the only way to clean up this mess and put it behind her. So she could focus on taking care of Rosa. Which had become the only thing that mattered.

"I'm not going to help you feel better. About what you did. If that's why you came here. What you did felt terrible."

She needed to smack this thing home.

"It felt like incest."

Leslie jerked back in her seat. She sucked in her breath.

"I, um... That's..."

A hand went up and smoothed her hair.

"Well. That's... really serious. I guess... I... I can see why... why you might... If... but... that's a big thing. One of those... those major social constructs. That—"

She took a deep breath. Her eyes found Esperanza's.

"It was only a kiss, Essie. Just a kiss."

Esperanza felt what she knew slide out of balance. She believed despite what happened that Leslie was an honest person.

"Just a kiss."

"Yes!"

"That's all."

Leslie frowned.

"Yes."

Esperanza nodded.

"I see."

266

They stared across the table. Leslie's eyes darted away and back again. Then slid down to her hands. A car went past outside. Esperanza listened to it climb up the road toward the hills beyond the village. When it was almost out of earshot she leaned forward and said—

"What about your tongue down my throat. That didn't happen?"

Leslie froze.

"Your hands on my ass? That didn't happen either? Trying to grab me again after I pushed you away?"

Leslie grimaced.

Esperanza sat back in her chair.

"None of that happened then."

Leslie filled her lungs. She held her breath for a moment before letting it out. She opened her mouth and shook her head.

"I don't know what to say."

"You can say it was more than a kiss."

"But—"

Esperanza waited.

"But what?"

She waited again.

The answer came to her in a flash. A memory that popped into her head like a snapshot. Of Leslie on that night in her casita.

With a glass of wine in her hand. The empty bottles on the table.

"You don't remember."

Leslie frowned. Esperanza pointed.

"Because you were drunk."

"I guess I was."

"Is that supposed to make me feel better?"

"No. It's just the truth."

"Do you have a drinking problem?"

Leslie startled.

267

"What? No."

"I think maybe you do. If you get drunk and molest your students and don't remember. That sounds like a problem to me."

"No, Essie. Please."

Leslie raised her hands and reached forward. She gestured as she spoke.

"I swear to you. I've never done anything like that before."

"So you admit that you did it."

Leslie sighed and lowered her hands.

"I don't remember clearly what happened. I thought it was just a kiss. I swear that's the truth."

"Are you saying that I'm lying?"

"No. I know you're not. I can see that. But it's not like—"

Leslie raised a hand and gestured over the table.

"It's not like I'm some creepy bull dyke mashing on the freshman girls. I swear to you that is not me."

She put had hand down again.

Esperanza studied the woman seated across from her.

"Right now all I have is your word on that."

"And my word is suspect."

"I can't help that."

"But wouldn't I have a reputation? If I did this all the time? Other professors do. You've heard about them?"

"I have."

"So please believe me that I haven't done anything like this before. You know me. You know I'm not like that."

Esperanza shook her head.

"No. I don't know you. I thought I knew you. I was wrong."

"Please don't say that, Essie. You *do* know me."

Leslie eyes were wet.

268

"You might know me better than anyone."

Esperanza almost asked Leslie to repeat what she just said. She stared across the table and remembered being overwhelmed by how much she admired this woman. Overawed by her brains and her poise. Agitated and scattered in her presence. She could not comprehend this was the same person. That seemed to have happened to other people in some other world.

She heard her own voice as if it came from someone else—

"Then I feel sorry for you."

Leslie swallowed and blinked and wiped a hand across her cheeks. She stared down at the table. Then raised her eyes again and searched Esperanza's face.

"Now I get it."

"Get what."

Leslie smiled. But her smile did not last. She was frowning when she said—

"Why they call you La Soldadita."

❖   ❖   ❖

She shared her childhood nickname during a moment of camaraderie around the campfire during their time in Colorado. When she felt that the people around her were the best on all the earth. And that her mentor Leslie Davidson was the very best of them all.

How far away that seemed now.

Having her nickname thrown back at her felt hostile. She had been working to contain her anger. Now she let it go. Heat rushed over her. She set her jaw and her nostrils flared as she filled her lungs. She narrowed her eyes and raised her chin and scowled imperiously across the table. Then let her breath hiss out between her teeth.

"What of it."

Leslie recoiled into her seat. She shook her head.

269

"I never saw how tough you are."

"Does that disturb you?"

Leslie nodded.

"Yes. It does."

Esperanza smiled.

"Maybe that pleases me."

Leslie managed to smile back. Her smile looked fragile.

"Maybe it should."

Esperanza smiled wider. Her teeth gleamed.

"So. Now that things are clear between us. Are we done?"

Leslie shook her head.

"No. There's something you need to know about."

She paused.

"There's a woman in the law school. A professor."

Leslie paused again.

"A friend of mine."

Esperanza raised an eyebrow.

"You mean she's a lesbian."

Leslie frowned.

"Okay. Obviously you're very angry."

"You think?"

"I'm trying to protect you."

"Is that what you call it?"

Leslie turned away. Esperanza pointed across the table.

"I think you're confused. I think you better have another talk with your law school friend. Because the law would call it sexual harassment."

Esperanza put her hand down.

Leslie turned pale. Her face became drawn. She spoke in a shaking voice—

"Can we put that aside for a moment?"

"How do you propose we do that?"

Leslie closed her eyes. She raised her hands and cupped them over her nose and mouth. Her voice sounded breathy in the hollow behind her hands—

"Are you going to file charges?"

She opened her eyes and took her hands away.

"Are you?"

Esperanza was slow with her answer. She knew what it was but took her time giving it—

"No."

Leslie sighed. A moment later she sighed again. Then she nodded once, very deeply, almost bowing over the table.

"Thank you."

Esperanza shook her head.

"No. That I will *not* accept. *No* gratitude."

Leslie nodded.

"I understand."

"I sincerely doubt that you do. Now tell me whatever else it is you have to say."

"My friend from the law school—"

"Who I assume is a lesbian. Since you won't answer my question."

"Does that matter?"

Esperanza shrugged.

"I don't know yet. You tell me."

"Give me a chance and I will."

"Go ahead."

"I'm trying to!"

Esperanza threw her hand at Leslie.

"So talk then!"

Her bark filled the kitchen. Leslie waited until the ringing sound of these angry words had passed and silence was restored. Then she leaned forward and said quietly—

"This is about your uncle."

Chapter 55

There was probably nothing Leslie could have said that would have been more unexpected. A cold flush passed over Esperanza. She sat up straight as the ice climbed along her spine and leaned forward over the table as it swept out across her shoulders and down along her arms.

"What about my uncle."

"He's being investigated. By the Justice Department."

Esperanza could not make sense of this.

"What?"

"The federal government."

"I know what the Justice Department is. Why are they investigating my uncle?"

Leslie shook her head.

"I don't know."

Esperanza sat back in her chair. She shook her head.

"That's a lie. You're making this up."

Leslie frowned and then the hurt showed. For a second her mouth trembled.

"You know I wouldn't do that."

Esperanza raised a hand and pressed her palm toward Leslie.

"If you want me to hear anything more you have to say then you need to stop insisting how well I know you."

She closed her hand and pointed.

"One more time and I will ask you to leave."

Leslie blinked and swallowed. When she blinked again her tears began to roll. She wiped at them. She bowed her head and looked down at her hands folded together in her lap and whispered to herself—

"What have I done."

Esperanza disapproved of her heart thumping around inside her chest.

❖　　❖　　❖

Leslie spoke quietly. She kept her head down while she explained that she spoke with her friend from the law school on their way home from Colorado. Esperanza remembered watching Leslie at the pullout overlooking the valley when they were coming down off the mountain. And how she felt about her then. How badly she wanted to know her better.

Watch out what you wish for.

Leslie raised her head. She blinked and wiped her cheeks.

"And I... when she told me I felt..."

She smiled.

"I felt so protective of you. That was..."

She took a deep breath and let it sigh out.

"A big part of it. My wanting to protect you."

She paused. Licked her lips. Then winced before she said—

"That protective feeling. Was a big part of..."

She lowered her head and whispered—

"Why I did it."

Esperanza raised a hand.

"Okay. You can stop now."

Leslie kept her head down.

Esperanza smacked a hand against the table. Leslie jumped.

Esperanza shook her head.

"I'm not listening to any more of that crap. You tell me what you know about my uncle. And then we're done."

"That's everything. She didn't tell me anything more. Except that... I'm not supposed to know about it. She told me in confidence. She doesn't know about you. So she doesn't—"

Leslie grimaced. Esperanza finished for her—

273

"She doesn't know you could tell me. And I could tell my uncle."

Leslie nodded.

"Yes."

"So why did you tell me? Trying to make up for what you did?"

"I was going to tell you. Before what I did."

"But when you had the chance to tell me, you *did* what you did."

"I am *so* sorry."

"Good for you. Now answer my question. Why did you tell me about this?"

Leslie shook her head.

"I don't know. What does it matter?"

"You must have had a reason."

"I guess so. I can't remember."

"You think I should do what? Get away from here?"

"Maybe. I didn't know about your aunt."

"Where would you have me go? If I left here. Should I come stay at your place?"

"You can if you want to."

"You are so out of your mind."

Leslie recoiled.

"That wasn't necessary."

"You're right. It wasn't. Is there anything else?"

Leslie looked down at her hands.

"No. Just that I really am sorry. About everything."

She frowned and bit her lip.

"If there's anything I can do."

She looked up at Esperanza.

"Please just tell me."

Esperanza sat back in her chair. After a moment she nodded.

"Okay. There is something you can do for me."

❖   ❖   ❖

Leslie sat up straighter. Her eyes were wide. Expectant. She raised a hand to her mouth and cleared her throat.

Esperanza leaned forward.

Then knocked her knuckles on the table with each beat of what she said—

"I *want* you to *leave* me a-*lone*."

She raised her hand and pointed.

"No more phone calls. Don't show up here again."

Leslie stared. Her mouth was open.

Esperanza jabbed her finger across the table.

"Do you understand me?"

Leslie kept staring.

Esperanza repeated slowly—

"Do you. Un-der-stand. Me."

"Yes! You don't have to be—"

Leslie shook her head. Esperanza smiled.

"Such a bitch?"

"Yeah."

Esperanza shrugged. Leslie shook her head.

"You're being kind of juvenile," Leslie said.

"I can be however I want. I didn't make this mess. I'm not going to pretend I like it."

"Well if you—"

Leslie sighed.

"I just—"

"Out with it."

"If there's anything I can do."

Leslie took a deep breath. She exhaled and raised her hands. She gestured toward Esperanza as she spoke—

"*Please* call me. I mean that."

Leslie put her hands down.

Esperanza nodded once.

"Okay. I seriously doubt that will ever happen. But you have my word. If I ever find myself in such desperate circumstances that I would accept *your* help—"

She nodded again.

"I promise I will call you."
Esperanza pointed at the door.
"Now I want you to go."

Part XVI:
Lizard Thing

Chapter 56

The day began clear and bright and beautiful. A spectacular Friday morning late in autumn. I arrived dressed as a working man. A dark blue jumpsuit with a black roller bag slung over my shoulder.

My real beard had been replaced with a fake one. I didn't want to shave at his place and leave all that DNA in the sink drain. But I also didn't want to draw the attention of anyone at the motel. If someone had noticed that the guy in #307 had a beard on Thursday and happened to see him again on Friday I wanted that beard to still be there.

The locks were old and worn out and no challenge even to a neophyte. They practically fell open when a pick was inserted. About fifteen minutes after he left for work I was standing in his kitchen. Given his habits and nature that seemed more than sufficient time for him to turn around if he was going to.

His kitchen was sizable. Especially so for a small house. I would guess it was added on to the main part of the building about thirty years before. The same white gas stove installed then was still in service.

Beyond the kitchen was the living room, the ground floor of the original structure. Beneath the living room was a damp low-ceilinged basement with an uneven cement floor, an old oil heater and the tank that fed it, some bags of road salt, and a vast amount of cobwebs. I did not see a single live spider anywhere. They must have eaten all the bugs and died too.

Above the living room was a small master bedroom, a tiny second bedroom that served as an office, and a large bathroom. About twenty years before a claw-footed bathtub had been replaced with a metal shower stall. Which left an excess of empty floor space. When the metal shower stall rusted out it had been replaced with a plastic one. This history was written in the stains on the floor and the patched-in linoleum where the old tub had been.

Tucked under the second story roof was a cramped unfinished attic. Above the kitchen was a crawlspace. Both were empty. All of the windows were small. Making the house dark.

Every aspect of the place was dingy and worndown and depressing. Despair and fatigue seemed pressed into the walls and the floorboards. The kind of house that people do not live in but just occupy on their way to death.

I was eager to be done and gone.

❖   ❖   ❖

The fake beard came off as soon as I stepped inside. It itched terribly.

Two packages were opened and waiting on his kitchen table. Both were from specialty automotive suppliers. He had ordered parts for his vintage Ford pickup. Which told me how he had planned to spend his time off. Before his fall from that ladder left him temporarily one-handed.

He kept his truck out in the detached garage. Still turquoise and recently repainted. Apparently he was fond of that color. It did not seem to be in running condition. He had not to my knowledge started the engine while I had been watching him. Although he spent a fair amount of time under the hood. Maybe he was taking his time getting things exactly right.

Or maybe he was just a lousy mechanic.

His breakfast dishes were in the sink. Fried eggs with ketchup and white toast with margarine. I wondered if he woke up early to give himself time to cook breakfast one-handed. Or that maybe when his arm wasn't in a cast he had time to do the dishes before he left.

I confirmed that among those dishes there was no mug for coffee or tea. Just a small glass that had contained orange juice. If the exiled Mormon was a secret caffeine addict he would definitely imbibe in the morning before he went off into the world. But there was no coffee or tea or even any chocolate products to be found in his kitchen.

Or elsewhere in his house. Which I searched as thoroughly as one can while taking pains to avoid leaving evidence that a search has occurred. I wanted what happened here between the two of us to be our secret. And for those who appeared in the aftermath to never suspect I was ever present.

I dreaded what I might find. A stash of child pornography. Trophies from past atrocities. Although I also wanted proof that linked him to what he had done. But if he had anything incriminating it was well hidden. I had plenty of time to look and didn't uncover any mementos.

That is not to say that I found no items of interest. In the master bedroom a Colt 45 was handily located in the nightstand drawer. I was pleased to see his vial of Vicodin waiting in the bathroom medicine cabinet. And there was a small Beretta semi-automatic stuffed down beside the seat cushion of the recliner in his living room.

Both pistols were loaded but not recently cleaned or fired. Judging by how many of the pills were missing he had been following the prescription closely and had taken just enough with him to get through the day. Which meant he was likely to want his next pill when he arrived home.

I would thoughtfully have his pills waiting for him.

I was relieved to secure the guns. I suspected he would own at least one. But finding the Vicodin was the greatest stroke of luck. To have it already in my possession when our interaction commenced. That would simplify things. And in such pursuits simplicity is always best.

❖   ❖   ❖

It was a long painstaking day searching his house then setting the stage and waiting in ambush. The kind of concentrated work that could make one ravenous. But although I had not eaten since early the previous day I did not experience hunger. Small doses of a long-lasting amphetamine eliminated my appetite. A laxative had made sure my bowels were thoroughly moved before I left my own quarters. While in his house I urinated in a plastic container brought for that purpose. I wore surgical gloves and a hairnet at all times. As much as possible I would keep my DNA on my own person.

Of course the time between when I was ready and when my host was due to arrive passed the most slowly and the most painfully of any period in that long stressful day. Even at the low dosage I was taking the speed made me jumpy. When I wasn't doubting the wisdom of the entire endeavor and my sanity for undertaking it and debating whether to abort the whole damn thing I was imagining I had forgotten or overlooked some important detail. I must have checked that I was fully prepared at least a dozen times.

Then finally Sorenson pulled into his driveway. About five minutes later than was usual. But I had expected as much. Traffic was always a little worse on a Friday. While I watched his headlights pivot across the neighbor's yard I wondered for the hundredth time what a janitor with his dominant arm in a cast could spend an entire workday doing. Maybe he had polished the chrome around the mirrors in the bathrooms? And the stainless steel of the paper towel dispensers? Whatever it was he found to do I was grateful he chose to go do it. And left his house unattended.

An hour seemed to elapse between the moment when I saw his car slowing down on the street before his house and the sound of his key in the door. Which opened into the kitchen. He hit the light switch beside the door frame and the fluorescent fixture in the kitchen ceiling hummed and flickered on. Light came through the doorway into the living room where I waited and pushed shadows into the corners.

Otherwise the house was dark. Twilight was almost spent. Night would soon be fully upon us.

His lunch box and thermos clunked down onto the table. Then apparently he had trouble shrugging off his jacket. Still learning how to live with that cast. I almost laughed when he muttered—

"Gosh darn it."

Capable of the basest depravity but he swears like a Sunday school teacher.

He sighed when the jacket finally slipped off. Then sighed again when he dropped it to the floor. He picked it up and tossed it down with a little force onto the table beside his lunch box.

Then his footsteps came across the kitchen.

Chapter 57

He shuffled into the room with his head angled down. His good hand was raised and busy rubbing the back of his neck.

A few steps past the doorway he stopped. He stared at the objects I had arranged on the side table next to his recliner. Then slowly lowered his hand. For another moment he kept staring.

Then his head came up. Just as slowly as his hand went down. He turned and saw me and took a half-step backward. His eyes went to his Colt 45. Which was in my hand and pointed at his chest. His eyes stayed there. His mouth came open. He breathed heavily through his open mouth.

I waved the gun at his recliner.

"Sit," I said.

His eyes stayed on the pistol. He stared for another second. Then crept over to the chair and lowered himself into it. He grimaced while he settled his injured arm across his lap. I watched his eyes cut down and to his right. A second later his fingers began flexing at the end of his cast.

With my free hand I pulled his Beretta from my pocket.

"Wishing you had this?" I said.

His fingers flexed once more and stopped.

I held his Beretta up in the air.

"You should thank me for finding this. Imagine what could have happened. You shooting at me left-handed. You're no good with your left hand. Clumsy as all hell, actually. But I would've had no choice. Self-defense. Then maybe you'd be dead already."

He blinked. I returned the Beretta to my pocket.

A moment later he sighed.

"I don't have much money."

A falsehood I chose to ignore. I had seen his bank statements. They were in his desk in the spare bedroom. He was a frugal man. Saving his pennies and stacking them on top of that inheritance.

He sighed again.

"I'm just a janitor."

As if maybe pity might stop me?

I pointed the Colt at the side table that stood next to the recliner. He turned to look. Among the objects waiting on the table were two of his pills beside a glass of water.

"Before we get started you should take those," I said.

I couldn't help grinning at what I said next. And putting a little sneer into my voice. In retrospect these theatrics seem crude and gratuitous. But that's what I did when I told him—

"The directions say you can take two when the pain is bad."

Sorenson glanced up at me. Something flickered across his face. Hatred or anger or fear. I couldn't tell. Whatever it was his expression came and went too quickly.

He eyed the pills. Breathing heavily through his open mouth. Then looked away and shut his mouth and breathed through his nose. Every breath rasped in and out of his head.

I watched him and thought how terrible he looked. So aged and shrunken. A shadow of the strapping thing he had been when I first saw him. I wondered if he was ill. Maybe cancer was eating him up from the inside. If that was so I wished I could let it finish the job. But maybe knowing death was drawing near he would only rush after more little boys.

He stopped breathing. Then exhaled loudly. He turned back to the pills and reached out slowly and picked one up and placed it in his mouth. He raised the glass of water and gulped. Then lowered the glass back to the table.

A moment later he did the same with the other pill.

He did not look at me when he asked his first question—

"So who are you?"

"We'll get to that."

I pointed the gun at the side table again.

"Pick up the remote," I said. "Turn on your TV."

Another stroke of luck was his forty inch flat screen LCD television with an HDMI connection. Which made it easier to hook up my laptop.

The remote waited not far from the glass of water. Sorenson stared at it for a second before he did as he was told. His television came on. I tapped the spacebar on my computer. We saw a map of the United States with six red dots on it. The dots were scattered across the Midwest and the West.

"What do you see?" I said.

Sorenson stared. A second later he shook his head. I gave him another few seconds to say something.

He chose not to.

"Come on now," I said. "Don't be coy."

He shook his head again. But he couldn't pull his eyes away from what was displayed on his television. He was consumed by that map.

"So you're going to make me do all the work?" I said.

He just blinked. Once and slowly. So very reptilian.

"These are all places where you have lived. Since your missionary years. Which were cut short. I don't know exactly what happened over in the Philippines. What you did to make your people disown you. But I can guess. Because I know what happened in the places where you see those red dots."

His mouth came open. He sighed. And then he stared.

"In each of those locations. Right around the time that you moved away. Either a little while before."

I paused.

"Or a little while after..."

I let my voice trail off. I watched him and waited.

Finally his face twitched. I waited a little longer.

He sighed again. But still he said nothing.

I gestured with his gun.

"Are you going to make me say it?"

Another twitch contorted his features. But he still wouldn't speak.

I trotted out that old familial nickname—

"Okay, Fenny."

This time his whole body shook. But his eyes did not stray from that map up on his television.

"Have it your way then. I'll keep going without your help. As you know, in each of those places marked up there on that map, those places where you have lived, a young boy went missing right around the time that you left."

I tapped the spacebar. A name appeared beside each red dot.

I pointed to where it said Elden Morris.

"Only one of them ever reappeared."

I waited a beat. But he just wouldn't play.

"Now do you know who I am?"

He turned his slack face toward me. His mouth hung open. He stared for maybe five seconds before he finally had something to contribute—

"You're too young to be his father."

This tacit admission gave me gooseflesh. I needed a moment to recover. I tried to look stern while I regained my composure.

"Correct. Besides his father is dead. As is the boy."

I pointed at Sorenson with his Colt 45.

"And you killed them both."

"No."

"Yes."

"No, I mean..."

He sighed. All his pathetic sighing was starting to jar my amphetamine-jangled nerves. He sighed again before he spoke again—

"How do you know they're dead?"

Much of the research I did in prison was unpleasant. There was the boring stuff that came with tracking down Sorenson. Determining where he had lived as he wandered around the country. And then there was the disturbing stuff. Uncovering what he had done along the way. But the worst of it was when I decided to find out what had become of the Morris family. Because of the personal connection I had with Elden.

A magazine article told me about the deaths. An investigative piece into the management of that Catholic charity hospital in California. The one that Elden Morris was sent to when his condition failed to improve. Which was closed about six years after he became a patient there. In part because a little more than three years earlier Elden strung himself up in a broom closet. A janitor found him hanging by a short length of electrical cord. Two months later Mr. Morris blew his head off at a campground in a state park. He used the same shotgun he once brandished in the backcountry of Doña Pero.

That article also told me what became of Señora Morris in the aftermath of those horrible events. She finally had too much. She suffered a nervous breakdown. During her recovery she moved to Tucson to live with a sister. Where she found work in another hospital cafeteria.

I had to dig deeper to find out what became of her after that. Legal records and then later social media. A church newsletter posted online.

Four years after moving to Tucson she married one of the cooks from the hospital where she worked. He was a few years older and had a son from a first marriage. Together they had two daughters. Señora Morris was reborn as Señora Hernandez. She found strength she did not know she possessed. She became the rock of her new family and a trusted and respected member of her new community.

Some of us can be reborn. And some of us cannot. Some of us are destroyed and must wither and die. As did poor Elden. As did his father. I learned in prison that I am one who can be reborn. As was Elden's mother. We were both clay that could be reformed and re-fired.

Which made me feel that the combination of my regained freedom with my new wealth charged me with a solemn duty—

Those who *can* must do for those who *cannot*.

Chapter 58

With one hand I kept his Colt trained on Sorenson. With the other I tapped the spacebar on my computer. A form appeared on the television. With my free hand I gestured at the screen.

"The Social Security Death Index record for Elden Morris."

I waited while Sorenson scanned it. Then I tapped again. Now we saw an article from a newspaper website. The headline made it clear what we were looking at. But I stated the obvious anyway—

"His obituary."

I paused.

"It says he died after a brief illness."

I paused again.

"Very brief. About six inches."

Sorenson frowned.

"He hanged himself," I said.

I gestured with his Colt.

"Because of you."

Sorenson looked away. I tapped the spacebar.

"Death record for his father."

I made sure Sorenson was looking. Then I tapped again.

"Obituary for his father."

Sorenson sighed. The sound of it grated on me. I imagined how it would feel to smack that Colt across his face.

"Would you like to see the crime scene photographs from when Mr. Morris shot himself?"

I didn't actually have those images. I don't know if they even existed. I never made any effort to find out. That wasn't something I wanted to look at.

But my captive did. Which was why I asked. To see if the lizard thing would reveal itself while it forgot to appear human.

Yesss, it wanted to hiss. Show me some gore!

288

Then it was gone again.

A moment too late Sorenson replied—

"That won't be necessary."

❖　　❖　　❖

When Sorenson entered his living room that evening he was sloughing off his everyday skin. The guy who mopped floors at New Faith Holy Gospel. And went to the supermarket to stock up on frozen dinners and store-brand breakfast cereal. The skin he wore through his day-to-day life.

He wasn't good at quickly shifting appearances and mindsets. As some are. This one needed time. Like a chameleon that is slow to shift colors. When he had recovered from the surprise of finding me waiting with his pistol in my hand—and maybe with some help from the hydrocodone that might have begun calming his nerves—he assumed one of his other skins.

Maybe this was the one that abducted little boys. Or took over after he had completed his unspeakable acts and managed the damage control. I don't know how many skins he had and precisely which one he wore now. And I don't care. I have no curiosity about the details of his fractured psyche. No academic interest in what made that freak tick.

But I will say the transition was noteworthy. And if you knew to watch for it, strikingly obvious. His slack face abruptly tightened. His voice came back with an edge—

"So I lived in those places. Where some boys disappeared. What does that prove? Kids go missing all the time."

He looked younger. And stronger. He regained some of his formidableness.

But I also saw it was more difficult. This skin demanded more of him.

He waved a hand at the television.

"Another man was convicted. For that Morris boy. You should go talk to him."

His statement presented a decision I had anticipated but not resolved—when to reveal my identity. I could now inform my captive I was the man he had just referred to. And have the satisfaction of his knowing why I was putting him through what would follow. Or I could remain anonymous. And minimize my risk if I failed to achieve my primary goal. I could always reveal myself later. When my safety was more certain.

I decided I was unwilling to postpone that particular pleasure. That I wanted Sorenson to know who I was for the duration. To be aware in each of those coming moments why I was doing what I did to him.

I smiled. He frowned.

I made a little bow.

"At your service," I said.

His frown cut deeper.

"Excuse me?"

I laughed a little bit. Maybe I even snickered.

"Are you really so dense? That you still don't know who I am?"

❖   ❖   ❖

His frown remained frozen for at least fifteen seconds. Realization was slow in dawning over the ruined landscape of his face. Which in his youth had been so clean-cut and all-American.

"You can't prove anything," Sorenson said.

"That is true. But I am not the FBI. They have resources that far exceed mine. And that is one option. I could turn you and everything I know over to them."

I nodded at Sorenson. He eyed the Colt in my hand.

"How do you like that option?" I said. "Does it appeal to you?"

290

His eyes came up to mine.

"Sure," he said.

"So you would take your chances with the law."

He blinked.

"Yes."

He made a point of looking me in the eye.

"I haven't done anything," Sorenson said.

Maybe this particular fragment of a person actually believed that was true. Because I have never seen a lie delivered more believably.

I took a few moments to let him stew. I pretended I was actually considering what I would do next. That I was not already certain what course of action I would pursue.

As if this was all improvised.

Then I shook my head.

"I have trouble with that option. Personal issues, you could say. I do not have much faith in the law. After what the law did to me. Which is too bad. Because I would like you to go to prison. There are things that would happen to you there that I would like to have happen. I can tell you from personal experience that a man like you is a complete pariah on the inside. The very lowest of the low. Fair game for everyone. To do whatever awful thing they might want to do to someone. And needless to say prison is full of people who like to do awful things to other people. And especially to a man who has done the awful things you have done. Do you know why that is?"

Sorenson frowned and shook his head. He looked very stupid doing it.

I waved the gun at him.

"Because so many men on the inside have suffered at the hands of a man like you. And they are very eager to pay that back."

His white face became a little whiter.

"And I would know. Because of you. Because I was blamed for what you did. And had to suffer

291

through those things they really wanted to do to you. Maybe it makes me not particularly noble of mind and spirit. But I would very much like those things to actually happen to the man they were intended for."

His eyes cut sideways and came back again.

"What if that's not me?" he said.

"Please let's not play that game."

I pointed toward his garage.

"You still have the truck I saw you in. It's still even painted turquoise."

I lowered my hand and clutched it with the other one around the Colt. As if I was restraining my violent impulses.

"I have thoroughly documented your life. I know your pattern. I have seen it played out too many times. Coincidence is not any possibility here."

I shook my head.

"So I must dismiss the option of turning you over to the law. It is too likely they won't find enough to convict you. And even if they did they might bungle the case. That happens all too often."

I paused and frowned.

"And even if they did not, the wheels of justice grind slowly. I have already waited too many years. My patience is exhausted."

I paused and swallowed. I gestured with my free hand.

"And knowing firsthand what would be done to you. In prison. How it could go on for year after year. A hell here on earth."

I lowered my hand and sighed.

"It would be less than Christian of me to subject you to that."

There was a flicker of hope in his eyes.

"As much as I want to see it happen. As much as I would like to see you suffer as I did."

I waved the Colt at Sorenson.

"Did you know I actually saved his life? I found him out where you dumped him. And what did I get for my trouble?"

I gave him my most murderous look. He shrank back into the chair.

I nodded once.

"Which brings us to my second option."

I smiled and showed him my teeth. I put fresh energy into my voice. As if this next idea excited me—

"I could do those terrible things to you myself."

His white face became whiter still. Even his pale brown hair seemed to turn a lighter shade.

I nodded at him. My teeth were still bared.

"We have plenty of time before you will be missed. Two whole weeks before they expect you back at work. With weekends that makes sixteen days before anyone might even pick up the telephone and give you a call. No one will come looking for you. You are alone in this world. You have no family or friends that might want to see you."

My laugh was horrible.

"Face it, Fenny. You're all mine."

Part XVII:
All Roads Lead to Vegas

Chapter 59

Matt parked on the shoulder of U.S. Route 95. A divided four-lane highway in the southern tip of Nevada. Ahead of him State Road 156, also called Lee Canyon Road, ran off to his right pointed southwest toward Charleston Peak in the Spring Mountains.

What brought him here was something that can only happen in such a place. An event that requires a highway laid out in long straight lines and an absence of human habitation. A particular kind of desolation endemic to the modern American West.

He stepped out into the rising heat. Late morning and the sun had everything on fire. A hundred feet away the asphalt shimmered and shook.

While he circled the intersection Matt divided his attention between the ground at his feet and the distant hills and mountains. If he was looking for something it was unclear where he thought it would be. Among the dirt and gravel and debris at the side of the road. Or off in the distance on one of the ridges and peaks.

❖   ❖   ❖

He was crossing the Thousand Islands Bridge when he realized his mistake. He had told himself he had nowhere to go and nothing to do. No reason to be anywhere. But he had started something in his departure from Walker City. Tentatively and on a limited basis. Then forgotten while he lost himself in his summer of unlove. Descending the span that connected Wellesley Island in the United States to Hill Island in Canada he saw that his correct destination was Las Vegas.

A new map purchased at the first opportunity led him to the west and the south above Lake Ontario and Lake Erie. After a consultation with a trucker during lunch he chose to bypass Detroit and the Ambassador Bridge or the Detroit-Windsor Tunnel in favor of the Blue Water Bridge at Point Edward.

He was in the vicinity of Lansing, Michigan, on 69 South planning to connect with 94 West near Battle Creek when he learned that a massive pileup at Paw Paw had closed 94. Which was confirmed at the interchange by the Michigan State Police cruiser blocking the on ramp.

He almost stumbled into a *descanso* in the northern corner of the intersection. Two simple pieces of sun-bleached white wood with "Juan" painted in black script on the horizontal beam. Paper flowers of faded red and blue fluttered where the crucified's hands would have been nailed.

Matt wondered how exactly the lost Juan had died here. If he had been killed by someone else or was the pilot of his own demise. And then Matt wondered who had constructed this memorial. What member or members of Juan's family had come out here to this lonely place and rooted this cross and decorated it. Matt wished he had a family who would gather here with him and erect another such offering.

With Matt she had always been gentle and kind and nurturing. Almost a second mother in how she treated him. The age difference shaped how they interacted. He came along late. His parents called him their happy surprise. He wondered if his sister had missed him after she left. He added up the years and realized he had missed Glory for half of his life.

He continued south toward Indiana. Where he intended to connect with I-80. Which would carry him all the way across the Midwest to I-76 just past Big Springs, Nebraska, and just shy of the Colorado border. From there 76 would take him to Denver where he would catch 70 to Sulphurdale, Utah, and from there 15 into Nevada and Sin City.

Or at least that was the plan. But not how events unfolded. Of course Matt did not realize he was about to make a lengthy detour when he stopped for gas and food. How could he? If he had been told that was true he wouldn't have believed it. His mind was very much on the road ahead and his intended destination at the distant end of it. He had found a purpose. Which he sorely needed.

But it was only a purpose that he needed. Not the particular purpose he had selected. Which meant that another purpose could readily supplant the one he had in mind. Especially if that new purpose was more attractive. And what could be more attractive to a lonely young red-blooded man than a shapely and charming young woman?

Watching the sad paper flowers dance on the arms of that faded *descanso* with the desert blistering around him, Matt tried one more time to reconcile the sensitive young woman he knew and loved with the hardheaded fast girl who battled against their parents. And once again that contradiction refused to be resolved. When the ferocious heat would no longer allow him to keep trying Matt continued his loop around the intersection.

Back at the car he stood beside the driver's door with a grip on the handle and let his eyes roam over the mountains rising to the south. Then he turned and looked back across the road at the *descanso*. Finally as he readied himself to leave and pulled the door open his gaze fell on the ground about twenty yards away. Where he saw a patch of burnt earth. Blackened soil and rocks and at the perimeter scorched cactus.

Matt stared where his eyes had fallen while he recriminated himself for not looking for this very spot. For what he had found by chance. Then decided that maybe by chance was the best way to find this.

He pushed the car door shut again and slowly made his way around his mother's old red Toyota and off into the desert. Carefully picking his way across the earth. To stand in the center of the burn and contemplate the ashes beneath his feet. Some of which might be his sister's.

They met in the checkout line at the Tekon Travel Plaza on the outskirts of Tekonsha, Michigan. Eyes were caught and smiles exchanged. A comment about the artwork on a bag of chips made her laugh.

Concerns were shared about the pileup at Paw Paw. Which was prompted by the local news coverage blaring from the television behind the cash register. Inquiries and information were exchanged about destinations and origins and alternate routes of travel.

A denunciation of Canadian drivers made her howl. The television began reporting on the inaction of Congress which prompted rants about politics and politicians that continued out through the glass doors into the parking lot. Where the conversation went freewheeling for most of an hour.

And ended with an invitation to follow her out to Oregon.

Down at his feet Matt saw what he thought was melted glass. And wondered if it was from the windshield. Or maybe a bottle that was waiting here. When the Honda was pushed out to this spot and burst into flames. Then he hoped it wasn't a bottle of booze that had been in the car with his sister and that she wasn't drunk when she died and maybe partly at fault in the collision. Her life had ended cheap enough as it was. Her final moments didn't need to be made any cheaper.

Matt walked slowly back to the red Toyota. With his head down watching his feet collapse onto the desert. Behind the wheel he sat staring ahead along the highway. He couldn't say what he was waiting for. At one point he put his key in the ignition and sat there with his hand ready to turn the engine over. But he took his hand away and sat back in the old worn out driver's seat that used to ferry his mother around Walker City on her errands.

His emotion came on quickly and without warning. For several minutes Matt was overwhelmed. Then just as quickly his feelings were spent.

He wiped his face and started his car and pulled out onto the highway. As he drove away Matt did not look into the mirrors that would have shown him the place where Gloria died growing smaller as it receded behind him.

Chapter 60

Her behavior had been out of character. She got carried away in the moment. The unexpected encounter in those unlikely circumstances. Her chemistry with this attractive and charming young man. But in the main, Abigail White was a quiet kind of girl. And since Matt was accommodating by nature he adapted his ways to her quietness. Which made for a quiet kind of romance. Hours passed in book stores and movie theaters and long slow walks on the streets of Downtown Portland. They quietly shared her third floor studio in the Ongford Apartments on Southwest 10th Avenue. Abigail attended classes at Portland State. Matt waited tables in a brew pub on Flanders Street.

And wondered if it would ever stop raining. He never got used to the rain. Walker County was made to seem dry.

The quiet of their relationship proved an effective antidote to the noisy sting of Meredith. But then the months began piling up. And Matt no longer required healing. Now the quiet grew oppressive. And the rain became unbearable. He could swear he was growing moss in his armpits. And would die of acute boredom if he lived this way much longer.

Once toward the end he heard his father's voice inside his head. Telling him bluntly he should either ask this nice girl to marry him or stop wasting any more of her time. Then an afternoon came when he was heading home from running errands and through the glass store front of their favorite coffee shop he saw Abigail waiting at the counter. She was talking with one of the baristas. A handsome guy that Matt knew only in passing. But from where he stood now he could swear that Abigail knew this fellow pretty well. Much better than Matt would have guessed.

She clearly had a crush on this barista. Who was far from indifferent to her. Matt stood out on the sidewalk watching them flirt and wondered how he had been so dense as to miss their mutual interest. And told himself these two would make a better couple. Like Abigail this guy was the quiet type. And a fellow student at Portland State. Not just a futureless waiter.

Matt pulled himself away and continued home. That night they would have The Talk. He would tell her he was leaving.

Which did not happen. And then a month had passed and still The Talk had not come to pass. But in that month Matt had witnessed Abigail enjoying her moments with the barista a few more times. And not by accident. He had placed himself outside the coffee shop when he guessed she might be there. Each time he saw them together he told himself that night he would end it.

Then one night Abigail said they needed to talk. Which meant that mostly she talked and Matt listened. She talked for some time. A lot of talk for a quiet type of girl. She did not mention the barista. When Matt had his turn and managed to utter a few words neither did he.

The end came with a soft lingering kiss. After that much time together, no matter how uneventfully spent, the kiss at the end had best be a lingering one. Or better not to kiss at all.

Then Matt was on the road again. Wondering what had happened to him. Where he had been for the last eleven months. He could have sworn that only a week ago he was in Michigan standing in a checkout line making time with a pretty girl. Then he blinked and almost a year was gone. Without a single noteworthy event worth recalling. The best he could come up with was that one night he got drunk with his coworkers and *almost* got a tattoo. But he didn't even go so far as to select the tattoo he didn't get.

Otherwise it was the brew pub and the studio apartment and the bookstores and the movie theaters and the long slow walks.

And all that damned rain.

And the quiet shapely girl. Who was definitely worth remembering. She had been nothing but kind and thoughtful and generous with her affections. Always good company and always good to be in bed with.

But Abigail White would be better off without Matthew Walker. And did not seem all that heartbroken to see him go. Despite all the kind things that she said as he was packing.

Why should she be sad? He was a loser.

No. He was a *fucking* loser.

And now she would be fucking the barista.

And her parents would be rejoicing that the loser was finally gone.

And her friends would all finally tell her what a loser he really was.

A loser who kept losing his girls to other guys.

First Meredith. Now Abigail.

He started crying just past the city limits. Then wept on and off for the next hundred miles. At first about Abigail. And what a loser he was for losing her.

Then about his parents. And how much he missed them. And how unfair it was that he had lost them. And how their hopes were wasted on a loser like him. And how their lives had been spent fruitlessly raising him and those other two losers, his brother Jack and sister Glory. And how he wished he had just one family member who was still alive. And wasn't a loser like him.

He even cried about Meredith. Over what a bitch she had been.

And then he cried about Abigail some more. With even more feeling. She was a good soul and he would miss her. He did not want to forget her goodness. Worse yet he did not want to forget her goodness and still remember the evil that was Meredith. Because he doubted he would ever forget that one.

This time when he was done the tears stopped for good. He was all cried out. But that is not to say he was out of pain. Actually the opposite was true. He had drugged himself with girls and now the second dose was wearing off. Which put him right back where he was before the Abigail drug numbed him pleasantly and the Meredith drug knocked him senseless.

He was back to being lost without his family.

He pulled off the highway near Eugene. When his tank was full and his bladder empty he sat in his car staring out through the windshield doubting there was any point in continuing on. With this trip or anything else. He was already played out. His young life a hollow ruin.

What would he do once he was done in Las Vegas? When he had seen the places where his sister had lived and died and his tour of his dead was concluded. He had nothing beyond that. After that was done all he could see was the great void beckoning.

About which he made a resolution. He resolved that it was too soon after ending things with Abigail for him to take his own life. Or she might blame herself. Which would be unfair to her. And could haunt her forever. Especially given her kind and caring nature.

He decided he should wait at least a year. A time frame that allowed for an unwanted thought to go fluttering around inside his skull. One he tried to catch and kill. Like a pesky fruit fly that won't be crushed. A year seemed long enough that if by some miracle his luck happened to change—and let that change be for the better since he acknowledged a change for the worse remained a distinct possibility and might even be probable—that something good could happen. Something good enough even to keep him alive.

A guy could hope. Even if he didn't want to.

And if after that year had passed he still felt about his life as he did at this moment...

Matt decided not to think about that. Or he might find it impossible to observe his year-long moratorium on suicide. Which would be so terribly unfair to Saint Abigail.

He got back on the highway. And drove until the dial on his dashboard said his tank was empty. Because now that Matt was back on his tour of his dead he was determined not be diverted. No pretty girls would waylay him this time. His object was in range and he would achieve it.

Chapter 61

Matt pushed through the deadly afternoon sun down a long row of paupers' graves. An email had brought him a plot number and a map showing the grave's location. He had tracked this information down when he decided what he would do when he left Portland.

When he found where she was laid to rest Matt tried to grieve for his sister. For himself but more importantly on behalf of his parents. If they had known where she was buried they would have come here. They would not have let their daughter go without making this gesture. Matt felt it was his duty to make the gesture for them.

But the anonymity of her grave would only allow Matt to feel the immense shame his parents would have experienced. That their only girl had come to this. That shame overwhelmed Matt and pushed him away.

Lawrence "Duck" Kingreal of Rodessa, Louisiana, was headed northwest on U.S. Route 95 in his Kenworth pulling a load of frozen chicken parts when he fell asleep and angled off across the median into the oncoming lanes. His rate of speed was estimated at approximately eighty miles per hour when he plowed into a Honda Civic subcompact approaching from the opposite direction, crushing the sedan and shoving it off the road.

Mr. Kingreal suffered a mild concussion and a bloody nose. No criminal charges were filed against him. He sold his rig to a dealer in Las Vegas and returned to Louisiana. He later became an evangelical preacher.

The driver of the Honda was incinerated in the resulting explosion and fire. Her driver's license and any other identification she might have carried were all destroyed. The vehicle was registered to an Earl James at an address that was no longer valid. The authorities were unable to locate him.

The Clark County Coroner attributed the cause of death to multiple trauma. Which meant there would have been too many injuries sustained in the crash to determine which one actually killed her. If they could have examined an actual corpse instead of cinders and ash.

He felt compelled to see where she had lived. Maybe as punishment for running away from her grave. What he found was a small tattered cluster of low sun-beaten apartment buildings. Dominated on that blazing afternoon by the endless droning bark of a solitary dog. A dismal and oppressive sound that provided the only sign of life.

He told himself he should go look at her apartment. Wander through the complex and find the one where Glory had lived.

Then do what? Stare at her door?

He didn't even get out of his car.

He reproached himself as he drove away. For hurrying through these last two stops on his tour. For not having done something to keep his sister alive.

What could have been done he had no idea. But he felt somehow culpable in her death. As if his eagerness to put these sad places from her life and death behind him made Matt retroactively guilty for his sister being gone.

❖   ❖   ❖

He was out on The Strip after dinner. Two sailors approached him laughing in their white uniforms under their white caps. One of them looked a little like his brother Jack. He watched this sailor and realized his tour of his dead would never be truly complete unless he went to Korea and saw where Jack rolled that jeep and snapped his neck.

"How the fuck will I ever get to Korea?" Matt said.

The sailor who looked like his brother glared at him. Matt looked away.

The sailors passed on.

The only way he would set foot in Korea was the same way his brother did. He could find an Army recruiter right here in Vegas. Joining up in the city where his sister lived when she died to get to the country where his brother lived when he died seemed fitting.

For an instant the military exerted the pull it can have over lives that feel purposeless. But Matt knew there was no guarantee he would actually be stationed in Korea. He had heard a hundred times from numerous sources that any promises made in the recruiter's office were bullshit. So as quickly as it came the idea was dismissed. If there was no Korea there was no point.

Where Jack died would not be part of his tour.

"Fuck Jack anyway," Matt said. "Piece of shit."

He had never admitted to anyone that he hated his older brother. Matt was small when Jack left but he remembered his brother clearly. The guy was a big selfish animal. A large stupid beast that chewed and screwed wherever and whatever it wanted.

So fuck Jack and fuck Korea. Here in Vegas on the glittering garish Strip he would officially conclude his tour of his dead. Which would be limited to the dead that he cared about.

He would end it tonight. At the Agropoli Hotel and Casino. Where Gloria had been employed as a cocktail waitress when she died. Then he'd get a good night's sleep and tomorrow morning he would decide what was next. In what direction he would point his life when this one was exhausted.

And exhausted was what he felt.

He hadn't been prepared for what this day would do to him.

A sign in the lobby pointed him toward the bar. Where he stopped just inside the doorway and let his eyes adjust. Then pictured his sister moving through this dark space dressed in the same form-fitting black outfits worn by the women currently on duty. One of them passed by and he almost stopped her to ask if she had known Gloria. But there was a hardness to the woman's face that made him not want to know.

A bartender was watching him. Tall with long thick arms. Close-cropped hair on a round head. Glancing at Matt while he monitored the action.

The scrutiny made Matt want to leave.

Instead he went over and stood at the bar.

"What can I get you?" the bartender said.

"Actually, nothing. I just have a question."

The bartender scanned the room.

"Okay."

"My sister used to work here. Gloria Walker? Maybe you knew her as Gloria James."

The bartender shook his head.

"Sorry."

"Yeah, well. It was a while ago."

"How long?"

"Six years. Maybe closer to seven."

"Yeah, that's before my time."

Matt nodded. He watched a couple get up and leave. Smiling at each other and holding hands. One of the waitresses glided past. She offered a lot to look at. Matt managed not to stare but it wasn't easy.

"Well thanks," he said.

The bartender shrugged.

"Sorry I couldn't help."

"That's all right. It was a longshot."

"So you're lookin' for your sister."

"No. Not exactly."

The bartender frowned.

"So what then?"

"I'm, um. Paying my respects. I guess you'd call it."

"Excuse me?"

"She died."

"Jeez. I'm sorry. Me and my big mouth."

"It's all right."

"You want somethin'? On the house."

"No, that's okay. Thanks."

The bartender nodded.

"Is that why you're in town? For your sister?"

"Yeah. That's why I'm here."

"Where you from?"

"Pennsylvania."

"I'm from Jersey."

The bartender extended his hand.

"Mike."

"Matt."

"What chou do back in P-A, Matt?"

"I'm not there anymore. I left."

"Where you goin'?"

Matt shook his head.

"I don't know yet."

"Sounds familiar. You ever tend bar?"

"A little. Mostly I waited tables."

The bartender smiled for the first time. He looked ten years younger.

"Do yourself a favor, kid. Don't go nowhere."

He nodded his round head at one of the waitresses.

"Can't beat the scenery."

Which made Matt picture his sister as part of that scenery. And how the men would have looked at her. Every night when she worked.

Chapter 62

As Matt crossed the lobby he pictured himself working at a place like the Agropoli. Entering one of these gaudy pleasure palaces every working day. And wondered if Las Vegas would be good for him. The antidote to rainy Portland. Sun and fun in Sin City. Maybe that was what he needed. Maybe his sister had the right idea. Maybe she liked being lusted after. Maybe sex was just sex like people said. And he needed to get over himself. And get over his hang-ups.

Then Matt felt he was being watched. And with surprise found the woman who was watching him. If she was what Vegas had to offer then he wasn't going anywhere. Then he put how she was dressed together with how she conducted herself. The direct look she gave him. And added all of that to their location. The lobby of a hotel and casino. Not just any hotel and casino but the notorious Agropoli. Which he had heard of long before he arrived on The Strip. All the way back in Walker County.

He wondered if this woman might be a prostitute. If so she was way out of his price range. Zeroing in on him didn't make any sense. There was some big money walking around in here. He was maybe her worst possible bet at this moment. Matt smiled, wondering if she needed glasses but didn't wear them when she was working. Then stopped smiling when the thought struck him as stupid. Clearly she could afford contact lenses.

Meanwhile he and this mystery woman had been walking toward each other. With Matt making his exit. And her making an entrance. Even in the lobby of the scandalous Agropoli she made the kind of entrance that turned heads. Matt was not the only one watching her saunter across the marble floor.

Then the distance between them became short enough for Matt to recognize with a dizzying jolt who this mystery woman was.

❖   ❖   ❖

Those big wide-set surprised-looking green eyes. The same thing that struck him the most when they first met. That was what knocked him a little bit senseless again now. Those green eyes had not changed. But when he last saw them—Was it really only a year ago? That was tough to wrap his mind around—they were not perched atop the fully formed curves of an adult woman. Back then her figure had been disturbingly childlike.

"Speak of the devil!" Meredith said.

They stopped and stood facing each other. Matt shoved his hands into his pocket. Meredith pointed a scarlet-tipped finger at his chest.

"We were just talking about you."

He waited for her to explain. Because Meredith appeared to be alone. He was the only one standing anywhere near her. But she offered nothing more. She just stared with those glassy green eyes.

"Who?" Matt said.

Meredith tapped that red claw against his chest.

"*You*, silly!"

She pointed it at his face.

"We were talking about *you*."

Her eyes slid down to his crotch and back up again. She put some smoke in her voice—

"Or part of you anyway."

Matt felt warm and then cold.

"Who were you talking with. There's no one else here."

Meredith looked to her right, then to her left, then spun around to face the lobby entrance and had to steady herself. Her red-tipped hands came up and one high-heeled foot stabbed the marble.

310

When she turned back to Matt she was frowning.

"She was here just a second ago."

"Who are you talking about."

"Cheryl! You remember her."

"No."

"Sure you do. We were waitresses together. Dark. Italian."

Meredith grinned and cupped her hands before her chest.

"Big boobs."

A gesture that succeeded in making Matt notice again Meredith's own boobs. And how they had become much more abundant since he last saw her. And in convincing him that she was drunk.

But her gesture did also assist in bringing Cheryl to mind. He recalled a short busty hard-bitten brunette that he did not like.

"Ah yes. And did you two enjoy Europe?"

"What?"

"Europe. I heard you went there. With Cheryl."

"No. Who told you that?"

"What's his name."

"Who?"

"One of the busboys. The pothead." He waved a hand in the air. "The one she went out with."

"What?"

He shook his head.

"It doesn't matter."

"We went to Disneyworld."

Matt snorted and shook his head.

"Of course you did."

"Is that funny?"

"No. Actually it isn't."

"Then why did you laugh?"

"Was that a laugh?"

Meredith frowned again.

"She was right about you. You're kind of weird."

"I'll take that as a compliment."

"We're starting law school. Then we're going into practice together. After we graduate."

She paused and smiled—

"Trusts and estates!"

I had a trust once, Matt thought.

❖   ❖   ❖

At that moment it seemed entirely unreal. That moment which had no right to exist. When he was drifting across the country trying to pretend he had a purpose and for no good goddamn reason bumped into the last person he would ever want to see again.

But yes, it was true. Once he had been the beneficiary of a trust fund. Set up for his education. So he wouldn't have to consider waiting tables at a hotel and casino. But the worthless piece of shit who stole the money his father died for had died himself not long after. Somewhere here in this very city. Drugged up in a hotel swimming pool. Matt wondered if that hotel was this same one he was now standing in. Where his sister had worked. Where he had just imagined himself working.

He became aware that Meredith was yammering at him. Something someone had said about something. Matt had missed what that was and tried to infer it from her prattle but that was fruitless. He tuned her out again when his thoughts jumped to a moment he shared with her back in Sackets Harbor.

When she told him about the life she had planned. How as an attorney she would crusade for good and save the world. Help the poor and the animals. Babies and puppies and rainbows. Now here she was looking like a high-dollar hooker in the gaudy lobby of a Vegas casino telling him that her career would be protecting money and therefore the people who have lots of it.

312

Matt wanted to remind Meredith of her former good intentions. But there was absolutely no point. And he was tired. Interrupting her would require far too much effort. His eyes went to the doors. Maybe Cheryl would return and provide cover for his escape. But there was no sign of any sawed-off buxom bitches coming his way. He'd have to get out of this on his own. He let Meredith's torrent of words come pouring back in again hoping he could find a place to stop her—

"I'm doing this kick-ass internship? The best! In New York. Mega-prestigious firm. Where are you staying? We're here. At the Agropoli. Isn't Vegas fantastic? I love it!"

She stopped and stood beaming up at him. Matt debated which of those statements and questions he should respond to first. Meredith reached out that red-tipped finger again and tapped him on the chest.

"You look great!"

Matt smiled despite himself.

"Thanks."

Not wanting to be rude he added—

"So do you."

Meredith lit up. Her eyes sparkled. She pushed her chest out and looked down at her breasts. First one and then the other.

"I finally got boobs!"

She looked back up at Matt and her face radiated delight.

"Did you notice?"

Matt searched for a way to deflect that question. The devil on his shoulder told him to answer honestly and watch her clothes peel off. Which he could imagine happening right there in the lobby. That red dress slithering down to her feet and pooling on the gleaming marble.

Meredith poked him again. Her red claw stabbed his chest.

"So where are you staying? You should come up to my room! The view is fucking awesome!"

Part XVIII:
Vinnie the Butcher

Chapter 63

I let him wait. While that hydrocodone seeped into his veins. Two pills on an empty stomach. That would hit quick and have some impact.

He kept his mouth shut. He blinked and stared. Dead-eyed lizard mode.

Then his eyes slid closed. He took a deep breath. His head rolled to one side. His breathing slowed down.

And now he wanted to talk—

"So what're you going to do to me?"

"Nothing."

He opened his eyes and straightened his head. We stared at each other.

"Nothing," he repeated.

"That's right."

He frowned.

"Then what's going to happen?"

"We're going to get some help."

His eyes twitched.

"Help."

"Yes."

"What kind of help?"

"The kind that has some real enthusiasm for the task at hand. Unlike you I'm not a sick bastard who enjoys doing those kinds of things. The nasty stuff that should be done to you. And in this case, with you, I just feel that I don't have sufficient motivation. To get over my inherent distaste for that sort of thing. And really dish it out."

I smiled and showed my teeth.

"So I was thinking. Maybe I should tell the families of those boys you raped and murdered who you are. And where you can be found. Then I'll wrap

315

you in that chair with about three rolls of duct tape. And be on my merry way."

His eyes twitched. They went off to one side and drifted down in small jerking motions. Then came slanting back. When his eyes met mine I could almost see that scaly little lizard thing inside of him running furiously on its tiny tread wheel.

That lizard was thinking as fast it could.

He made an expression that I guess was intended to express indifference.

It only made him look constipated.

"Go ahead," he said. "Do it."

The lizard had gone where I predicted. In seeing how this could play out. Best case he could overpower me while I was busy with the duct tape. Or maybe I would do a lousy job and he could escape after I was gone. Meanwhile one or more of his victims' families would almost certainly contact the law. And instead of murderous revenge-seekers he would be found by Denver cops.

He might not remain free. But he could probably count on remaining alive.

After all he could afford a good attorney.

I gave him a few moments. To enjoy his high from the hydro. To believe he had dodged a bullet. That he wasn't going to suffer horribly and then die. That worst case he was probably only going to prison.

Then I explained why broadcasting his name and whereabouts to all of the families was off the table. How it was too likely one of them would go to the law. He already knew how I felt about getting the law involved. How it was too likely he would get away somehow. On a technicality or some bullshit.

He tried to hide his disappointment. But for a habitual criminal he was a terrible actor. You would think with all that practice he would have gotten better at it. But there was just that lizard inside there. Doing the best it could with its limited abilities.

When I told him there was a variation on telling the families that I felt had potential his hopes rallied again. It showed in his eyes.

How could he possibly think this might be good news?

I tapped my spacebar. We saw a photograph of a man crossing a parking lot. A bullet-headed bruiser. Beefy and powerful. Wearing sunglasses and a black bowling shirt. Caught mid-stride looking angry and determined.

"Do you recognize this gentleman?" I said.

Sorenson shook his head.

"His name is Vincenzo Galuzzo," I said. "Does that name mean anything to you?"

He shook his head again.

"Vinnie the Butcher," I said. "Made man in the Genovese crime family. One conviction for assault. Charged with murder but the key witness recanted just before the trial. And also the uncle of..."

I tapped the spacebar. We returned to the map with the red dots and the names beside them. But now one of those names and dots and a blue oval around it.

"Kenny Landrieu," I said. "Of Saint Louis, Missouri. To be precise, the suburb of Kirkwood."

Another tap on the spacebar. Now we saw a portrait of a smiling boy. He was a little bucktoothed and had pronounced dimples.

"A cute kid. The neighbors said he was a sweet boy. Never caused any trouble. Helped the elderly woman who lived across the street with her groceries. Walked her dog too."

Sorenson stared at the television. His face was pale.

"Not only was Vinnie the Butcher this kid's uncle," I said. "But also his godfather."

Sorenson frowned at me.

"What?" he said.

"I don't mean in the Mafia. I mean his godfather in the Catholic Church."

Sorenson stared at me. I still wasn't sure if he understood what I meant.

I decided I didn't care.

❖   ❖   ❖

I hit the spacebar again. A video clip began. The bullet-headed man sat at a metal table in a bare room. The camera faced him at an angle. He glowered at someone or something. He gestured in the direction he was facing.

"Yuh wanna know wud I'd do? If I cawt dat bastid?"

He put his hand down the table.

"I tell yuh wud I'd do. I'd staht wid his han's. Toot'picks an' sewin' needles unda da nailz. Each an' eve'y one a dem. When he can't feel dat no moah I'd smash da enda each finguh. Crush dat bone. When dat pain woah off I'd break da bones below da fust knuckle. Den below da secon' knuckle. Den I'd smash da knuckles demselves. Den I'd break each a da bones in his palms. Den take a hammuh to wus left. I like a dawg-head hammuh fuh dat. Crack up his wrists while I'm addit. Dem liddle bones in dere. His hands'd be moosh. Let 'im live wid dat. F'maybe a day. Den cut his hands off. Wid a bone saw. Real Civil War shit. So he's got dese rough bloody stumps. Fust yuh salt da stumps. Den cawderize 'em. But do it slow. A liddle bit adda time."

The man canted his head to one side.

"An' dats just 'is hands. We still got all da rest a him."

He gestured like he did before, in the direction he was facing.

"I won't go inta alla it. We could be here fuh hours wid me spellin' it out. But yuh can bet he'd git it up da ass. Wid a cattle prod. Nice jolt a juice up in dere. Wait a few minutes. Do it again. Fer a day.

318

Maybe longer. If yuh got time. An' da final touch. Dat's impo'tant. Slice his belly open an' let 'im watch his own guts spill out."

He nodded once.

"I like dat touch. Den fer da end I like strang'lation. Dat way he really knows he's dyin'. When he feels his breat' cut off."

The bullet-headed man fell silent. He looked thoughtful. Then he grinned.

"So dere yuh go," he said. "Dat's wud I'd do."

I tapped the spacebar again. The video stopped with the bullet-headed man still grinning.

"Would you like to guess who he's talking about?" I said. "Who the bastard is that Vinnie the Butcher wants to torture and strangle?"

Sorenson stared and said nothing.

"No?" I said.

He scowled at me. I tapped the spacebar.

The video resumed playing.

The bullet-headed man grinned for a few seconds. Then he glowered.

"I can't buh-lieve creeps like dat even exist. Dat one who took my nephew? My godson? How can God let dat happen? I don't geddit. I'd like some priest explain dat shit tuh me."

He shook his head. His glower cut deeper into his features.

"An' when it's all done? An' he's dead? Den I wish I could bring dat bastid back tuh life. So I could do it all ovuh again. Maybe about ten times. Before I'd get sicka dat shit."

We watched the bullet-headed man glower for another five seconds or so. Then the video stopped and the screen went black.

"Mr. Galuzzo lives in Las Vegas," I said. "He owns a restaurant. You can find him there every Friday night. Should we give him a call? He could hop on a plane. Rent a car. Be here in a few hours. Make you suffer horribly in all the ways you heard him mention. And in many other ways he didn't. Maybe he would stay here and work you over for all of those sixteen days before anyone would miss you. He could even bring some help. He has a number of colleagues who are very skilled at that sort of thing. Not that he would need any help. He's one of the best himself. At that kind of work. Which, as you may have guessed, is why they call him Vinnie the Butcher."

I paused.

"We could try the number at his restaurant. Casa di Palermo. He might be working the front desk. Greeting his customers. Or back in the kitchen. He enjoys cooking."

I paused again.

"But just in case he isn't there, which happens from time to time, if business calls him away—like the business we have here—it would probably be best to call his cell phone."

I paused a third time.

"I have the number on speed dial. Should I ring him up? He knows to expect a call."

This time I allowed more than a pause. I waited for Sorenson to break the silence. Which did eventually happen. He sighed before he said—

"Do I have a choice?"

I feigned consideration of his query. I frowned at Sorenson long and hard until he finally flinched and turned away.

Only then did I respond.

"You want to know if there is another option."

He turned back to me. His eyes went over my face, then to the television, then back to me again. Finally his eyes went down to his Colt in my hand and back up to my face. He nodded.

"Yes," he said. "Another option."

I repeated my long hard frown. Sorenson turned away again.

"There is," I said.

His eyes came back to mine. I pointed both my gaze and the Colt at the end table beside him.

"It's under that cloth," I said.

Chapter 64

Sorenson looked where I indicated. For a long time. As if he was afraid what was under the cloth might bite him. Then he carefully removed the dishrag I had found in his kitchen and draped over one of his soup bowls. Inside the bowl was the rest of his Vicodin. He stared at the pile of white pills. Which were set off brilliantly against the chromium blue of the shallow bowl. His eyes remained fixed on the bowl of pills the entire time that we were both silent. And only left the beckoning drugs as he said—

"What if I won't do it?"

His eyes went wandering around the room. I waited until they found their way to me. Then I smiled at him. I didn't want to waste that smile while he was looking somewhere else.

"Is there any need to ask?" I said.

I waved his pistol at the television.

"After what you have seen?"

Then I pointed it at his broken wrist.

"Do you remember how badly that hurt?"

"Of course."

"Well I can assure you that was nothing. From personal experience. When they put on the cast, did you experience great relief?"

He frowned. A moment later he nodded.

I shook my head.

"With Mr. Galuzzo there will be no relief. Not even for a moment. Only different levels of extreme misery. Your torment will go on long after you have come to wish for death. You will beg him to kill you."

Sorenson's eyes returned to the television. He frowned at the black screen.

"Why don't you just shoot me?"

"Would you really prefer that?"

His eyes went from the television to the gun in my hand. A moment later they went to the pills in the bowl. Finally they returned to the television and remained there while I spoke.

"I am trying to be humane. A lethal dose of drugs has been deemed the most civilized way to commit an execution. Which is why it has replaced electrocution, the gas chamber, hanging—"

With my free hand I gestured at the Colt.

"The firing squad."

Sorenson stared at the pistol. Then his eyes came up to mine before they turned away.

"I didn't do anything," he said. "To those boys."

I sighed and shook my head.

"Really, Mr. Sorenson. This won't do. One way or another you will soon enter your final moments."

He looked at me. I nodded at him.

"Do you really want to lie so grievously at a time like this?"

He turned pale. I gestured with the gun.

"Is that how you want to meet your God?"

Sorenson slowly turned ashen. His mouth came open. His breathing became heavy.

I pointed the pistol at the pain killers.

"The pills, Mr. Sorenson."

His eyes cut over to the bowl of Vicodin and back to the black television.

"The pills," I said again.

❖   ❖   ❖

He closed his mouth and clenched his jaw. Now each breath rasped in and out through his nose. For a full minute or more he did not vary his position or engage in any actions other than his labored respiration. Finally his nostrils flared as he inhaled deeply. He held his breath for a few seconds. Then he opened his mouth and let all his air escape.

Only then did his eyes return to the pills. His good hand came snaking out and went to the bowl. When he turned his hand over two pills were in the palm. He stared at them. Then his hand went to his open mouth. When his hand came down it went to the waiting glass of water.

I watched his Adam's apple jerk up and down as he swallowed.

"Next time let me see them on your tongue," I said.

He glared at me. Then repeated his motions only altering them to honor my request, then repeated them again twice more. Including the two he took when he first sat down, if all the pills had actually been swallowed, he now had ten of them in his system.

After his last swallow Sorenson sighed and closed his eyes. I gave him a moment with his thoughts. Then I said—

"Perhaps you have considered doing this on your own."

His eyes came open and he glared at me. He kept glaring while he swallowed another ten pills. When he paused at the twenty mark he said—

"I'll need more water."

I gestured at another cloth-draped something waiting on the end table. His good hand removed the cloth revealing another three full glasses.

"I guess you thought of everything."

"I have endeavored to."

When he looked up at me I pointed the pistol at yet another cloth. This one lay flat across the end table. He lifted the cloth and beneath it waited a fresh pad of lined white paper and a brand new blue ballpoint pen. The pen rolled a little across the table when the rising cloth disturbed it.

His eyes came back to mine.

"What's that for?" he said.

"Do I really have to tell you?"

His attention returned to the paper and pen.

"Think of the families," I said. "You could bring them some measure of peace."

I paused.

324

"This is the best thing you can do with your remaining time."

Sorenson did not look at me. His eyes went from the paper and pen back to the television.

Then he took another ten pills. Which made thirty. And paused again at this next milestone.

❖　　❖　　❖

His eyes went out of focus. He let them slide shut. Then forced them back open. Another ten pills went down his throat. He paused for a few moments. Then the remainder of the pills followed without interruption.

"Your confession," I said. "While you still can."

His voice was a little slurred when he responded—

"I have my own family to think of."

I didn't know what to make of that. I knew he had never married. As best I was aware he had no children. I wondered if I heard him correctly.

"What did you say?" I asked.

He did not answer. A moment later his eyes returned to the paper and pen. I thought it best to not delay my only instructions—

"And of course you should leave me out of it. Or I will only have to destroy it."

IIe looked at me. IIis head wobbled.

"What?"

"Don't mention me. In your confession."

"IIow could I?"

Now I was confused.

"What?" I said.

His eyes closed heavily. And slowly reopened.

"I don't know your name," he said.

I needed a moment to comprehend this. Then my fury took me suddenly and by complete surprise. At first I didn't know why I now wanted to pull the trigger of his Colt. Maybe after smashing the heavy pistol against his broken wrist. Then I sorted out my feelings and understood that my anger came from having gone to prison for a crime this man had committed and he had not even bothered to memorize my name. Not the false name under which I was convicted. Or the real one under which I was set free.

I tried to frame my words for informing him of this. But he spoke first—

"I thought you were Mexican," he said.

I licked my lips and swallowed.

"Is that what you heard?"

"You don't sound Mexican."

"Don't I?"

"No."

"How do I sound then?"

"You sound Spanish."

This unexpected comment left me momentarily silenced. I licked my lips again before I replied—

"Really," I said.

His wobbling head nodded.

"I knew some Spanish guys. Back when I was a missionary."

He raised his good hand and pointed at me unsteadily.

"You sound like them."

This odd little exchange affected me greatly. I should have dismissed it as the ramblings of a drugged man and a doomed soul. And felt pity for him at how he wasted his final moments. When a confession would have done so much more for his peace of mind. Not to mention any prospects he might have had in the hereafter. If inside of him still lingered some fragment of a religious man.

But instead what I felt was outrageously flattered. By the same individual in the previous instance I had strongly wanted to murder outright. Whom I had laboriously persuaded to overdose on pain killers. My heart pounded and I felt light-headed. I seriously considered that maybe this man before me had some worth after all. Just because by the workings of inexplicable chance he had offered a small offhanded remark that made me feel complimented by feeding my ridiculous enthusiasm for all things Spanish. Perhaps if he had said I looked Spanish too I might have repented on the spot. And tried to save the life I had worked so hard to bring to its end.

But he did not. In fact Sorenson never spoke another word. His eyes were soon closed and would forever remain so.

And I quickly remembered who he was. And what he had done. And what he was planning to do again. And to do soon.

Most likely to that boy I had watched romp with his dog.

Chapter 65

While I waited for his death something he said came back and nagged at me. You may recall that Sorenson claimed he had his "own family to think of" when he refused to write that confession. Which was as close as he came to admitting his guilt.

I was puzzled by that. To the best of my knowledge he never married and did not have children. I realized as he was slipping down toward death that the family he referred to must be the one who disowned him when he was exiled by the Mormon Church. His parents were still alive. He had numerous siblings and nephews and nieces. A small army of aunts and uncles and cousins. Apparently he wanted to protect them from the stigma of being related to a man who admitted raping and murdering boys.

The disowning seemed complete. I saw no evidence his family played any current role in his life. Nothing indicating any interaction between them turned up when I searched his house. In his peregrinations he never returned to Salt Lake City. Where he was born and his family continued to live.

But when facing death he protected them. He chose the welfare of his own family over the welfare of his victim's families.

So even with a monster, blood can be thicker than water.

Not having that confession was a bitter disappointment. I very much wanted to offer what little peace might come with it to the families of his victims. I could have tried to beat it out of him. But I just wasn't capable of that.

You may wonder why I didn't simply call Vinnie the Butcher. And have him extract that confession. A task he would have savored.

But maybe you already suspect the truth about our vicious restaurateur.

Vincenzo Galuzzo was a fabrication. He was portrayed in the photograph and video by Salvatore Romano. A mild-mannered embezzler that I knew from Salazar's woodshop in the prison. Salvatore was paroled a few years before I was released. And died a few years after he did me that favor. A massive heart attack sitting poolside in his uncle's backyard on Long Island. Another named added to the column titled "Good" in the great balance sheet of souls who have departed.

But he was a criminal you say. An embezzler. Which is only a fancy kind of thief. And all that is true. But Salvatore Romano only became a thief when he realized the health insurance company he worked for was routinely denying its customers the coverage they had paid for. And that people were dying as a result. The money he stole went to charities that helped the very kinds of sick people that his employers would let die. When he was caught the authorities recovered only twenty-seven thousand of the thirteen million he had siphoned away.

So to me Salvatore Romano is a true American hero.

When I changed my plans to take advantage of Sorenson's injury my friend was only too glad to email me the materials I requested.

He even called to urge me on.

"You get that bastard," Salvatore said to me.

As Vinnie the Butcher he would have said that with a growl. As himself he made those words sound almost forgiving.

But now at least I had done that much.

I had got the bastard.

❖   ❖   ❖

He looked terrible. Sallow and waxy. I wondered again if he had been ill. And if that contributed to his decision to take the pills. Since death was already coming for him.

I remained with his corpse for an hour after the pulse oximeter I attached to his fingertip told me his heart had stopped beating. Just to be certain he was gone. By then his flesh was notably cool.

So was the sad house. The thermostat for the oil burner down in the shallow basement was on a timer and had turned back for the night. Making the old pile start to creak and groan as it contracted. Which my jangled nerves found jarringly difficult to endure. Silence would have been a blessing.

I left dressed as a woman. Wearing a full-length overcoat and a long brunette wig. Now pulling that black roller bag behind me on its little wheels. So even the bag appeared to be different.

In an alleyway near where I had parked there was an abandoned building where I changed back into my workman's uniform. This was for the benefit of the security cameras mounted in the parking garage where I left my car. I did not want them to record the same car exiting with a woman behind the wheel. Meanwhile I had hopefully covered my trail, if anyone was watching, by going into and out of Sorenson's house in two different disguises.

Which was probably an unnecessary ruse. But an easy enough one.

Best to make your trail as cold as you can.

I was making my way out of Denver when the rain began. It turned to snow a few hours later. Then fell on and off for the next two weeks. Ending in a blizzard over the weekend before New Faith Holy Gospel was reopened. Two feet of snow entombed Sorenson in his decrepit house.

I could have seen this weather as more evidence of God's handiwork.

If I was so inclined.

His employers were surprised not to see him Monday morning. He usually braved any weather. When he didn't appear again on Tuesday someone gave him a call. They left a message and were surprised again when Wednesday rolled around and there still wasn't any sign of him.

But no one bothered to go see if he was all right.

When he hadn't appeared by the start of the next week they assumed he had moved on. That he was a drifter who had drifted away again. As the kinds of men who might work as janitors have been known to do. The church hired an older Spanish man to take his place. To mop the floors and scrub the bathrooms and change the light bulbs.

The Florida landlord of the sad house did not miss the rent check for the first two months. She was away at the time and busy with other matters. She called and added to the messages that went unanswered. When a third month passed without a check she wondered if something had gone wrong. And called the Denver police.

A patrol car was sent to that sad house in that rundown neighborhood.

The Office of the Medical Examiner concluded the death was a suicide.

The remains of Kirtland Fenimore Sorenson were shipped to Salt Lake City.

He was buried in the same cemetery as his ancestors. But was denied a place in the family plot. His grave stands in a long row of others who died without acknowledged kinship. In a solitary state of being.

Alone in life they remain alone in death.

Part XIX:
Be Careful With Him

Chapter 66

The last thing Esperanza could remember was being disappointed with the garlic at the supermarket. While simultaneously worrying about Rosa. They had spent most of the day at the hospital for more tests. Then stopped for groceries on the way home. Between then and now was blank. A sense of time passed but left empty.

She closed her eyes and tried to think. Nothing more came to her.

Maybe she should go back to sleep. Time might fix itself if she left it alone.

Sleep would not return. Her mind wanted answers.

She opened her eyes again. This time she forced them into focus. And saw she wasn't in her room. The ceilings at home were white plaster and brown vigas. This one above her now was white textured rectangles in a metal grid. An institutional drop ceiling. Complete with obligatory brown water stain in the corner of one panel. Like spilled tea.

An electronic chime dinged in another room.

A woman's voice came over an intercom.

She flexed her hand and found an IV in her arm.

She stared at the plastic fixture attached to the needle piercing her flesh.

Motion drew her eyes away. Someone was rising from a chair beside her bed. The young deputy who drove her home from the city. He drifted away out of the room. She wanted to ask what was going on. But she couldn't make her voice work.

The woman's voice came over the intercom again. It was still just sound. Esperanza couldn't understand what the woman said.

Her uncle appeared. He stood beside the bed looking down at her.

"How are you feeling?" Josef said.

They were interrupted by a nurse. She bustled into the room and bent over a machine beside the bed. Esperanza hadn't noticed the wires connecting her to this machine. She studied them while the nurse bustled back out again. When the nurse was gone Esperanza turned to her uncle. She thought her voice might not work again. She was trying to remember how to form words when they came out of her—

"What happened?"

Her uncle took the seat the deputy had vacated. He sighed while he settled his bulk into the chair.

"There was an accident," Josef said.

Her mind jumped. She went past the supermarket and the sad garlic back to her anger at the kitchen table. Leslie Davidson was seated across from her. Esperanza frowned and shook her head.

The nurse returned with a cup of ice water. A doctor followed right after her. He used a pencil light to examine Esperanza's eyes. When he was done he moved to the foot of the bed and made notes on her chart. He exchanged medical jargon with the nurse. They left together.

Esperanza took a sip of the water the nurse brought for her.

"I heard something," she said. "About an investigation."

Her eyes cut to the door and back again. She lowered her voice.

"Against you, Tío. By the Justice Department."

Her uncle frowned at her.

"We talked about that," Josef said.

333

Esperanza didn't hear him. Her thoughts had returned to the kitchen. Where Leslie was still stubbornly present.

"You called me," Josef said. "Do you remember?"

She looked at her uncle.

"Right after your friend told you," Josef said.

"She's not my friend."

She shook her head. Leslie disappeared.

"You said there was an accident."

"Yes."

"Was I driving?"

"Yes."

She wanted to ask. She didn't remember asking. Her voice hadn't reached her ears. But she must have asked. Because her uncle answered her question—

"Rosa is still unconscious."

Unconscious. Not dead.

She felt like she was floating.

"The investigation," she said. "Against you."

Josef shook his head.

"Don't worry about it. You just get better."

"Did you know about that?"

He nodded.

"Forget it. Nothing to worry about."

"Tell me what you know."

Josef sighed at his niece.

"You wake up after a car crash and this is the first thing on your mind?"

Esperanza frowned.

"She's unconscious?"

"Yes."

"So was I."

"That's true. And now you're awake."

"How is she?"

"They don't know yet."

Her head felt warm.

"When have they ever known."

"What?"

"They never know how she is."

Her uncle nodded.

"That's true. Very true."

"Tell me what you know."

Josef frowned.

"Maybe you should rest, mija. You seem confused."

"Tell me."

He raised his hands.

"I just told you. They don't know yet. She's still unconscious."

"About the investigation."

His hands came down and his eyebrows went up.

"Okay then. Since you won't let it go. The feds are always looking for someone to push around. Make into an example. This time they think it's me."

"You're not worried?"

"Why should I be? I've done nothing wrong. Anything they could find would be some minor technicality. Small potatoes. Not worth worrying about. Not worth them even charging me."

Josef made a mountainous shrug. A slow heavy gesture worthy of Ajax that proved beyond words how well he could bear the vast weight this world bore down upon his shoulders.

"What can I do. It comes with the job. A man has to take his lumps now and then. The trick is to keep up on your feet. And no one is going to knock me down anytime soon. You can be sure of that."

What her uncle said and how he said it and his presence seated beside her were reassuring beyond all human measure. Her concerns on his behalf were utterly obliterated. She felt foolish for having suspected anyone could harm her invincible Tío. He stood as a giant among men. A Titan among dwarves.

"When can I see Rosa?"

"As soon are you're up and about."

"I can do that now."

She tried to sit up.

Instead she fell asleep.

❖   ❖   ❖

She woke up again and her uncle was still there. Or maybe he had left and come back again. She looked for clues. She didn't find any. Her uncle looked the same. She saw the deputy out in the hallway and he looked the same. The room was too strange for it to ever look the same. She looked at the needle in her arm. That was far too weird. She hated it being there.

"How long was I asleep?"

"Maybe an hour."

"I thought maybe it was days or something."

"That's probably the drugs."

"I guess it must be."

"I heard from the doctors. Rosa is stable. They like that."

Esperanza took a deep breath.

"Okay. Good."

"Yes."

She found her water on the tray beside her bed. She lifted the cup and emptied it. The ice had all melted. She returned the cup to the tray and watched droplets slide down inside the clear plastic. Running into each other. Merging together. Gaining weight and momentum.

Josef cleared his throat. She kept her eyes on the cup and the droplets.

"I was thinking about that friend of yours," Josef said.

"She's not my friend."

"The professor."

"I know who you mean."

"You know she goes with women."

Esperanza jerked her head around. Pain flared in her neck.

"You looked into her."

"To protect you."

"From what?"

336

"I didn't know. I had a hunch. Did she hit on you?"

Esperanza look away.

"You could press charges," Josef said.

Esperanza remembered telling Leslie she wouldn't.

"That's a crime," Josef said. "She shouldn't get away with it."

Esperanza knew exactly how that would go. There was no proof of what happened. No witnesses. No evidence. Just her word against Leslie's. And Leslie would be an enormous idiot to admit what she had done. That would ruin her life. Just having Esperanza say she had done it could wreck her life bad enough. She might lose her job over it.

Esperanza did not want to ruin Leslie's life. And she did not want to tell what had happened to a bunch of strangers. Men watching her and listening to the sex stuff. That would be disgusting.

She said her piece at the kitchen table. She was done with that mess.

But her uncle wasn't. He cleared his throat again.

"Don't you see what this is about, Essie?"

Esperanza put her eyes back on the plastic cup. She watched a droplet slide down. Clean and straight. No others in the way.

Esperanza wanted to be a clean solitary droplet.

"She's trying to turn you against me," Josef said.

A clean solitary droplet with a clear straight path.

"And not just me," Josef said. "Against men in general."

Esperanza closed her eyes. Her uncle's voice floated at her—

"That's how they work, mija. The gays. They try to turn you against the natural order of things."

❖　　❖　　❖

The hallway was empty. The silence and stillness told her it was late. The last thing she remembered was thanking the nurse who brought her a pill.

She looked down at her bare feet. The floor was cold beneath them. Square white linoleum tiles.

She looked behind her and wondered how far she had gone. If she was just outside her room or halfway across the hospital.

Then she knew why she was out of bed. The feeling that got her up on her feet almost knocked her back down.

She found the elevators just past the nurses' station. The desk there was empty. No one to tell her to get back into bed.

Up or down? She punched down. Machines whirred behind the metal doors. The doors slid open and she stepped inside and punched the button for the ground floor.

The doors slid shut and the car dropped. Air moved against her back. Her gown was open. She reached around to tie it and something stabbed into her arm. She looked down at the IV needle. No tubing. She must have pulled that out back in her room.

She knotted her gown. The car stopped and the doors slid open. A sign on the wall pointed to Intensive Care. She jogged along the hallways. Scanning for obstacles. People who worked here that might try to stop her.

An alarm sounded. She ran toward it. Around a corner she almost collided into a nurse barreling out of a doorway. A doctor charged toward them from the opposite direction.

The treatment rooms had windows onto the hallways. Esperanza stopped before the window of the room where the alarm blared. The knot she tied in the elevator was pulled loose when she ran. It came undone. Her back was naked while she watched the doctors and nurses scramble. They ignored her. Too focused on the patient that the machines told them could soon be dead.

An orderly came past rolling a mop bucket. An older black man who had become accustomed to finding unsettling things in the white halls and rooms in the middle of the night. He stopped beside the young woman standing in the hallway when he saw the next mess he would have to clean up.

"Miss," he said. "I think you best come with me."

He was a big man. She looked up at him. She did not resist when he bent down and lifted her up. As he carried her away she looked over his shoulder and saw a pool of blood on the floor.

Chapter 67

Running along the hallways tore the stitches out of a deep wound in her right thigh. Tore it open and made it worse. The surgeon who went in there to fix it was surprised she remained upright. He stitched it closed again and they replaced the blood she had lost for a second time. Then kept an eye on her for a few hours before they sent her back upstairs.

She was discharged three days later than initially planned. Because of the reopened wound and the second transfusion. And because of the behavior that made those things happen. Her attending physician ordered her held for psychiatric observation.

She went directly from the hospital to the funeral. There was no time to stop at home and do anything to make herself appear normal. Roberto came to get her and took charge of her. He muscled her wheelchair up and down the steps of the village church and across the uneven ground of the graveyard. He remained at her side until the time came for him to help bury his mother.

The grave was dug the old way. By hand. With one shovel. Passed between the men of the family. Now they took their turns putting the dirt back in.

Josef stood with a group of men a short distance from the grave. When his turn came he was called over and handed the shovel. He worked for a few minutes then handed the shovel off again.

Esperanza watched her uncle return to the men who waited for him. All of them men of significance in Doña Pero. A judge and a businessman and two county commissioners. The village mayor and a state senator. She wished that for just this one day there could be no power and politics in the lives of the Armijos. And felt dread at knowing how soon she would be sucked back into that vortex. Maybe she would be tossed around by it even harder than before. Without Rosa around to share that jarring ride.

She closed her eyes and listened to the shovel do its work. Cutting into the pile of earth. Then the earth hissing off on its way into the grave.

❖   ❖   ❖

She became aware of someone approaching. Maybe she heard footsteps. Now this person was standing beside her. She told her eyes they might want to open. Her eyes chose not to. A hand settled on her shoulder. An instant later she startled.

The hand disappeared.

Then the voice of the old village priest—

"How are you, my child."

She looked up into his face. She saw a man who worked hard at being kind. Because that was his job but it was not his nature. She told herself she was being cruel in her grief.

"Do I still look like a child to you, Father?"

"No, Esperanza. You are certainly a woman."

"And yet you call me your child."

The priest smiled. His eyes looked displeased.

"A figure of speech. Meant as an endearment."

"All of the people who could really call me their child are gone. My parents died when I was so young I can't remember them."

"That was a terrible thing."

Esperanza gestured toward the men taking turns with the shovel.

"And now my Tía. Who had the right to call me her child if anyone did."

"Don't forget your uncle. You still have him."

"I could never forget my uncle. But my uncle forgets me. Until he thinks of some way I can be useful to him."

"Words spoken in pain. You will regret them."

"No I won't. Because it's the truth. My uncle is a selfish man."

"A position of power can make one preoccupied."

"What about before?"

"I'm sorry?"

"He was preoccupied before he became powerful."

She watched one of Josef's brothers hand the shovel to Roberto.

Then saw Rosa's face on that day at the hospital. When they went for more tests. The pain and suffering that had carved itself into her features.

"I want to believe this is an act of God."

"An act of divine mercy."

"Yes."

"Do you feel responsible?"

"I do."

The priest's hand returned to her shoulder. She didn't want it there.

"You are not at fault," the priest said. "The man who hit you. He's the one who needs forgiveness."

"I want to believe that God made it happen. To spare Rosa. That the man who hit us isn't anymore to blame than I am."

"You want to forgive him."

"No. I want him to be blameless."

"A very different thing."

"Yes."

"That only God can know."

"I hate that."

The priest removed his hand.

"God's ways are mysterious."

"If he's to blame then I am too. Because maybe I could have done something. I should have seen him coming."

"He was clearly at fault. There was nothing you could do."

"There's always something you can do."

"You mustn't torture yourself."

She looked up at the old man.

"What else can I do? Stuck in this chair. The stupid drugs."

She returned to watching the men shovel.

"I can't focus. Thoughts come at me and I can't do anything."

The hand returned.

She wanted to bite it.

❖   ❖   ❖

Josef was taking another turn with the shovel when Esperanza remembered seeing the pool of blood on the hallway floor. When the orderly lifted her up. She had forgotten the blood until this moment. Another moment passed before she realized the blood came from her. She felt feverish while she tried not to wish more blood had followed. Enough blood flowing out of her to take her with it.

She wanted to tell this to the old priest. That she was fighting against a desire for death to take her. But she turned and he wasn't there. Instead he was approaching the men around the grave. He spoke with them and shook their hands and then moved on to the group waiting for Josef. He did the same with them and then he left. She watched his stooped back as he receded across the graveyard.

She turned back to the grave and watched Josef hand off the shovel again. He said something to one of his brothers. Then returned to his colleagues. Watching her uncle hold court at the grave of his dead wife Esperanza could see what was ahead. As clearly as if it had already happened.

With Rosa gone her uncle would need someone to keep his house. And the someone he would turn to would be her. As soon as she was on her feet again he would want her to clean and cook and pay the bills and make sure the house didn't fall down. Maybe eventually he would get around to finding another wife. But until then he would want her to do all of that.

What else could she do? She was completely dependent on her uncle. If he wanted her to keep his house how could she refuse?

Going back to college wasn't an option. At least not anytime soon. The full scholarship that took her there was gone. When Rosa became ill Esperanza surrendered her financial aid. They warned her that once you left the track that made the money flow, getting it to flow again wasn't easy. That didn't seem to matter at the time. All that mattered then was Rosa.

And back at school there would be Leslie to contend with. Who by fate's perverse hand was the one person who had offered her a way out. A place to live other than with her uncle. Imagining herself invoking that overture made her cackle. She sounded like a heckling crow. Heads turned. Faces frowned. Her laughter died and her cheeks burned.

She watched her uncle talk and his cohorts listen. And wondered if he was right about Leslie. That she told Esperanza about the investigation to make her think badly of her uncle. To turn her against him. He was smart that way. Seeing why people did things. Figuring out their dark motivations.

But maybe that was because it took a manipulator to know one. She watched her uncle and wondered what sides of him had been hidden from her. Or she had refused to see. She knew those were the sides that made Rosa argue with her husband. And now with Rosa gone maybe she would have to see those sides. She didn't want to.

And then Esperanza hated herself for not choosing sides. For letting Rosa battle Josef alone. Every time she saw them fight it was always Josef who was in the wrong. She should have said so. Her Tía was the one who cared for her. Who had earned her allegiance. She should have been more loyal. Instead of remaining studiously neutral. Giving her uncle deference he didn't deserve. Just so she could hold onto their runt end of a relationship.

Her feet were swinging up off the floor. The orderly was lifting her into the air. She was safe in his strong arms.

She was stuck in this damned chair. Watching the blood pooling around her.

Furious with herself for wanting to be rescued.

Chapter 68

Her uncle hired a woman from Juárez to clean the house. She appeared once a week and tuned in a station from across the border then sang along while she scrubbed and scoured. She gave it her all with the sad love songs. Esperanza wondered if her uncle paid extra for this. Because if anything might get her back on her feet faster that would do it.

The daily chores were handled by the women of the family with help from a few neighbors. The cooking and shopping and light cleaning and taking care of the invalid. Esperanza tried to be a good patient but was too irritable. Everyone accepted her bad temper and that irritated her more.

Before the accident she was the caregiver. Now she had to tolerate being the patient. That role reversal was a constant discomfort. It served as a daily reminder that the accident had spared her from caring for Rosa when death became inevitable. She was glad to no longer be facing that future torture. And felt guilty for her relief. Another layer of guilt among the many piled one atop another.

In those rare moments when she attempted to be positive Esperanza tried to convince herself that her aunt had been spared from unnecessary suffering. That her death was coming anyway and her remaining days were all bad ones. It was valid to suggest that Rosa could be better off. Her condition had steadily deteriorated. All of her recent tests had been bad news. None of the treatments helped. The only therapy that could claim any success were the painkillers that left her benumbed. Making her final days a blur. Moments endured but not lived.

Much like many of the moments Esperanza experienced now. Days were lost staring at the television. Nothing that happened on the box got past her ears or her eyeballs. If anyone had asked her what was going on in any of the shows that she watched she would have been unable to tell them.

❖   ❖   ❖

Eventually crutches appeared and the wheelchair was pushed into a corner. Esperanza noted that now she had sufficient mobility to properly kill herself. She could crutch into her uncle's bedroom—all his now with Rosa gone—and find one of his pistols before she became too tired to keep looking.

She had sold her own gun when she went off to college. A cousin had an eye on it and made her an offer. If she hadn't said yes she might have already blown her brains out.

But she didn't go looking for a gun. Instead she got to work. Doing what she could around the house. She was in the kitchen at the sink washing dishes when her mind finally climbed up out of the despairing rut it had slogged through since the funeral.

And picked up a few steps before where it left off. When she was wondering if her uncle was right about Leslie trying to drive a wedge between them. Now she turned that thought on its head. And wondered if her uncle was trying to push her away from Leslie. Always like the schemers and scammers to accuse others of their own sins. Those being the sins they know best. If the devil is in the details then the details are how the devil reveals himself.

He had maybe gone too far with his "that's what the gays do." He had never before given a damn what the gays did. As long as they didn't do any of it to him she knew he could care less. So what he had said just didn't sit right. His suggestion that Leslie was trying to turn her against men.

If that idea had been put to him he would have been the first to say what people do is always personal. That the individual is not a political actor.

The bomber throws bombs because he likes throwing bombs. Not because he feels oppressed. Even if he does feel oppressed that isn't what makes his bomb-throwing arm itchy.

Maybe he thought she might learn the truth about him. Or some kind of truth anyway. Some part of the truth. If she stayed in contact with Leslie Davidson. Why else could he want to keep them apart?

Esperanza felt like she was seeing her uncle clearly for the first time. That she had finally stripped him of all the baggage she heaped on his head when she was a wounded child and needed someone to worship. When she had to build him up because her world had been torn down.

But she decided that feeling was probably just the drugs.

Slowly burning a big hole through her brain.

A week after she switched to crutches Esperanza woke up one morning and out of habit reached for her painkillers. Then looked down at the pill waiting in her hand and decided not to take it. By then she was making her own breakfast and lunch. And it was not the singing Juárezian's day to clean. Which meant she had the house to herself until dinner time. When someone would show up to feed her and Josef.

She spent the day thinking. There were other things she appeared to do. Personal hygiene. Light chores. Crutching around out in the yard. Tossing a stick for a neighbor's dog. But those things were not what she really did. All of the real action went on inside her head.

She thought and she dug into her thoughts and she remembered and she dug into her memories. The most important accomplishment of this was to recall a conversation she had with Rosa. How she labored at unearthing it. Slowly excavating it from the earth of her brain.

It was the end of a long day spent in the hospital. For another round of tests. Esperanza was driving Rosa home. When her aunt raised the subject no one wanted to discuss—

"After I am gone," Rosa said.

Essie couldn't hear it. Not at that moment. Traffic was bad and her nerves were shot. She knew at some point they had to discuss this. But she wanted to do it at home. When the house was quiet. Preferably in the fortress of the kitchen.

"Please Tía," she said. "You're going to be fine."

The lie burned in her throat and scalded her tongue.

"About Josef," Rosa said.

She paused.

"Be careful with him."

The oddness of those words enveloped Esperanza. For an instant she felt paralyzed by them. Then that instant had passed and now she wanted to rip open those words and grab at their meaning. She took her eyes down from the traffic light she had been staring at and turned to Rosa. Who sat peering straight ahead with her drawn face looking carved out of stone. Esperanza hesitated before she said—

"Do you mean I should take care of him?"

The truck behind them blasted its horn. Which sounded like the booming trumpet call of a great ship leaving harbor. Esperanza jumped in her seat. Her eyes went back up to the light and now a green arrow said they could go.

She stepped on the gas and they lurched forward into the intersection.

Esperanza needed a few days to be certain what happened immediately after. To accept why her memory went blank after she stepped on the gas. In those same few days she convinced herself that her hesitant and unconfirmed first interpretation of what her aunt meant was correct—

That Rosa's last wish had been for Esperanza to take care of Josef.

By the kind of coincidence that persistently shapes our star-crossed lives her uncle chose the end of those few days of intense contemplation, when her conclusions were freshly solidified and had their greatest possible influence on her thinking, to make his own wishes known. Now that her healing was almost done. When she was feeling just about back to normal.

And it was time to discuss what she would do next.

"I need you, Essie," her uncle said. "Right here at my side."

Fulfilling what Esperanza had foreseen at Rosa's graveside.

Like a key in its lock.

Fitting perfectly with what she now believed Rosa wanted.

Part XX:
Doña Pero Revisited

Chapter 69

On the slab of gleaming black marble was inscribed one of his treasured *refranes*. For his epitaph nothing else would possibly do. Here is what they carved into his tombstone—

Por la boca muere el pez

A phrase I found entirely incomprehensible. To make sense of these words I tried translating them. And spoke my attempt aloud—

"Through its mouth the fish dies."

My bewilderment remained. Only later would I come to know the meaning of this ancient phrase. When I found a wonderful book by the renowned linguist Rubén Cobos that anthologizes and translates the old Spanish sayings of the American Southwest. Here is what that good scholar had to say about the *refrane* quoted above—

> People who talk too much often give
> themselves away or put their foot in it.

It is foolish to argue with centuries of convention. But indulge me in doing so anyway. Why a fish? Which are silent. I would choose a bird. Preferably one that actually speaks. A parrot or a magpie. I guess because a fish gets caught on a hook in its mouth? But then it comes flopping up out of the water and dies without uttering a sound other then perhaps a muted gasping. So I just don't get it.

Later, when I learned how he met his end, I saw those words in a new light. And wondered if he chose them himself. In the long days when he worked at his death. In a slow-motion suicide of excessive drinking. Through his mouth this fish did indeed die. But not from talking too much. He cannot be accused of ever having been particularly garrulous. At least he never was in my presence. I certainly wish he had spoken more during my trial.

He was awaiting a trial of his own when he died. For a crime previously mentioned in our narrative. I will offer a hint by eliminating the obvious choice: his criminally negligent defense of your narrator. Not for that would they have put him in prison. Maybe a fine. Perhaps disbarment.

The charge instead was vehicular manslaughter.

He ran his old Cadillac through a red light while thoroughly inebriated. At far above the speed limit. Where it plowed into and completely demolished the sedan driven by Esperanza Armijo. Causing the extensive injuries that killed her good aunt Rosa.

❖ ❖ ❖

But of course I was there because of what he did to me. Offering such a worthless defense in my trial. By which I felt personally betrayed. Because on a personal level I liked old Bill. Even through that cloud of liquor he floated around in, I found him sympathetic. And consideration must be given to the fact that he was already a defeated man when I fell into his charge. And I doubt anyone else then employed by the Public Defender Department would have done any better. The deck was very heavily stacked against me. By all the power in Doña Pero County.

I don't think Bill was too lazy or too wasted or too apathetic to do the work needed to gain my freedom. I think he was bribed and/or threatened. Both seems most likely. Armijo would be the type to apply both the carrot and the stick. And having accepted the bribe would be another thing Bill could be threatened with. But I don't know why Bill did what he did and at this point there is no reason to find out. The cause is immaterial.

The research that set me free revealed that Bill spent the weekend when he claimed to have gone looking for my aunt in the drunk tank of a town halfway to where she lived. Apparently he began but failed to complete what he intended to do and claimed to have done. Because the drink overcame him on his way there. And I assume it was his fear of crossing all that power back in Doña Pero that made him crawl inside the bottle.

And in the end he let the drink overcome him for good.

In the end he surrendered to the drink and was gone.

When I was done visiting with Bill I found a pebble and placed it on his tombstone. Adding it to the row of others already waiting there. I did not at that moment know why I did this. Or why others had done it before me. It simply seemed like an appropriate way to honor the time he and I had spent together in this life.

I have learned since that this is considered a Jewish custom. And is practiced in the American Southwest by *conversos* and crypto-Jews. Whose ancestors hid their Jewishness to escape imprisonment, torture, and execution. Numerous explanations have been offered for the origins of this practice. But the source is irrelevant to our narrative. All that matters is its ethnic association. And therefore the suffering of the Jewish people.

I look back now at the sad specimen that was Bill Jameson and see him as the end product of persecution stretching across the centuries. His ancestors sent fleeing across the Atlantic to the New World by the horrors of the Spanish Inquisition. Only to flee again from the horrors of the later Mexican version. Pushing his people out to the very edges of the empire. Which was to them, at that time, the very end of the civilized world.

Do I know for certain that Bill Jameson was a crypto-Jew? Or descended from *conversos* with long-forgotten Jewish heritage? No. I do not. Short of approaching his relations to see if any of them would participate in DNA testing I will never be sure. But I choose to believe one or the other was true. Because placing him in that context I find it easier to forgive. To accept his sins against me as the result of innumerable sins committed long before he came squalling into this world. That struggling beneath the weight of all the evil that befell his ancestors the poor man stumbled and fell.

And Bill could very well have been a Jew. I don't know that he wasn't. How else to explain that line of pebbles atop his tombstone? And there was his persistent fatalism.

And after all he was a lawyer.

The afternoon light was stretching thin when I found the other grave. Hidden in a half-abandoned corner. I stumbled on it by chance after giving up and starting back to my car.

There was nothing grandiloquent carved into this tombstone. No cryptic *refrane* inscribed there to puzzle me. Just the deceased's name and the years in which he was born and died. Who unlike Bill was not someone I had ever met. And who therefore never had any chance to do me harm.

I was there because of the others he had injured. Most specifically Hermán and Adelita Armijo. The young parents of infant Esperanza. Killed when their car plummeted from that high mountain road. Knocked down into that stony gorge by "Halfbreed" Henry Pennycoat.

The man who laid buried at my feet.

For the record his gravestone omitted "Halfbreed".

And to be honest I did not go there to visit him.

I went there to meditate on the nature of my adversary.

Who had found a use for this dead man. A role to play in the myth of Sheriff Joe Armijo. Because every successful politician must have a myth. Armijo's portrayed him as a resolute defender of justice who was also kindhearted. Tough with the bad guys and tender with the innocents. A strong hand against the villains. A soft touch with his loved ones.

Henry Pennycoat helped create that myth. Always the opportunist, Armijo saw how to exploit his family's misfortune.

Not loudly and directly as he did with myself. Turning me into a Mexican bogeyman stalking the children of the borderlands. Whom he had single-handedly brought to justice. A broad swath of his myth that now lay in tatters. He would have to do some spinning and reweave his myth.

Instead Armijo maintained a wall of silence about his family's tragedy. His surrogates were the ones who did all of the talking. Who turned this family catastrophe into a cornerstone of his legend. Broadcasting his loss and how he had honored his family duties. Making sure every profile of Armijo, longer than a few sentences, mentioned that his brother and sister-in-law were killed by a drunk driver and that he had adopted his orphaned niece.

Who stood beside him in every campaign. And on occasion delivered a rip-roaring speech that made her uncle out as no less than a superman. Some even said she was the one who got him elected the first time.

I wanted to see the grave of the man who made that happen. Who set those events into motion. Get a look at where he wound up. Since that was part of where this whole thing began.

Two graves to visit upon my return to Doña Pero. Of the two drunks who crashed into the life of Esperanza Armijo. And took away those who loved her most dearly. The ones who birthed her. And the one who raised her.

I considered also visiting the grave of Rosa Armijo. Along with the graves of her in-laws Hermán and Adelita. But I felt to do so would be in poor taste. That I did not have the right to intrude on the Armijo family. Even the ones who were dead.

My quarrel was with the fat man. I would leave his family out of it.

As I walked away from the grave of Henry Pennycoat I thought of another burial place. One lost out in the backcountry. And the family tragedy that went with that one. I considered how this mess kept piling up dead people.

And how maybe if I wasn't careful I would become one of them.

Chapter 70

I was not alone in the graveyard. On that afternoon shortly following my return to Doña Pero, there was an old man wandering about. I caught him turning a few glances in my direction. And thought that perhaps he looked familiar. But his type was common enough in that part of the world to attain a certain anonymity. A man you notice but cannot place because you have seen too many who resemble him. And the aged are more frequently found visiting graveyards. Being more likely to pay their respects to the dead. Since they know so many more of them.

His presence could have seemed entirely natural.

But I suspected he was there watching me.

Which was one of the reasons why my thoughts turned to avoiding my own death. As I counted up all the dead already present in whatever this thing was that I found myself caught up in. Which started with my father's death and kept marching me past a long line of graves.

Later that night I realized who he was. When I was in bed unable to sleep.

Let me describe him to you. Maybe then you will remember him too.

He was tall and pot-bellied. His face was ruddy and cragged and he wore a gray shaggy mustache. And an old battered cowboy hat that had long ago been white. Snowy hair stuck out from beneath it.

Does this man from the cemetery sound at all familiar? Can you spot him in an earlier passage of our narrative? If so then you possess a most remarkable memory.

I was surprised by how little he had changed over the years. More belly to him. A little more sag to his shoulders. But still standing tall and upright.

Still an imposing figure.

❖　　❖　　❖

That imposing figure stood before me a few days later. In the produce section of my local supermarket. I had my head down and heard someone approach. When I looked up there he was.

He did not take me entirely by surprise. I had seen his truck follow me into the parking lot. The same truck I had seen every day since the cemetery. One time parked across the street from my new house.

"I can't let you kill him," the old man said.

Right down to business. I could respect that.

"Why? Do you have first dibs?"

The old man laughed. He reached up and pushed his hat back.

"He didn't put me in prison."

"No. He just stabbed you in the back and stole your job."

"That was a long time ago. If I wanted revenge I've had plenty of chances to take it. You're just getting yours."

"Maybe you've just been lazy. Now I show up and you think you better get moving."

He laughed again. Then shook his head.

"I'm not interested in revenge."

"Then what are you interested in? There must be some reason we're having this conversation. Just you me and the vegetables."

"I want justice. Don't you?"

"Suppose I did. Why should I discuss that with you?"

"I'm a professional."

"You *were* a professional."

"I've kept my oars in."

So this was a sales pitch. Okay. I'd hear what he was selling.

"Doing what exactly?"

358

"Private investigations."

"Are you licensed?"

"The people who hire me don't care about that. So no. Never got around to it."

"There you go being lazy again. Always putting off till tomorrow what should be done today. What are you hired to do?"

The old man frowned at me. I think I lost him when I called him lazy for a second time. Once was acceptable but twice rubbed him the wrong way. He was too busy being irritated to hear my question.

"Excuse me?"

"What kind of investigations do you specialize in? Since everyone is a specialist these days."

He tried to see my game. Whether he saw it or not, eventually he answered—

"Smuggling. Companies looking to plug a leaky border. Goods stolen on one side and sold on the other."

"They still do that?"

"You thought they stopped?"

"I thought NAFTA made us one big happy family."

The old man snorted.

"Not by a long shot."

"Good. I'm glad to hear that."

"I don't follow."

"You don't have to. But I like Mexico to stay where it is. How do I know you're not working for him?"

The old man took a moment to absorb that one. In the process some color came to his cheeks. Then he said quietly—

"When hell freezes over."

I liked that answer.

Maybe he wouldn't mind a little revenge after all.

❖   ❖   ❖

Clarence Eugene McElvy. The former Doña Pero County Sheriff. Elected to five terms before Josef Armijo unseated him. The man who hired Armijo and trained him and promoted him. The man Armijo repaid by running against him and taking his job.

The man who was Sheriff when I was framed.

He gave me one of his business cards before he left. Asked me to think over what he said. Then give him a call once I had.

The card put him in the cattle business. Those investigations of his were apparently kept very private indeed. Later I would learn that his presence in the beef trade was a return to the family enterprise. The older brother who had taken on the ranch left it to Clarence when he passed.

I would learn much more about the ex-sheriff. Which certainly had not been something I anticipated when I returned to Doña Pero County I intended to maintain a solitary existence. To remain unnoticed. As I had in Denver. And for the same reason. I wasn't there to do anything I wanted anyone to know about. Not in advance anyway.

And in Doña Pero I faced a much greater chance of being recognized. Not by anyone who knew me when I lived there as a boy. That was far too long ago and I was far too changed. But perhaps by a guard from the state prison. Or a former inmate. Or someone who worked in the courts and was involved in my release. All of whom I might encounter by chance. Meaning that even more so than in Denver I was compelled to go about disguised. A beard and fake glasses and some gray in my hair. Pressed shirts and slacks. Jackets and ties. The professorial look that had already served me well.

But it wasn't the possibility of a chance encounter that kept me vigilant. It was because I knew Armijo would be on his guard. Watching out for me. That was one of many factors that sent me to Denver first. To give the fat man time to decide I wasn't a threat. And call off the dogs I knew he would have out sniffing after my scent.

❖   ❖   ❖

McElvy told me I was right to be paranoid. In our next conversation. When once again he appeared before me in the produce section at my supermarket. Which was a week or so after the first time. He opened up with it—

"Good call not coming back right away. I meant to tell you that last time."

I had no idea what he was talking about. I told him as much.

"It was smart not to come back right after you got out. Back then I wasn't the only one looking for you."

Now I understood.

"But his guard is back down again," McElvy said. "He figures you would have made your move already. After all those years of waiting for the chance. I have to admit I thought the same."

"So you still have yourself convinced that's why I'm here."

"We can play games if you like. But I for one have no interest."

"Should we be discussing this in public?"

"We're just two guys standing in front of some red peppers. Maybe that's all we're talking about."

"There could be surveillance. Security cameras. That would leave a record of our meeting."

"Not in this aisle. The camera over here is a fake."

"And how would you know that?"

"I know the guy who did the security. We go way back."

He nodded at me.

"I know Doña Pero better than just about anyone. That could be very useful with what you have planned."

"All I have planned is buying some groceries."

"You still got my card?"

"Maybe."

The old man laughed.

"Damn if you aren't playing this close to the vest."

"Whatever do you mean?"

McElvy laughed again. Then he smiled and pushed his hat back.

"But I suppose you'd be a damn fool to play it otherwise."

He grinned and pointed at me.

"And from what I hear a fool you ain't."

Chapter 71

He knew his last line would get under my skin. Tipping his hand that he had looked into me. Asked around about me. Leaving me to wonder whom he had spoken with and what was said. It was a challenge not to bite down. But I managed to keep myself off his hook.

Meanwhile I considered delaying my plans. Leave Doña Pero while I waited for the old man to give up on me.

Or die. Which couldn't take too long. He was old as dirt.

But I had already waited a long time. And there was no compelling reason to quit just yet. I had done nothing criminal. And McElvy was not the law. Armijo had that privilege. Although if the old man was actually working for the fat man then I could possibly wind up dead myself. But that risk seemed miniscule. McElvy's antipathy for Armijo seemed second only to my own.

And maybe not even. My history with Armijo was extremely brief when he betrayed me. McElvy had been far more deeply deceived. And although the price I had paid seemed much greater, I had regained both my identity and my freedom—plus a cool ten million dollars. McElvy's identity as sheriff remained stolen. And he had received no cash settlement.

What did the old man hope to gain from me?

A paycheck? That seemed unlikely.

He didn't play his cards much looser than I did. We both hugged our hands close. But he had opened the game and forced me into it.

Which really pissed me off. He mucked my plans up big time.

That old pushy bastard.

❖　　❖　　❖

He had the advantage of knowing me better than I knew him. That score needed to be evened. So I got busy doing research. I started with what could be found online and at the local library. McElvy had been a public figure. What he did and thought were once news.

I went over all of those old stories. Including the ones from the unpleasant episode of Armijo's ascension. In some old video from the local news the first thing I came across was a press conference following the Elden Morris abduction. In which Armijo stole the limelight from his boss. And there was McElvy's pained concession speech. He conducted himself like a gentleman and wished Armijo success as the new sheriff. Words that came haltingly and at obvious cost. I couldn't find any suggestion that he ever spoke ill of his usurper. Despite one aggressive reporter who tried to bait him into putting some blood in the water.

"I'm not here to tear down Josef Armijo," McElvy said. "I'll leave that to jackals likes you."

The old man stuck to the high road.

Meanwhile I did not. I tapped my criminal contacts and McElvy was hacked every way to Tuesday. I peered under the hood and banged all the doors and kicked all the tires. As best could be determined he was clean in every way imaginable. And had no apparent ties to the fat man.

❖   ❖   ❖

I rebuffed him once more. At the supermarket again. This time we stood catty-corner to each other at a sale bin of jalapeños. And this time he did not take me by surprise. Now I was ever vigilant for the old man. When he came and stood near me I continued to examine the large dark green pepper in my hand while I said to him—

"If I want to speak with you, you will hear from me."

When I looked to where he had been he was gone.

Later I saw him at the checkout. He was ahead of me in the express aisle. In one hand he carried a gallon can of Maxwell House. The other held a half-gallon bottle of Jim Beam. I stood there behind him picturing a ranch life of black coffee and straight whiskey. And wondered if the whiskey ever came before the coffee. And wondered if McElvy had spent his forced retirement from the law medicating his wound with his booze.

A thought that gave me pause. I had already seen my life destroyed by the incompetence of one drunk. Letting another repeat that favor would be too cruel indeed. Fool me once, shame on you. But fool me twice...

I went back and dug around again. This time specifically looking for signs of drunkenness. DUIs, DWIs, public intoxication. A sloppy performance at a political event. Any little scrap that might indicate the old man spent too much time with the bottle.

Nothing. Not the slightest hint. The only thing I found that even mentioned McElvy and alcohol was a reminiscence posted online by an old woman now living in North Carolina who waxed nostalgic about a party from her youth when McElvy drove her home because her date got loaded and passed out. And how she had wished many times since that "handsome Clarence" had kissed her.

Riding the high road even then.

I decided to hear the rest of his sales pitch.

Chapter 72

The view from McElvy's front porch seemed to end in Texas. I was enjoying that view one evening when he came up the drive. If he was at all surprised to see me waiting he didn't show it. We said hello like nothing was out of the ordinary and I helped the old man bring groceries in from his truck. This time he had purchased much more than just coffee and booze.

When that was done we sat on the porch with a couple of beers. Spent a few moments staring into the distance. Then he said just as casual as you please—

"What's on your mind."

"You tell me."

"You showed up here. That makes this your dance."

"You want to sell me something. Start selling."

"I'm not selling anything."

I put my beer down and got to my feet.

"My mistake."

"Don't be hasty."

"So you'll stop popping up among the produce? Since you don't want anything from me."

He chewed on his lip.

"I never said that."

I sat down again. He kept chewing.

A moment passed.

"Start talking or I'm gone."

"Hold your horses."

He chewed for a little while longer.

Then sighed and shook his head.

"Ten million dollars is one hell of a war chest. I don't know how much of it you're ready to spend. But you didn't show up here not intending to part with any of it. I'm guessing you bought that house. And maybe that office building across from the department."

He paused. Waiting for confirmation was my guess. I didn't give him any.

But he was right about both pieces of real estate. I had acquired the house where I was living. And a three story office building across the street from the Sheriff's Department.

I did not want him to know those things.

Not him or anyone else in Doña Pero.

He was really fucking up my plans.

❖   ❖   ❖

We didn't speak for several moments. I watched the evening march across the desert and thought about all the many other evenings just like this one that I had missed being locked away. I don't know why that weighed on me just then. I haven't spent much time since I was released dwelling on those stolen days. I try to forget them and move on.

McElvy raised a hand and gestured in my direction.

"Look. Andreas. Let me shoot straight here."

He wiped his hand over his mustache. Then lifted his beer and drank. The mustache got wiped again.

"My wife has been gone twenty years now. God rest her soul. All my friends are dead or just so damn decrepit they ain't no fun. Sit around bitching about how they can't taste nothing and can't pee right. My daughter is in Oregon and never had a family. And now she's getting old herself. Truth is she's just damn weird. Mad at the whole damn world. Every goddamn thing is a thorn in her paw. My boy lives in Florida and I see him once a year if I'm lucky. He used to play minor league ball and now he sells Jaguars. Got to say I liked him better when he was a ballplayer. He was a lot more fun back then. He's divorced now and his ex-wife hates his guts. Hates mine too. Which means I hardly never get to see the grandkids. My prostate is as big as a grapefruit. The doctors keep nagging at me

367

to let them rip it out. I don't know what the fuck for. I'm gonna keel over soon anyway. Why start taking parts out now? Let me go down in one goddamn piece."

He turned to me and his eyes burned into mine.

"This is the one thing I want done before I'm gone. Even it up with that bastard Armijo. If you got any questions start asking. I'll tell you whatever you care to know."

He exhaled sharply and looked away.

"Hell. I probably just said way more than you care to know."

"You haven't said what you want from me."

"Isn't that clear?"

"I prefer not to make any assumptions."

McElvy rocked his head back and laughed.

"You are something. I'll give you that."

"I'm glad I amuse you. Now what do you want from me?"

"A well-heeled partner."

"Why."

"Because Armijo isn't someone to mess with. He already got the better of me once. The better of both of us. Don't forget that. And he has that whole department to throw around. Not to mention a bunch of powerful friends. I'm just one man. And a broke-down old one."

"You're doing a great job of selling yourself."

"Fuck it. Either you'll buy the horse or you won't."

"Why me? Why not someone you already know."

"You know anyone else with ten million dollars who wants to go after him?"

"It's a big risk. Throwing in with a stranger."

"You get where I'm at, risks start looking smaller."

"That does not reassure me."

"Because you're careful. Like they said. And like I've already seen."

There they were again. These mysterious people he had mentioned before. The one who were talking about me.

This time I took the bait—

"Like who said?"

"A fellow such as yourself doesn't exactly go unnoticed. I hear you're smart too. And disciplined. And determined."

He nodded at me.

"And sitting on one great big pile of cash."

I smiled. Then I laughed quietly. My beer needed to be drank. After that was done I smiled again.

"So it's the money you're after."

"And the man who comes with it. But the money wouldn't hurt. War ain't free."

"So this is war?"

"You better know that. Or you best quit now."

"And how do you see this war ending? With his head on a stick?"

"With his ass in jail."

He let that image sit with me for a moment.

"Wouldn't that suit you?"

I nodded.

"Yes. That would suit me just fine."

"Then we want the same thing."

Maybe he wasn't such a bad salesman after all.

There was one more thing I wanted to accomplish. One remaining reason why I drove out to his ranch. I wanted an answer to that damned question. The one he kept bumping against and not addressing. The one he had stuck under my skin and left there to fester.

"You've mentioned things people have said about me."

McElvy frowned.

"I suppose I have."

"Who have you been talking to?"

He pulled at his mustache.

"Guards at the prison. Some people in the DA's office."

"Did they want to know why you were asking?"

"I didn't have to ask. Just bought drinks and let them talk. Steered things around to your release. Natural enough subject. All of us having a history with it. Then they jabbered away."

I pictured the old man in a bar with a trio of uniformed prison guards. I gave the guards faces from my past. I imagined them all drunk and blathering. I wanted to punch each of them. One after the other.

McElvy smiled. He extended a hand toward me. Apparently he decided the horse could use a little selling after all—

"That's exactly what I bring to the table. I'm a friendly old geezer who's locally planted. I know a whole crew of people who matter in this. I got eyes and ears and a big old nose. And I can go out and about without anyone batting an eye. You have to go around all disguised and pretending you're someone else."

"And you have experience with this sort of work. Tailing people. That sort of thing."

"Exactly right."

"Are you always so bad at it? I saw you coming a mile off."

The old man grinned. Like the fox who ate the hen.

"You saw me when I wanted you to. At the graveyard. Across the street from your house. Pulling into the supermarket parking lot. You didn't see me when I followed you to your new office building. Or watched you drop your clothes outside the drycleaners."

The sun had been sliding down behind us. Long shadows stretched out across the desert. I told myself when my beer was finished I would leave.

The old man started up again—

"Got to admit it would be handy to have a pair of seasoned boots out there on the ground. Wearing down the shoe leather. Seeing what's what and who's doing what. While your holed up hoping no one figures out who you are."

I decided my beer didn't need to be finished. I got to my feet. I stood over the old man and looked down at him.

He looked wary.

I pointed at him.

"We met before you know."

McElvy watched me.

"At the hospital," I said. "When I found the boy."

The old man nodded.

"I remember. That was a terrible day."

"Why should I trust you? You were part of all that. Of what was done to me. It was your department."

"And the buck stops with the boss."

"It sure as hell does."

"I'm not arguing with you."

"Why did you let Armijo run the investigation? That was a big case. You must have considered running it yourself."

"I did. But he caught it. And he was an experienced lawman. He had done good work in the past."

McElvy paused.

"It was time to let him step up."

"You trusted him?"

"I had to. I hired the bastard."

We stared at each other.

McElvy nodded at me.

"Anything more you want to ask?"

"How can I be sure you're not working for him?"

The old man frowned. After a moment he shrugged.

"I guess you can't."

"So why should I trust you."

"I don't know you. But you came here."

"A mistake I can fix."

McElvy grimaced.

"Come on, son. Don't be like that."

He pointed at the chair I had left empty.

"Sit the hell back down. Finish your damn beer."

"What an appealing invitation. But no thank you."

He was still on his porch when I drove away.

Part XXI:
Canyon Girl

Chapter 73

Matt watched the waitress approach through the plate glass windows. Tall and blond and old enough to be his mother. But very much not his mother. At his age she had been a showgirl. She still moved like one.

She unlocked the door and pulled it open and smiled when she told him to sit anywhere. He chose a booth in the front. He spent a moment with the menu and asked for coffee and "The Winning Hand"—two eggs over easy, home fries, bacon and sausage, toast and two pancakes.

The waitress smiled while she took his order. One eyebrow arched up a little higher than the other. When she left he found himself watching her.

He made himself stop.

❖   ❖   ❖

He told himself this was a mistake. That he should have learned better from his first impulsive detour. The one that consumed eleven months, left him contemplating suicide, and had only ended two days ago. A fact he had trouble comprehending because those two days seemed just as long as those eleven months.

Next he berated himself for being sentimental. He wouldn't be returning if he hadn't gone there with his parents. Which was true. But he didn't see anything wrong with that. Why shouldn't he revisit a place where they were happy and had fun? When would he be this close again?

He tried to convince himself that wasn't healthy. That he was wallowing in the past. His parents and his siblings were all dead and he needed to accept that sad truth and move on. He was using the past as an excuse to avoid the future. To drift from place to place and job to job. Not to mention from girl to girl. He needed to find a path and stick with it. Instead of letting life push him around. And here he was letting it push him across the map again.

He felt his future could wait another day or two. That no harm would be done by a little sight-seeing and reminiscing.

The voice in his head had run out of arguments. It tried embellishing the ones already offered.

Matt remained unpersuaded.

He had his maps with him, including some new ones he found at the motel. He spread them out across the table. Staying in Las Vegas was out of the question. He went to sleep with that thought and woke up with it.

Maybe his sister didn't hate it. Maybe she actually liked living here. But Matt wasn't made for life in the neon Gomorrah. Seeing Meredith looking like she was born to stalk prey across a casino floor had thrown that into stark relief.

There was California one state over. He figured he could reach Los Angeles in time for lunch. But he had heard that out-of-work actors wait tables. All that competition might make it hard to find a job.

Maybe San Diego would be better. A beach town meant tourists and tourists needed to eat. He could try LA first and see how that went. Then head down the coast if it didn't work out.

Or he could go the other direction. He remembered that his father liked San Francisco when he set port there in the Navy. Matt liked the idea of a city full of hills. He knew it was expensive. All that Silicon Valley wealth. Which he guessed meant lots of fancy dining. Maybe he could bus tables at a high-end joint to get his foot in the door then work his way up. He knew a waiter at a top tier enterprise could make serious money.

Finally in exasperation the voice in his head told him he was only doing this because the tall blond waitress gave him a boner. Which in his present state almost made sense. And reminded Matt of the waitress and almost gave him another one. Prompting his only laughter during the four hours and fifteen minutes he spent driving there. Making the voice indignant and prompting it to inform him if he had any guts he would go back to Vegas and try to ball that waitress if he wanted her so bad.

The voice was still yammering at him when he paid his entrance fee and rolled through the park gates. Adamantly repeating what had already failed to prevent him from coming here. No reprieve as he stepped from his car and crossed the parking lot at the Visitor Center and right up to the moment when he approached the rim and the canyon opened before him.

Then the voice had nothing to say. San Francisco could wait. Or wherever else he decided to go. So could finding a job when he got there. That future he had been so desperately worried about became instantly insignificant. And entirely manageable. All that would take care of itself in due course.

All that mattered now was what he saw and couldn't comprehend. What Matt thought he knew about this place—his memories of what the canyon looked like and how being here had made him feel— those were like x-rays of the actual experience.

He felt stunned and couldn't take it in.

"Where you going?" the waitress said.

She was standing beside him. He turned toward her and was confronted by her bosom. He forced his eyes up.

There was that smile again. That one eyebrow curving up just a little higher.

"I don't know yet," Matt said.

"On vacation?"

Her voice was like silk.

"Not exactly."

"So you're on the road."

"I guess that's what you call it."

"Ever been to the Grand Canyon?"

Matt felt a jolt. Like he had been poked somewhere tender.

"When I was a kid."

As if the trip had been so long ago. Like he was too small to even remember it. He started to explain but the waitress was laughing. Warm throaty laughter that washed all over him.

She put a hand on his shoulder and he stiffened.

"Sweetheart, you're still a kid."

Her hand stayed where it was. With the other one she pointed at his cup.

"Refill?"

"Sure. Please."

His shoulder felt cool when her hand was gone. He watched her step to the counter and bend over it then felt flushed when he looked away.

She returned with a full steaming pot. Her hand returned to his shoulder and heat came with it. She filled his cup slowly. With the hand that was off duty just resting there. Before she left, that hand gave him a little squeeze.

He had to make himself stop watching her again.

He found the canyon on one of his maps.

❖   ❖   ❖

He was startled when he realized almost an hour had passed. He had spent it wandering along the rim not thinking about anything but what his senses fed into his brain. Shadows from the passing clouds shifting across the canyon. The scent of pine washing over him as a breeze came and went. The colors of the stone faces always changing. A raven clacking overhead. Sunlight gleaming on the river twisting below.

The most untroubled hour he had spent—

"Since before everything went to shit."

He hadn't meant to speak. And hated that he swore.

Like a stain splashed onto something spotless.

Chapter 74

His mother would have hated his cursing. It only became a habit after she died. Alive she would have shamed him out of it. Matt felt ashamed that he let her death excuse him from maintaining her standards.

Helen Walker saw routine profanity not as a moral failing but an intellectual one. She may have been a housewife without a higher education married to a blue-collar worker in a town of no consequence but she refused to be stupid. She spoke rarely but when she did her words mattered. They were precise and carefully chosen. There was no room in her sentences for filler.

Matt saw that in some ways his mother was much like Abigail. And that she would have become quickly attached to the quiet girl from Portland. His father too. They would have been more than a little heartbroken when it was over. And disappointed in him that he didn't end it when he knew he should. That he hung around until she made the hard call.

But oh how they would have hated Meredith. He could imagine them grimly staring at her as she blathered disjointedly within her narcissistic bubble. Still they would not have approved of how he treated her at the Agropoli. They would have wanted him to be a gentleman and politely decline her invitation. How he behaved was just lowering himself to her level.

"You've been fucking up," Matt said.

He then literally bit his tongue. Hard enough that he tasted blood.

He got her room number and said he would meet her there. That he needed something to take care of first. She seemed to have an idea what that was. Maybe she thought he was going to buy condoms.

He started running just past the lobby doors. And didn't stop until he arrived panting at his motel room. He gasped for air while he fumbled with his card key. By the time he got the door open his breathing had slowed enough for him to gulp some cold water. After that he collapsed on the bed.

When he had recovered he tried to distract himself with the television. He went through all the channels without any success. He turned off the set and the lights and lay on his back and stared up at the ceiling. Which was dimly visible in the glow that filtered in around the drapes from all the illumination humming out in the street.

He tried to grasp how all the pieces had to fit. How all the events of his life and many other lives had to have been ordered so that on this day of all days he ran into Meredith of all people in of all places the same hotel and casino that had employed his sister when she died. And that she showed up there transformed into a woman who turned heads in Las Vegas.

None of that made any sense. And all of it disturbed him.

"Help me out here, God," Matt said. "Are you trying to tell me something?"

As if in response sirens came wailing across the city. Those sirens told Matt to look back out across the desert to what had brought him here. And he imagined sirens screaming up the highway toward the desolate intersection where his sister was being incinerated. He saw her crushed car burning beside the highway and hoped she was unconscious when that happened. After being plowed into by a semi that seemed likely. He felt he could count on that mercy from whatever forces guide our universe.

What he also felt, so strongly that this feeling was a form of knowing, was that his sister's life had

379

been short and painful and lonely. Being here had made that clear. Seeing where she lived and where she worked and where she died and where she was buried. All of it was sad and ugly. Her life had been anonymous and her death even more so.

And that was why he came here. As unpleasant as it had been he wanted to know his sister better. Now he did. He could decide later if that knowledge was worth the cost of acquiring it.

But did Glory have to be a piece of meat hung out for display? Parading around in those slut clothes. Tips for being trash. He heard his father's voice saying those things. While his mother frowned and shook her head.

❖   ❖   ❖

He was disturbed by how he had gone from girl to girl. Depending on them for shelter. Adapting to their routines. That wasn't who he wanted to be. That wasn't who his parents raised him to be. He was better than that. Or at least he used to be. He wanted to believe that he used to be better than that. Wherever he went next—San Francisco was fading away and California was going with it—he wasn't going to let a woman take him in again. He would make his own way and find his own place.

And if that was important then maybe the smart move would be back to Portland. Where he knew people who could point him to available situations. Where he knew which parts of the city were good and which ones to avoid. Call this a mental health break and go back to where he wouldn't have to start over from scratch. His boss at the brew pub told Matt his job would be waiting for him.

But there were days when he had looked out at all that rain and wanted to be obliterated. To have never existed. He only got through all the damned rain because of Abigail. Because she seemed to thrive on it. Like a plant that couldn't get too much water. He clung onto her to survive the soaking.

But maybe that would be true anywhere. Even somewhere it never rained. Maybe he needed a woman to stay in this world. Maybe without Meredith he would have drowned himself in Lake Ontario. Maybe instead of Portland with its killing rain he should return to Las Vegas and its bracing sunshine. See if that tall blond waitress would take him in. Like a lost puppy looking for a new home. Encouraged by a little petting.

He knew she could teach him a thing or two. More like a million things. She could teach him a whole plethora of life lessons. But he was getting enough of those on his own. He didn't need any help getting them faster. The tall blond waitress could be the death of him.

He was starting to see there were a lot of good things about Portland.

Chapter 75

He was trying to convince himself that the rain wasn't really a problem. That he had blamed the weather for the sense of confinement that came from being with Abigail. That on his own things would be different.

Then a spectacle appeared before him. Banishing all other thoughts. When a sparkling white cloud unfurled a silver veil that dropped shimmering into the red and orange canyon. At first Matt did not recognize what he was seeing. When he realized that was rain glistening and glittering into the abyss his heart thumped around inside of his chest.

A moment before he thought he had been ruined for it. That the sight of rain would forever depress him. Now here it was, falling as if on grand display just for him, and he had never seen anything so beautiful. Not that the rain back in Portland ever looked anything like this. Nothing he had ever seen of any rain anywhere even approached what he witnessed at this moment.

And there was more to come. From the sparkling white cloud came a vivid bolt of yellow lightning. Then across the silver veil spread a perfect rainbow. Matt felt he was experiencing the very crown of all creation. That to absorb more natural splendor was not humanly possible. His swollen heart burst open. Tears filled his eyes. He blinked them away and wiped them away and stared ahead until they filled his eyes again.

He wanted to feast undisturbed on every second of this miracle.

❖ ❖ ❖

He decided he wasn't going anywhere. Not just yet anyway. He needed more time here at the canyon.

To get pointed in the right direction. Maybe the canyon would cure him.

He would stay and see the canyon at sunset. And lit by moonlight or starlight or whatever kind of light tonight offered. Then he would see it lit again by the sun at tomorrow's dawn. Only then would he decide where he was going. Until then he would be entirely here.

Before now he wasn't sure he had ever been entirely anywhere.

That needed to change.

He only left to get food. The rest of the day he was on the canyon rim. Sometimes his mind was cluttered but more often he kept it clear. Staying in the here and now. Looking and listening. Letting it all in.

The colors at sunset seemed to move through him. He felt scrubbed clean as they swept across the canyon. By the end he was exhausted. His last energy drained away as the sky and canyon lost their oranges and reds.

He found a place to park where he didn't expect to be bothered.

In less than a moment he was asleep.

He awoke feeling someone had been with him. Here in his car seated beside him. Not an invader. No sense of panic. A sense of loss that this someone was gone. He stepped out onto the pavement and pushed his door shut and looked around. No one in sight.

A flash of motion across the parking lot. Followed by a shadow thrown from a light streaming through the trees. He started that direction. Not sure if he was following someone. Not sure if he had actually seen anyone.

He stopped where he thought the person had been. Looked around not knowing what he was looking for. When he moved again he went toward the canyon. Not knowing why but knowing he should.

He felt cool and then almost cold. Sensed the canyon before he saw it. At the rim trail he had another glimpse of motion. This time to his right. Again he went toward it.

There was no moon overheard. Half the sky was covered with clouds. The other half was full of brilliant stars.

He rounded a bend and stopped when he saw her. She stood facing him. In a white dress down to her ankles. No more than forty feet away.

There was a voice behind him. The muted slam of a car door. He glanced over his shoulder. All he saw was distant light filtering through the trees.

When he turned back again she was gone.

For a moment he waited. As if she might rematerialize. Then he closed the space that had been between them and stood where she had been. He felt stupid for looking around him. Like he was searching for clues.

He didn't need any evidence to know who she was. And there wouldn't be any. Nothing to reveal her identity. Or where she could be found. He knew he wouldn't see her here again. Not tonight anyway. She wasn't going to reappear while he waited for her.

There was a bench nearby. He went over and sat down. And remembered how she haunted him for the rest of that vacation. It was even worse when he got home. He shredded a sneaker while lost in a daydream of being with her. Ran a lawnmower over his foot and almost lost a few toes.

Then she came to him in that vision. Right after he lost his virginity with Meredith. And told him to stay with the green-eyed girl. Despite how much Meredith disturbed him.

"Why did you do that?" Matt said.

He tried to imagine how she would answer. But again he had no clues. He did not know this canyon girl. All he knew was that he loved her. And had from the moment he first saw her. Whoever she was. Wherever she was. He would always be in love with her.

Which meant that he was good and royally screwed.

And totally fucking nuts.

This time he had finally really snapped.

❖   ❖   ❖

He hated having Meredith back in his head again. He had banished her while in Portland. Hid her memory behind Abigail. Ever since he hit the road she had been with him again. As if he knew she would come stalking him across the gaudy lobby of the Agropoli. Like a vampy starlet in a trashy Hollywood spectacular. Looking entirely unreal.

Everything about that experience was unreal. The marble floors gleamed too much. The glass doors sparkled too much. There were no shadows. Light seemed to shoot at him from all directions. Everything was too garish and too glaring. A hyped-up version of what was already overhyped.

And especially there was her new body. As if the devil pulled out all the stops trying to lure Matt back into bed with that crazy girl. Only supernatural forces could affect such a transformation.

It couldn't be real. It couldn't have happened. One moment he had been in reality. And then the next moment he wasn't. If it hadn't happened—if it was impossible—and it seemed impossible looking back at it now—then it was all in his head. The whole experience had been delirium.

What he thought happened with Meredith at the Agropoli—that was insane.

His encounters with the canyon girl—two and counting—also insane.

Being *in love* with the canyon girl—that was a whole new level of crazy.

He would wind up one of those babbling homeless people. Living in filth.

He realized he was already homeless.

He felt cold and numb.

❖   ❖   ❖

The abyss opened before him. Looming malignantly in the dark.

He felt it pulling him forward—

Up on your feet! Get a good running start!

Over the edge. The sickening fall.

Then nothing. The torture is over.

His father's face appeared. Floating before him with eyes blazing fire. Frank Walker re-imagined as a disembodied old-testament prophet.

Frank opened his mouth and words streamed into Matt's brain—

Suicide is a coward's choice!

Matt grinned at the fire-and-brimstone version of his dead old man.

"Like father, like son? Is that what you're telling me?"

His anger surprised him. White hot rage that boiled his brains and his blood. How could his father have been so stupid? Trading his life for money. He should have known that money would vanish. With the streak of bad luck they were fighting against.

How could he leave him to fight alone?

How could his father have abandoned him?

Like he had any clue out here on his own.

Look how badly he was fucking up.

Then his anger was gone.

Drowned by an infinite sadness.

❖   ❖   ❖

The lightning was pure white. Shooting down and dancing across the earth. Incomprehensibly stark and beautiful against the blue-blackness behind it. The storm cell splitting the darkness open with its bolts was in the east, off to his right. For a minute or two it had the night sky to itself.

Then another cell began firing off blue lightning over in the west. These bolts went crazily across the sky and down to the earth like electric strands of a vast demented spider's web. Crackling up and down and around and over.

For several minutes the two storm cells took turns. One would fire and then the other. Back-and-forth across the canyon and the night.

Then both went at once. In stereo the lightning flared open the sky.

They stopped at the same time.

He waited for a few moments.

"Thank you," Matt said.

He thought hours of darkness still remained. Then the birds started calling. And the photographers arrived. Soon the sky in the east was paling. And the glorious light came pouring forth. Making the colors of the canyon bloom.

He wanted to stay and savor the dawn. But hunger pushed him onto his feet. Dinner had been meager and far too long ago.

He stood yawning before the bench where he had been seated half the night. Then twisted his back to stretch out a knot.

That was when he recognized where he was. When the setting became familiar. He went a few paces in both directions along the trail. Just to be certain. Then returned to the bench and sat down again.

He stared. Then shook his head. He frowned before he shook his head again.

He tried to credit his subconscious with guiding him here. Through the dark. Along a trail he was unfamiliar with. To a place he had been to only once. And remembered as if in a dream.

He told himself she had been a figment of his imagination. A hallucination induced by his stress. His mind created her because it needed her.

But that wasn't what he felt. What he felt was that she had been sent to him. A vision to guide him back here. To where it started. To where he and the Hispanic girl had connected. At his core he knew this to be true. Despite how much his rational mind protested.

He believed in her.

She was real.

Part XXII:
The One-Armed Brother

Chapter 76

In Doña Pero my operation was on an entirely different scale from the one in Denver. A bigger fish requires larger tackle. I had shell companies that owned shell companies that owned yet more shell companies and so on until finally down at the very bottom layer there were companies that actually owned things that were real. Nothing being more real than real estate. Such as a nice house well situated in a very private aspect in a quiet neighborhood not far from the center of town. Discretely hidden behind walled gardens.

And an entire three story office building across the street and just down the block from the headquarters of the Doña Pero County Sheriff's Department. Within that building two office suites leased to yet another shadowy entity in my myriad and byzantine holdings. Occupying the entire top floor. Giving no one I did not approve of any reason to be up there. A buffer from the outside world.

And in the corner office nearest to the nerve center of the fat man's fiefdom the latest and most sophisticated surveillance equipment. So I could monitor all telecommunications in and out of the Sheriff's Department. Along with constant video observation of all entrances so I knew who was coming and going at all hours of the day and night. Plus an excellent vantage point for taking photographs of who came and went through the parking lot.

And once all this was set in place I reshuffled my deck. My shell companies bought and sold each other and some disappeared and new ones came into being. Making them even more impenetrable. As an aside let me mention that the collapsed real estate market proved entirely to my advantage. These properties and others were acquired at very agreeable prices and terms. In the end I actually made a profit on this aspect of my enterprise. A welcome fringe benefit I never anticipated.

But back to what matters. What was I after? What form of pain did I hope to inflict upon my prey? My object was not death. I had no intention of killing Armijo. Which may seem strange since I was willing to kill Sorenson. But the lonely janitor was an immediate and ongoing threat to innocent children. A threat I felt had to be disposed of. And as soon as possible.

Armijo was a threat of a different kind. Evil in an office that was supposed to be in service to the general good. People might lose their freedom or even their lives at the behest of such a man. But as best I knew little boys were not being raped and then murdered by Armijo himself. Instead any rapists and murderers who pursued such activities in his jurisdiction might go free. If it was not in Armijo's personal best interests to pursue them.

But without an immediate threat to an innocent party I was not willing to kill him. So what then was I after with my complicated preparations?

My goal was to assemble evidence against him. To know Armijo better than he knew himself. And build a case that could be turned over to whatever entity proved most appropriate—the FBI, the DOJ, the ATF. I was not particular by whom he was prosecuted. Just as long as the law was used against the lawman. Because instead of murdering him physically I wanted to murder him symbolically. To strip away everything he had made of himself. And leave behind just a corpulent bastard growing long in his years with a long time to suffer for his sins. His death would come soon enough. As it comes to us all. His suffering I wanted more.

That said and my disclaimer given I will confess that if events had brought us into closer conflict I do not know what I might have done. I have known no hatred even remotely approaching the scale of what I felt toward Armijo. In the heat of the moment I may well have become his murderer. And might have enjoyed being the one who made him dead.

❖   ❖   ❖

Time passed. In which I learned nothing of consequence. Long days spent in my roost peering down on the comings and goings of Armijo and his men with my ear cocked at their radios and cell phones. Including some days that stretched into nights when I had a misguided presentiment that something significant was about to happen. I setup a makeshift bedroom in an office of the suite to be closer to the action I kept hoping would occur.

And of course there was plenty of action in the conventional sense—men rushing out to address acts of violence and larceny. Or to direct traffic away from fire and flood when the monsoons were upon us and could strike the tinder of dry grass and trees with their lightning or fill the streets with their torrential rains. I had a spectacular view of the coming storms from my aerie and sometimes found myself distractedly watching the thunderheads march across the desert. There would be a burst of activity down below and I would miss half of it before my attention shifted away from the magnificent white clouds against the brilliant blue and back to my purpose in being there.

But all I saw and heard was routine law enforcement. With perhaps more political business being conducted then would be acceptable under campaign finance regulations. I looked into those regulations and concluded that a man of Armijo's standing would receive a light sentence that would most likely be commuted to parole. A blemish on his record that would not even force him to leave office. He could in fact retain his position while imprisoned. As had happened a few years before in a neighboring county. When the sheriff ran his department from his cell at the county jailhouse after being convicted of embezzlement. A statute to prevent another such embarrassment to the rule of law was stuck in committee at the state house. So all I could reasonably hope for was a slap on the fat man's wrist.

I began to grow frustrated. Spending your days watching others do things that do not matter to you while you hope they will do something that does is a trying way to pass the hours. And too much like my time spent in prison. Where you are also forced to wait while others act out the events of major consequence in your life. Which made watching Armijo a source of stress I was ill prepared to handle.

One of my contacts knew of an expert who could be brought in from Los Angeles to wire the sheriff's headquarters on the inside. And while he was here I could have him do the same to Armijo's house. Even his vehicles. Then the fat man couldn't take a piss without me recording the splash. I was about to commence negotiations with this expert when the man was arrested. Nothing to do with his line of work. A domestic violence charge. Such are the quality of people you work with when you work outside the law.

And sometimes within it. What better place for the devil's own to hide than behind a badge? I was certain that was the case with Armijo. I could sense it radiating from the fat man. Every time he came and went down below me I could almost see it in the air around him. An electric charge of evil.

With the expert from LA unavailable I considered recruiting another. But a search of that kind can tip your hand. Too many people hear that someone with a specific set of skills is being sought and word leaks into the ear of some law enforcement mole buried somewhere. And slowly but surely they work the thread back until the next thing you know the hunter is being hunted. Not a risk I was willing to take.

Which pushed me to reconsider killing Armijo. If I couldn't take him down maybe I should just take him out. Even if that would be less than completely satisfying. One day I saw the fat man in his parking lot and fantasized about being a sniper and putting him in my crosshairs. I even started to consider ways I could escape from my third floor office faster than the law could get to me. Maybe bungee jump out a back window to my car waiting below. But then Armijo got in his SUV and drove away and my contemplation of the scheme vanished with him. That wasn't what I came here to do.

Focus, I told myself. Eyes on the prize.

The next day I went the other direction. And considered giving the whole thing up. Just forget about Armijo and what he did to me and turn a fresh page. Go have fun. Travel the world. Then maybe settle down somewhere tropical. Find a nice woman to share my life with. Have some kids even. I was a wealthy man. And still young. I had options. Why risk all of that to ruin the fat man? He would manage to ruin himself eventually. He wasn't smart enough to avoid his own destruction indefinitely.

Another day passed and this idea did not pass with it. Instead I was another day closer to packing it in. I felt as if I was emerging from a fog. One that had covered a third of my life. But the fog was still lifting. It hadn't entirely lifted yet. So I remained in my groove.

The next afternoon I sat in my office looking down at the command center of Armijo's empire and considered how I would unwind this operation. Disposing of the equipment and the properties. Or maybe I should keep the properties. There could be profit in holding them. Stop thinking like an assassin and start thinking like a businessman.

Such were the thoughts that occupied my attention when a black SUV rolled into the parking lot down below. Out of habit I moved to my camera and peered through it and found the vehicle as it came to a stop. My mind was still pondering the details of abandoning the long-held objective that had brought me here when the driver's door of the SUV swung open and a man in a dark suit stepped out onto the asphalt.

I worked the zoom to get in tight.

In that instant, when his face came into focus, everything changed.

Chapter 77

I tried to get a room at the place where Armijo stuck me when he set me up. Just for old time's sake. But that place had been bulldozed. All that was left was the concrete slab with some pipes sticking out.

While I was parked in front of where I guessed my room had once been a coyote went loping past out in the desert that rolled away behind the slab. He looked young and vigorous. I wondered if he was a descendant of the ones I went looking for on that night long ago. The night before the morning when the fat man came to arrest me.

When the coyote was out of sight I went and found another motel. One that was still standing and still in business. I checked in and called McElvy from my room. Twenty minutes later he pulled up out front. When he was inside and the door was closed I said—

"Take off your clothes."

The old man blinked.

"Excuse me?"

"You heard what I said."

He blinked again.

"Is this a deal-breaker? Get naked or get out?"

I nodded. He grimaced.

"Tell me this ain't nothing kinky."

I frowned at him. He made a little grin.

"Guys pick up some weird habits in prison."

I kept frowning. He nodded.

"Okay."

❖   ❖   ❖

He started on the buttons of his shirt. I pointed at his hat. He handed it to me. I put it on the round table before the curtained window.

"How did you find me," I said.

McElvy frowned.

"What's that?"

"How did you track me down?"

He undid another button and then stopped.

"You mean in the graveyard?"

I nodded. He nodded back and his hands resumed their work.

"A hunch and a bit of luck. One thing I'm good at is picking the man out of the crowd. Height. Build. I can spot it."

He gestured at my bad leg.

"A slight limp."

There it was. Like a fingerprint on my every action.

"I watched for that," McElvy said.

He gestured at my face.

"I saw past the beard and the glasses."

McElvy shook his head.

"Little things like that don't throw me. So I just kept watch."

His hands went back to his buttons.

"Drove around town. Went to bars and stores. The post office. Watched who came and went at the motels. Just kept looking. Didn't figure I stood much of a chance. Told myself I had quit a couple of times. But even then I kept an eye out. As I went about my business. And when I found myself with time on my hands..."

He shrugged.

"I went right back to it. Got in the truck and drove around. Guess I liked it better than watching TV."

He finished with his buttons. I reached out my hand.

"Give it here," I said.

"Tell me you're gonna give it back."

I nodded. McElvy didn't move. I gestured at the shirt.

"It's not like it would fit me anyway."

"Nice of you to point that out."

396

He put the shirt in my hand. Then pointed at my chest.

"I spotted you first at that supermarket. Where I found you again later. Followed you from there to the graveyard. You were picking out apples when I saw you."

He nodded at me.

"But it's the redhead you would remember."

The redhead was hard to forget. Especially for a man who was living like a monk. I remembered her every day for a week afterward. And could still recall with too much clarity how she moved when she walked away from me.

But I wasn't ready for small talk. I gestured at his undershirt.

"Come on. Keep moving."

McElvy sighed. His tee shirt went up over his head. When he handed it over I pointed at his pants. He sighed again before he sat on the edge of the bed and untied his shoes.

"I'll take those too," I said.

He pulled his shoes off and passed them over.

"And the socks."

McElvy handed them to me. Then stood up and dropped his pants and stepped out of them. He handed his pants over and I took them away.

All the old man had on was his shorts.

"You need some new underwear," I said. "Those are disgusting."

"If I knew what you had in mind I would have worn my lingerie."

"And perhaps a girdle?"

"Now that's just plain cruel."

I waved at the wretched underpants.

"As much as I regret it. Those too."

He peeled off his shorts. For a moment he used them to cover his genitalia. Then he sighed and handed them over.

❖   ❖   ❖

I made McElvy get naked for two reasons. The first and most unsavory was to establish my dominance. The second was so I could check him for bugs.

I removed my scanning device from its black case and had him turn around slowly while I waved the wand up and down beside him. Then I made him spread his legs and bend over. Which was, of course, very pleasant for both of us. Next I went through his clothes and waved the wand over each piece before handing it back to him.

When he was dressed again McElvy scowled at me.

"Nice to have my dignity back."

"Can't be too careful."

"They were right about you. No unnecessary chances."

I had nothing to say to that. I still didn't like that I had been discussed. Especially by the guards from the state prison. I wondered if one of them had mentioned my limp. Thinking that might be the case didn't help. I was starting to make myself mad.

"So is that it?" McElvy said. "Are we done?"

"No."

I could see that wasn't the answer he expected.

Inside the black case that held my scanning gizmo was a white cardboard envelope. The type used for mailing large format photographs. I handed it to McElvy. Inside he found three pictures. Glossy eight by tens from the brand new high-resolution photographic printer I had in my office overlooking the Sheriff's Department.

The one on top showed a man with a broad face. Under his eyes stood thick Apache cheekbones.

"These are recent," I said.

McElvy squinted at the image. Then moved over to the lamp on the night table beside the bed and held the photo under the light. At the moment of recognition his head jerked back and his squint

398

disappeared. His face opened wide. Before it crowded into a scowl. He glanced my direction then put his eyes back on the photo.

"Hell if that don't look like Danny Ortega."

"Doesn't it though."

"Where did you take this?"

"Outside the Sheriff's Department. In the parking lot."

McElvy snorted and shook his head.

"Shit. Yeah. I see that now."

He shook his head again. His eyes stayed on the image.

"Hell of a gamble."

"And yet there he is."

McElvy shuffled to the next photo. He stared for a moment before he shook his head.

"I don't buy it. Too damn brazen."

"You think so?"

The old man didn't answer. I pushed him on it—

"Even for Armijo?"

Chapter 78

McElvy shuffled the images again and looked at the last of them. In this one Ortega was not alone. He and the fat man stood facing each other. McElvy snorted and shook his head. He held up the photograph so I could see it.

"Come on now. This is just asking for it."

"Yes. I agree. But remember who you're talking to. He sent me to jail as someone else on a case that was total bullshit. Are you going to tell me there weren't a hundred ways that could've blown up in his face? Clearly he's willing to take chances."

McElvy was shaking his head again. He held up the first image. The one that was closest on Ortega.

"This could be his brother. That's a hell of a lot more likely."

"You met his brother. Do you think that's him?"

The old man gave me a wary look.

"Can't say. We met a long time ago."

"True. And back then his brother still had both of his arms. Shame what happened to him a few years ago. That motorcycle accident."

I pointed at the other photographs.

"Look at the second one. See any missing arms?"

The old man scowled at me.

"That's a fact. You're not messing with me now."

I produced another envelope. This one was manila and contained a single sheet of paper. But not photo stock and with no images. Just plain paper and standard text. A printout of a newspaper article. I handed it to the old man.

"If that's not enough you can look him up. He lives here in town. The whole arm is gone. All the way up to the shoulder."

McElvy hissed and shook his head. He skimmed over the article then looked back at the photo of Ortega.

"Shit. This is big."

"Getting cold feet?"

"What? Hell no."

"Let me ask you something."

"Shoot."

"Who brought Ortega into the department?"

McElvy raised his head and turned to me.

"What do you mean?"

"Who recruited him?"

"Yeah. Now I got you. Armijo did."

He nodded at me.

"But you knew that already."

"I had an idea."

I pointed at the newspaper printout.

"His parents live here too. Not far from the brother."

"Yeah. Think I met them once too."

"So be careful when you go sit on them. Maybe they remember you better than you remember them."

"What about the brother?"

"I say it's the parents."

"I know a good man. We could sit on both of them."

"That's nice for you. That you know a good man. But I don't know him. And I don't want to. Truth is I don't really want to know you. So no additional help. You'll have to do."

McElvy scowled at me.

"Yes sir."

"Unless you don't want in after all."

His scowl cut deeper. McElvy growled at me—

"Now did I say that?"

❖   ❖   ❖

You might remember him as Señor Fuzzy Lip. Which was what I dubbed him during my trial. The deputy who assisted Armijo when they arrested me as I was leaving town. And looked like he very much wanted to shoot me and smile at my blood and guts being splattered about.

It was the official opinion of the District Attorney's Office of Doña Pero County that Deputy Daniel Ortega acted alone in contriving the fraudulent evidence that put me in prison. Planting the fake driver's license that presto-change-o made me into a magic Mexican. Distributing incriminating items "found" among my belongings. The worst being a pair of shredded and bloodied boy's underpants. When the District Attorney announced the results of the investigation into this shocking corruption of justice he said—

"We will never know why Ortega did it. He took his answers with him."

The DA shook his head and waved his hand.

"All that is lost to us now."

Lost in a high-speed single-vehicle accident out in the backcountry. Deputy Ortega's truck was found smashed up and rolled over in a wide shallow wash with a corpse that was identified as his strapped in behind the wheel. Cause of death was determined to be internal bleeding.

Whether the dead man identified and interred as Daniel Ortega had any assistance in achieving that condition is yet another thing in all of this which it appears we will never know. Maybe they had an unclaimed corpse at their disposal. Maybe they made one out of someone who was disposable. Maybe their contacts across the border provided them with one. Anonymous dead bodies are easy to come by in Old Mexico.

Whatever his origins he became that patsy I had envisioned. Back in prison while examining all the scenarios that could unfold. When deciding what course of action to pursue. Here was the scapegoat who would allow Armijo to slip away. Some poor sap who was dead under another man's name. Can you get any more anonymous than that? Can you be any more used?

I think Armijo planned on my death at the state prison. Instead the very man he probably expected to make me dead became my protector. Thanks to the serendipitous arrival of Tranquilino Rojas. A development Armijo could never have anticipated. Under Silvertone's protection the fat man couldn't touch me. And then he learned I was looking for legal help. I had become a ticking bomb. He needed some way to contain the explosion. So he threw that corpse claiming to be Ortega over the blast he knew was coming.

What a cocky fat bastard he was. To believe he could get away with it.

McElvy was of course familiar with Ortega's story. So we didn't need to discuss what his presence meant. Or mention to each other that if anyone could lead us into the bloody beating heart of whatever dirty business Armijo was up to it would be Señor Fuzzy Lip.

Whose lip was no longer fuzzy. He had a decent mustache now. It was a handsome young supposed-to-be-dead man that I sent McElvy out after. I keep calling him young when in fact I was a few years his junior. Although I looked much older in my professorial getup. And felt older too. But I would have felt older wearing diapers. There was an eternally boyish quality to Danny Ortega. As if he would always retain a child's rash foolishness and mindless cruelty.

I let McElvy in out of necessity. Like it or not I needed help. I couldn't be in two places at one time. And like it or not I had gotten almost nowhere on my own. Before Ortega showed up I had nothing.

And for weeks after he appeared I had nothing more. Ortega didn't show at his parents' house.

McElvy lobbied to sit on the one-armed brother instead. I was almost ready to let him.

But then one evening just after dark a black SUV came down the block and parked across the street. Ortega stepped out and placed an envelope in his parents' mailbox. Then McElvy followed the black SUV across most of the county to an isolated ranch down near the Mexican border. Doing this undetected required him to drive for about twenty miles through the backcountry with his headlights off.

Not something I personally would have attempted.

The next day it was the old man's turn to show photographs. This time we looked at them on a computer display in my office. Luckily there had been a nice bright flood lamp turned on outside that remote ranch house which allowed for some good shots of Ortega and the men that he met there.

After a little online research allowed me to identify one or two faces in those images I had an idea where Armijo got his money. I decided McElvy had earned the right to know what we had. When I told him he stared at me blankly. An expression I misinterpreted.

"What's the matter?" I said. "You want out?"

He stared for a moment longer before he shook his head.

"No," he said. "Just trying to wrap my head around this."

Then he grinned at me.

"This is starting to get interesting."

I grinned back at him.

"We're two crazy bastards," I said. "You know that."

He grinned some more and nodded.

"That we are," he said. "Crazy as all hell."

Then we were quiet while we enjoyed our moment of self-satisfied bravado. Savoring what we believed was the impending destruction of our mutual foe. Brought to bear by the knowledge we had so recently and artfully acquired. By dint of our daring and our intelligence and our stealth.

Looking back I would say that was the moment when our friendship began.

If you can call it that.

Part XXIII:
Stand With Me

Chapter 79

Cooking and cleaning would have been more than enough to ask of her. When she had just recovered from serious injury. And was still struggling with profound emotional loss.

But Josef also wanted Esperanza to help with his next campaign. Election time was coming around again. And unlike last time he faced a real fight.

All the signs indicated that the well-respected and well-liked police chief of a town down near the Mexican border would be nominated by the county Democrats. He had yet to formally announce but was doing what should be done. Presenting himself to the electorate. Meeting with potential backers. Building a network of committed volunteers.

The kind of opponent who could make an election actual work.

When he asked for her help Josef took her hand in both of his. And peered gravely into her eyes.

"We have a big fight ahead of us," he said. "I need all the help I can get."

Esperanza did not hesitate. She immediately agreed to do as she was asked. But not for her uncle's sake.

She agreed because of Rosa.

Because she intended to martyr herself to the last wishes of her dead aunt.

Esperanza was not consciously aware that martyrdom was her objective. In her confused and distraught state she had buried that truth so deep it was hidden even from herself. Entombed far down in the depths of her young and impressionable soul.

Where a voluptuous self-pity had begun to spread its roots. A delicious sense of being doomed that she reveled in during the lonely hours spent cleaning and cooking and keeping her uncle's house.

Esperanza never revealed to anyone that her commitment to her uncle was secondary. That her primary devotion was to the memory of her Tía Rosa. She knew exactly how well such a conversation would go. How she would be implored not to waste her life living for the dead. No matter how holy she believed her dead might be.

Life is for the living, mija, her uncle would have said.

She also never shared that she had remembered her final conversation with her aunt. That sacred memory—the inspiration for her belief in the self-sacrifice required by her destiny—became a precious and powerful secret. One that compelled her to live sealed off within herself. Divorced from the world of the living. Dedicated to serving the memory of her beloved Tía.

Dutifully paying down the sin of getting her aunt killed.

For a couple of months Esperanza made this life of penance work. She kept her uncle's house in order. Did more than was asked of her on his campaign. Put out political fires while she stoked the domestic ones.

Then Josef announced they were moving. And everything she had worked so hard to hold together threatened to spin apart.

She stared at him openmouthed.

Her uncle frowned back at her.

"What's wrong?" Josef said. "You don't like it?"

"Of course I don't."

"Why not?"

"You have to ask?"

"It's too far from town. I need to be closer to work."

"Since when? It was never too far before."

"It's always been too far."

"Then why didn't we move before?"

"You know why."

"Because of Rosa."

"That's right."

"And already you turn your back on her."

She told herself she should regret those words. But she didn't.

Josef narrowed his eyes.

"You should take more care with how you speak to me."

"Then maybe I shouldn't speak to you at all."

Josef snorted. Beyond that he didn't reply.

When a moment had passed he gestured impatiently.

"There's a lot of junk. All that crap she squirreled away. I want you to get rid of it."

"Those things were important to her."

"Well they're not important to me. Are they important to you?"

"Yes."

"Then you can figure out where to put them."

"I'm not getting rid of them."

"Suit yourself."

"Where are we going?"

"I have my eye on a place. If I can get the right price. But wherever we go all that crap is yours to deal with. Are you good with that?"

For the first time in her life she wanted to hit him.

"Yes."

"You don't sound sure."

"I'm sure!"

"Good. You better be."

❖   ❖   ❖

The next morning a realtor came with a *For Sale* sign to plant in the front yard. Esperanza spied on him past the curtain in the kitchen window while he sweated in his brown suit trying to make the thing stand up straight.

Eventually the realtor gave up and left. Esperanza stared out at the tilted sign and felt as if her soul was bleeding. How could she make a life for herself away from here? Some days the strength she took from this old place, the memories she had of feeling safe and secure within these familiar walls, of everything she and Rosa shared here—that was what kept her going.

Without them who would she be?

Chapter 80

They moved into a new development in a broad wash at the edge of town. Where the houses all stood far apart on sloping rock-strewn and arroyo-cut lots studded with sagebrush and mesquite. And every one of them looked imperious and resentful. Like scattered forts that would independently face off against an impending Armageddon.

Esperanza first saw the house on the day her uncle took possession. She stood in the driveway and pictured far too many rooms. And too many windows. And too many toilets.

"You expect me to clean all of this?" she said.

Josef went past her without answering. She watched him unlock the door and disappear inside. Then she looked back up the freshly paved road that had brought them here into this wash where no one should live and wanted to walk away. If she had some money in her purse maybe she would have.

There was an embarrassment of space for their belongings. The heirlooms and artifacts that had belonged to Rosa only took up a corner of the vast attic. The immense living room devoured every scrap of furniture they could heave into its gaping maw. The enormous kitchen swallowed their pots and pans and plates and bowls and cups and glasses and every other item they possessed related to food and cooking. And still the huge room with its array of cabinets and cupboards looked bare and empty.

Even all the Armijo women couldn't fill that kitchen. When they gathered there at the housewarming. Surrounding Esperanza were the wives of Josef's brothers and sons and nephews. In two generations she was the only female born with her surname.

They all cooed at how wonderful it was. Such a big room! So much counter space! What a wonderful

410

dishwasher! What a wonderful refrigerator! What a wonderful stove!

Esperanza hid her disagreement behind a smile. She thoroughly despised this new kitchen. Where Rosa had never been. Where her aunt's good cooking had not saturated every surface. She could make all the recipes her aunt ever taught her a hundred times over in this hopelessly sterile environment and still everything single thing about it would remain entirely wrong. Cold and dead. Without a soul. Without her Tía's warm loving essence cooked into it.

❖   ❖   ❖

When the wife of one her cousins asked how she was doing for the first time Esperanza let herself express frustration with her circumstances. How there was no room in her life for herself. For her own interests and concerns. Only for her uncle and what he needed from her.

The women clucked.

The wife of another cousin shook her head.

"Men," this wife said. "That's how they all are."

"Isn't that the truth," someone added.

"Only ever think of themselves," a third voice said.

An aunt sighed at Esperanza.

"You're so young," this aunt said. "There's plenty of time."

A second aunt's eyes beseeched her. With light fingers she reached out and touched Esperanza's arm.

"Think of all he's done for you."

The women all clucked again. Collectively invoking the great burden of her guilt. Her original sin of being orphaned.

Esperanza wanted to say that she *had* thought about that. She had thought about it quite a lot. But other than taking her in so that Rosa could do all the work of actually raising her—what was it exactly her uncle had done on her behalf? Paid for the food in her belly and the clothes on her back. That was certainly something. But nothing that required him to alter his own life. To accommodate her presence or her needs. What had he ever done that was specifically for her?

And assuming a debt remained, when and how would that debt be paid? She had worked hard for him. Not just recently but when she was still a child. Getting him elected for the first time. Out on the stump giving speeches. Which made her so sick with nerves she thought she would die.

Which is it, ladies? Esperanza wanted to say.

Do men only think of themselves?

Or has my uncle really done a lot for me?

Because you can't have it both ways.

But Esperanza didn't say anything like that. To the Armijo women gathered in the new kitchen that they thought of as hers. Which she thought of as having been foisted on her by Josef.

"You're right," she said instead.

And wished that she believed it.

❖   ❖   ❖

When everyone was gone the house seemed even more absurd. All those people parading through left the rooms feeling that much more numerous and outsized and empty. Esperanza moved through them turning off lights and making note of what needed to be cleaned when she wasn't so tired and wished she was somewhere else. Preferably far away.

She thought of her conversation in the kitchen with the other women. And admitted to herself that she had mentioned her frustrations hoping one of them would offer to help. Hopefully invite her to go live with them. Give her someplace else to stay while she restarted her life. Away from her uncle and his demands.

But that hadn't happened. Instead she was encouraged to keep putting her uncle first. Which she had feared but expected.

Maybe she should ask. Tell them outright that she wanted to get out of here.

But she knew how they would answer. They would all tell her to stay put. Because they all wanted her to keep Josef happy. She had never seen that before. But now there it was. Like an enormous billboard mounted on the roof of this awful house. Proclaiming in huge letters why she was stuck here. Why no one would lift a finger to help her leave.

Because none of them wanted to cross Josef.

No one in her family had asked if this was what *she* wanted. Because it was what *they* wanted. And they didn't want to hear that she didn't want it. She had been chosen by default to serve the patriarch.

Like musical chairs. The music had stopped when Rosa died.

Chapter 81

Up at the head of the road, beside the entrance to the development, there was a strip mall. And in that strip mall were drycleaners. Which was where Esperanza was waiting. While the young Chinese woman who worked there looked for Josef's blue suit. Which he wanted for an event that weekend.

The Chinese woman had been reading the local newspaper. She left it on the counter. After a moment Esperanza turned it around so she could scan the headlines. Only to be confronted by—

CONVICTION IN MORRIS CASE OVERTURNED

The Doña Pero District Court today overturned the conviction of Manuel Ortiz, a Mexican native, in the abduction and molestation of Elden Morris, a crime that transfixed the region a decade ago. In a stunning development it was revealed that the man sentenced as Ortiz was in fact a United States citizen and former resident of the area named Andreas Delmorales. The court ordered his immediate release. How Delmorales came to be convicted under a false identity will be the subject of an investigation by the District Attorney. Meanwhile the true perpetrator in the Morris case remains at large.

Esperanza stopped and started over. She was not able to read anything more. That first paragraph insisted on being hammered into her head. She was reading it for the third time when the clerk returned.

Esperanza struggled with her purse and scattered change across the floor. An hour seemed to pass while she picked up coins with her shaking hands and fumbled through paying the clerk and stumbled across the room and out the door. Halfway to her car a voice called out behind her—

"Miss! Yew fahgit soot!"

Another hour seemed to be lost in her trek back to the waiting clerk. And in the return to her car. Where she screamed and beat her fists against the steering wheel until they began to bleed.

❖   ❖   ❖

For the rest of the day she waited.

First she waited in the parking lot for her grief and anger to pass. There was a supermarket down at the other end of the strip mall. She had intended to go there next and buy groceries for the week. Eventually she looked at her bloodied hands and decided that wasn't going to happen.

Instead she drove home and waited in her bedroom for her mind to clear. So she could call her uncle and ask him what was going on. What had happened all those years ago and what was happening now and why hadn't he told her this was happening?

When the day was almost done and her mind still hadn't cleared and she still hadn't called she went to the kitchen and waited at the table for her uncle to come home.

An hour or so later the front door swung open. He called out her name. She answered calmly—

"In here."

He sat beside her and at first said nothing. When he finally spoke it was to ask 'about her hands. She had forgotten how she abused them back at the strip mall. She inspected the scabs on her knuckles and decided she would not answer her uncle's question. Not about the condition of her hands or anything else he chose to ask. She would remain silent until he addressed what they both knew must be discussed.

Another minute passed before he began. Then Josef told her he had been deceived just like everyone else. That at the time the evidence had appeared solid and overwhelming. And that he would not rest until he got to the bottom of this despicable act.

"Justice will be served," Josef said.

He placed his hand over his heart.

"And my name will be cleared. I *swear* to you."

He took Esperanza's hands in his. His grip hurt her cuts.

"Will you stand with me?" he said.

Esperanza stared at her uncle. And remembered how she saw him when she was a child. When she believed he had wrought holy vengeance on the evil one who destroyed Elden Morris. A myth that had sustained her through the awful aftermath of that terrible crime. Now here she was looking at just a man. And worse than that. Now he was a frightened man. Who needed her. She could see that fright and need pouring out of him.

He was not a mountain. He had never been a mountain.

The dirty Mexican was a hoax. The villain she had repeatedly and devotedly prayed cast down into the deepest recesses of hell had never even existed. It was terrible for her to learn this. To have the scales torn from her eyes. How important those lies had been to her.

And how dependent she was upon her uncle. Having only him to rely on in this world. For a sense of belonging to something more than just herself. For the food in her belly and the clothes on her back and this roof that she hated over her head.

She did what so many others have done. When similarly overwhelmed. When otherwise the transition would be too abrupt and too jarring. A trauma that could shatter and destroy.

She reached for those scales and put them right back on again. So she could look out once again through eyes that saw what she needed to see.

Now her doctored vision told her that however far her uncle had fallen he could never fall so low to have actually framed the man sent to prison for the abduction of Elden Morris.

He was just a man. Not a mountain. But he was also not a monster.

Her uncle could not be that wicked. Not the uncle who took her in when she was orphaned. Who raised her as his own.

"Of course I will stand with you."

What else could she say? What else could she do? Where else in this world could she go? She had no one else. And nowhere else. This was her entire world. Right here in this awful house. Just the two of them and their life here together. This was all that she had.

And she could see no way to escape from it.

So she stopped looking.

Part XXIV:
Arizona Knockabout

Chapter 82

Matt decided to begin at the top. Which meant the dining room of El Tovar. He stopped outside the entrance of the grand rustic lodge and wrestled his excitement down to a nerve-prickling jitteriness. The promise of a fresh start at this extraordinary place seemed to hang thick in the air around him.

He stopped again inside the lobby. Halted by a moment of déjà vu. Then he remembered stepping in here with his parents. For just a quick glance around. Which was enough to make them all wish they could have stayed here. Then the tour herded them off again.

He waited at the front desk. Then began to wilt while explaining to the stone-faced Havasupai woman behind the counter that he came in search of employment. The look she gave him could have frozen Lake Powell.

Which was nothing compared to the reception he received from the manager of the dining room. Who told him brusquely and with what Matt would have sworn was profound spite that there were no positions currently available. And if there were he would have to apply through proper channels. Which would be the human resources department at the contracting firm that ran the lodge. He should not expect to get hired "just walking in off the street."

The manager did not wait for a response. He went striding away across the sizable floor of his fiefdom with his hands behind his back. Matt looked around at the magnificent room and failed to convince himself that he did not really want to work here.

418

As he retreated across the lobby the Havasupai woman called out from her fortress behind the desk —

"Any luck?"

Matt stopped and turned and shook his head. The Havasupai woman finally displayed an emotion. She slitted her eyes and smiled like a cat.

His luck was no better anywhere else at the canyon. Although the receptions he received were less frosty. After El Tovar no one seemed to take pleasure in sending him packing.

A clerk in one of the gift shops explained how to apply for work with the contractor who ran the facilities. But also told him there was nothing available on short notice.

"There's always a waiting list," the woman said. "People want to be here. Like me. I came here twenty years ago and that was it. I had to be here the rest of my life."

Matt then spent what seemed like twenty years enduring her account of how she came to the canyon on vacation from Iowa; had an epiphany on the flight home; which became an episode of mania when her plane landed; followed by a nervous breakdown; after which she was hospitalized for a time; leading to the loss of her job as an office manager for a construction supply company; and the end of her ten-year marriage, which had produced four children, including a set of twins; followed by another epiphany that brought about her permanent return to the canyon.

"I've never left. Been right here every day since."

She smiled and waved a hand in the air.

"Well not *exactly* right here. I spent a few months down in Winslow. Thank God not for long."

What about your kids? Matt wanted to ask her. Did you leave them back in Iowa?

As if on cue she said—

"I do miss my kids. They grow up so fast. But they're happy back in Des Moines. The schools are better and they have their friends."

The canyon was more important to you than your children?

Matt wondered if maybe her kids would like to come out here to see mom and go for a stroll with her along the canyon rim. So they could find a nice place to give her a quick shove.

The woman frowned. Matt glanced at the door.

"Things were easier back then," she said. "It was easier to find work. Not just here but pretty much everywhere. And just easier in general. A dollar went a lot farther. Life has gotten so hard."

She nodded at Matt.

"I feel bad for you young people today. Everything is just so..."

She sighed and shrugged and shook her head.

"So gosh-darned hard."

You have no idea, Matt almost said.

But he managed to stop himself. Now was his chance to escape. He offered his thanks and said goodbye and almost ran out the door.

"Good luck!" she called after him.

In the nearby village of Tusayan he met the same lack of opportunity. And was pointed further down the road by a convenience store clerk. Who told him the closest place he could expect to find work was another seventy-odd miles away from the canyon.

In Flagstaff. Where Matt walked the main drag in the downtown historic district ducking into bars and restaurants.

Despite spending the greatest part of his time indoors speaking with anyone who would listen long enough for him to say he was looking for work, Matt managed to be outside at the start of the only bone-chilling cloudburst that occurred on that particular afternoon. While he stood freezing and dripping before the bar at the next joint he entered, a patron who overhead him talking with the bartender mentioned that a woman he knew had just that morning quit a job waiting tables at an Indian restaurant down in Sedona.

A hurried consultation with his map put Matt back on the road again. A little less than an hour later he was shaking hands with the owner of the Indian place. Ten minutes after that he was hired.

One of his new coworkers knew of a room that was available. Matt called the number he was given then went over there to see the place and speak with the landlord. By evening the room was his.

He had in one day secured all the major arrangements of a new life. And that life was set amid the scenic splendor of the red rock high country. Not right at the canyon as he had hoped. But still. Close enough.

That feeling of excitement and promise returned. The one he lost back in the lobby of El Tovar. This time it stayed with him.

When night came Matt couldn't sleep until the sun was almost up.

Chapter 83

He had a good month in Sedona. Then a day came when during the setup for lunch a furious argument boiled out of the kitchen. It was conducted mostly in Hindi. Leaving Matt clueless until one of the other waiters explained what was being said. The owner had been informed that two of his cousins would arrive that night from Mumbai. And that he was expected to employ them.

The considerable amount of shouting that went on between the owner and the other family members who were his senior employees made it clear that the owner was not pleased by this development. In a burst of expletive-laden English he described one of the arriving cousins as a "less-than-worthless piece of goddamn fucking pig shit".

Eventually the shouting stopped. The owner emerged and stood outside the kitchen doors. For a minute or so he remained there with his head down. Then he looked around the dining room and frowned when he saw Matt.

The owner asked Matt to join him in his office.

The owner said that adding one cousin to the staff could have been achieved by rearranging the schedule. Most of the employees were family. They would make room for another of their own. Matt and his fellow non-relatives would have been asked to accept a slight reduction in hours. Everyone would be taking a cut anyway since the summer high season was coming to a close.

But making room for both cousins would require letting someone go. There wouldn't be enough work for all those hands. Matt was the last one hired. Long-held custom in the owner's family dictated Matt should therefore be the first one terminated. The owner said he had presented strong arguments against holding with tradition in this case. Which Matt took to mean there were other workers he would rather fire.

But tradition had triumphed. Matt received one weeks' severance and the promise of a glowing recommendation. The owner walked him to his car and while shaking his hand said—

"This saddens me Matthew. I like you. You're an excellent worker. If it were up to me I'd tell my cousins to go to hell. But you know how it is with family. What you want doesn't always matter."

Matt tried to imagine having such a family. One powerful enough to dictate how you ran the business that belonged to you. Even when you and your business were on a different continent from most of your family.

The owner clapped him on the shoulder.

"Don't be a stranger," the owner said.

Then he turned and walked away. Matt watched him go.

The owner did not look back.

Matt had spent his off hours in Sedona hiking the trails. For the pleasure and also for the exercise. His run across Las Vegas fleeing Meredith had made it clear he was out of shape. Which wouldn't do if he was going to explore the canyon. And the canyon wouldn't let him not explore it. He was planning his return when he was fired.

With the summer season over, jobs in Sedona were tight. Even tighter than his finances. Which didn't allow for much time without work. He had just spent most of his available cash on tires and brakes. He didn't want car trouble to ruin his trip to the canyon.

When the next month's rent came due he was still unemployed. He packed up his things and followed the search for work south again. Further away from the canyon. Down into the dusty sprawl that filled the Valley of the Sun. Three days later he landed a job at a fast food joint in Mesa. The next day he rented a one-room apartment in a converted motel.

His immediate neighbor was a meth head. The day after Matt moved in the skeletal figure with the scraggly teeth confronted him as he was coming in and pulled out a hunting knife. Matt surprised both of them by knocking the blade out of the addict's shaking hand.

The meth head ran away. Matt never saw him again.

❖   ❖   ❖

A week passed and nothing notable happened. Then Matt went to work on a morning that was already blazing hot despite summer supposedly being over and sat in his idling car staring openmouthed at what the day before had been his place of employment. Overnight the little building where he worked the grill and the counter and took takeout orders over the telephone had burned to the ground. All that remained was the concrete slab foundation and a pile of black char.

"You gotta be kidding me," Matt said.

But no one popped up out of the ashes and shouted "Surprise!"

When he tried his employer's phone number there was no answer. He kept trying over the next three days until he finally got a recording that told him the number had been disconnected.

"You gotta be kidding me," Matt said again.

❖   ❖   ❖

Weeks of scrambling failed to produce work. Matt skipped paying his rent to have money for food and gas. When the eviction notice came he moved his scant belongings back into his car and drove away from the converted motel where he had once been cheered by his triumph over the meth head who had lived next door.

That evening he hid behind a shopping center that had never been occupied. The entire complex had gone directly from construction into foreclosure. He drove slowly across the vast barren parking lot with his heart in his throat waiting for a siren to whoop out at him and cops to appear with their guns drawn. Or at least a fat security guard holding a Taser.

Meanwhile the plate glass storefronts glowed incongruously glorious shades of golden coppery bronze as they reflected and refracted the setting sun. Before them the little red Toyota inched forward throwing a long shadow across the black asphalt toward the warm vibrant colors slowly blending and fading as the day slid down to its close.

Chapter 84

He parked out of sight behind one of the empty stores. Living like a fugitive stealing across the diseased cityscape. Dinner was the second of two apples bought that morning and the last of some almonds purchased on sale a few days before. He chewed slowly and stared out the open window of his car at a loading dock that had never been used.

He told himself that tomorrow he would start back to Portland. That at this point he really had no other choice. Maybe Abigail would give him a loan when he got there. If his former boss at the brew pub rehired him he could repay her in a month or so. Six weeks tops.

The canyon would have to wait. Maybe, like it or not, the canyon was gone out of his life. Maybe he would never see the canyon again. His life showed signs of being far more difficult than he had anticipated. Apparently losing his family was just the beginning.

Or tomorrow he could go to the canyon. And throw himself in. A few hours' drive and then a quick jump and his troubles would be over. A thought Matt found unexpectedly comforting.

And then it disgusted him. Worthless self-pity. He wasn't going to give in to that. He needed to be strong.

He fell asleep to the sound of the expressway from which he had spotted the spectral shopping center. Deep into the night, traffic still hummed vigorously beside this new growth that had been stillborn at the city's bleeding edge.

Matt dreamt that the Hispanic girl sat beside him in his car. He realized she was older now. That she had been older when she appeared before him wearing that white dress. She had become a woman since he first saw her.

They said things to each other that made no sense even in his dream world. Eventually they stopped speaking and he started the motor and they drove away. Then she was gone from beside him and he was alone again out on a desolate highway.

He missed having her beside him and hoped he had become a man. As she had become a woman. But he had doubts about that. He reminded himself he had been manly when the meth head came at him with that knife.

He awoke with his dream forgotten but a lingering sense that something had happened during the night. The sun was rising behind the mountains. Hunger clawed at his entrails.

Back on the expressway he was debating how much breakfast he could afford when he passed a sign for a local restaurant chain that sent him across two lanes of the light early morning traffic. At the next exit he doubled back and found the restaurant and stopped just inside the parking lot entrance to stare up at the sign where a brightly feathered rooster took a prancing step.

Beneath the strutting cock was written "El Gallo Bonito". Matt heard his Hispanic girl's voice from his dream and repeated something she said to him that made no sense at the time—

"The rooster is pretty."

He parked and got out of his car. Then stopped as he approached the door. Beside it taped inside the plate glass was a Help Wanted sign. He continued inside and went to the counter where an older Hispanic gentleman smiled at him and said—

"May I help you?"

Matt smiled back.

"Yes and I hope so," Matt said.

The man frowned and raised his chin but his smile remained in place. Matt pointed up at the menu board and said—

"Yes because I would like one of your burritos."

He brought his hand down and used his thumb to point back over his shoulder at the sign in the window.

"And I hope so because I need a job."

Now the man smiled and frowned at the same time.

"You want to apply for the job," he said.

"Yes sir."

"¿Habla español?"

"Sí señor. Y aprendí en la cocina. No sólo en la escuela."

Yes sir. And I learned in the kitchen. Not just at school.

The man smiled and nodded his head.

"Bueno. ¿Lava los platos?"

Good. Do you wash dishes?

"Sí. Y las ventanas. Y los pisos. Lo que sea."

Yes. And the windows. And the floors. You name it.

The man nodded again and kept smiling. Matt hoped he had made the right impression. That maybe this older Hispanic gentleman with the happy open face would take a chance on him.

"But first you must eat," the man said. "What can we get you?"

Matt wanted to ignore his budget and get the biggest burrito they sold. Instead he ordered what looked like the most calories per dollar. No meat. Eggs and cheese and a lot of starch. Fuel to keep him going.

"Take a seat," the man said. "We'll bring it right out."

Matt did as he was told. A few minutes later the man put a plastic tray down on the table before him.

"When you are done we will talk," the man said.

"Yes sir. Thank you, sir."

The man went back to his business. Matt bent over his food. He had to stop after every third or fourth bite and remind himself to slow down.

As he was finishing his last bite the man returned and sat across from him. For a quarter of an hour the man asked questions. At first he inquired after Matt's work experience. Then made a few gentle probes into his personal history and current circumstances.

At the end of their conversation Matt was hired. Six weeks later he was promoted to shift manager. Three weeks after that he sat across from his employer again—for the older Hispanic gentleman who had hired him was the owner of the El Gallo Bonito chain—and this time Tomás Martínez asked Matt if he would like to be in charge of an entire location. Across the valley in Tempe.

"At ASU," Señor Martínez said. "We get all those hungry college students. We do good business there."

"Yes sir," Matt said. "Thank you *very* much, sir."

He had lived in his car for two weeks after first being hired. Then had rented a room from a coworker's aunt. Two days after his second promotion Matt moved into a small but comfortable and entirely spotless apartment in a decent building in a respectable neighborhood within walking distance of where he now worked. Not a single meth head in sight.

This new place was owned by a cousin of Señor Martínez.

"We are slowly taking over your life," Señor Martínez said.

Matt smiled and shook his head.

"Not so slowly," he said.

Señor Martínez laughed and patted Matt's shoulder.

Chapter 85

Matt made the Arizona State University location of El Gallo Bonito hum. Which kept him occupied and he liked it that way. He was friendly with the customers and his employees. But he didn't make friends. The closest thing Matt had to a friend in this new life that had sprung up for him was Señor Martínez. But the Señor was his boss first and foremost. And that placed strict limits and constraints on their friendship.

Matt wasn't aware that he needed a friend. Or wasn't allowing himself to be aware. He glued his eyes and ears to his work and blocked everything else out of his mind. He had come close enough to being literally penniless to make concerns other than his survival seem presently superfluous.

But his reduced expectations and the limitations they placed on his concerns could not endure. When the belly does not ache and there is reliable shelter at hand the heart will again seek companionship.

That moment came for Matt when one day during the lunch rush a young woman entered who looked unsettlingly familiar. In his second glance he saw how much she resembled the girl he had met at the Tekon Travel Plaza in Tckonsha, Michigan. With his third glance he thought she might even be Abigail White.

But then she opened her mouth and out poured a thick syrup of Texas drawl. Prompting Matt to sigh out his relief. He wasn't ready for Abigail. Not taken by surprise at least. With some warning maybe. With a little advance notice maybe he would even want to see her again.

Then he remembered what it had been like to share her life and her bed. And his loneliness descended upon him like a shroud. Cutting him off from all the humanity bustling around him. For the rest of the day he watched his employees and customers as if they lived in another world. Which he could interact with but never join. Young men and women his own age with lives so very different from his that they could belong to a separate species.

❖   ❖   ❖

As he made his way home through the night it seemed everywhere Matt looked young lovers strolled hand-in-hand. Or laughed inside their automobiles. Or kissed passionately on street corners.

He couldn't help comparing his life to theirs. Even though he told himself not to. The contrast made him shudder. Not inwardly or figuratively but in an actual physical tremor. One that stopped him in his tracks in the middle of the sidewalk. He felt as if a cold wind had blown through his soul.

When the trembling passed he looked up and down the street. At the cars going past. The buildings looming around him. The young people strolling past. He felt nailed to the spot by how everything and everyone here was entirely oblivious to him. To who he was. He was completely unknown.

He craved familiarity. To know and be known. To not be lost in a world full of strangers. And there was only one person in all the world who could give him that. Because there was only one person who knew him well enough.

He took out his cell phone. And then hesitated. For ten or fifteen seconds Matt scowled down at the blandly dangerous-looking device in his hand.

Then he called her.

"Matt!" Abigail yelled. "Is that really you?"

He assured her that it was.

"Where have you been? You promised you would stay in touch."

He remembered making that promise. Outside her apartment before he left. And his good intentions in that moment. Now he apologized for vanishing. Then struggled under the barrage of her questions. Where was he, how did he wind up there, what was he doing with his life. He kept his answers short and omitted any details that would have hinted at how desperate things had been. And how lonely he was now.

Then this question brought him up short—

"So. Busy breaking hearts since you left me?"

He couldn't even stammer out a nervous laugh.

But no matter. Because no response was needed. The Oregon girl began talking again. The awkwardness of his silence having failed to penetrate all the waves and wires of cellular telecommunications to her little handheld unit off in Portland.

Into which she blurted out that she was getting married.

Of course the lucky guy was none other than the barista at that joint around the corner from her apartment. Who else could it be? Matt was tempted to interrupt and say—

You don't have to explain. I know who he is.

In the next moment he was tempted to hang up.

He didn't do that either.

What he did do was congratulate her. And sincerely. He had left her and Portland partly to get out of their way. Why be a bad sport about it now? Even if this unexpected news unexpectedly hurt like hell.

Thankfully their conversation ended quickly. Because she was at a party to celebrate her engagement.

At the brew pub on Flanders street where Matt had waited tables.

When they said goodbye and hung up Matt found himself outside a bar. He looked back to where he had brought out his phone and called Abigail and had no recollection of crossing the space between here and there. At some point during their brief but debilitating conversation his feet had decided to start moving again and carried him away down the block.

The bar door swung open and a trio of blondes spilled into the street. He watched them stumble away laughing. All three wore short skirts that left their scissoring legs naked. He wondered at a life that made room for things like getting drunk with your college friends. Since those three were decidedly ASU girls. Let alone a life in which you had friends. And could go to college. And felt safe enough to wander around drunk in clothes that said *fuck me*.

And could get married.

He pulled the bar door open again and went inside resolved to get drunk enough to push the Oregon girl and her barista boy out of his head. But while seated before a beer that wasn't as cold as he would have liked Matt looked around at the carelessly inebriated college students carrying on all around him and felt that he had become very old. Far older than anyone else here. Even the fat guy down the bar who looked to be about forty.

And so very much older than the girl he had just spoken with. The one he lived with back in Oregon. Who was now engaged.

Matt asked himself why he cared what she did and who she did it with. He had been bored sharing her quiet life. He was itching to leave the moment it became clear that he should go. So what if she took up with some jerk who worked in a coffee shop?

And the guy was not a jerk. He actually seemed pretty decent. They made a nice couple. He had seen that in the first moment when he caught them looking at each other.

434

And the life he lived now—was it more exciting than the one he had shared with her? That life he had decided was too quiet for him? While he had been on the road he could say that was true. On his tour of his dead. But now that he was settled into Tempe? With his barren little apartment and his busy little job? Now he lived like a monk with no monastery. An urban hermit. No friends. No girl. No relationships that weren't work-related. A social life of coworkers' birthday parties and Martínez family events. Where he stood on the periphery and only talked when he was spoken to.

She was the only person in his life outside this cramped little sphere. And now she had made a big change. One that could only take her further away from him. Slight as their connection had been, it was all he had.

The thought of losing her made him feel destroyed.

Chapter 86

He didn't notice when the girl seated beside him rose unsteadily to her feet. He didn't hear when she laughed and yelled something to someone down the bar. He wasn't aware of her presence until she stumbled and fell against him.

Suddenly her face was next to his. She was Hispanic and very pretty. He looked at her blurred laughing features and the attractive young woman pressed against him disappeared. Instead he saw the girl from the canyon. The one who had come to him in visions and dreams. And had sent him into whatever this life was that he was now living.

She leaned forward and whispered in his ear—
Soon we will be together.

Then he heard the real words from the real girl—

"Sorry. I'm a little drunk."

Then she was laughing again.

He helped the real girl in the present moment onto her feet. And rose to his own feet while doing so. Then stood planted beside his stool watching her go tottering off. When she disappeared into the restroom Matt abandoned the warmish beer he had barely touched and went back out into the street.

Where he stopped on the sidewalk just past the door and felt paralyzed by an all-encompassing anxiety. His life seemed to be happening all on its own. He felt no power over the events of the world that churned around him and the things he did as part of the chaos. As if he was a stick tossed downstream by a rushing torrent.

His vision closed into a tunnel. He felt he was about to pass out. And realized he had stopped breathing. He forced air into his lungs. Hot dry dusty Tempe air that tasted of burnt gasoline.

When his vision had cleared Matt needed to hear his own voice—

"Get a grip," he said.

And then wondered if he was already too far gone.

❖   ❖   ❖

He slept fitfully. Shallow restless sleep full of anxious dreams. His parents were there. His siblings too. A handful of friends from back in Walker City. When he went to school like his peers and led a normal life. Unfortunately Meredith also put in an appearance. Naked to reveal those new curves he had lusted after in the Agropoli.

It was the Hispanic girl who had tumbled against him that last visited his dreams. They were again seated at the bar but now they faced each other. She began telling him about a movie she had just seen. She told him he had been the star. While her hand slipped inside his pants. This being a dream her hand did that effortlessly. No fumbling with zippers or buttons.

And then the dream ended and Matt was awake. He sat on the edge of his bed with his erection aching between his legs and shook his head. Then went and stood at the toilet waiting for his penis to deflate so he could pee. Which took far longer than he could remember that ever taking before.

Back in his bedroom he pulled some clothes on and stared out the window. He had no view to speak of. There was no reason to stare. He didn't see what was out the window. What he saw was the moment when the Hispanic girl at the bar became the Hispanic girl from the canyon. And what she had said to him. And how very much he wanted to believe her. And what he would say to her if she was real. How he would profess his insane devotion.

But instead he said this—

"You are really losing it."

437

And then his telephone rang. On beat and as if on cue.

❖   ❖   ❖

The only calls Matt ever received were from work. Today was supposed to be his day off. Maybe Señor Martínez wanted him to come in. He had gotten that call before. He asked himself what would happen if he didn't answer.

Then asked himself how he would fill up an empty day. With all these girls rattling around in his head. The ones he had left behind that were now getting married; and the ones who fell against him in bars and felt so very good; and the ones who came to visit him in his head making him think he might be mad.

He reached for his phone. The caller ID confirmed that Señor Martínez was on the line. Matt braced himself to yield this day that was supposed to be his to El Gallo instead. And tried not to admit he would be glad to.

But that was not what Señor Martínez wanted.

"Forgive me for calling on your day off," the Señor said. "But we have a problem. And I hope you can solve it. Otherwise I wouldn't bother you. Let me ask you something. Would you be willing to relocate? One of my cousins and I bought a new place. Sit-down service. Lunch and dinner trade. Southwestern food. The kitchen is solid but the service needs work. We want you to manage it. What do you say? Would you be willing to do that?"

Matt did not hesitate. Here was escape. A door had opened and he went charging through it—

"Absolutely," was Matt's answer to Señor Martínez.

"Good! That's great. Let me call my cousin back. After that I'll get you all the details."

Matt had just one question he would have liked to ask. But before he could do that Señor

438

Martínez hung up. Matt sat looking down at his now-silent phone and wondered where he had just agreed to go live.

Part XXV:
Bold Coyote

Chapter 87

He was a local boy. The star quarterback of his high school team. Which he led to a state championship. An injury ended his college career.

Now he was a decorated former member of the United States Army Special Forces. Who decided that being retired was just too boring. For a bit of fun with a week left before the filing deadline, he tossed his green beret into the Republican primary ring. The sound bite that dominated the local media for the next news cycle featured him growling to the gathered press—

"Turns out I'm not done kicking ass."

The big grin he offered the cameras was full of large square white teeth set in large square jaws. His large square head was set solid upon large square shoulders riding high atop a very large square body. His legs were square and his torso was square and his arms were square. And up in that high square head his nose and ears and eyes were all square and his hair was cut square around them. The photograph that appeared on the front page of the local newspaper seemed to scream—

Behold and venerate my all-American masculine squareness!

"He looks like something out of a movie," Josef said.

He waved a hand at the image.

"After I fight off a man like him. Assuming that can be done. What will I have left against the other one?"

Esperanza had never seen her uncle so discouraged. She heard something new in his voice—a note of panic.

But she remained calm. Sometimes the soldier has to steady the commander.

"He has no experience in law enforcement," Esperanza said.

Josef snorted.

"You think people will care about that? They see someone like him and they go blind to what matters. Before we can convince them he would be a lousy sheriff we have to make them realize he isn't a superhero. Because he sure as hell looks like one."

"Then we will work hard."

"Yes. We will. We will work *very* hard. Which will mean spending a lot of money. And chances are good we will beat him. He is new at this and we are not. But then we will already be bloodied. And even worse we will be broke. Just when we have to go fight again. Against someone who does have experience in law enforcement."

Now Josef was referring to the Democratic candidate. Who they would have to face after the Green Beret. That well-respected and well-liked police chief from down near the border.

"What the hell will we say about that one? The one who could actually do a good job. And not make a hundred stupid mistakes right off the bat."

"We'll think of something."

"Sure, sure. Punt it down the field."

"What else can we do? We have to focus on what's in front of us."

"Exactly."

He waved his hand at the Green Beret again.

"I'm gonna lose because of this asshole."

Esperanza rode beside Josef in the back seat of a departmental SUV. At the wheel was the young deputy who came to fetch her home from the city and who had been waiting beside her bed when she awoke in the hospital. The morning had just begun on another day full of The Campaign.

They were listening to a local conservative radio show. This morning's guest for the rush hour was none other than the Green Beret. Who overnight had become the darling of every right winger in Doña Pero. The host opened by asking about the candidate's combat experience. The Green Beret answered by trumpeting his success against insurgent forces in Iraq.

"Which is basically the same situation as what you have right now, right here, where we live," the candidate said. "With these drug cartels coming across the border."

The host leaned into his microphone—

"You're saying we're at war."

This was his trademark moment. The signature of his show. Filling up the speakers as his deep resonant voice delivered an ominous pronouncement. Implying once again that doomsday was at our doorstep. Leaving a weighted pause before he expanded on his subject—

"What you're saying, if I understand you correctly—and I believe that I do—is that these Mexican drug lords are waging war against us. Right here on American soil."

"Yes sir. That's exactly what I'm saying."

"Now what can we do about that?"

"Well the first thing I can tell you is that when you're at war you need to put a warrior in charge of your forces. You don't send your men into battle under the command of just any lawman. Because the law won't protect you against hostiles."

"Very interesting. Let's hold that thought. We need to take a station break. We'll be right back—"

Josef had a big voice of his own. He used it now to fill the SUV and drown out the radio.

"That was nicely done. How they dodged his complete lack of experience with the law. By talking up a threat that is beyond the law. One a lawman can't do anything about. A war requires an army. Which a lawman does not have. So what will his experience leading combat troops do for him when he has a few men with pistols against many men with assault rifles? If he finds a cartel force here in Doña Pero. Which has never happened. He wouldn't be able to do a damn thing to stop a cartel if they came in here. And he knows that. Unless he is even more of a fool than he seems already."

Josef waved a hand at the radio and the men who had been talking on it.

"But still. That was nicely done."

A few minutes later the show was back on. No one spoke in the SUV while the host and the Green Beret took turns implying and alleging that at any moment the drug cartels would come swarming across the border and turn Doña Pero County into Mexico North. Headless bodies hanging from every overpass. Piles of heads dumped before the courthouse. Mountains of drug money turning their government into an addicted whore.

And only one man could stand in the way of this Armageddon.

Esperanza wanted to tell her uncle the Green Beret had torn a page out of his playbook. That this was exactly how Josef Armijo had become sheriff. Taking the incumbent by surprise. Proclaiming that he was the only man who could save Doña Pero. From a threat south of the border.

But of course she did not mention this. She only smiled to herself while she thought about the parallels. And what one could say about them—

What goes around comes around.

Karma is a bitch.

That sort of thing.

When the two on the radio had finished their tag-team reduction of Doña Pero into a post-apocalyptic wasteland, it was time for another station break. The ads seemed to blare out at them for an hour. Esperanza's thoughts moved on to other things. Then she realized the two men were talking again.

She jolted when the host said—

"Now about this Morris case."

The weighted pause.

"The conviction that was overturned. A notable case. A tragic case. And an outrageous miscarriage of justice."

A second weighted pause. This was a big deal.

"Armijo was deeply involved. We have a deputy, who is deceased, being held accountable."

A third weighted pause! Lock and load, fellow patriots.

"Tell us what you think about that."

The Green Beret could be heard taking a deep breath.

"I'll tell you what I think."

"Shut it off," Josef said.

Esperanza yelled—

"No! We need to hear this!"

The Green Beret leaned in close. Any closer and the square lips of his square mouth would have brushed against his microphone—

"Now that to me just does not pass the smell test."

"That's it!" Josef said. "We've heard enough."

The deputy pushed a button and the radio went silent.

Chapter 88

Sheriff Armijo was surrounded by a knot of supporters who were all women and for the moment he could not have looked happier. His eyes sparkled and his smile flashed and pleasure lit up his fleshy face while he offered little jests that set his audience to tittering. Esperanza watched and saw the man she had grown up with and not the man he had become. She liked him again while that moment lasted. And remembered with sad fondness how her Tía Rosa used to laugh at her husband's delight in the company of women.

Josef concluded his exchange with his admiring lady friends and rejoined Esperanza at their table. As he pulled out his chair his cell phone rang. He remained standing and dug the phone out of his pocket. It rang again while he was frowning at the display.

"What good is caller ID when it just tells you the number? I need a name."

"What's the number?"

Josef ignored her and put the phone to his ear. Esperanza watched him and listened to his half of the conversation—

"Armijo."

"I'm good. Thank you. How are you?"

"I'm sorry to hear that. You will be missed."

"I hope you're not getting cold feet?"

"If you say so."

"Let's not be too hasty. That was just—"

"Come on now. After a little thing like that?"

"Tell me you're not putting your money behind him instead."

"Well that's something at least. Do me this much more. Wait a little longer. He just got started. So he's strong out of the gate. But he's new at this game. Let's see how he does after we go a few more rounds. *Then* make your bet on who will be first over the finish line. Will you do that for me?"

"Good. I have your word then?"

"I'll hold you to it. You know that."

"Okay."

Josef disconnected the call and took his seat. He sat staring at his phone.

"Son of a bitch. One damn interview with this joker and the money starts drying up."

He put his phone away and turned to the man seated on his other side.

"Did you catch that?" Josef said. "We're bleeding."

The Executive Manager of the Campaign to Re-elect Sheriff Armijo spoke in hushed tones. So his every word sounded like it was shared in close confidence. Making what he said now inaudible to anyone but his boss.

"That's good," Josef said. "But we need to do more."

There was an edge to his voice when he continued—

"We need to cut him off at the knees."

Esperanza was looking at her phone when he sat down beside her. The one she had been trying to keep an eye on. He of course sat too close. And managed to poke the side of her breast with his elbow. Even as she was busy moving away from him. He leaned almost into her lap when he held out his check. Upon which she could see actual grease stains. Ovaloid blotches marked by oily fingertips.

Then his reptilian voice came slithering out of him—

"I hope you don't miiind," he said. "Your uncle told me I could give this to yooouuu."

Esperanza felt like she had been licked all over by the slimy tongue of a scaly beast. She wanted to go home and shower. She did not want to take the proffered check. That would put her hand very close to his.

"Of course," she said. "I will see that our treasurer gets it."

She reached for the check but he did not release it. His other hand quickly covered hers. His skin was cool and clammy. She imagined her own flesh turned fetid by the contact.

Out came that licking voice again—

"Many thaaanksss. What would he do without yooouuu?"

Pay someone, Esperanza wanted to say. Actually a couple of someones.

Now let go of my hand.

She felt his moist breath lap against her cheek as he slowly released his grip. Then her hand came free with the check in it and she turned away from him. She had an envelope in her purse for any donations that might be offered by those who chose to deal with her. Among whom she knew the greasy one seated beside her would be first and foremost.

She felt his eyes all over her while she retrieved her purse from the seat back where she had hung it and dug out the envelope and tucked the check inside of it and then slipped the envelope back into her purse. She decided to keep her purse in her lap while he remained beside her. A layer of protection and a handy weapon if it came to that.

He leaned close and whispered in her ear that he wanted to meet in private.

No shit really? was how Esperanza would have liked to reply.

Instead she merely cleared her throat and leaned away. But he followed close behind. Now his lips were even nearer to her ear. And he was claiming not to harbor any untoward intentions.

Like hell you don't.

He only desired to assist Esperanza in whatever she chose to do after her uncle's campaign

447

had concluded. During which she had demonstrated such a notable gift for political operations. Her hard work had impressed certain influential people. To whom he would be glad to introduce her.

After they had a chance to meet. In private. And discuss her goals and objectives. To determine where the best opportunity might be found. To meet those goals and objectives. Which they would meet to discuss. In private. At her earliest convenience.

He was by now markedly stimulated. Apparently the idea of being alone with her was too much for him.

Esperanza graciously thanked the greasy one for his kind offer. Then said that for now her uncle's campaign absorbed all of her available time. That she would be happy to discuss her future once the campaign was over. And her uncle was re-elected. But until then it was simply impossible.

And if by some freak chance we ever have that conversation I will tell you to go to hell.

Let us end with one last reproduction of his grating speech—

"Ah your Tío is lucky to have such a good one as yooouuuu."

Then he excused himself. For the restroom.

Which Esperanza wished he had not mentioned.

The campaign manager said something that made Josef laugh. Not down in his belly but snorting through his nose. It was not the most appealing sound that her uncle had ever made.

When Josef turned to Esperanza he said—

"Did he give you a check?"

Which brought back the man she was trying to forget. She wanted her response to be cutting. Maybe mention that ugly noise her uncle had just made. Tell him never to do that in front of the cameras and microphones.

Instead she just nodded. Josef nodded back.

"Good," he said.

"Yes. Good. It's all very good."

Josef frowned. He leaned closer and whispered—

"Is there a problem?"

Esperanza whispered back—

"You didn't wonder why he insisted on giving it to me?"

"What? Come on. Don't give me that."

"What should I give you then?"

"Don't be like this. We need to make him happy."

"How happy should I make him?"

"Excuse me?"

"What do you think he wants from me?"

"What are you saying?"

"He wants me to sleep with him."

"What? Don't be disgusting."

"I just want to make it clear exactly what you expect me to do."

"What has gotten into you?"

"You're not the one he wants. If you were in my position you would ask these questions too."

"He really wants that?"

"Don't be simple, Tío. Of course he does."

Josef hissed out his breath.

"I didn't think that snake had it in him. Can you keep him off?"

"So far so good. But as soon as he gets me alone it's all over."

"Then don't let him get you alone."

"That will only happen if he catches me by surprise."

"Then make sure he doesn't."

"There's only so much I can do. If he keeps stalking me. At some point he might get lucky."

"Damn. I really don't need this."

449

"*You* don't need it?"

"I'm sorry, mija. Of course you don't need it either."

"I think I don't need it a little more than you don't need it."

"Calm down. You know what I mean."

"That's not a good idea."

"What?"

"Telling me to calm down."

Josef stared at his niece. But offered no response. The expression Esperanza saw on his face was one she had never seen caused by her. For the first time she suspected her uncle was afraid of what she might do next. And then her uncle laughed. Which confirmed her suspicion. Because she knew her uncle laughed when he was confronted by something he feared.

Good, Esperanza thought. It's about time.

Chapter 89

They were approaching the day's final event. A fundraising dinner that had already suffered the withdrawal of the deep pockets who had been impressed by the Green Beret's radio interview. Not the biggest sponsor they had but close to it. Josef seemed to have forgotten that loss in the hours since. But with the dinner now immediately before them Esperanza could tell he was thinking of nothing else.

"There will be consequences," Josef said.

Esperanza watched her uncle and waited. He had his eyes pointed forward. Looking past the deputy at the wheel out at the road before them. When a moment had passed Esperanza almost asked her uncle what he was talking about. Then decided maybe she didn't want to know.

That was when he told her—

"If I lose," Josef said.

He turned to Esperanza.

"Things will change for us. Me. You. Our family. My men."

He waved a hand through the air.

"This whole place will change."

He lowered his hand and sighed.

"Maybe someday the people will understand. How I tried to protect Doña Pero. From forces beyond our little world. Here in this small corner of our big country."

He shook his head.

"The borderlands are never easy."

He sighed again. With all the weight of the world that had cruelly descended upon him. To straddle his round shoulders.

"There is so much the people do not know. How everything works. The deals that are made. Between light and dark. If the people knew they wouldn't be able to sleep at night."

Esperanza had no idea what her uncle was talking about.

"What consequences?" she said.

Josef frowned at her.

"What?"

"You said there would be consequences. If you lose. What did you mean by that?"

Josef stared for a moment. Then grimaced and shook his head. A sound of disgust came hissing from the back of his throat—

"Ahhhh..."

Then he turned toward his window and was silent. Esperanza watched him and waited for more. Even though she knew nothing more would follow. He was done. The subject was closed.

"That's not fair," Esperanza said.

No response. Her uncle remained turned away.

She raised her voice and tried again—

"Tío. That's not fair."

He turned toward her. His face said that his thoughts were far away.

"Hunh?" Josef grunted.

"You can't tell me there will be consequences and not explain. Then go on about the world and how bad it is. Without telling me what you think could happen."

He watched her with a solemn face. She waited but he said nothing.

"That's not fair," Esperanza repeated one more time.

Josef snorted softly. Then he sighed. For a moment his face lightened. He almost smiled. Before his features collapsed back down into their burdened heavy fleshiness. He spoke quietly—

"Ah mija. You have no idea how unfair things can be."

And with that he turned away again. Pointing his eyes out the window at the world that went sliding past.

452

Over on her side Esperanza did the same. Where she was busy thinking she had a pretty good idea exactly how unfair things could be. And did not care for her uncle asserting that she was still an innocent. Given that this world had been taking away the people she loved since she was an infant.

❖   ❖   ❖

She wanted to leave it alone. To pretend he never said anything. That his gloomy little oration on the complexities of living in this world of good and evil had never happened.

But something he mentioned kept nagging at her.

Finally she couldn't stand it any longer.

"What deals?" Esperanza said.

He ignored her.

"What were you talking about?"

No response.

"I'm not going to stop until you tell me."

He shook his head. But didn't speak.

"What?" Esperanza said. "Out with it."

"Forget it. It's nothing."

"A few minutes ago you made it sound like the end of the world."

"It doesn't concern you."

"Does it involve this campaign?"

Josef went silent again.

"So that's how it is," Esperanza said. "I work like a dog for you. But you keep things from me."

"This isn't anything you need to know about."

"So why mention it?"

"I shouldn't have."

"You're right. That was a mistake."

"There are things you don't *want* to know about."

"And you're the one who decides. Which things I want to know. And which things I don't."

"Of course. Who else?"

"Right. Of course. Who else?"

"Don't get like that with me, Essie. You're still my responsibility."

"Really? That's how you see it? Like I'm still little and great big you is taking care of me?"

"You know what I mean."

"I run your *life*, Tío. I keep your house. I make sure your bills get paid. Do everything on this campaign that you can't get someone else to do. And what do you pay me for all this? Hunh? Nothing. Not one stinking cent. So who is taking care of whom here?"

"Okay. You do a lot for me."

"I do *everything* for you."

"Let's not get carried away."

"But still there are things I don't get to know about."

"That's how it is."

"Well I don't like it."

Josef's voice came back hot—

"Who said you had to like it?"

Esperanza stared at her uncle. And remembered that look of fear she saw on his face. Back at the luncheon when he wasn't sure what she might do next. She wanted to put that look back on him. And knew how to do it. She could insist on being let into her uncle's complete confidence about his campaign. Right here and right now. And threaten to quit if he didn't.

But that would be poking the bear. His anger was starting to show. Then this dinner looming ahead of them could go even worse than already promised.

And there was the deputy at the wheel. Witnessing this rupture. Maybe her uncle didn't want to speak in front of him.

La Soldadita was too much of a good soldier to push any further.

She would hold her tongue. And resume marching.

❖ ❖ ❖

The coyote came out of nowhere. One moment the road ahead was clear and the next moment the animal was standing there. The deputy jammed on the brakes. They screeched to a halt. Everyone was tossed violently forward.

The coyote didn't budge. It stood like a statue on the pavement. Bold and brazen and defiant. Esperanza felt the animal was staring at her. Which she tried to dismiss as an optical illusion. A trick of the light and the angle that made the trickster appear to unnervingly hold her gaze.

But that was not what she felt in her gut. Her gut said the coyote was there because of her. That the look it gave her meant—

I am watching out for you.

The animal turned and loped away across the road. Making its exit through a break in the traffic. Without as much as a glance in either direction to see if the way was clear. From across the boulevard the coyote looked back again.

Then it vanished. One moment it stood before a low brick wall in the office park across the road. The next moment it was gone.

"What the hell was that?" Josef said.

For the first time in days Esperanza heard the deputy speak—

"You can't kill a coyote. It's bad luck."

"Is that so?" Josef said. "Who told you that?"

"My abuela. She's Diné."

"Of course she is. Good for her. Now get going."

The deputy got them moving again.

Esperanza became aware she was breathing rapidly. She took a deep breath and tried to calm herself. She kept seeing the coyote staring at her.

Josef extended a hand and pointed ahead. Her heart jumped again. She expected to see the coyote.

455

Instead she saw the sign for the restaurant. Where the fundraiser was being held.

"Look," Josef said. "Here we are. And it only took a lifetime."

Esperanza turned to her uncle. He smiled at her.

"Yes?" Josef said.

"What is up with you?"

Josef pointed at his chest.

"With me?"

He spread his hands.

"Not a thing! Couldn't be better."

His grin was full of teeth.

"Right as rain."

The SUV slowed for the turn into the entrance. Esperanza scanned the cars in the parking lot and hoped many of them belonged to willing donors. That they would get lucky and just the one who called wouldn't show. That everyone else on their list would arrive with checks in hand. Then maybe her uncle would shake this off and get back on track.

She looked back at her uncle. He was still grinning at her.

Esperanza hissed and shook her head.

"Yeah, you're great Tío. This is gonna be a real good time."

Josef laughed. The sound he made was hard and cold and unamused.

The deputy found a spot near the entrance. Esperanza was the first one out.

She was eager to gain some distance from her uncle.

Part XXVI:
El Leñador

Chapter 90

It was an inauspicious start. On the morning he was supposed to leave Matt found a nail sticking out of his flattened right front tire. One of the tires he had bought back in Sedona. When he was planning his return to the canyon. Not that the tires were new anymore. But the money he spent on them still seemed freshly enough surrendered that seeing a big fat nail protruding from between the tread felt like a violation.

He had hoped to arrive at his new home that afternoon. Instead, getting the tire patched took the rest of the morning and it was past noon before he left. With everything he owned once again stuffed into his mother's little red Toyota. He had sold the few pieces of furniture he acquired while in Tempe and rented a furnished place at the other end. Keep it simple. Travel light. Who knew when and if ever he would really settle down.

He arrived just before dusk. His new place was a small square adobe casita in a complex of about twenty others more or less like it. Some were a little larger and had a second bedroom. A few had covered patios.

He had grown accustomed to the Sonoran Desert. With its odd abundance of bizarre plant life. This place was starker and sparer. No saguaros standing sentry. Outside of town, low scrub was scattered across open country. Rocks and dust stretched away toward jagged mountains.

He wasn't sure if he liked it.

It looked like a good place to get lost.

❖   ❖   ❖

His race wasn't a problem. Despite most of the staff being Hispanic. Neither was not being a local. No one seemed to care where he was from. It was his age they didn't like. Most of the staff were at least a few years older and visibly resented reporting to this new kid. The source of their displeasure was made clear when he overheard one of the cooks say—

"Can you believe this shit? How old is he? Twelve?"

Matt turned around and went back into the kitchen.

"You want to know how old I am?"

The cook scowled.

"I didn't mean anything by it."

"Go ahead and ask me."

The cook raised his chin.

"Okay. How old are you?"

"Old enough to fire you. Which is all you need to know. Are we clear on this?"

The cook nodded.

"Yes sir."

The rest of the day no one said anything to him unless Matt spoke first. He felt eyes follow him everywhere. And caught more than a few glares when he turned around quickly.

The staff that was incompetent had to be weeded out and dismissed. Which left them shorthanded. So new staff had to be hired. Then everyone required various degrees of training. Even the best had to be taught how things could be done better.

The cook Matt quarreled with proved to be one of the good ones. Tino was smart and worked hard and was willing to learn. Fortunately he also didn't hold a grudge.

When a month had passed Matt fired the head cook and put Tino in charge.

A decision he had to sell to his boss.

Matt called Señor Martínez right after it was done.

"I was told the kitchen was in good shape," Señor Martínez said. "That was one of the reasons we made the purchase."

"It was. Now it will be better."

Señor Martínez laughed. But he didn't sound happy.

"I should know better than to second guess you. And if we didn't want bold thinking I would have sent someone else."

He paused.

"But why am I only hearing about this after it's done?"

"Would you have tried to talk me out of it?"

Señor Martínez didn't answer.

"I need to make my own decisions," Matt said.

Still no reply.

Matt wondered if they had been disconnected.

Then he started to hope they had been disconnected.

Finally Señor Martínez responded—

"Yes. I see your point."

He sighed and the line crackled.

"But next time tell me first. There are other investors to consider. Are we clear on this, Matthew?"

Matt had to swallow to get his voice back.

"Yes sir. Very clear."

Two of the busboys got into it over a waitress. They stepped outside to settle their differences. Matt heard the shouting and went to break it up. He got between the combatants and was clocked on the cheek. The fist that punched him was wearing a ring. That ring tore open a deep gash.

459

Tino cleaned it up and inspected the damage.

"That's going to want stitches."

"Fuck. Are you sure?"

"If it was on my face. When was your last tetanus shot?"

"Fuck!"

Tino taped a wad of gauze over the wound. Matt told everyone to get back to work and drove himself to the hospital. A nurse in the emergency room told him he'd get faster and less expensive treatment at an urgent care clinic. She told him where the nearest one was located and he got back in his car.

At the clinic he waited to be admitted. Then a nurse took his information and directed him to a second waiting area. Where he waited to be treated.

And wondered how his life had come to this.

He was struggling every day to turn El Leñador into a functional restaurant. Although he deeply appreciated everything Señor Martínez had done for him and the confidence he had demonstrated in selecting Matt for this, job the assignment was starting to feel like a curse.

Last week he lost his best waitress. She eloped to Wyoming with a wildcatter. Called to quit two hours before the dinner shift. He still hadn't found anyone to replace her.

The week before that one of the cooks was arrested. Despite having been born in this country before Matt could bail him out, the cook was transferred to an INS detention center because he had the same name as someone who actually was here illegally. Getting him out of that mess required enlisting a local legal defense organization that specialized in handling such cases. Matt hated to admit that if the man hadn't been a good cook he might not have done all the work needed to get him out. And Manuel could be stuck down in Mexico right now. With no money and no one to turn to.

And these problems just kept coming. One right after the other. On top of all the everyday stuff that had to be done to remain open for business. He worked seven days most weeks. Six days when he caught what passed for a break. From twelve to sixteen hours every working day. Mostly spent on his feet solving immediate and unpleasant problems.

Like last night. When a busboy called in sick at the last minute and Matt had to cover the shift himself. While still managing everyone else. In the middle of the dinner rush someone clogged up a toilet and flooded the women's bathroom. While he and the other busboy were in there with a plunger and a mop, the tables piled up with dirty dishes and customers filled up the waiting area and began turning away. A good chunk of their dinner business was lost. And paid for with some bad word-of-mouth.

There was nothing good to be said about a night like that.

And he had far too many of them.

Chapter 91

A nurse came and got him. Then left him waiting in a treatment room. Which was air-conditioned to near Artic conditions. The chair he sat down in was directly under the vent. After a few moments of suffering in the frigid blast he got up and moved to the examination table.

Where he asked himself what could he expect to get out of all these bad days and nights. Where were this job taking him? Other than here to see a doctor? What would he do after El Leñador was in decent shape? Assuming that ever happened. How long would he be stuck running it?

And when he left would he repeat this same miserable process somewhere else? Kill himself all over again unknotting some other clusterfuck? After that would there be another one? Would he spend his life turning places around for Señor Martínez?

Or was he being groomed for something better? Was there anything better to be groomed for? Did he want to be groomed?

He could look for another job. But how would that be any better? Doing the same shit for someone he didn't like as much as Señor Martínez.

He could try going out on his own. Find a place that needed to be turned around, put together a business plan, line up some investors, and make the jump. Would Señor Martínez back him if he did?

He told himself he had options. And tried to find that reassuring.

But none of those options appealed to him. The truth was they all sounded horrible. Because they all involved restaurants. And he was sick to fucking death of fucking restaurants. Sick to goddamn fucking death. What good were options that kept him doing work he had grown to hate?

But it was the only trade he knew.

And he was presently failing at it.

El Leñador could take his options away. Kill off any career in management. Bust him back down to waitstaff.

Then maybe he would have to do what he considered back in Las Vegas. Move to a major city and try to work his way up in a top tier restaurant. Which sounded almost as unpleasant as what he was doing now.

And like it or not he wasn't willing to give up. He didn't want to disappoint Señor Martínez. But if he didn't show some real progress soon he would fall all the way out of favor. His former shine was already marred by prominent scuff marks. Like that scolding he got over Tino.

At least that gamble had paid off. The kitchen was turning out better food faster and with less waste. Which would be great if Matt had been sent there to improve the kitchen. And not the waitstaff. With which he was flailing like a drowning man.

Maybe he should look for a place with good waitstaff and a bad kitchen.

Now he was really shoveling some bullshit. Like he knew enough to actually run a kitchen. He wasn't a cook.

But Tino was. Maybe he and Tino should look for a place.

His phone rang. He looked at the display and saw Tino's number. Maybe this was a sign. That they should become partners. Maybe it was more bad news. That seemed far more likely. But most likely of all was that Tino was just calling to check on him. He had been gone for a while now.

"Hey," Matt said. "I'm still waiting for someone to sew me up."

"We got a problem."

Matt heard sirens in the background.

More bad news it was.

What fun he was having today.

463

❖   ❖   ❖

A dishwasher spilled a pot of grease on a countertop. He was new and still learning his way around. While he was looking for what he needed to clean up the mess a waiter stuck his head in the kitchen and asked if Matt was back yet. That led to a cook recounting for the dishwasher how the boss got injured breaking up the fistfight between the busboys.

Meanwhile the grease was spreading. Oozing across the counter which was next to the stove. Where a pot of water was waiting to boil. When the grease crossed the stovetop and reached the burner it burst into flames.

Tino returned to the kitchen just as the fire erupted. He began shouting at everyone to get outside and made sure the building was emptied. If anyone deserved credit for no one being hurt he was the one. He also shouted at the cook who had distracted the dishwasher to call 911. Which meant that the fire department arrived quickly.

The kitchen was gutted but the rest of the interior only suffered smoke and water damage. Insurance covered everything. Including the installation of superior fire suppression equipment. Which reduced the premiums paid by the owners going forward.

Changes suggested by Matt and Tino allowed the renovations to improve the layout of the kitchen. Especially the staging area used by the waitstaff.

When El Leñador reopened, all of their problems vanished. The turmoil that had plagued the waitstaff came to an abrupt halt. Not just in the work done there by the waiters and waitresses and busboys and now busgirls (Matt replaced the two brawlers with a pair of young women). But also in the lives of those individuals. They stopped eloping. And almost getting deported. The weekly crises came to a halt.

A waitress attributed the transformation to *feng shui*. She said the restaurant had become harmonized. Resulting in vastly enhanced flow. That affected everyone who entered there.

Either that or it was just a coincidence.

Meanwhile the fire inspector had determined that a defective valve in the old fire suppression system had failed. So despite the system being properly installed and having passed all of its inspections, instead of blasting out forceful jets of smothering water the sprinkler heads had merely spurted and sputtered. Allowing the fire to advance unimpeded.

The owners of El Leñador immediately joined a class action lawsuit against the manufacturers of the valve and the system that employed it. Which settled soon after they signed on. What the owners received as their portion of the settlement more than offset the costs of closing El Leñador during the three weeks required to complete the renovations.

At that point Matt thought he might have to start believing in miracles.

In a show of faith that left Matt feeling emotional, the owners approved a suggestion by Señor Martínez that the proceeds from the lawsuit be used to increase the promotional budget for El Leñador. A couple of weeks later he heard the first advertisement on the radio. It gave him goosebumps.

"Hot damn!" Matt said.

He was in the kitchen with Tino. Who made a face at him.

"Hot damn? Who the hell says that?"

"I do."

"You never said it before."

"Not that you've heard."

"So you only say it when I'm not around? You save that white-ass shit for your white-ass friends?"

Matt started laughing. When he didn't stop Tino looked worried.

"It wasn't that funny."

"It is to me."

"Why?"

Matt almost explained that other than Tino he didn't have any friends.

White-ass or otherwise. Or other-assed.

That last thought made him start laughing again.

He laughed about those two thoughts on and off for the rest of the day. And wondered if he could ever explain to anyone why they were funny. He was laughing about them again when the day was over and he was home standing before his mailbox glancing through his mail. Which was where and when he discovered he was wrong. He did have a friend other than Tino.

And she had sent him an invitation to her wedding.

❖   ❖   ❖

He carried the invitation inside like it might break. Then sat on his bed staring down at the thick ivory-white envelope. Where his name was written in her impeccable hand.

Abigail was really getting married. And really did want him there. Nothing had ever seemed more touching in his entire stupid life.

He carefully peeled the envelope open. The invitation included a plus one. Which meant plus zero. Because he didn't have anyone to take with him.

The date that was surprisingly soon. Only a month away.

If they were in love why wait?

Of course he wouldn't go. He couldn't afford to fly and driving would take too long. He couldn't miss that much work. Not now when everything was finally coming together.

Which was very convenient. Because being there would hurt like hell. Seeing her make that big

466

step. With someone else. Even if he never thought that was a step they would make together. The entire time he was there he would be ready to slit his throat. He might get drunk and say stupid things. Be the jackass who makes an inappropriate toast. Or maybe he would just stand up and start crying.

Not because he had lost the girl. But because he had lost his hope of having a girl. And therefore of having a life. Because he felt like he was drifting slowly away from all the good things a wedding represented.

He wondered if the barista had moved in with her. Taken Matt's place in her studio in the Ongford Apartments on Southwest 10th Avenue. He couldn't imagine her giving it up. He checked the return address. She was still there. Which meant the barista was there too.

Should he feel jealous? At least a little? Wouldn't that be normal?

He didn't. What he felt was overwhelmingly alone. What they had was more than he and Abigail ever had. Or he and Abigail would have been the ones who sent out invitations. So they had something that was more than anything he had ever known. More than anything he ever expected to know.

Which made him feel impossibly lonely. Impossible because he should only feel this lonely if he was alone in the entire universe.

Maybe he was. Maybe he was lost in his own universe. And everyone else lived in another one.

Chapter 92

He was exhausted. That was why he was having such idiotic thoughts. Why he couldn't stop laughing back in the kitchen. And made Tino wonder if he was losing it. Because he was losing it. Maybe he had already lost it.

He got himself up onto his feet and pushed himself through getting ready for bed. Then stared up into the dark and obsessed over what was ahead. What he could expect from this life he was leading if he kept living it.

He would gradually make more money. But he wasn't going to get rich quick working in the restaurant trade. If nothing went too seriously wrong in ten years or so he should be able to save enough for a down payment on a little house in a lousy neighborhood. But what was the point of buying a house if there was only him rattling around inside of it?

All the women he knew worked at the restaurant. Most were Hispanic and most were waitresses. A few worked in the kitchen but they were all older. The busgirls he had just hired were still kids.

A lot of the Hispanic women had no eye for Anglo men. He saw it in their faces. Not just when they looked at him. When they looked at any man who wasn't one of their own.

The waitresses around his age that were single all had baggage. Children from absent fathers. Substance abuse problems in their families. Family members off in prison. They were the ones who worked while parents and siblings and uncles and aunts and cousins fell down in the dirt. Sometimes they stopped to help. Other times they sighed and shrugged and kept going.

They presented a stark contrast to Abigail. Emphasizing how she remained unfettered and unscathed. Largely unaware of the privilege with which she lived. Matt saw that since he left Portland a great distance had opened between them. That the difference already present had grown enormous.

He remembered when she told him she was getting married. On that strange and disturbing night back in Tempe. How her news had knocked him off balance. Now here it was knocking him around again. Sparking off another one of those troubled nights.

When the thoughts in his head began to seem dangerous.

Which of course made him think of the canyon girl. She being the most dangerous thought of all. The one best equipped to finally drive him mad.

He remembered what she said to him on that night back in Tempe. The last time she visited him. When she whispered in his ear—

Soon we will be together.

Matt stared up into the dark and resented the canyon girl. For always dancing away from him toward some distant magical future when they would finally be together. She was starting to seem like an inveterate liar. Even the most generous definition of "soon" had been stretched terribly thin.

"Show yourself or get lost," Matt said. "For good."

The darkness remained undisturbed.

He wished he could believe that was an answer.

In the morning something was different about the face staring back at him from the bathroom mirror. Maybe it was the scar made by the busboy's ring. Which looked darker than he remembered. Even a little menacing.

When he was getting dressed he saw Abigail's invitation. And had an impulse to burn it. Then felt feverish with a flush of shame.

The traffic light at the corner was a short yellow and a long red followed by a flash of green. It went yellow as he approached and the truck behind him honked when he chose to stop instead of hurrying through.

He looked ahead at his day and wished it was already over. Then heard his father's voice in his head. Telling him to get his ass into college. If he wanted any hope of a life that wouldn't crush him. Matt decided he was finally ready to attempt making that happen. With loans and work-study and whatever else was necessary to cobble together enough money.

Not just because he hated being poor. He did. But compared to the people he worked with and lived among he was doing pretty well. So he had trouble feeling truly impoverished. Although one quick glance at his life made it abundantly clear he wasn't rich. Still driving his mother's old Toyota. Living in a neighborhood where food stamps were common currency.

But he needed college for more than just a better living. He needed it because his mind was starving. Slowly shriveling up into a desiccated raisin rattling around inside his thickened skull.

Maybe he would study history. Which had always been his best subject.

He imagined himself as a professor. At a small college with a leafy campus in some bucolic setting. Spending his hours outside the classroom writing books. Not about the big names. The famous people everyone already knew about. But the regular ones. Those who were excluded like they didn't matter. He wanted to write about what life was like for the average unsung Joes and Janes. The working stiffs.

Like the people he worked with. And people like his parents.

People like he was right now.

❖　　❖　　❖

470

He jumped when the truck behind him honked again. Then stepped on the gas when he saw the light was green. His mother's little ancient Toyota sputtered and lurched and before he could clear the intersection the truck zoomed around him. Blasting its horn again as it went flying past.

"Fuck you!" Matt yelled.

His heart kept pounding long after it should have settled down.

He entered El Leñador with trepidation. A sense that on this day events might go terribly wrong. He did his best to hold it in check. He smiled and called out hello to the kitchen staff as he entered.

Thankfully the rest of the morning and then the afternoon passed quickly and without event. At the end of the day he sighed out his relief.

Tonight was what mattered. They needed to be in good shape for it.

Señor Martínez called promptly at five o'clock. Which had become his habit. To find out what the night had in store. When the telephone rang at that time Matt no longer had to check the display to know who wanted him.

Especially not today. When Señor Martínez would not fail to check in. Given who had booked their banquet room. This marked a turning point. When the power players were willing to display themselves in your establishment. That meant your moment had arrived. And you needed to grab onto it.

"How is my miracle worker?" Señor Martínez said in his jolly tone.

This had become his standard greeting.

"Doing very well, sir. How about you?"

"Yes! Very well, thank you. And how do we look for this evening?"

"We look great."

"Excellent! Of course we do. With a man like yourself in charge."

"Thank you, sir."

"Is everyone excited?"

"Absolutely."

"Excellent! Today is a big day for El Leñador!"

"Yes, sir."

"Very well then. I will quit chewing your ear and leave you to it. Let me know how it goes!"

"I will, sir."

"Very well, my friend. Speak with you later!"

"Goodbye, sir."

When Matt hung up he stood looking down at his phone feeling deeply moved by this exchange with his employer. Brief and limited as it was. He knew Señor Martínez had failed twice in the restaurant business before making a success of it with El Gallo Bonito. And had seen his personal life marred by misfortune and tragedy.

But the man kept a smile on his lips and a song in his heart.

"How the hell does he do it," Matt said.

And was extremely grateful that this good man did. Because it was this same positive attitude that had led the resilient Hispanic restaurateur to take a chance on a homeless Anglo kid. Which had turned Matt's life around.

He might be dead now. If not for Señor Martínez.

Matt blinked and his eyes were moist.

Then motion drew his eyes outside. An SUV went rolling past the plate glass windows. On the side was emblazoned the official markings of the Doña Pero County Sheriff's Department.

Their special guest for this evening had arrived.

The moment had come to make Señor Martínez proud.

Part XXVII:
No Kind of Love Story

Chapter 93

The coyote that appeared before the departmental SUV, delaying its progress, caused events to be so ordered that Matthew Walker saw Esperanza Armijo before she saw him. The delay was exactly sufficient for Matt to recognize the young woman who came charging out of the vehicle across the pavement and be overwhelmed by knowing who she was.

Here was the magic girl he had seen all those years before. The one who had returned to him in visions and dreams. She actually existed. He had precisely enough time for this knowledge to knock him senseless and have his senses return before she saw him watching her.

Which meant that Esperanza saw Matthew at the exact moment when his love for her began pouring out of him. Because that was what followed in the immediate wake of his astonishment. His love came welling out like a flowing river pouring from an enormous spring.

Which she felt surging toward her. While she was still adrenaline-shocked from the lurching halt before the coyote. And still angry with her uncle for his odd and annoying behavior. For what she was coming to see as being tediously self-involved and far worse to be self-pitying.

Although later for that she would be grateful. Because her uncle was too preoccupied by his own selfish concerns to notice what was happening right under his bulbous nose. When to the young lovers it felt like a lightning bolt had just struck. And by that spiritual blast they had been fused into one.

473

Esperanza knew who Matt was the instant that river of love came flooding over her. As if every fiber of her being had been in wait for that moment. Not that she could say how she knew. It wasn't as if she recognized his face. She couldn't even see him clearly yet. He was only half-visible behind the glare on the plate glass. And yet she was certain that was him.

About time those two were finally reunited. Wouldn't you say?

And about time Rosa Armijo was proven to be prophetic and not insane when all those years before at the Grand Canyon she said that Esperanza would see Matt again. Of course neither of them knew his name at the time. The mystery boy they briefly encountered along the rim. The one Rosa insisted her niece must never forget.

I could show you their reunion. Or at least capture the major details. Provide a sketch of the rough outline. A schematic of what Matthew and Esperanza experienced when they were brought back together again. When love crashed like a tsunami through their young lives.

Maybe with great luck and the full employment of my meager skills I could possibly manage to convey the slightest hint of the enormous happiness that filled those first exquisite days of their blossoming romance.

But to do so would be to pretend that this is a love story.

Which it most definitely is not. This is some other kind of tale.

I will let you be the judge of what to call it.

I am at a loss.

Part XXVIII: Contact

Chapter 94

We chose a diner in the city. Near the university campus. With plenty of tall plate glass that offered nice clear sight lines. I arrived early and told the waitress that someone would be joining me. Then indicated my desire to be seated at a particular booth near the front. Where I could watch the comings and goings of who came and went. The waitress smiled before she led me over there. Then smiled again before she left me alone.

McElvy crackled in my ear—

"Damn nice rack on that one."

He was out in the parking lot in a van loaded with surveillance equipment. Before I went inside he wired me for sound.

"Dirty old man," I called him.

"Well I may be old. But I'm not dead yet. So I can still enjoy a look or two. And I sure liked the look of her two. It's nice when you can see the twins moving around like that. Giving each other a bit of a tussle in there. The way she wagged 'em about I'd have to say she likes you."

"And that's what's on your mind right now."

"When I see a fine pair like that."

"How about you keep your eyes on your work."

"Don't sweat it, boss. I got ya covered."

The waitress appeared beside me. When I looked up my eyes met hers. But my thoughts went to where I knew McElvy was looking.

"Can I get you anything while you're waiting?" she said.

And she offered another smile.

"No thank you," I said.

She smiled again before she sashayed away.

"You could have at least asked for some water," McElvy said.

"Why?"

"So she would come back."

"Keep your eyes off her tits and on her job."

McElvy laughed out in the van. I felt like I could hear him both through the tiny speaker in my ear and through the plate glass.

A truck pulled into the parking lot. Tinted windows in the cab and my angle of view made it impossible for me to see who was inside.

"Not her," McElvy said.

The truck parked. An old Spanish man in a cowboy hat stepped out. He hitched up his blue jeans before he started toward the door.

McElvy was in my ear again—

"You know what I'm gonna start calling you?"

"You know that I don't care."

"Señor Killjoy. Bleeding the damn fun outta everything. Always nothing but work with you. A man can't live by work alone. He needs to cut loose now and again. And that waitress, now she looks like a *whole* lotta fun. When was the last time you get your wick wet?"

"You want to have this conversation? Here and now?"

"What else we gonna do while we're waiting?"

"Ignore each other."

"Spoilsport."

McElvy tried a few more digs. He called me an "old dishrag" and a "dried-up schoolmarm" and "one lifeless bastard". But I gave him no reaction and after a bit he quit jabbering.

And then we waited. In silence. Which was blessed.

And we watched.

Then McElvy was back in my ear—

"I have visual."

"Meaning you see her."

476

"Better get with the lingo amigo. If you're gonna go in for this kinda work."

"I do not plan on doing any more of this than I have to."

"She brought company. Young adult male in the passenger seat."

A moment later the car came into view through the plate glass beside the booth where I sat watching.

"And now *I* have visual."

"There you go. Gettin' with the program."

The young woman parked the car and the young man bounded out of it. He went around to the driver's side where the young woman waited with her window open. They exchanged a few words. The young man glanced toward the diner. Then bent down to kiss the young woman.

"Boyfriend," McElvy said.

"Looks like it."

When they were done kissing the young man reached inside the car and placed his hand on the young woman's cheek. Spying on that intimate gesture embarrassed me in a way that watching their kiss had not.

"Definitely the boyfriend," McElvy said.

The young man started across the pavement. Halfway to the door he turned to glance back. The young woman smiled and waved. I saw her boyfriend's hand rise as he started to wave back. But he was still in motion and as his hand came up he disappeared out of view. From my vantage point he would remain obscured until he entered the room where I waited to speak with his girlfriend.

I studied the young woman. I wondered if she was afraid.

You should be, I wanted to tell her.

❖   ❖   ❖

477

Our meeting was the result of an unexpected email. One that I had received a week before. When my attorney wrote to tell me that she had received an unexpected email of her own.

From a young woman named Esperanza Armijo. A name I was of course already familiar with. As you know from my visit to the graves of the men who caused the deaths of her parents and the aunt who raised her. I was in my office across the street from the Sheriff's Department watching none other than Armijo himself exit the driver's seat of his departmental SUV when my computer beeped at the arrival of this message. A moment later Armijo was inside the building.

And I was reacting to Daniella's name in my inbox. Hearing from her always agitated me. My suffering was of course even worse when she called. Any contact made me want to stop barring her from my personal life. And instead pull her in. Despite the front I put up with McElvy I'd had about enough of this living like a monk.

But all that is neither here nor there. Let us return to what matters.

My attorney's email said that Esperanza had requested to be put in contact with me. She wrote that she was a close friend of Elden Morris who wanted to express her condolences for the injustice I had suffered. And that she would be in my debt if I was willing to discuss what had happened. She was hoping to find some closure on those painful events from her childhood.

I was so stunned by this entirely unforeseen development that I had to discuss it with someone. And of course the only someone I could possibly discuss it with was the old man. He being the only soul on earth who knew where I was and more importantly what I was doing there. Making him also the only one who could possibly comprehend my reaction.

So I called him. And his reaction was immediate—

"You should meet with her," McElvy said.

"What? Why should I do that?"

"Don't get stupid on me. She's on the inside. Or at least damn near. You got any other way to get this close?"

"It could be a trap. Maybe her uncle put her up to this."

"A trap how? So you meet with his niece. He can't arrest you for that. Meanwhile we lure the fox out of his hole."

"What if I run into her afterwards? Somewhere around town. There goes my cover."

At that point McElvy began to lose patience—

"How far are we getting with that exactly? With your precious cover all pristine and unsullied."

"I can do it by email."

"Like hell you can. This kind of relationship needs a pulse. Eyeball to eyeball. You need to make this girl trust you more than him."

"More than her uncle?"

"Who the hell else?"

"You're talking about the man who raised her."

"Esperanza is one smart cookie. And from what I hear a good egg. By now I'll bet she knows what kind of man her uncle is. Or at least has some powerful suspicions."

"You know her?"

"We've met."

"So you do it. You go talk to her."

"No good. I'm old news. And an old foe. She's gonna feel disloyal enough going against her uncle. Doing it with me will be a few steps too far."

"I still say this can be done by email. Or at least get started that way. Get a feel for how willing she is to talk. That way I keep my cover. If she wants to talk we can meet later."

"You lose the element of surprise. Gives her time to grow wary. She just reached out. That means she is open right now to having contact and, if we're almighty-God lucky, maybe providing some information. Now is when she is most likely to talk. So now is the time to jump."

I hated that he made sense. And had far more experience in this sort of thing. While I had nothing to refute his assertions. I chewed my lip while I tried not feel crammed in a tight little corner.

Then the old man fired his fatal shot—

"So what's it gonna be, cowboy. You gonna man up?"

They were so painfully young. Even though by the measure of years I was not much older. Only a decade. Not old enough to be a father to either one of them. Just enough to be a world-weary uncle. Still they looked so fresh-faced and innocent. Although as I learned later, and as you have already seen, life had already thumped their young hearts more than once.

That was what went through my head in the brief moments while Matt was out of sight. How young and carefree they looked. Then the door swung open and he stepped inside. He did an admirable job of ignoring me. While my eyes were only on him. I openly stared while he crossed the floor and took a seat at the counter and busied himself with a menu. The poor kid had no chance whatsoever to get a look at me.

Now it was her turn. Esperanza Armijo was on the move. She stepped from the car out onto the pavement and pushed the door shut and started toward the diner. She was not a girl who would catch my eye while standing still. To be honest I would have described her as plain-looking. But in movement the force of this woman became evident. And she was definitely moving when she came toward that diner.

I rose as the door swung open. She angled straight at me. What Matt was doing I did not notice. The force was in the room and I was consumed by it. And then she slid onto the bench seat across from me. And I resumed my seat now facing her.

In hindsight I believe my reaction to Esperanza as a woman made me more curt and aggressive than I would have been otherwise. As was evident in how I greeted her. The first words spoken between us came from me—

"I see you brought your boyfriend."

I could picture McElvy wincing out in the van.

Be nice, he had told me. You catch more flies with honey.

Who the hell wants to catch any damn flies, I said back to him.

That's a bad attitude, had been his last words on the subject.

While he shook his whitened old head.

Having already gone rogue I pressed forward—

"You can acknowledge that is true. Or we can end this right now."

"Yes. He's my boyfriend."

"And he is here to protect you."

She nodded. I nodded back.

"Because you brought him—"

"I didn't. He insisted on coming with me."

My eyes went to the young man at the counter. I watched him sip from his glass of ice water. He managed to keep his eyes away from me. I looked back at his girlfriend.

"That speaks well of him. But his presence here makes me wonder what you are afraid of. Or what he is afraid of. And if that is anything I should be afraid of."

Esperanza bit her lip.

"Let us try again," I said. "And come at this more directly. Why did you agree to meet with me?"

"Why did you ask me?"

481

"Why do you think?"

Esperanza blinked.

"Because you want information."

Smart girl, I almost said.

"And what do I want to know," was what I did say.

She frowned.

"I'm not sure."

"Give me your best guess."

She didn't hesitate—

"If my uncle framed you."

I shook my head.

"Almost. But not quite."

I nodded at her.

"Try again."

She bit her lip again. But only for a second.

"You want proof. That he did it."

Which was exactly what I wanted Esperanza to believe—that I was out to correct the injustice of my imprisonment and set the record straight. Better she did not know, at least not yet, that I was casting my net wider. That I wanted anything I could use to bring her uncle down. Her willingness to meet with me did not indicate a readiness to destroy the man that raised her for any sin he may have committed. Only the one that brought us together. So for now it was best to keep his other transgressions off the table.

I nodded at my guest. And even smiled a bit.

"That's better. Now we're getting somewhere."

The door swung open. An older man entered and made his way down the room. I waited while he passed.

"So," I said. "We have established why *I* am here."

I extended a hand in her direction.

"I'm sure more than idle curiosity made *you* agree to this."

"Yes."

"Well?"

Her mouth was open slightly. White teeth glistened. She lowered her chin and peered directly at me.

"Do you know who did it?"

I pretended not to know what she was asking. Frowning as if the meaning of her question was not at first apparent. Then let my mouth drop open and dragged my eyebrows up as if understanding had just dawned on me. Then I unnecessarily declared what it was we were now discussing—

"You mean who actually did those terrible things."

I paused. Then I nodded once.

"To your friend."

She swallowed before she nodded. I turned my eyes away as if considering whether to tell her. Then brought my eyes back again when I said—

"And what would you do with that information? If you knew who it was. Would you go after him?"

She stared back at me.

"Would you want him to face the law?"

Her stare did not waver.

"Or would you want to kill him yourself?"

Her response was immediate—

"I know part of me would."

No hesitation. I found that impressive. And a little intimidating.

I knew how the different parts of you could want and not want to kill. I thought about that before I asked her my next question—

"And could that same part of you kill him?"

Chapter 95

McElvy scouted locations, then we went around together to the ones he liked. The diner was his first choice but he saved it for last. He said that with the others as reference I would see how the diner clearly knocked them out of contention. We parked in the lot and he went over all the advantages of sight lines and escape routes. Then we took turns going inside. The old man went first. He was gone about five minutes and came back looking jolly. He grinned at me as he slipped in behind the wheel of his pickup.

"There's a booth in the front where you should sit," McElvy said. "Clear view of most of the parking lot and right next to the door. Plus if you're lucky it might come with benefits."

"Benefits?"

He pointed toward the nearest plate glass window and smiled at the bosomy waitress standing behind it.

"Maybe she'll be on shift then. And hot dog if she ain't a looker."

I hissed through my teeth and shook my head.

"That's what's on your mind."

"As long as I have a pulse."

I hissed again as I stepped out. Then slammed the door behind me. McElvy leaned out his open window.

"Ain't you a good time," he said.

I hissed again. Which was pointless. By then he couldn't hear me. I was halfway across the pavement.

The waitress smiled as I came through the door.

"Hello," she said.

I waved a hand at the interior.

"I'm just looking for someone."

Her smile was undimmed.

"Help yourself."

A minute later I was back out in the truck.

"That was quick," McElvy said.

He sounded disappointed.

"What'd you expect me to do? Make sketches?"

"I expected you to chat up that waitress."

"Well you expected wrong."

"In the future my expectations will not be so grand."

"Are you mocking me?"

"Someone has to."

He started his truck. We didn't talk again until the city was behind us. And when we did it was to argue over the locations. An argument from which you already know the old man emerged victorious. For no good reason I argued against the diner for half an hour. I had nothing against it. I was just dragging my feet.

Because I still wasn't sure about this.

Even an actor in the most minor of roles can significantly shape the course of dramatic events. As we have seen with the coyote that leapt out into the road before the departmental SUV as it approached El Leñador. Thereby ordering events so that Matthew saw Esperanza first and his reaction to her was written across every aspect of his being when she first saw him. Which set the all-important tone of their life-altering re-meeting.

Perhaps I dwell on that moment too much. But I am deeply attached to it. No other event outside of my own life has echoed so profoundly within it.

That waitress in the diner was my coyote. When she approached to ask if we were ready to order, she also halted a thought making its way from my mind to my tongue. In response to Esperanza expressing that part of her wanted to kill the one who had all those years ago assaulted her friend. Here is the thought I was about to give voice—

When you kill someone, all of you is present. Not just part of you. So all of you has to do it.

While I listened to the waitress inquire what we would have and Esperanza answer I imagined myself sharing my thoughts about murder and felt panicked at how close they came to escaping from me. Hinting at the greatest secret of my past. Even just a hit tip toward what happened up in Denver was a terrible idea.

The old man was listening in. If things went bad between us he could use Denver against me. A wall could have been thrown up between me and my guest. She could have heard those words and known I wasn't theorizing. That I spoke from experience. She could have bolted in the next moment.

If I had been left to keep going, if the waitress hadn't arrived and saved me, the rest of our lives— excluding the waitress who will soon exit our narrative never to return just like her predecessor the coyote—but my life and the life of my guest and the life of her boyfriend waiting at the counter and let us not forget the old man outside in the van—the four of us and others too would have been gone off in a very different direction.

Like Esperanza I ordered only coffee. Before the waitress turned to depart she smiled down at me. Then cast a quick and critical eye at my guest. None of which was lost on Esperanza. When the waitress had started away she leaned forward over the table and said—

"She likes you."

Then raised an eyebrow and smiled.

"And that makes her not like me."

Comments that of course made me turn to look at the departing waitress. More to have somewhere to point my eyes away from Esperanza then to confirm her observations. There was after all no confirmation to be had in the sway of the waitress's hips. Which it seemed could not move without undulating.

I did of course register their provocative motion. And that her form was arousing. And then I wanted to punch the old man.

"Maybe you like her," Esperanza said.

I felt heat on my skin. The truth was that I had no reaction to the waitress beyond that simple animal observation that sex with her was something my body wanted to try. Like or dislike had nothing to do with it. The reaction that really had me flustered was how I felt about Esperanza. So once again—despite being just a bit player and entirely unaware of the drama she was only peripherally involved in and soon to exit forever from this chronicle—the waitress helped shape the course of events in our narrative. By providing a decoy source of my distraction. I was only too happy to let Esperanza believe it was the other woman who had me worked up.

Luckily behind all those layers of consideration and reaction my mind had managed to recover and refocus on my objective in being here. And even achieved an insight that had previously escaped me. By asking why at this particular junction Esperanza wanted to know who the real villain was in the crimes against Elden Morris. She could have reached out to me back when the news of my wrongful conviction first emerged. So what made her wait? Or more to the point what could have pushed her to act now?

I thought maybe I had an answer to that. And decided to gamble that my guess was correct. I turned back to Esperanza and what I said next peeled that imperious smile about the waitress off her face—

"Maybe you suspect someone already. In that long ago tragedy with your friend. And that's why you're here. To find out if your suspicions are correct."

She blinked and her eyes narrowed. I pressed on—

"You have asked yourself who gained from what happened. And found the answer to be painfully obvious. Not to mention extremely unpleasant. I can only imagine how it must feel to live and work with a man—the very same man who took you in when you were orphaned, and then raised you into the young woman you have become—to live and work with him so closely. When you now suspect he is the very one who destroyed your best friend. And did so from the shadows. While pretending to be the one who enforced justice for those crimes. And then rode my back into the office he now holds. The same one you are now working hard to help him hold onto."

Esperanza did not answer. Her face had become a cold mask. Behind which her flickering eyes implied I had either struck a nerve or been profoundly irritating. I added one thing more—

"What you are carrying is much to live with."

Chapter 96

The waitress brought our coffee. Mine arrived with another warm inviting smile. A pale one went to Esperanza. Who said thank you. Shaming me into recalling my manners and offering my thanks as well. Which turned that smile radiant and welcoming again when it was directed back at me.

The waitress departed. Esperanza showed me her cold mask again. Which was unpleasant to look at so my eyes sought refuge elsewhere. They drifted out the window into the parking lot where they settled on the car that had brought my guest here. Which returned to my mind that tender exchange shared by this young woman and her lover. And sent my gaze back inside to the counter where her boyfriend sat waiting.

The sight of whom disturbed my testosterone beast. In my belly turned the dark worm of jealousy. How dare he be so young. And so quietly handsome. And most especially how dare he be so white. With his entire—I mistakenly believed to be—unblemished life still stretched out before him. The living embodiment of unquestioned privilege. Taking this young Spanish woman across from me as his entitled birthright.

And that was how my relationship with Matthew Walker began. With me dismissively assuming that his young fair Anglo self had never known any trouble or grief. That his life had been and would always be nothing but ease and delight and endless comfort. And that nothing but good days were behind and ahead of him. As you know I could not have been much more wrong about this already long-suffering young man. But for me, at that moment, he was yet to become an actual person. He was merely a lightning rod for my own passions and prejudices. A screen on which I projected my own frustrations and dissatisfactions.

Another rash impulse took hold of me. Or more accurately the same one as before but now in a ruder form. Now I wanted to tell Esperanza explicitly that I had tracked down the man who did those terrible things to her friend. And reveal how I had so very cleverly made him dead.

The force of the desire to make that boast—which would also have been my confession, delivered both to her ears and to the old man's listening in—was almost unbearable. But following so closely after its first manifestation—which fate in the shape of the shapely waitress had chosen to save me from—I managed to see this for more idiocy. And steeled myself to let it pass. So once again the waitress had influenced the course of these events that took place under her nose but outside of her awareness.

After the impulse passed I was ashamed by its motivations. I wanted to impress this unsettlingly formidable young woman who sat across from me. To show her I was more of a man than this boy she went with. And because I could not have her I wanted to intimidate her.

Nothing but rank male vanity. Which left me feeling petty and mean.

I silently thanked my present angel. The curvaceous one who kept saving me from my stupid self. Which sent my eyes searching for her undulating form. But she was not in sight. So I wished her in absentia a good life for the good she had done me. Then brought my gaze back to Esperanza.

And saw something going on behind that cold mask. A hint of vulnerability in those fierce eyes. I glimpsed for an instant how very young she still was.

A glimpse that decided my response. This girl had come here wanting an answer to a powerful question. And a very simple one. That required a yes or no answer. I could respond with the truth. Which would gain me nothing that I could perceive at the moment. Or I could lie. Which might turn her into a tool that I could manipulate. But then how would I be any better than that unholy fat bastard I had come here to destroy? Exploiting innocents to my benefit. Just as he had done with me.

So that was part of what pushed me onto the high road—a desire to be better than him. But mostly it was just that glimpse behind the mask. Seeing her youth in all its fresh glory.

"Your uncle had nothing to do with it."

The mask held for an instant longer. Then relief broke it open. She put a hand to her mouth and sighed. Clearly she had not been prepared for how much weight was resting on my answer.

I tempered her reprieve with this—

"Other than taking advantage of it. But you already knew that."

The mask quickly reassembled. She frowned when she asked me—

"Do you know who did it?"

I frowned back at her. Then I nodded. And then I stared.

The mask blinked.

"Will you tell me who?" she said.

"Why do you want to know?"

The mask blinked again.

"I'm not sure I do."

"Then don't ask."

Esperanza turned away. She looked out through the plate glass beside us and I studied the side of her impeccable face. Because that was how I now saw it. The plainness I had perceived before had been replaced by faultlessness.

I could not stop myself from wanting to offer her some peace—

"He can't do those things anymore."

She turned back to face me. I answered the question in her eyes—

"He's dead."

Relief swept the mask away. She looked directly into my eyes and I saw her soul peering into mine.

❖   ❖   ❖

I almost offered the big lie about how the villain committed suicide. But I could feel that any falsehood might put the mask back up again. And we would be done. And if the mask remained down the untruth would soon rot in my belly. And with enough time maybe even poison me.

A moment later the mask had reassembled. At first I felt what had begun to form between us was now slipping away. But then I saw in those fierce eyes which were busy flickering again that a decision of consequence was being wrestled with inside that sharp restless mind. We did not speak while I let her alone with whatever calculations she was performing.

Then the mask vanished.

"I don't have any proof," Esperanza said. "That he framed you."

I was unprepared for the depth of my disappointment. Despite extensive attempts at framing prudent expectations I had hoped beyond all reason that this would not be her answer. And had entertained fantasies that from this little meeting of ours would flow forth the ready solution to the achievement of my grand objective.

"Maybe there isn't any," she said.

I pretended to consider this. A moment later she added—

"Are you sure it wasn't Ortega?"

I thought of our photographs. Especially the one I took of the former deputy who was supposed to be dead standing with Armijo in the parking lot of the Sheriff's Department.

"Did you know him?"

She nodded.

"He came around the house a few times. I saw him at the office."

"So not very well."

"No. But he made an impression."

She paused.

"I never liked him. He seemed cruel."

She shook her head.

"My aunt didn't like him either."

I wondered how she would react if I slid that photo across the table and then told her when I had taken it. What seeing this cruel one she never liked still alive and in conference with her uncle would do to her.

But I hadn't brought any photographs with me. And what good would they do if I had? Why disturb her with proof of her uncle's deceit? To make her feel as used and disappointed as I did? She was already beaten up enough. Or she wouldn't be here sitting across from me.

I forced a rueful smile. Then I shrugged.

"I'll probably never know what really happened."

She nodded.

"Probably not."

Her eyes went over to the counter. Then she looked past me down the room. When her eyes came back again she leaned forward.

"I heard a rumor. About a Justice Department investigation."

I nodded. The same rumor had found its way to Daniella Magallanes. My lovely lawyer had chased down more details. Including the end result.

Esperanza frowned.

"You heard that too?"

"Yes."

"Do you know what it was about?"

"Election fraud. Part of a larger investigation."

I thought that was enough. Apparently it wasn't. Esperanza stared at me.

"They didn't find anything," I said.

Her relief was apparent. She nodded and looked away. I watched her and saw that having helped with his campaigns how it would hurt to learn that her uncle had cheated his way into office.

Then for no reason I was aware of this came out of me—

"How is the campaign? Going well I presume."

I thought I was making small talk. I picked up my cup and sipped my coffee and forgot what I had just said.

Esperanza exhaled sharply.

"We dodged a bullet with that Green Beret."

I had no idea what she was talking about. I put my cup down. Then I smiled across the table.

"How's that."

Esperanza wasn't looking at me. Her eyes were somewhere else.

"People liked him. He was a natural."

"What happened?"

She frowned at me.

"You didn't hear?"

I shook my head. Esperanza lifted her water glass and drank. Then glanced around inside the diner before she turned back to me.

"Haven't you been following the election?"

I nodded indifferently. In truth I had barely been paying attention. Which in hindsight was a gross omission. Given that the man I was after was a local politician, I should have been all over local politics.

"Then you must have seen the news," she said.

It took me a moment. But then I knew exactly what she was talking about.

And exactly how badly I had screwed up.

Chapter 97

On another day the story would have gone national. But there was an oil spill in the gulf and high-profile corruption hearings in Washington and wildfires in Colorado. All of which clamored for attention behind what dominated our worthless trash-filled culture's attention—that the it-girl Hollywood starlet of the moment had been found passed out behind the wheel of a Ferrari at a stoplight in Miami with three grams of heroin in her purse.

So the story never broke out of the local market. Despite the incredibly lurid details. A decorated combat veteran commits posthumous self-cremation by pulling the trigger of the Glock 19 inserted in his mouth at the same instant that he flicks the butane cigarette lighter held in his other hand thereby igniting the gasoline he had splashed all over the interior of his Hummer H2 in the same instant that a bullet tore through his brain.

To call the act desperate does not even approach taking its measure. How far one must be driven to desire such utter and complete self-annihilation. But such is the depth of the shame that can be experienced by a man of conservative leanings and patriotic values and outsized chest-pounding machismo when threatened by being exposed as a homosexual.

When he retired from the Army, the Green Beret spent a few years doing security work based in San Diego. Where he met a young man on the beach. He bought the kid clothes. Then a motorcycle. Helped him with his college classes. Wrote him mushy love letters. Let his chiseled face be captured in some homemade sex tapes. Told the kid they would always be together.

Then one day the Green Beret was gone. Took a job overseas and didn't bother to say goodbye. And when a few more years had passed and the Green Beret emerged as a candidate for the Republican nomination to be sheriff of Doña Pero County, the kid from back in San Diego—who was not really a kid anymore—was still looking for him. One night he found his former lover and sugar daddy giving a stump speech on YouTube. One in which the Green Beret went full-throttle rightwing homophobic and blamed a number of the nation's ills on "the gays".

The used-to-be-a-kept-kid contacted a local news station. And shared with them a few love letters. And a relatively innocent clip from one of the sex tapes. The news station sent a reporter and a camera crew to visit the Green Beret. From whom they received a stunned-into-silence non-response.

The next day the Green Beret reduced himself to char.

Or at least that was how the story was told.

Later I would attempt to blame our failure on Señor Fuzzy Lip. If he had not led us so persuasively down one path we might have seen the other right in front of us. But that remains the very lamest of excuse-making. McElvy and I were entirely at fault for this most enormous of all errors. We should have been all over that Green Beret. Knowing that Armijo would be all over him too. And could have been there to scoop up evidence of what the fat bastard did. To find proof after the fact was far less certain.

The night the story broke McElvy called me. But not to discuss it. We talked instead about some details of things we were working on while I ate dinner in a taqueria. On the television hung from the ceiling behind the counter, the local news had a clip of the smoldering Hummer in heavy rotation. Every few minutes there it was again. As if showing it a hundred times would make something further happen.

But of course nothing further ever did happen. The Green Beret had made a splash in the local election and now he was scandalously dead. Wasn't that sad. But if we had been paying attention maybe we could have made much more happen. For all we knew a virtual gold mine of information that could be damaging to Armijo had come and gone right before our gaping faces. If we had been looking the right direction maybe we could have taken our target down before he got to his target. And that great big hypocritical homo dickhead of a Green Beret would still be alive.

If he really was gay. If the young man who claimed to be his lover hadn't been paid to say those things. Because of course the fat man was behind that. He had to be. And the old man and I had been too busy scratching our balls to even notice. While discussing our pathetic efforts to take Armijo down, I remained absurdly oblivious to the implications of what I saw up there on that screen. I paid more attention to my damn tacos.

But now those implications had been made obvious. By someone who had also apparently managed to miss them. Here she was seated right across from me while she delivered the news that had just ruined my day. All it took for me to connect the dots was thinking back to how Esperanza had initiated this subject—

We dodged a bullet with that Green Beret.

Like hell you did, I wanted to tell her.

Armijo never dodged bullets. He was too fat to jump out of the way.

Instead he bent their flight.

I wanted to pound my fists on the table. Run out to the van and grab the old man by his shirt while I screamed into his gray weathered face—

Why the hell can't we catch one fucking break in this goddamned mess?

497

None of which I did. Of course not. I remained seated and quietly listened. Waiting for Esperanza to acknowledge what was blatantly obvious.

But she talked about other things. I won't pretend that I can remember what else she said. I assume she shared more about the campaign. All I know is what she did not know. Because it astonished me.

How could she not see that her uncle had the Green Beret killed? Or at least badgered him into doing it? How many dead man, real or imagined, had to pile up around him before she noticed he had reason to want them dead?

Was I going to tell her? Hell no. Leave that for someone else.

Maybe her boyfriend waiting over there.

If he could get his head out of his ass long enough to notice.

The waitress returned to refill our cups. If she dispensed any smiles no one noticed. When she was gone it was clear the fresh coffee would be wasted. Our business was done. We had nothing more to discuss on the subjects that compelled us to meet.

But before we parted there was one more thing I wanted to mention—

"You know that we have met before."

I could see that Esperanza was surprised by this.

"You don't remember?" I said.

She shook her head. I prompted her—

"At the hospital."

Now she frowned.

"On the day that I found your friend," I said.

Her frown cut deeper into her face.

"We sat together," I said. "In the hallway outside his room."

498

Her expression became frozen. But not like the mask she showed me before. Then she blinked and her eyes were moist. She nodded once and then spoke in a whisper—

"I was with my aunt."

"Yes. I'm sorry that you lost her."

If my knowing this disturbed her she did not show it.

"Thank you."

I nodded once. Bowing slightly over the table between us.

"You thanked me then as well," I said. "For finding your friend. I have never forgotten that."

"I'm sorry. I don't remember."

"It was a long time ago. You were young. And in shock."

Esperanza nodded. Then she blinked and her tears started down her cheeks. She reached for a paper napkin from the dispenser beside the menus and used it to dry her face. When she was done she crumpled the dampened paper and clutched it in her hand while with the other she reached across the table and grasped my wrist. Her palm was soft and warm. The contact made me feel feverish.

"I used to pray for your damnation," she said.

I had to swallow before I could speak.

"You had good reason to."

She smiled and I felt paralyzed.

"Please forgive me," Esperanza said.

Chapter 98

La Soldadita did not look back. But her boyfriend did. When she appeared at his side and put her hand on his shoulder Matthew glanced in my direction as he rose to his feet. I wonder what he made of my expression at that moment. I never thought to ask. I wish that I had. I would like to know if the man he saw looked as stunned as I felt.

As they went out the door I wondered when and where I would see them again. I had no reason to believe that I would. But some instinct told me our lives had just become inextricably intertwined. That our fates were now fused together. The feeling was strong enough to keep me planted in my seat for a minute or two after they had left.

I had no further contact with the waitress. Esperanza had tried to insist on paying for our coffee. But I reminded her our meeting came at my invitation and therefore I was her host. I left a nice crisp twenty dollar bill for those two cups we drank and the two that we didn't. And maybe for all those smiles the waitress kept giving me. Those were worth more than what I tipped her. Even if I had done my best to ignore them.

Out in the van McElvy greeted me with a big grin. He could not have looked more tickled if Esperanza had handed us her uncle's guilt all bound up in a legal dossier embossed with gold leaf. He was about to speak when I beat him to it. And slapped that irritating grin off of his face—

"How in hell did we fuck this up so badly?"

I ranted about what we missed with the Green Beret. When I stopped for air McElvy smacked me down—

"Don't be a goddamn baby."

"What?"

"You're crying over spilt milk. Get over it."

I felt exposed and stupid. He grinned at me again. I had a strong urge to hit him.

"What we got was better," the old man said.

"And how do you see that?"

"She likes you. She trusts you. And much more importantly she feels that she owes you. For all those years of hating your guts."

"And she also has nothing we can use."

"You must like the taste of shit."

"Excuse me?"

"Must be why you keep your head up your ass. So what that she hasn't got anything. Right now. Off the top of her head. When she just met you. And came here with her own questions. She sits at that fucker's goddamn elbow! Only a matter of time until she has something. Especially if we get her to start looking."

"So what is it you want me to do? Call her up every few days and chat? Then by-the-way mention could you please spy on your uncle?"

"Kept your head up there so long now it's shit for brains."

"Watch yourself old man."

"We got ourselves a mole. And a goddamn good one. You gonna walk away from that?"

I was silent and glowering. McElvy sighed and shook his head at me.

"You know what you need?" he said.

I wanted to hit him again. He pointed and said—

"Don't go nowhere."

He was out of the van and halfway across the parking lot before I calmed down enough to wonder what he was up to. Five minutes later he clambered back into the van and handed me a slip of paper. I glanced down and saw that it was torn from a restaurant order pad.

I looked at McElvy and he pointed at the paper.

"There," he said. "*That's* what you need."

I looked at the paper again. All I saw was a blank order check.

"What is this," I said. "Some sort of riddle?"

"On the back, stupid. Turn it over."

Scrawled across the back in swirling blue ink was a woman's name and a telephone number.

I looked at McElvy again.

"Who's that?"

"Are you really that much of a moron?"

"The waitress."

"Damn right it's the waitress."

"Why would I want this?"

"Why the hell do you think? Because you need to get laid you stupid jackass!"

"You need to mind your own fucking business."

McElvy reached out his hand.

"Okay. If you're not going to use it. Give it back."

I recoiled.

"That's even worse."

"Hand it over."

"You're old enough to be her grandfather."

He shrugged.

"My pecker don't know that."

The old man snatched the piece of paper out of my hand.

I had no idea he could move that fast.

Part XXIX:
Shadows and Strings

Chapter 99

The old man and I had nothing to say to each other as we made our way out of the city. And still had nothing to share when we were back in Doña Pero. The first day of no contact became a second and then a third. After that they piled up like dead leaves.

Maybe we had overdosed on each other and a break was inevitable. Maybe we were fundamentally incompatible. Maybe he got lucky with that waitress and she put him in the hospital. Whatever the cause of our split I was now on my own. My efforts felt unclarified with no McElvy around to argue with. Over what we should do next. Or how to go about it.

Left to my own devices I tried connecting Armijo to the death of his rival. Scrambling after that big old hunk of red meat to toss at the media and the higher authorities. If I could find something fast enough I might even knock him out of office. But more importantly I was convinced there had to be a conviction in there somewhere. For something that would put him away. Murder. Racketeering. I would take anything that wouldn't let him plea bargain his way out of jail time.

I found absolutely nothing. Not one single scrap. Which convinced me that we had missed it. That if we had been paying attention all along we would have had him by the balls. There was no reason to think that but I thought it anyway. I was determined to believe God had granted us a golden shining moment and like complete idiots we had been looking the other way.

The primary ballots had already been prepared when the Green Beret died. He received 3.07% of the vote. A poll released a few days before his former lover went public put his support among registered Republicans at 42.8%. His sexuality and his lurid death apparently convinced approximately 40% of the Republican base, or roughly 93% of his previous supporters, that there was no cause to honor his memory at the polls. Leaving only an ardent few to make that quixotic gesture. Where they were perhaps joined by one or two addled extremists who remained unaware that their candidate had died. Let alone that he had been homosexual.

The scandal around the Green Beret took the heat off of Armijo. Everyone seemed to forget that he stank of corruption. Which left him facing the main event stronger than ever. A poll published in the local newspaper two weeks before the general election had Armijo ahead of that Democratic police chief by fourteen points.

❖   ❖   ❖

Thankfully the day that poll appeared also presented an excellent distraction. One that brought me out of my hermetic perch high above Armijo-land. Which was becoming a very uncomfortable cage.

There was however one gray cloud to this silver lining. My errand took me somewhere I had hoped to never see again. And which looked every bit as grim as I remembered.

From the outside it appeared nothing had changed at the state prison. On the inside I knew things were very different. Silvertone was dead. The cartel presence had grown strong enough that they decided dealing with him was no longer in their best interests.

They left his head in the middle of the yard. The rest of him they managed to dispose of somehow.

Glad I hadn't been around for that.

I had to wait longer than expected. There was a delay while the guards dealt with a disturbance.

What exactly required their attention we never found out. And once the gates rolled open we didn't care.

I forgot how much I hated that place and how my split with the old man gnawed at me and how much it was going to hurt when the coming election returned Armijo to office and how my loneliness was starting to feel pathological when the gates parted and out stepped Tranquilino Rojas.

I looked at my good friend striding toward me and tears came to my eyes.

Now there was a face I was very glad to see.

"Look at you," I said. "A free man again."

"Free enough. A paroled man hasn't got all his freedom back."

"Don't be greedy. Right now you got more than enough."

His grin spread wide across his broad face.

"More than enough is right."

His release was unexpected. Tranquilino thought of himself as such a hard case that the possibility of parole hadn't occurred to him. But when he began carving, Daniel Salazar saw to it that the dramatic *santos* that came flying out from beneath his hammer and chisel took wing from the shop and the prison and sailed out into the world. Where they immediately began gaining notice. And winning awards. And being sold in prestigious galleries. Which Daniella Magallanes used to convince the parole board that Tranquilino Rojas had been transformed from a habitual miscreant into a worthwhile citizen. One who would henceforth contribute to society. Or at least to the general coffers. And that he therefore no longer required further incarceration.

(A little sidebar before we continue. Since this is the last we will hear of our uxoricide let me mention that Salazar not only survived the transition from state-run to privately contracted management but actually increased the size and profitability of his operation. Which in hindsight makes perfect sense. He and his new overlords spoke the same language.)

When Tranquilino arrived before me I was crushed in his thick arms.

"How I missed you, amigo!" he bellowed in my ear.

When he released me and I could breathe again I told him I had missed him too. But while he was hugging me I could not speak.

I won't bore you with all our catching up. Suffice it to say that it went on for many hours. The afternoon was stretching out into evening when we finally turned to matters that concern this present narrative. So no, in case you were wondering, I did not bring my good friend back into the story just so I could mention him. He has work to do here like the rest of us.

❖   ❖   ❖

We were in my office overlooking the Sheriff's Department. I had already told Tranq what little I had managed to learn about Armijo's empire. Now we were crowded together in front of a computer display reviewing the many photographs McElvy and I had taken. Hoping Tranquilino could put some more names to the many faces. We had before us the picture of Danny Ortega in the parking lot across the street. I reminded my friend how Armijo had slipped away from what he did to me. That this man in the photograph had taken the blame and was supposed to be dead.

"One loyal soldier," Tranquilino said.

Then he frowned.

"Or else he got himself something he really wanted."

"Like what?"

Tranq shook his head.

"Your guess is as good as mine. Maybe a lot of money."

"Then why is he still here?"

"A good question."

Tranq nodded at the photo.

506

"Any idea what he's been up to?"

I loaded up the photos McElvy had taken on his midnight run when he tailed Ortega. The ones that filled us with hubris when we first got them. When we had gone through a few of them I pointed at the man who had done all the talking that night outside the remote ranch house down near the border.

"I was hoping maybe you knew who that was," I said. "Since he seems to be in charge."

"Nope. Never saw him before."

That wasn't what I wanted to hear. Ever since I heard Tranq was getting out I had hoped he would be able to identify this one man in particular. That at some point in my friend's rather extensive criminal past he had crossed paths with this individual. Because Tranq never forgot a face. And I really needed a name for this one.

Or at least I thought I did. I was so busy being disappointed he didn't know this guy, I almost missed what my friend said next—

"But he doesn't matter."

It took me a moment to digest that.

"He doesn't?" I said.

"Nope. Not him."

"But he does all the talking."

"Because they want your boy here to think that. Ortega. They want him to think that one is the boss. But he's not."

Tranq pointed at a man standing in the background.

"That vato there is the one calling the shots."

I peered at the man Tranq pointed out. And saw nothing that distinguished him from any of the others.

"How do you know that?" I said.

"Because I know who that guy next to him is."

The one Tranq said he knew was turned toward the first man, leaning in close to say something.

"So who is he?"

Tranq grinned at me.

"Wouldn't you like to know."

"Just tell me already."

Tranq laughed and squeezed my shoulder. I pretended that didn't hurt.

"Benny Vallejo. Met him when I was still a kid. On a roofing crew. We worked together for a couple months. After that I didn't see him again for maybe six or seven years. Then a cousin of his married a cousin of mine. So we saw each other when the families got together. Weddings. Quinceañeras. That kind of stuff. And since it's family you hear things. First I heard he was with El Frente. Don't know how he got in with them. But I know he has family across the border. So maybe that's how. Then later I heard that only close family and a few good friends still called him Benny. That anyone else better call him Benecio. And if you didn't know him and liked how your face looked you better call him Señor Vallejo. Because now he was high up in there. In El Frente. Which means whatever went down, that guy he's standing next to there is one serious heavyweight. Because that guy outranks him. So this had to be some big deal."

Tranq pointed at the man beside Benny Vallejo.

"I'm telling you. From that one's lips to El Viento's ears. He's gotta be that high up. In all these pictures that guy never looks at Benny once. He always has his eyes on the action. But Benny looks at him a couple times. He's waiting to hear what that guy says. Because Benny answers to him."

All this was more than I could readily process. I frowned at the photograph and the man in it that Tranq had just told me was in charge.

"So this is cartel business," I said. "Whatever they're doing here."

Tranq frowned at me. Then jabbed a hand at the image on the screen.

"Benny Vallejo. Out kissing ass in the middle of the night. And in the middle of nowhere. I kinda doubt they're planning a picnic."

Chapter 100

What I had envisioned was comparatively small scale and strictly domestic. Like most things in Doña Pero I believed this one would reflect the limited resources and population of the region and its disconnect from the larger world. One or two local operators paying Armijo to look the other way while they moved their relatively modest amount of product. From where and to where and in what quantities of which intoxicants had not crossed my mind.

But instead there was only a single degree of separation between the fat man himself and the top ranks of a Mexican cartel. Which put a whole new light on his operation. And very much not in a good way. Small time is usually pretty stupid. And therefore not so likely to get you killed. But big time is almost always very smart. And never not deadly.

Of course in retrospect this made perfect sense. And made me feel perfectly stupid. I should have immediately suspected he was involved with a cartel. Because that meant not just big money but truly goddamn huge money. The type of money that would explain how Armijo could practice the kind of corruption that sent me to prison and keep him in office. You don't pull off with what he got away with without having powerful friends. And the surest way—truly the only way—to obtain powerful friends is to purchase them. And they can never be bought cheap. How else could he have kept the FBI and the Department of Justice and any other federal agencies who might take an interest in something that stank all the way to high heaven from sticking their noses way up inside of his fat ass? The "Ortega-did-it" cover-up reeked all the way to Washington. A congressman or senator or someone equivalent behind the scenes must have been deep in his pocket.

It's true that money tends to show itself. Someone can't resist that flashy car. Or goes on a vacation way above his pay grade. Buys too many hookers and too many drugs and says the wrong thing while drunk in a bar. But just because Armijo and everyone around him lived exactly like they made the meager salaries available in a backwater like Doña Pero didn't mean they weren't riding a river of cash. That river was leaving plenty of other erosion along its banks. I should have seen that.

Imagine you are driving on a highway. And decide to change lanes. You are under the impression there is no traffic around you. You check your mirrors and what you see confirms your path is clear. But at as you move to turn the wheel at the very last moment, another glance into your side mirror reveals a tractor-trailer barreling at top speed out of your blind spot. Now magnify that sensation a hundred times. And that was how I felt when I learned that Armijo was in contact with El Frente. Which meant he worked for them. Because when you do business with a cartel they own you.

Two things became uncomfortably clear. First and foremost that I had been dangerously incompetent. I should have chased the money. Not seeing any didn't mean there wasn't any. And second that I had just caught a very lucky break. My good friend had left prison just in time to save my sorry ass a second time.

God bless Tranquilino Rojas. My rough-and-tumble guardian angel.

When I could wrap my sorry head around what Tranq told me I finally got on the phone and called McElvy. To warn the old man who we were dealing with. If he was still in this thing. I got his voice mail and asked him to call me back. The next morning I called again and left a more urgent message before I took Tranq home to his mother.

Where that good and long-suffering woman wept over her prodigal son. And would not let me refuse breakfast. Only when Señora Rojas was satisfied I had been stuffed full enough was I permitted to leave.

I was barely out the door when I tried the old man again. This time I didn't leave another message. Instead I hung up and drove out to the ranch. Where I did not find McElvy. I parked in the empty drive and sat on his front porch with my eyes off into that long view toward Texas for almost an hour. By then telling myself not to worry wasn't working. And my concern wasn't purely disinterested. If the cartel had the old man they were probably after me. At that point I didn't know much about El Frente but it seemed safe to assume they were good at making people talk. All the way back down the old man's drive I kept watching for his truck coming toward me. But no cloud of dust appeared ahead to announce his approach. All the life I encountered was one lone coyote loping away across a field off to my left.

Back in town I went to my office and tried to resume my surveillance. Just to give myself something to do. But nothing was happening across the street. And I didn't really care if there was. So I gave up watching nothing happen and listening to nothing happen and instead I stared at the photos McElvy had taken of the midnight meeting down near the border. Where something had definitely happened. And wondered what that was.

Then I wasted a few minutes trying to convince myself Tranq could have misinterpreted those frozen moments. That maybe he was wrong and that wasn't even Benny Vallejo standing there in the background. But there was the stubborn fact that Tranq never forgot a face. All those years ago he had not forgotten mine even though I had been a child when he last saw me. And as for his reading of the

512

pecking order among the men in those photographs the more I looked the more convinced I became he was right. That vato beside Benny was very much the boss man.

When I couldn't stomach those photos anymore I fired up the Internet. And should have read the news or looked at pictures of naked women. Instead I researched the cartels in general. And El Frente in particular. Which could not have done less to make me feel better.

❖   ❖   ❖

Like many evil things in this all-too-wicked world that story of El Frente is the story of one terrible man. The proverbial bad seed. This one was born to a doctor and a schoolteacher in Jalisco. These two good citizens raised their son with loving care and tender devotion. By all accounts they were excellent parents. Kind and understanding but not overindulgent. Firm when firmness was necessary and forgiving when forgiveness was called for.

And yet still their only child grew up to become a notorious narcotraficante warlord. So much for nature versus nurture in the case of Hernando Lopez.

His parents hoped he would follow his father into the field of medicine. But halfway through his undergraduate studies Hernando abandoned that path and instead obtained a degree in political science. Then to the great dismay of his mother and his father he joined the Mexican Army. Where he rose quickly through the ranks to become one of the youngest Teniente Coronels (Lieutenant Colonels) in the nation's history.

But shortly after attaining that rank he resigned. And went to work for the Juárez Cartel policing their disputed borderlands with the Sinaloans. A few months in the field and he became known as El Viento, or The Wind, for his ability to move forces at considerable speed over very rough terrain.

After he succeeded in clearing out their enemies, and had secured the region for a full year, the Juárezians rewarded El Viento with semi-autonomy. In exchange for holding the Sinaloans at bay he was permitted to control the human smuggling in his domain and on a limited scale to participate in the drug trade. He had already become feared. Now he also became rich.

A man does not make his bones controlling the no man's land between two infamously violent crime syndicates by offering a gentle touch. El Viento and his outfit—which became known as El Frente, or The Front, for the position it occupied in the Juárez Cartel's territories—were infamous for the ruthless zeal with which they decimated any perceived threat. If you crossed them in any way shape or form, however slight that might be—say you accidentally stepped on a pair of sunglasses one of them dropped and wasn't even aware you had done that—they would kill you and everyone who knew you and anyone who looked like you.

And if the transgression was more complicated and information had to be obtained they were known as enthusiastic and effective torturers. They could push you repeatedly to the brink of death and bring you back again to extract whatever it was they wanted to know. Or thought they wanted to know. Or maybe were just somewhat interested in. They would do that to you and everyone you knew and anyone who looked like you until they got what they wanted. *Then* they would kill you and everyone you knew and anyone who looked like you.

Please excuse my jocularity. While incongruous as it may seem, is often the only reaction one can sanely have to such horrors as this world routinely presents. Yes of course I exaggerate. But then again I do not. To carve out a place between the two warring cartels, El Frente had to be faster and nastier and more vicious and more brutal than the monsters on either side.

The environment always dictates the qualities of the organism.

Chapter 101

The polls had barely closed when the Democratic police chief from that town down near the border made a short gracious concession speech and it was all over. He did the right thing. There was no reason to drag it out. Armijo had trounced him good.

I may have taken the candidate's loss harder than he did. He at least had the satisfaction of being in the ring throwing punches. While I only stood on the sidelines watching. Dreaming of what my fists could do. If I had any fists to make and punches to throw.

At first I attempted to put aside the overwhelming sense of failure that came with the election results. I pretended to remain resolved in my purpose. And pretended that I was busy pursuing my objectives. But I was just filling time. Holding off the wolves at my mental door. In each and every waking moment I felt the fat man slipping away from me.

This went on for about a week. Then after another day spent watching the fat man's kingdom and accomplishing a big fat zero I went home and prepared my dinner with hostility and indifference. Which was exactly how it tasted. So I left it on my plate and watched the last daylight fade at my windows. When it was dark I did the American thing and got in my car and drove. If I had any sense I would have gone somewhere crowded. A movie theater or a shopping mall. I should have buried myself in the multitudes. But instead of meandering around employing the therapy of watching others live normal lives I went where there was almost no one.

Out on the edge of town. Where the construction stopped and the raw desert began. And my latest acquisition sat waiting. A few days before a deal long gestating in my shadowy empire had finally achieved fruition. One of my myriad companies purchased a distressed property that overlooked the Armijo place. Which I had of course wanted so I could spy on him when he was at home. I went out there that night to decide if I would go through with those plans. To survey the battlefield while I debated whether to give battle.

The house was not in the same neighborhood as the Armijo place. Instead it belonged to another struggling new development immediately adjacent and to the north. Where it sat alone on a cul-de-sac above the bend in the road on which the fat man's house was situated. The back of the lot ended in a bluff opposite his driveway. So although the two houses were a little more than a hundred yards apart they were on different residential streets leading out to separate connections with the main road. When I came and went he would not see me come and go. We would be neighboring but not neighbors. A highly advantageous arrangement for my purposes. And since the housing market had collapsed, all the places nearby other than his were still vacant. Therefore being free of prying eyes.

The brand-new streets were all empty. As I wound my way back through them I passed all of three houses that were inhabited. I pulled into the drive and parked at the end of the fresh black asphalt that was like an oil spill in the falling night and went up the stone walk and unlocked the front door.

The foyer was enormous and enormously loud. My footsteps banged against the walls and off the ceiling and back down upon the floor. The din was almost enough to make me turn around and leave. An impulse strengthened by the chemical stink of paints and adhesives that still hung in the stale air.

Unfortunately this place wasn't any more appealing than I remembered it.

❖　　❖　　❖

I wandered the ground floor and pictured the rooms filled with things. Furniture and artwork and lighting and electronics and maybe some books on some shelves. All of which would be impersonal and generic. Because that was what you got when you had no actual personal involvement with the objects in question. A façade of life being lived. Which I would have to provide to disguise my covert operation.

There were mailmen and meter readers and cable guys to consider. And maybe the occasional cop looking for anything suspicious. I found myself actively bored and even depressed by the prospect of setting all that up. And once in place it would need to be maintained. Dust and cobwebs couldn't be allowed to collect and hiring someone to clean up was not an option. They might wonder about the surveillance equipment. And if I kept that room locked and off limits that would intrigue them all the more.

When the ground floor had thoroughly sickened me I climbed to the second and stood before the broad window in the master bedroom. Which afforded the best view of the Armijo residence. A vantage point I had planned to exploit thoroughly. But now while I stood there looking out through the deepening night at the lights on over at the fat man's place I saw that without being completely dedicated to this enterprise, proceeding any further would be a colossal mistake. Inviting the kind of error that could make me dead. Which meant that not wanting to do this anymore was in and of itself a compelling reason to stop. Before it all blew up in my face and the cartel uncovered my game and did what evil it would to me.

And McElvy too. Maybe they had their hands on him already. I was still waiting to hear back from the old man.

To my internal judge I would have to rest my case on taking out Sorenson. And ask how many villains I must dispose of for the public good. To earn my ten million. Which was an issue. Feeling that I deserved the money paid. Somehow just being locked up and beaten wasn't quite enough.

So my decision was made. Not entirely without reservations. But determined nonetheless.

I would not return to this ugly house. I would stop spying on the fat man. I would take what I had and consider what could best be done with it. Which federal agency was most likely to pursue the scant and almost entirely inadmissible evidence I could provide. Maybe just send it to everyone who might give the slightest damn. Not the representatives of our corporate-controlled and largely dysfunctional and oxymoronically named news media. But the independent organizations that still performed actual journalism. Any blogs and web sites that could serve as productive irritants. Then hope and pray someone who could do something would get outraged enough to bring some significant heat. And like dominos set in motion maybe I could provide the initial impetus that would bring down the fat man.

Not so decisively as I had hoped. Without a smoking gun found clutched tight in his sausage-like fingers. But still achieving my ultimate objective.

I will admit to feeling shame at my surrender. But also that a great weight had been lifted. I even managed a smile standing there before that broad window in that darkened room. A moon waxing near full had begun its transit. Despite the signs of contemporary civilization scattered here and there about the landscape before me, what I saw appeared eternal in that pale ghostly light. And it is an ancient characteristic of man to take particular satisfaction in feeling we have defied the gods. Which was how I felt at that moment. That I had slipped a painful fate decreed to me.

I did not need to chase after Armijo. I could set that burden down. Put the past behind me and move forward into a better future. Where Mexican drug cartels would not want me dead. The relief I experienced was immeasurable. And I planned on enjoying the hell out of it. There was much of life to be lived and I was now free to go live it. As if awakening from a long nightmare. Here I was, rich and still young and I was told not unpresentable. My good friend Tranquilino was once more a free man. There was a sky overhead and earth to be trod upon and the great wondrous entirety of human experience to be celebrated.

The last time I had fully experienced the pure delight of existence and the staggering potential of the life granted to us was as a small child. Now as an adult that feeling swept back over me. And my mind and soul both reeled.

I reached for the window wanting to open it and fill my lungs with the night air. To clear my nose of the chemical stink that had clogged it since I stepped inside. But once the window was unlocked I found it was painted shut or jammed closed or in some other way sealed tight by shoddy modern workmanship of one form or another. A moment of irritation that I managed to let pass. I wanted to hold on with all I had to the good feeling that had come over me.

Chapter 102

Outside the night had turned crisp. In the east above the mountains the pale silver moon was almost full. The timeless spectacle of its rising drew me away from my car across the back of the property and down the bluff and out into the middle of the street below. Where I stood in that wide open space drenched in impeccable moonlight savoring my sense of liberation. And feeling brazen to be so boldly positioned before the fat man's house while I said goodbye to chasing after him.

All of which seemed very romantic. Determined to change the course of my life away from the dead past toward a living future. While standing in the light of that glorious moon before the lair of my relinquished enemy. And all that romance demanded thoughts of love. So my mind gladly began fantasies of romancing Daniella Magallanes. Why not? Why deny myself what she was so eager to give?

But at that moment Esperanza Armijo appeared before me. At a window in their kitchen. Just as quickly she was gone again. But she was present long enough to remind me of our meeting at the diner. Which I had already recalled many times. Growing ever more baffled by why I kept revisiting it. Feeling in my bones she and I would never be lovers. When a lover seemed perhaps what I needed most. But unshakably certain there was a connection between us. That we shared a common path.

Which made me admit there was no common path with Daniella. And that all the hope I could muster would never make it so. Exposing my fantasies of making a life with my beautiful attorney as nothing more than self-indulgent self-delusion. In other words I snapped out of it. And felt some of the luster had been rubbed off my jewel of a moment. When my life was supposedly realigning toward bliss.

❖   ❖   ❖

A light came on in an upstairs room. Armijo's bulk appeared framed in a window. Where he remained long enough for me to experience the sense of omnipotence that can come from watching others when they are unaware of your presence. The predator eyeing its prey experiences the demigod's power.

In that moment of heightened clarity I was struck by an insight that arrived feeling painfully delayed. One that should have been obvious the moment Tranquilino informed me that Danny Ortega had been deceived about who was in charge of that midnight meeting. The one at that isolated ranch house which McElvy managed to photograph. That deception meant Ortega might not even know those men were with El Frente. Which meant Armijo could be ignorant as well. Oblivious to being used by a notoriously lethal Mexican drug syndicate. Just as he was unaware of me as I stood watching him.

I had seen Armijo as the puppet master. Because that was how things were when he put me into prison. But maybe in this he was only a puppet himself. Dancing herky-jerky while El Viento pulled his strings. Being played just as he had played me. But unlike how it was back when he pulled on my strings Armijo had no idea he was being made to dance. And therefore how much danger he was in. I might have felt sorry for the fat wily bastard if I hadn't been so busy laughing up my sleeve. Not literally of course. I didn't cackle into my shirt standing in the moonlight before his house. But I did smile. For the moment that these thoughts amused me.

Unfortunately I was strongly unamused by the thoughts that followed. If Armijo was unaware who he was dealing with then he was also unaware of how much risk he was exposed to. And if he was in danger then so was his niece. If El Frente came for Armijo, if he was perceived to jeopardize their operations and they wanted him eliminated, there was no better place to kill him than here in this secluded and therefore opportune spot where the fat man had stupidly chosen to live. Anyone else who happened to be present would also be murdered. Especially any relatives. To eliminate witnesses and also to send a message to others who might think of crossing them—

We will not only kill you but those whom you care about.

And of course Armijo presented a risk to El Frente. Everyone involved in that business is always a risk to each other. There is never any safe way to deal drugs. Any one of Armijo's schemes could blow up on him and his partners. How he went about framing me. That sloppy business with the Green Beret. The fat man kept getting lucky but luck never lasts forever.

With these perceptions vanished the romance of my grand moment. Just to drive the point home a cloud slipped before the moon. The plunge into darkness felt sinister. The chill that a second before had been pleasant now said winter would soon work its jaws upon the desert.

I had to warn Esperanza. Knocking on the front door had a certain appeal. Instead I behaved more sensibly and took out my phone to call Daniella. While I anticipated watching Esperanza drive away. As surely she would after my lawyer related her mortal danger. I knew how persuasive Daniella could be. But then I saw there were no little bars glowing on the display. I had no coverage out there in that broad wash on the edge of town.

My useless phone went back into my pocket. I glanced up as the light went out in the window that had framed Armijo. A change that struck me as foreboding. I tried to dismiss this concern as a melodramatic overreaction. But I watched closely and listened intently. And my anxiety grew stronger.

Shadows moved in the kitchen. I heard raised voices. Then a woman's shout. Followed by stillness and silence. Then a man's voice bellowed and a shadow moved and someone seemed to cross the kitchen and exit. Slowly and with deliberation. A moment passed then a second shadow followed after the first. Moving quickly and without hesitation. I can't say how I got all that from watching shadows. But that was what my mind made of what my senses related. Some animal part had kicked in and taken over my understanding of what I witnessed.

For several moments all I heard was a breeze stirring the mesquites. My eyes scanned the house, darting over it and coming back to the kitchen window. The only one that was lighted. But now nothing happened there. No shadow play to be interpreted. My eyes went darting out again searching for light or for motion. For several moments there was nothing.

Then I jumped as a yellow flash filled the bay window in the living room. At the same instant came a muffled thump. An instant later I realized what I had just witnessed was a gunshot. The muzzle flash of a pistol in a darkened room accompanied by the muted blast.

I wish I could report myself running heroically headlong toward these signs of present danger. Proving myself valiant by charging to the rescue. But I remained firmly planted in the middle of the street.

From where I watched as Esperanza burst out the front door and ran almost straight at me. Then stopped short about twenty feet away. And stood staring in my direction. I couldn't tell if she saw me. Or saw anything at all.

What I remember most distinctly was how the moonlight made the blood on her white blouse appear black. And how even without color I knew what that was. What it had to be.

Then Esperanza doubled over and vomited across the pavement.

Part XXX:
Almost Like a Wife

Chapter 103

Another victory meant another insufferable victory celebration. With the same self-important people smugly strutting about. Esperanza once again noted that she preferred the fireworks and gunshots of the original. And remembered making the same observation last time.

But last time Rosa was here to keep her company. This time she was on her own. She hadn't even bothered to ask her uncle if she could invite Matthew. She knew what his answer would be. And didn't care to hear it.

Matt said that was reason enough not to go.

She agreed with him. And then said—

"This one last thing and I'm done."

And she meant it. With this one final payment she considered her debt paid. The obligation she felt to her uncle would be fulfilled. She would resume living her own life again.

Guilt had carried her here. From where and when we last saw her. Guilt at suspecting her uncle had been involved in the crimes against Elden Morris. When the man who had been framed for those crimes told her that her uncle had nothing to do with the horrors inflicted on the boy her first reaction was relief. But only briefly. Soon the guilt came rushing in.

How could she have thought her Tío Josef was such a monster?

If not for that guilt she wouldn't be here. She would be with the man she loved. Making plans for their future. In the new life she would soon lead. A life out from under the shadow of her uncle.

If not for that guilt she would have left her uncle weeks ago. Maybe even months. She might have bolted right after we last saw her. Because that was when her uncle's behavior became so intolerable.

At the end of the day he would come home and drink. The whiskey would go down his throat and the words would pour up out of it. Bemoaning how the greater virtue of his deeds would unjustly remain largely unrecognized. Lamenting how the enormous risks he had undertaken and the vast sacrifices he had made would forever be unknown to the innumerable beneficiaries of his herculean efforts. How all he had ever done in office was with one single goal first and foremost in his razor-like mind—to protect and serve the simple folk of Doña Pero. A torrent of bourbon-soaked rhetoric that made each evening seem endless.

Gone was the self-pity he indulged in when the Green Beret first appeared. Which despite being tedious had at least managed to humanize him. If only just a little. Now it was entirely non-stop preening and chest-beating and never-ending self-praise. To hear him tell it he was a colossus bestriding the earth. Every bit the great man his niece had once believed him to be.

At least he had once been some kind of a lawman. Not nearly so virtuous as she had imagined. But he did catch some bad guys along the way. And risked his neck doing it. But now for all his talk of all he did to protect the little people of Doña Pero she couldn't imagine what that could be. He didn't put in the kind of hours such heroics would require. Or spend enough time out in the mean world where the bad guys could be found. The kind of champion he claimed to be isn't home for dinner every night. But here he was bragging and boasting and boring her to death.

And where was the gratitude? She did everything he asked of her. Would it kill him to say thank you?

❖   ❖   ❖

And now another week had passed and she was still here. Still keeping his house. Still running his political life. And still not getting paid. Her uncle had dodged every effort on her part to discuss what she would do next. Insisting he was too busy wrapping up his campaign and transitioning into his next term to consider anything else.

Matthew was understandably disappointed. She made a promise and hadn't kept it. If she put him off much longer he would grow angry. Then she wouldn't blame him if he pulled away. She would in his position. She was determined not to let that happen. Today she decided she was done. Because Matt was too important to her.

And because today she saw that soon there would be a breach that could be permanent. That what she felt for her uncle would soon turn from anger and resentment into hatred. To save her relationship with the man who had taken her in and raised her—the only parental figure she had and the relative to whom despite everything she was closest— she would have to leave him.

Tomorrow she would move out. And move in with her boyfriend. She took solace in believing that Rosa would give her blessings. That her Tía would tell her to go. She wished again she could tell Rosa that the boy from the Grand Canyon was now her love. And wondered again at the mysterious forces that had moved Rosa to take her there. And set in motion the odyssey that brought Matt to Doña Pero. And therefore to Esperanza.

Tomorrow she would start her new life. She would find a job for which she would actually be paid. And not have two—campaign fixer and all-purpose domestic—for which she was not. She would save some money. Maybe she would even get two paying jobs. And save that much more money. She had proven she could handle it.

And most importantly she would complete her education.

Chapter 104

His rant over dinner began with how useless the local Republican party had been during the election. How he had dragged the county ticket behind him on his coattails. How the state party was little better and maybe even worse. How the Republican governor was nothing but useless. And owed the slim margin that returned her to office to his weight on the ticket here in Doña Pero. How she was a terrible embarrassment to the party and the state. Because around the state capital she was known as a drunk.

At this last remark Esperanza stopped her fork in midair. Then cast her eyes from beneath raised eyebrows at the glass of booze her uncle was rapidly emptying. She watched the glass rise from the table up to his mouth and back down again with a nice bite taken from away the contents. Then shook her head as she returned to her dinner.

"Maybe next time I will take *her* job," Josef said.

His fork went to his mouth and he spoke while he chewed—

"And show her how it should be done."

He swallowed and belched and reached for his glass. Then the glass went up and more whiskey went down. When the glass was back on the table he shrugged.

"And after that. Who knows. Maybe I could do some good over in Washington. Maybe a senator who knows what goes on in the real world could shake things up in that cesspool. Not like this no good bastard we have now. That one half-asses everything. I could show him a thing or two. How a man—"

Esperanza almost shouted—

"I'm moving out!"

530

❖   ❖   ❖

Josef blinked and narrowed his eyes. His mouth hung open. He closed it and swallowed and licked his lips before he spoke.

"What did you just say?"

"You heard what I said."

"No. What I heard is impossible."

He put his fork down and raised his hand and wiggled his fingers beside his head.

"My ears must be playing tricks on me."

He stared at Esperanza. Then bent over his plate and his fork went back to work. His food went in slowly now. He paused at each bite and chewed thoroughly.

He raised his fork and pointed it at Esperanza.

"It's that Anglo boy. That's what this is about. You're going to go live with him."

"And what if I do. That's my business."

"That's a sin."

"Look who's talking."

"Watch your mouth."

"Don't lecture me about sin. When was the last time you went to church? Forget about confession. Have you ever confessed?"

"Never mind what I do. You are still my responsibility."

"We've had this conversation. I'm not having it again."

"You forget who you're talking to."

"*You* forget I need a life of my own! I can't go on like this."

"You think you're all grown up. A real woman now."

"I know I'm not a child."

His fork was still in his hand and still pointed her direction. He held it there for another moment then tossed it down onto his plate. He stared at his glass then stabbed his hand at it and the glass went to

531

his mouth and came away empty. He wiped his lips and cut his eyes in her direction.

"What is it about him anyway? This Anglo kid. What's so special about that one? You never cared about any other boy."

"He's not just any other boy."

"He looks like it to me."

Esperanza debated if she should tell her uncle. Would it make things better or worse? Then she asked herself if she cared. And decided she did not. That she would tell her uncle because she wanted to—

"Do you know where I first saw him?"

"Of course. At that restaurant."

Esperanza shook her head.

"No. Not there."

Josef frowned. His eyes shifted over her face.

"So tell me then. If it's so important."

"At the Grand Canyon."

She could see that he didn't remember.

"I went there with Rosa."

"I know that."

He clearly didn't. Not until she reminded him.

He made a show of laughing. First the big grin. Exposing his gleaming teeth. Then his head rocking back and his mouth coming open.

When he was done he pointed at her—

"So you think that makes him special. You think that makes this punk you don't even know the only one for you. Because of a stupid coincidence."

"It's no coincidence. He came here looking for me."

She didn't want to explain all the complexities and subtleties of what that entailed. How Matthew chased a vision of a girl that started with Esperanza and became something otherworldly and in the end changed back into her. She knew how her uncle would delight in tearing that apart.

Josef scowled at her.

"He came back here to find you."

"Yes."

"Then he's insane. Only a crazy person would do that."

"Rosa didn't think so. She told me I would see him again."

Josef snorted. He threw a hand toward Esperanza when he spat at her—

"Then your Tía was insane too!"

He glared across the table.

Esperanza shook her head at him.

"Do you even miss her?" she said.

He scowled again. Then jerked back in his seat when he shot his breath out.

"What are you saying. Of course I do."

Chapter 105

That was the moment when he began to crumble. When what was human about her uncle started to fall apart. Because she knew that he was lying.

His eyes told her this. Those wet drunken eyes. They said that she should ignore what just came out of his mouth because the truth was he didn't miss his dead wife. Or anyone else. His eyes said that he never missed a single living soul because he couldn't. To do that he would have to feel something.

Esperanza looked into his eyes and saw those things and realized she already knew them to be true. All those ugly truths and many more about this man. Who had once meant so much to her. Only moments ago she had still felt deeply connected to him. Now in an instant that had vanished.

"You never cried for her."

"So what. So I don't blubber like a baby. A man has to be a man."

"A husband cries for his wife when she dies. If he ever loved her."

Josef hissed out his breath. A hand came up and pointed.

"You keep forgetting who you're talking to."

"I know exactly who I'm talking to. For the first time in my life I know exactly who you are."

His eyes told her he didn't like that.

She rose to her feet and stood over him. She shook her head.

There was nothing more to say. She doubted there would ever be anything more to say.

She began cleaning up. She was at the sink with her back turned when she heard the bottle clink against his glass. A moment later her uncle coughed. She glanced over her shoulder and watched him pour another. Then shook her head and turned back to her work. She ran the water and began scouring dishes and feeding them into the washer.

The running faucet masked the sounds he made as he came up behind her.

Suddenly he spoke into her ear—

"That boy can't give you what you need."

A hand grabbed her ass.

"What you need is a man."

She spun around and slapped him. He laughed in her face and pawed at her breasts. She pushed his hands away and slapped him again. He put his head back and laughed louder.

"You're drunk," Esperanza said. "Go sleep it off."

He grinned at her.

"You don't tell me what to do."

"When you behave like this I will."

His grin melted away. He stared at her with burning eyes. His hand came up and he pointed at her face.

"Like I keep saying. You forget who you are."

He jabbed his hand at her.

"You forget who you always will be."

Later she wondered why she stayed. Why she didn't walk out the door after he stumbled from the kitchen and get in her car and drive away. Come back tomorrow when he was at work to get her things.

Much later she wondered why she didn't see that the rumors could be true. Right then and there standing in his kitchen after they fought. That her uncle had intentionally put the wrong man in prison for the things done to Elden Morris. Then framed Ortega to cover up that frame. And killed him to make the cover-up stick. Then killed the Green Beret when he came along and got in the way. She had finally seen what kind of man her uncle really was. Why didn't she make the next step and see what he could be capable of? That the whispers might be more than just gossip?

Maybe she was overwhelmed. Maybe she was just too damned tired. Maybe she was put off the scent after she went the wrong direction and wondered if he had assaulted Elden. And needed some time to get her nose pointed the right way.

But even now she didn't see that he could be the monster behind all those terrible things. That he could be dangerous.

All she saw was that he had never behaved like such a jackass. Not even close. She couldn't believe he wasn't done. That he wasn't already passed out back in his bedroom sleeping it off.

So she continued cleaning up his kitchen. He was still her Tío. Still the man who took her in. Still the one who raised her. Those things still came first.

For now. Tomorrow was a different story.

One last time, she told herself.

In the morning she would be gone. And after that she might not speak with him anymore. What could they ever have to talk about? The break between them that she had wanted to prevent, that had seemed so unbearable only hours ago, now rose before her like a refuge. Somewhere she couldn't wait to escape into. Where she could finally be her own person.

The water was running again when he returned. So again she didn't hear him. And since her mind was elsewhere she reacted out of instinct. Pure physical reflex. If Josef had chosen another moment maybe things would have gone better for him. And therefore worse for her. But he chose when he did to grab her arm and spin her around.

He spat his words into her face—

"Eras casi como una esposa."

You were almost like a wife.

536

Then swung his big heavy pistol up over his head like a club. To bring it crashing down upon her skull.

But he was drunk and she was sober. And he was right-handed and she was left. So when his right hand came swinging through the air her left hand came up to block it.

And in that hand was a chef's knife with a fine blade of carbon steel. Kept sharp after the habit Esperanza learned from her mentor in the kitchen. Rosa did not hate many things. But she despised a dull edge.

Esperanza held the knife in her fist with a good tight grip. She was a strong young woman. She shoved the blade up through the air toward her uncle's approaching forearm.

And he swung his pistol down with the inside of his wrist toward his target. A roundhouse blow. Starting from behind him and looping up over his head.

The blade sliced his wrist open just below the joint. Flesh and muscle and tendons all cleaved apart.

And most significantly so did the ulnar artery.

He bellowed and stumbled away from her. A corner of her mind managed to wonder if his blood had been thinned by all that booze. Because it flowed out like water. She watched the gun that was tangled in the fingers of his useless hand and was ready to grab it if she saw the chance.

He staggered out of the room. When she could move again she hurried after him. Telling herself that was the wrong way to go. Once again out the front door would have been the right choice.

She stopped in the living room doorway. Watched him raise his left hand. The one that hadn't been rendered useless. Now this was the hand that held the pistol. She jumped when he fired and felt the bullet split the air next to her head.

The recoil knocked him off his wobbling legs. He went tumbling over onto the white carpet. From where he groaned and his breath rasped. She told herself he still might try to shoot again.

But the fear of being shot was not what made her move. What sent her out of the house and into the street where she was sick across the pavement was remembering her uncle's last words.

And realizing that he had been jealous.

Part XXXI:
The Sugar Man

Chapter 106

There was a lot of blood. A trail of it leading into the living room. And a great dark pool of it spreading across the white carpet. The pistol was still in his hand. The one attached to the arm that was not bloodied. The gash on his bleeding arm was still pumping it out. Then a breath heaved out of him. A second later the pulse from his wound stopped.

I entered thinking he had shot himself. So this was not the scene I expected. Instead there was apparently something sharp involved in his death. Which I found on the kitchen floor beside the open dishwasher. The chef's knife that was coated with blood.

I returned to the fat man. When I was looking down at him again my perception of space and time collapsed into a single moment. For I had seen Armijo fallen like this once before. As I was being led from the courtroom following my trial as Manuel Ortiz. Seeing this image both before me and in the past made time seem shockingly flexible.

Then my heart was pounding in my chest. This experience failed to satisfy as once had been imagined. No sense of victory came from peering down at his bloated corpse. Only fear.

Then I remembered having promised myself I would spit on Armijo's fat dead body. But just stepping inside had clearly been a mistake. Perhaps a stray hair had drifted from my head as I crossed the threshold and now waited to be plucked up and analyzed and my DNA added to the evidence. At that moment I was certain federal agents of one department or bureau or another would be crawling all over this place before the blood was dry. Of course

Armijo's murder would blow the lid off this mess. It would have too. How could it not?

And expectorating on his corpse could tell them I was part of that mess. In whatever role that may yet prove to be. So that was a pleasure I would have to forego.

I went back down the hall to the kitchen. Nothing I saw this time added to what I already knew about what happened. But as I turned to go I saw a purse on the counter. Maybe I had seen it before but it hadn't consciously registered and that was why I went back. Maybe my subconscious mind was hard at work.

I grabbed the purse and left.

❖   ❖   ❖

I found Esperanza at the wheel of her car. With the door open while she stared straight ahead. When I stood beside her and said her name she turned and looked up at me.

"I know you," she said.

"Yes. You do."

"Why are you here?"

"No time for that. We have to go."

I held out her purse. She stared at it before she reached out and accepted it. She looked down at her purse when she asked—

"Is he dead?"

Then frowned up at me waiting for my answer.

I nodded. She looked so stricken I thought she might be sick again.

"What am I going to do?" she said.

Before I could answer headlights swept across a rise behind the house. When the lights had come and gone I turned to look back up the road and saw that in about two minutes the car pushing those beams forward would round another bend and we would become visible.

I reached down and grabbed her shoulder.

"What you're going to do is run and hide. Because there are people who will want you dead."

Now she looked even more bewildered.

"What?"

"There is no time for that. Will you come with me?"

She hesitated for a second. Then she was out of the car slamming the door shut behind her and we were across the street and up onto the bluff. We reached the top as the headlights swept across the pavement beneath us. Behind the lights came an inky black SUV that swung in beside Esperanza's sedan. We turned and watched as the headlights and engine died and the door swung open and a man stepped out. The glowing ember at the tip of his cigarette was brilliant orange in the dark. He took a last drag on his smoke then dropped it to the pavement and ground it under his foot.

As he stepped away from the SUV, moonlight revealed his face. Esperanza's fingers dug into my arm. She whispered in my ear—

"He's supposed to be dead."

Which was how I recognized Danny Ortega. At that distance in just the moonlight and with my one eye partially blinded I would not have known otherwise. Seeing the dead risen seem to clarify Esperanza's thinking. Her fingers cut back into my arm and she hissed into my ear—

"Can we get out of here?"

A few seconds later we were in my car making ourselves gone. I had to force myself not to race away from there. We needed to be just any car making its meaningless way to nowhere special. Any moment now the sirens could start wailing their way along these roads.

❖   ❖   ❖

We didn't talk on the way to my house. I was too busy watching for the law. I assume Esperanza was too much in shock.

When we were seated in my living room all the talk came from me. I told Esperanza about the men who would come after her. Their reputation for extreme violence. Since her uncle had been of use to them that meant she had destroyed what they considered a valuable asset. And maybe the entire operation based around that asset. For which by their code she must pay with her life. And because of her proximity to that asset they would suspect she could have knowledge of their activities that would be of harm to them. So if they managed to catch her they would make her wish that she was already dead while they attempted to determine how much she knew about what her uncle did for them. Even though that might be nothing. And only when they were satisfied she had confessed all would they kill her.

Esperanza listened in silence. When I was done she peered at me with wide open, gleaming eyes. Then she wept. Which she did with great restraint. A few gasping sobs were the worst of it. I got up and brought her some paper towels from the kitchen.

And then her phone rang. Before I thought to stop her she had answered it. I averted my eyes while Esperanza tried to convince Matthew she was all right. Although clearly she wasn't. Which he heard right away. And he was clearly not buying it. She summarized her current state of affairs by saying—

"Things are kind of a mess."

I wasted a moment pondering exactly how much of an understatement that really was. Running my mind back over what I had witnessed and what I knew and where that left us. But fortunately I was only an idiot for a moment or two. A few seconds lost before I realized the mess Esperanza referred to had just gotten worse. And that it now included her boyfriend.

If they had her cell number they could be watching her calls. And there are ways to locate a cell phone from its signal. Don't ask me how. If you want to know, feel free to do the research. Right now I don't care to look it up again and learn it again only to forget it again. I am not and have never been a real tech geek. I know just enough to get me into trouble. And in this case to barely escape it.

I got Esperanza off the phone by scrawling—

hang up we have to go <u>right now</u>

—on a piece of paper and holding it up in front of her face. I grabbed what I needed while Esperanza found her purse and we ran out the door and back into my car. On our way out of there I told her why we had to leave.

Our first stop was beside a storm drain around the corner from my place. I handed Esperanza a burner phone and asked for hers in return. Then told her to call Matthew and tell him to meet us behind El Leñador in five minutes. Then I stepped from the car and dropped her phone onto the pavement and smashed it with a rock. The pieces went down into the sewer.

Then we more or less kidnapped poor Matthew. Esperanza told him there was no time to discuss what was happening and dragged him into the car.

Chapter 107

There were things I wanted at my office. Information which could prove valuable. Given the uncertainty of the situation it seemed prudent to arm ourselves however possible. While I was busy gathering what I came for, Esperanza explained to Matt what had happened. Which was how he and I learned the basic details of Armijo's death. When she was done recounting that horrifying experience and a moment of silence had passed afterwards Matt asked the same question that was plaguing me. A question he almost whispered and could not finish—

"Was he going to...?"

I stopped what I was doing and turned to watch her answer. And told myself I shouldn't intrude. But I kept staring.

"Rape me?" Esperanza said.

Matt did not respond. His eyes searched her face.

"Or kill me?" Esperanza said. "Both?"

She put a hand to his cheek and wiped away his tears. My eyes went back to my work. But I remained immobile while I pictured Esperanza fighting off her drunken uncle.

"I am so sorry," Matt said.

She answered in another voice—

"It's all right. We need to stay focused."

My head swiveled back in her direction. Her gaze was now pointed at me. With time I would come to recognize this other person I saw watching me.

La Soldadita was ready to fight.

"Are we done here?" she said.

"Not quite."

"Well let's get moving."

I turned back to my work. But there was nothing for me to do. The machine was still busy.

Things had been quiet down below. Now a car pealed out and a siren started up. Esperanza moved to the window and watched the car roar away. When it was gone she turned to face me again.

"We need to hurry," she said.

"Hurry where?" came from Matt.

"Almost done," was my response.

Matt's question hung in the air unanswered. We all left it there. Floating around like an explosive balloon.

Another car pulled out. No siren this time. Then about a block away its siren came on and the car went wailing across town. Another car followed the second one. Now a chorus of sirens was pealing here and there.

My cell phone rang. I pulled it from my jacket pocket and held the phone up while I said—

"They don't know this number so they can't trace it."

Then I looked at the display to see who wanted me. I expected it would be Tranquilino. Who was the only one calling me those days.

But instead it was Clarence McElvy. Which I was very glad to see. Those cars and their sirens made me doubt that the timing of his call was a coincidence.

"Talk to me," I said.

"The Department just put out an APB. Guess who they want."

I looked at Esperanza. While in my ear McElvy said—

"Esperanza Armijo. Any idea why?"

I didn't answer.

"So that's how it is," McElvy said. "Your name wasn't mentioned."

"It's a long story."

"Where are you?"

"At my office."

"Hunh. Kind of the hot seat right about now. What's wrong with your house?"

"Compromised."

McElvy paused at that news.

"Well shit," he said.

I didn't respond to that. I heard McElvy start his engine. I had assumed he was safe and warm and comfortable at home. Now I pictured the old man in his truck with the police scanner mounted under the dash. And I could guess a few places he might be parked. The old dog was still on the hunt.

"Go to the ranch," McElvy said.

"You're sure?"

"Does anyone know about me?"

"I don't see how. I left a clean trail."

"Not so clean if they found your house."

"I mean to you. I left nothing behind that connects me to you. All of that is with me."

"Then head on out. Where the hell else you gonna go?"

"I have no idea."

"You best put her in your trunk."

"Excuse me?"

"You heard what I said. They see a woman in your car they'll pull you over."

"They won't both fit."

"What?"

"She's not alone."

"I'll meet you downstairs. Gimme five minutes."

And with that the old man hung up on me.

Sirens were going everywhere when we stepped outside. We found McElvy already waiting in the parking lot behind the office building. He pointed toward the south and his ranch.

"They're putting up roadblocks," McElvy said.

He pointed at Esperanza and then at my car.

"You young lady are going into that trunk."

She offered no objections. I popped the lid and she climbed in.

McElvy pointed at Matt.

"Just to be on the safe side. We best stow you away too."

We hid Matt under a tarp in the back of McElvy's truck. When we were done the old man pointed at my chest.

"When I turn off my headlights you do the same."

"Got it."

We zigzagged through alleyways and back streets. Across town into an old neighborhood of small square casitas. As we crossed a boulevard off to my left, maybe five blocks away, I saw a squad car barrel past going the opposite direction with its sirens wailing and its lights flashing. When it was gone the sound of my heartbeat pounding in my ears muffled all the chaos screaming across Doña Pero.

We entered a newer development of ranch houses and territorials. A couple of turns brought us parallel to the main road at the south side of town. Where the road turns to the southeast and gradually descends before turning due south again. Off to our right the street lights for the main road painted the world in cold orange and deep shadows. The light poles seemed to grow shorter as they followed the road down and out of town.

We were at a stop sign when McElvy cut his headlights. I did the same before I followed after him. Now the lights for the main road were obscured behind a row of close-set houses with mature trees that still held most of their leaves. When we were past that clump of darkness across an open field I could see the flashing reds and blues of the roadblock. The vehicles were down out of sight on the main road but judging by the lights there were two of them parked sideways across the pavement. Shadows moved across the far side of the road from the movements of the men stationed there. I felt obvious and vulnerable. But with our headlights off there was nothing to betray us sneaking past.

At the end of the open field a sign marked the main entrance of Dominica Chavez Elementary School. Señora Chavez was an early advocate of public education in Doña Pero. That is all I have been able to learn about her. I wonder if she would have approved of the use we made of the school named after her. We turned in and wound our way through the cluster of buildings and across the school grounds to a gate at the back of the complex. When McElvy jumped out and bent over the lock I assumed he had a key. But when he had spent some time at his task I realized he was picking the lock.

The gate let us out at the top of a bank that descended to the main road. We were just out of sight from the roadblock behind the corner of a portable classroom. McElvy jumped out again to relock the gate. Then I followed him down the slope and we rolled out onto the main road. The road arched so that the roadblock was just out of sight past the crest to our right. The flashing lights glared against the night sky.

Then we turned away from town and the roadblock lit up our mirrors.

I felt an irrational amount of relief when McElvy switched on his headlights.

We were almost at the turn off for McElvy's place when swirling red and blues appeared behind us. A moment later the siren came on. I expected the squad car would charge up on my bumper, flashing its headlights to pull us over. Instead it veered into the oncoming lane and went barreling past. My relief made me feel like I had a fever. Sweat broke out all over.

At the top of the old man's drive McElvy pointed at Matt while he gave us the latest from his scanner—

"Now they want you too. So if you had any second thoughts about coming along get rid of them."

"No sir. I mean yes sir."

"So you're with us."

"Yes sir."

"Good."

Our host herded us inside. Where the first thing he did was turn on the scanner he kept on a bookshelf in his living room. He listened for a few seconds before turning to me. He didn't have to ask. I told him what I knew.

When he was done with me I left the old man with our two fugitives and went to set up my laptop on the dining room table. I knew how to log on to the old man's network because I was the one who set it up. Back before he and I had our falling out.

The old man came and stood behind me. I could feel him scowling at my computer screen.

"What have you got there?" McElvy said.

"My home security cameras."

"So if they show up at your place we'll know about it."

"Exactly."

"That's over the Internet I suppose."

"You suppose right."

"Anyway they can track that out to here?"

"My understanding is that maybe the NSA could. But even they would need some time."

He shifted his weight behind my chair and the floorboards creaked.

"How much time."

"By that time we will be gone."

"I happen to live here."

"Then maybe bringing us here wasn't a good idea."

The floorboards creaked again.

"Well keep looking," the old man said.

A few minutes later he was back.

"I'm headed to Walmart. You need anything?"

"You're going shopping."

"Clothes and whatnot. For our fugitives."

"Is that a good idea? Buying clothes in their sizes."

"Like you said. You won't be hanging around. So when they track me down you'll be gone."

"They'll know we were here."

"Do you need anything or not? It's kinda now or never."

He had a point. Anything we wanted to do out in public should get done immediately. Before the federal agencies showed up and took over.

I shook my head at him and went back to my machine. A moment later the door banged shut and he was gone. For another moment I wondered if I would ever see McElvy again.

Chapter 108

Matt and Essie wandered up behind me and spent a few minutes watching nothing of interest happen on my computer screen. Then they sat at the table and watched me and each other and the ceilings and the walls. When Matt asked after the bathroom I pointed down the hall.

He returned with a question—

"Why can't we go to the FBI? Or the DEA?"

Esperanza looked at me. I looked at her. We both looked at Matt.

"And what do I give them?" Esperanza said. "Because I have to give them something. I have to be useful to them."

Matt frowned. He glanced at me. Then he shook his head.

"I don't know if that's true."

"Well I know that it is."

"We know what your uncle was doing."

"No. We don't. We just know who he was doing it with. And that really isn't worth anything."

"You don't think the FBI would protect you?"

"Think about what I would tell them. That my uncle was connected to a drug cartel. Through a guy who was supposed to be dead. It's a lousy story. And if I'm lying then I'm a cop killer."

I waited for Matt to look at me. When he finally did I told him this—

"For all they know she could have been the one working for the cartel. She got into trouble with them and they came after her and her uncle got in the way. Or maybe her uncle figured out what was going on so she killed him. So they might arrest her and put her in prison. See if that changes what she tells them. Keep her there until her story changes enough to make more sense. And if it never makes sense then go ahead and hang it on her."

I let Matt digest that. When he was done and I had his attention back again I continued—

"I had a cellmate from the Juárez Cartel. Believe me. In prison is the last place she wants to be."

I paused again. Matt flinched when I said—

"Inside she's dead."

He looked at that table. Then back at me before he turned to Esperanza. Then he nodded.

Esperanza made a smile full of pain. Every ounce of her misery was written there. She reached across the table and took his hand in both of hers. I put my eyes back on my computer when she raised his hand to her mouth and kissed his fingers.

❖   ❖   ❖

I called the old man from his bathroom. I didn't want to share what I was thinking with the others just yet. Since McElvy might dispel my concerns. I didn't see the point in alarming anyone if that was the case.

I had checked the local news sites and found nothing. No mention of the roadblocks. Or any explanation for all the sirens wailing around town. And most importantly no mention that Armijo was dead.

"So they shut it down tight," McElvy said.

"Who did?"

"I don't know. Armijo could've done that."

"And without him?"

"You sure he's dead?"

"I thought of that. But even if he isn't he's not telling anyone what to do. He left enough blood around that house to kill a bull."

The old man needed to think. I didn't rush him.

"Maybe they got everyone to keep quiet for now. Suspects at large. Don't want to tip them off."

"With roadblocks up? Sirens blasting all over the place? It was like a war out there. How could they sell not wanting to draw attention?"

"Yeah. You're right. Forget that. Stupid thought."

"Either way it's a big story to sit on. Whether he's dead or just almost."

"You would think."

"It seems more likely they don't know."

"Yeah. I hear you."

"If they weren't told to keep quiet they would report something. Roadblocks are news. You at least mention them. Even if you can't explain their purpose. So who told them to keep quiet?"

McElvy didn't respond.

"Any ideas?" I said.

The old man sighed before he answered.

"Here's how that could go down. Someone in the Department is playing king. Passing along what the king supposedly says without bothering to mention that the king is actually dead. Or at present incapacitated."

"Why would anyone do that? Hell of a game to play. What's in it for them?"

McElvy took a few seconds before he answered.

"Can't say that I know."

I gave him a moment to change that answer. He declined to do so. Leaving me to say what he didn't want to—

"If Armijo belonged to El Frente. All the way. Not just some deal but they owned him outright. Then the people who were close to him, maybe they owned them too. Which puts the cartel in control of the Department. At least until it gets out that Armijo is dead or half-dead. And this play makes sense if the cartel is calling it."

McElvy took a good part of a minute to respond.

"Okay. I'm not arguing with you. But I just don't know that I'm ready to go that far."

"The fish rots from the head down. The rotten head is chopped off. But the body seems to rot all alone."

I could picture the old man's expression. How he would screw up his face like he bit a lemon. In his dislike of both what I said and how I said it.

"Okay," he said. "If that's how you care to put it."

❖   ❖   ❖

While McElvy was gone his scanner was quiet. A little chattering now and then but nothing dramatic. Five minutes after he returned the commotion began. As usual what the dispatcher said was Greek to me. A string of codes connected with words that seemed random. All a bunch of nonsense except for an address with a street name I couldn't place.

But that gobbledygook was intelligible to Esperanza. Having been raised in the household of a lawman. Matt turned to her.

"What's going on?" he said.

She listened for another few seconds before she answered—

"My uncle's house is on fire."

The scanner spat out some more. McElvy frowned at me.

"They're not covering their tracks," I said. "They didn't kill him."

The old man nodded.

"They're covering *her* tracks. So no one else can find her."

"Who else would be looking for her?"

The old man didn't answer. I looked at Esperanza. Her eyes were cast down. Beside her Matt was watching me. Our eyes met for an instant. I was the one who looked away. Back to the old man.

"Any other law around?" I said.

The old man narrowed his eyes.

"Like who? The DEA?"

"You tell me."

He shook his head.

"Not much chance. They go where the action is. And there ain't none here. Since we sit opposite no man's land. What we get is small time. Independent operators that wind up dead when El Frente tracks them down. The big stuff goes across on each side of us. Where one of the major outfits has control. The DEA only comes to Doña Pero when they chase someone here."

"So why is El Frente here?"

"I've been thinking on that. And I've got two answers. First is they're moving product. But usually that would show up. Border Patrol would stumble onto some of it. That hasn't happened. And one side or the other wouldn't like it. Depending on whether El Viento had permission from Juárez. So we'd see retaliation. But it's been quiet."

"So if not that?"

"El Viento used Armijo to ramp up his business. The one Juárez doesn't care about. Moving illegals."

"So maybe the INS."

"You're thinking they burnt down his house so the INS wouldn't find his niece."

"Yes. That's what I'm thinking."

"Could be. I guess."

McElvy frowned again.

"Maybe we're reading too much into it. They might be improvising. Just making it up as they go along. This has got to be new territory for them. Taking over a law enforcement department. Up here anyway. I know they control the law some places down on their side. But up here is a different story. They got no playbook."

"They torched the place because it seemed like the thing to do in the heat of the moment."

"Yeah. Could be. People are impulsive. Criminals even more so. If there's one thing I learned working as a lawman. That's it right there."

I didn't have anything to say to that. And for the moment McElvy was done talking. When he spoke again he posed a question to all three of us—

"How good are you folks on horseback?"

Chapter 109

After we answered his question the old man changed the subject. If he had switched to any other topic I probably would have challenged him. I wanted that horseback query explained. But he said this—

"Anyone hungry?"

And he made me realize I was starving. McElvy added that we were looking at a long night and an early morning and should eat while we had the chance. Esperanza volunteered to cook and took Matt into the kitchen to help her.

We ate in silence. A burning house is an ominous thing. The context made this one seem to overflow with ill portent.

I revisited the question of why the house was burning. And recalled the old man's assertion about the impulsive nature of the criminal mind. Which led me to contemplate the many criminals I had known. Who were in the most part extremely reckless. But the most notable ones were not. And could plan and wait as well as anyone. Better even. Prison being a training ground in waiting. And Silvertone being a prime example. But McElvy was right that that kind were the exception.

Then I considered the lone criminal I had seen at Armijo's. I remembered his stupid face when Ortega came with Armijo to arrest me. And chased me out of the shower in that crappy motel that has since been razed. Back when he only had some fuzz on that lip. It was easy to imagine him putting flame to Armijo's place on an impulse.

These thoughts of mine were interrupted when Matthew said—

"Maybe they're trying to flush us out."

He glanced my way and then looked at McElvy.

"I read this magazine article. A review of a book a guy wrote about being in the Army. He compared a tactic they used to hunters flushing out game. You create hell all around your target. Try to make them panic so they break cover. Maybe that's what their trying to do to us. Make us panic. They lit up the house to try and make us run for it."

The old man nodded.

"Could be. El Frente is run by ex-military guys."

"So we can't let it get to us," Matt said.

Esperanza joined in—

"I agree. We can't piss ourselves."

We men all turned her direction.

"What?" she said. "You don't agree?"

McElvy laughed.

"And here I am watching my mouth."

Esperanza snorted.

"Well don't on my account."

She waved a hand through the air.

"It's your house. Talk how you like."

"All right then."

I only listened to the start of this conversation. My thoughts went off on their own again. I watched their faces at first. Then my eyes drifted back to my computer. But what was on the screen did not occupy my mind. In my head I was back inside of Armijo's house. Where I watched Ortega.

In this vision of mine Ortega did not remain alone for very long. Nor was he the one who started the fire. That role went to my former cellmate. The one from the Juárez Cartel. I watched him move across the living room pouring gasoline on the white carpet. Then out of his pocket came a pack of smokes and a vintage nickel-plated lighter. He lit a cigarette and took a long drag and the smoke drifted around his face. He took another and grinned before he tossed the cigarette down and the flames jumped up.

Which gave me a different angle on our situation. I have no idea how one thought led to the next. But what that vision of the fire-starter pointed me to came straight out of my mouth—

"Maybe we're looking in the wrong direction. That instead of what comes here we need to look at what goes there. Which is weapons and ammunition. They get that from us."

I had interrupted the conversation. The others stared at me. I glanced from face-to-face as I kept going—

"Maybe El Viento decided it's his turn to run the show. And he needs his own supply lines because he's going to bite the hand that feeds him. Go up against Juárez. And if not then maybe he's working for them against the Sinaloans. Either way we have war."

I looked at McElvy.

"Maybe the law they're trying to avoid is the ATF."

The old man stared back at me. Then shot a glance at my computer.

"You get all that from watching those cameras?"

I smiled at his joke. But mention of the cameras sent my eyes back to the video feed. Where they landed just in time to see a black SUV come to a stop outside my house. Which must have registered on my face. Because the next thing McElvy said was—

"What is it?"

"We've got company."

While the others rose from their seats to gather around behind me I watched Ortega step out onto the street and stop to look both directions. The others joined me in time to see him cross the street and kick in my front door. Which was impressive. That was a good solid door and well mounted. When he had entered every room and I guess determined the place was empty he started tossing my living room. Why he chose to start there I still wonder. Isn't the bedroom the customary place to begin?

He treated my belongings very roughly. Cushions were slashed open. Books were torn apart.

"I really liked that house," I said.

Something made Ortega stop. He turned toward the street.

Another black SUV pulled up behind Ortega's. Two men got out and went inside. One of these newcomers seemed to be in charge. He spoke and Ortega replied. They talked calmly and did not seem to be doing anything other than working together.

An impression that was shattered when the newcomer who remained silent raised a pistol and shot Ortega in the head.

"I did not see that coming," McElvy said.

❖   ❖   ❖

I was disturbingly unaffected by the head-exploding gunshot. I kept telling myself to be horrified. But all I could think about was the mess. Which I was going to have to pay for. Someone had to clean that up. You can't sell a house with a man's brains all over the living room.

I really liked that house. It was the first nice place I ever lived in.

And I had hated Ortega. Almost as much as I hated Armijo. The shock and horror of his death and what that meant for our safety was counterbalanced by being glad he had gotten himself killed.

Exactly what his death did mean was uncertain. When I stopped for a moment to suggest to our self-appointed leader that he could possibly be overreacting this is what McElvy fired back at me—

"We don't know that it was her cell phone that brought them to your place. That's an assumption. Which belongs in our best case scenario. Worst case is they know about you. And then maybe they know about me. Which means they could show up here at any moment. And maybe you should consider they might've cracked your little empire. Which could put you in a pretty jam. Assuming they don't kill you first. When you need all that money of yours most it could be gone."

That sent me scrambling to check my funds. The various websites I had to visit offered no bad news. I had in fact made some nice gains in a few accounts. I tried to act cool and collected when I reported back—

"It's all there."

The look McElvy gave me was hideously demeaning. It said I was a piteous thing ignorant of my own enormous shame. To make me feel even worse he put a hand on my shoulder when he spoke—

"Maybe you didn't hear me. I said when you need it most. That's when they'll take it all away."

Words like ice water. Splashed directly into my stupefied face.

That money had been my security blanket. Which had now been abruptly yanked away. All through this business with Armijo I believed if events took a bad turn I could buy my way out. But the old man was entirely correct that now at any moment my money and the power it provided could both vanish.

Given who was chasing after us. Killing people in my house.

Oh I really did like that house.

But that did not make me like McElvy's plan. To this very day I still hate it. I only went along with it because we had no better plan. No other plan at all. And there was no denying the need to do something. I shared with the others in the general refusal to be fish waiting in a barrel.

McElvy's plan had six components:

Our young fugitives and I would go on horseback to a cabin he kept in the hills southeast of his ranch. Where we would wait while he—

Went north and created a paper trail that made it appear Matt and Essie had fled in that direction. When he returned he would—

Meet us at a general store located at a crossroads south of the cabin. And we would—

All go to a friend's place in Texas. Where we would—

Wait until the heat was off. And then—

Who the hell knows. The old man never said.

Watching him work was a glimpse into his past. When Sheriff Clarence McElvy ran the law in Doña Pero. It was impossible not to admire how decisively he laid out the course of action that would determine the fate of the four lives huddled together under his roof.

While he spoke I did not object. The old man went too fast and I was too busy just keeping up with him. But when he was done I wanted to tear his plan apart. But I also wanted to appear reasonable to the other two. If I was going to halt the momentum of his plan I would need allies.

So I prodded gently—

"I'm wondering about your cabin. Why should we hide there?"

"The only way in is on horse, ATV, or dirt bike. Can't get a truck or SUV down that trail. If they show up here, and assuming they have enough brains and knowhow to track your horses, they won't have any way to follow. Since you're taking all my horses with you. I doubt they'll show up equipped with ATVs or pulling a horse trailer. And it's a hell of a long walk. So they'll have to go get some mode of transport that can carry them after you. That buys time. And we need to buy time every way you can think of."

Damn it. I couldn't argue with that. I tried something else—

"About the paper trail. Tell me what you have in mind."

He nodded at Matt and Essie.

"I take their credit cards and drive north. Make it look like they're buying stuff. Food, gas, whatever. You want places where you swipe the card yourself. Gas pumps, self-serve checkout lines. Avoid places where you have to hand the card over to someone else. They'll be watching those accounts. And come right after me."

"I don't have a credit card," Esperanza said. "Not one of my own. The only one I have is on my uncle's account."

"That'll do," McElvy said. "They'll be watching his accounts."

"You're sure this will work," I said.

"Damn straight I am. Why wouldn't it?"

"If they know about us then they know these two have help. They could suspect it's a trick."

"But that's worst case. We don't know we're there yet. But they'll have to send someone out on it regardless. My bet is at least two guys and if they've got 'em they'll send more. However many they send that's the same number less we have back here. And I know from experience if you believe you have your target out on the run that takes your focus off other places. You can't help it. It's just human nature. Divide and conquer. That's what we're gonna do."

McElvy smiled and pointed a finger at my chest.

"There was this time I chased a couple up into Colorado. They split up out on the road. I had to decide which one to follow."

He was still pointing that finger. He frowned and the hand rose up and tugged at his mustache.

"How did you decide?" Matt said.

The old man turned and smiled at his questioner.

"I flipped a coin. Right there at the bar. A place in Loveland where they were last seen together. Followed the guy with the floozy he took off with up into Montana. And caught 'em in flagrante at a motel.

I could see why he went off with her. Over that other one."

"We don't need to know," I said.

McElvy turned back to me. His hand resumed pointing.

"That's right," the old man said. "You don't."

He jabbed his finger forward when he said—

"But what I need to know is that friend of yours."

His eyes gleamed as they bored into mine. Clearly he was enjoying himself. Must have felt good to be back in the saddle.

"What are you talking about?" I said.

"I'm talking about your buddy who just got out. He's going with me."

"No."

That hand jabbed forward again.

"With another man we can make it look like these two split up. Which means whoever they send will have to split up too. And if we get lucky maybe they'll even send more. Like I said, divide and conquer. I'm telling you. This is a good idea."

"Good idea, bad idea, I don't give a damn. I'm not dragging him into this. He doesn't need it."

"I'll tell you what he does need. Money. An ex-con just out of the joint is always short of cash. Pay him for his trouble."

"No. And you're wrong. He's making money."

"Legally?"

"Yes. So shut up."

McElvy was still pointing. I could see those gears up in his head grinding away. I raised my own hand and pointed back at him.

"Drop it," I said.

His eyes narrowed and mine narrowed back at him.

Chapter 110

And then my phone rang. The old man and I stood there in our stupid little face-off while it rang again.

"Well at least see who it is," McElvy said.

I took out my phone. And felt like I was holding a rattlesnake. The little display showed me the name of Tranquilino's mother. So either it was Tranq on the other end or they knew enough about me to go looking for him.

I put the rattler up against my ear.

"Hello," I said.

I heard my heart thud in my ears before his voice came back at me—

"So you're awake," Tranquilino said. "Why am I not surprised."

I felt lightheaded. Black dots appeared at the edges of my vision.

"I don't know," I said. "You tell me."

"Maybe it has something to do with what I just heard."

"What'd you hear?"

"That the fat man's place burned down. Went up like the Fourth of July. I thought you would want to know. Now I think maybe you already knew."

"Is that your friend?" McElvy said.

Since my situation meant cell phones might have to prove disposable I used cheap ones. With microphones that are not directional. Meaning they pick up every sound coming at them.

Which meant that Tranquilino could hear McElvy.

"You all right?" Tranq said.

"Yes."

"Well that's good."

"Ask him," McElvy said.

I was about to tell the old man to shut up when Tranq said—

"Ask me what?"

Of course he agreed to do what McElvy wanted. As I knew my good friend would. Which was why I hung up on him without answering his question. But he just called right back again. As I also knew he would. And the truth is despite my efforts to protect him I wanted the indomitable Tranquilino Rojas on our team. Any sane person would. He brought both strength in numbers and just plain strength in strength.

I put McElvy on the phone and he and Tranq made their arrangements. When they were done I tried again to punch holes in The Plan. And didn't get any further than I had before. Next we spent a few hours pretending to sleep. All of us except the old man. Him I heard snoring.

When we were crowding into the kitchen wanting coffee and breakfast I took another shot—

"About this place in Texas," I said. "Where you want us to hide. If El Frente might know about me, and therefore they might know about you, then what's to stop them from finding this friend of yours?"

Maybe the old man was still half asleep. Having been the only one who got any. He looked bleary enough. Whatever the cause, what he said revealed a bit more than he might have wanted—

"That's the beauty of it. No one knows that we know each other. And there's nothing lying around to connect the dots. It ain't the type of relationship where we're in each other's address books."

The old man and I stared at each other. He blinked first.

"And why is that," I said.

McElvy chewed on a corner of his mustache. The bleariness disappeared. Wary eyes slid over to Essie and then to Matt and then back to me.

"Maybe you and I should step outside," he said.

"Are we going to fight?"

The old man pulled his head back and frowned.

"Hell no. We're gonna talk."

"It's cold outside. We can talk in here. Where it's warm. I'd like to stay warm for as long as I can before you stick me on a horse. But maybe at the moment you find it's a little too warm."

"How about we step down the hall."

I glanced at Essie and Matt. They watched us like a pair of owls on a tree branch.

"Maybe if you want us to trust you and your plan you can tell all of us why you and this Texan have a secret relationship."

The old man raised his chin. With his white hair uncombed and askew, this attempt at imperiousness made him look even more ridiculous. When he spoke his voice was dry and cracked—

"Maybe you need me and my plan."

"Sure we do. Since at the moment it's the only plan we have. Let's just make sure it's a good one. Tell us about the Texan."

"I don't need to be any part of this."

"Too late for that now. You put us under your roof that means we're all in this together. We all face the same threat. Any one of us gets caught things are that much worse for the rest of us. So tell us about the damned Texan. Because we have a right to know. Given how important he is to your plan."

McElvy's eyes made another loop around the three of us. When he was done and his eyes were back on me the old man looked very pissed off.

"Why are you busting my ass," he said.

I shook my head at him.

"Don't even. Not gonna cut it."

He glared for another moment before he made his first attempt—

"So maybe—"

Then he hissed. I thought he might spit at me. He looked at Esperanza and back at me then at Matt and back at me again. He raised a hand and it stayed there for a second before he dropped it back down. He set his jaw. Then his eyes flared. When he finally spoke each word was bitten off—

"So maybe I haven't always been exactly lily white."

His eyes went around the three of us again. Then he poked his chin at me.

"Happy now?" McElvy said.

❖   ❖   ❖

I laughed like a hyena. Maniacal laughter that clearly disturbed the others. Then I laughed like I was choking to death. All that effort spent looking at McElvy. After he stuck his nose into my business demanding a piece of it. And still I managed to miss his extracurricular activities.

The old bastard was dirty. I was mad at him and then at me and then at him again. When I could speak I pointed at the old man's face.

"I should have known. Another dirty sheriff fucking up my life. Jesus Christ. How many of you sonsabitches do I have to deal with."

"Stop it," Esperanza said.

She didn't even raise her voice. But her tone stopped me cold. I turned to her and she frowned at me. Then shook her head. Like she was scolding a child.

"That's not helping," she said.

I pointed at McElvy and she shook her head again. I put my own head down and looked at my shoes.

"I want details," Esperanza said.

I looked at her and saw she was eyeballing the old man.

"Tell us what you did," Esperanza said.

McElvy shrugged. He pulled a face.

"Do the details really matter?"

"Details always matter. If you're dirty how do we know you're not working for them?"

Pow to the solar plexus.

"Now that's going a little far. There's dirty and then there's dirty."

"So how dirty are you."

"It was a long time ago. And it wasn't drugs. If that's what you're thinking."

"So what was it."

McElvy rubbed a hand over his whiskers.

"We don't have time for this," Esperanza said.

His hand stopped.

"Sugar."

We all watched him. No one spoke. The old man dropped his hand from his face and looked directly at Esperanza.

"To avoid the tariffs."

"How did you do it?"

"How many details do you need?"

"I'll let you know."

The old man spent a moment not liking that answer.

"There was a guy who worked for a Mexican shipping company. He saw to it that they lost track of shipments. And then made sure those shipments wound up just across the border. I made sure no one was looking when it came across. The guy I knew brought it over."

"How did you meet him?"

"I caught him at it."

"And then what. He talked you out of arresting him?"

"He offered me a bribe."

"Why did you take it?"

"Why does anyone?"

Esperanza shook her head.

"You're not anyone. You're the guy who wants our trust. So tell me why you did it."

"I got in a jam. After my brother died and I took this place over. Trying to hang onto it."

Esperanza folded her arms together.

"Keep going," she said.

The old man raised his chin.

"This place has been in my family for a long time. Too long to see it lost just because my brother was a stupid drunk."

There was a problem we could all relate to. It was easy to imagine how the old man had been pushed into crossing the law he was employed to uphold so he could undo the mess made by a worthless relative.

"We did it a half dozen times," McElvy said. "Then the guy at the shipping company was fired and we were done."

"And that's it?" Esperanza said. "Nothing else you want to share with us."

McElvy shook his head. Esperanza nodded.

"So we're good?" the old man said.

Esperanza nodded again.

"We're good enough," she said.

Part XXXII:
The Batmen

Chapter 111

Even when you may be riding toward torture and death, seeing pretty colors painted across the sky can make you feel better. Or maybe I'm just some kind of fool. Or maybe that's what ten years in prison did to me. Whatever the cause being out under that stupendous morning sky did me a world of good. As the ranch house receded behind us, the sun rose in the east and the heavens turned pink and peach and a delicate pale violet. I looked up and drank it in and felt blessedly drunk by the miracle of creation.

So that was the first surprise of the morning and the trail. To have my mood and perspective so radically altered. And so rapidly improved.

The second was who proved to be the best rider. My guess would have been Esperanza. I knew people still kept animals in the village where she grew up. It would seem only fitting if La Soldadita could ride like a *vaquera*.

But when our packhorse gave Esperanza trouble Matt rode up alongside her and asked for the lead as if he knew what he was doing. And it turned out he did. We continued on without further incident from the once-balky animal. And when we were halted before a portion of the trail that had collapsed into an arroyo, Matt was the one who saw how to best negotiate our passage. So within the first few miles it became clear who would be in charge while we were riding.

❖　　❖　　❖

When the morning was young we did not speak any more than necessary. Esperanza seemed occupied with private thoughts. Matt was busy with the trail. For my own part I was content to be left alone. Free to contemplate the great mystery of existence.

That famous quote from the first Don Juan book came into my head—

> For me there is only the traveling on the paths that have heart, on any path that may have heart. There I travel, and the only worthwhile challenge for me is to traverse its full length. And there I travel— looking, looking, breathlessly.

Words that made me wonder about the path I was on. If it had heart. And how I could know for certain. At that moment I felt the path of my life had a great big pounding giant of a heart. Maybe I didn't always like what that heart demanded. But I felt my path was true. How to know though? Feeling and knowing being two so very different things.

These ponderous thoughts made me want to talk. To hear my own voice and have it answered. To claim this life as mine and reclaim my joy at being out in the great wide open.

We were riding abreast in a section of trail that was wide and flat. Matt was in the middle. I was a little behind the others. I urged my horse forward. As I drew alongside Matt I turned to him and said—

"Am I the only one enjoying myself?"

Which I even thought was clever. An impression I was disabused of by the look Matt gave me. Which was promptly reinforced by my companions' failure to reply. It was soon abundantly clear I had been very much alone in finding pleasure in our present circumstances. Back when I still did. Which now I could not. Having gone and opened my very big and stupid mouth.

Matt had hidden Esperanza from my view when I spoke. A few steps further along, when he was ahead of us, my gaze met hers. Just as my discomfort had begun to recede. I glanced over to check on my companions and my distress came roaring back when I saw the pain on her face. I was too stunned to look away. She held my eyes for just a second. With no look of anger or resentment. Then was kind enough to avert her eyes when she said—

"I don't understand how my life came to this."

❖   ❖   ❖

So ended the first and for me surprisingly pleasant phase of our horseback journey toward an uncertain fate. With me being an insensitive bastard. I do not expect to ever feel like more of an asshole.

I dropped back to be alone with my shame. Self-imposed exile kept a few paces behind. I listened as Matt tried to dissuade Esperanza of believing she had murdered her uncle.

"It was self-defense," Matt said. "You did nothing wrong."

Her silent response was more heartbreaking than any words she could have chosen. She only lowered her head and rode on, slumped forward.

Witnessing this scene while still freshly disgraced by my grotesque behavior forced me to confront the unpleasant truth that although I had probably saved the lives of my two companions I had done exactly nothing to make them like me. Whining like a spoiled child at McElvy. Yodeling about my fun time on the trail. While they were dealing with far greater burdens than the ones we shared. In their places I would have wanted to strangle me.

So I resolved to stop being thoughtless about their difficulties. I hadn't killed my closest family member. Whom it turned out was owned by a drug cartel. That now wanted to kill me. There was no APB from a corrupt law department out on my ass. I hadn't walked away from my entire life because my girlfriend told me if I didn't I would die. My life could prove to be recoverable. I was still rich last time I checked. Compared to Essie and Matt my situation looked pretty damn sweet.

The truth was my chances would look a lot better if I wasn't with them. Just being in their presence was a liability. Which made me wonder why I was. And not with McElvy instead of Tranquilino. Why had the old man taken a chance on an unknown ex-con over taking me along with him? Why was I out here? To protect these two? Be the gunman if we got into trouble? My companions could probably handle the rifles McElvy sent with us better than I could. Just like they did with the horses. My pride was pretty severely wounded by realizing the old man may have dumped me off on the kids because he didn't want to deal with me. That instead he was willing to bet on someone he didn't even know.

But there was nothing I could do about that. The decisions had been made. The plan was set into action. What I needed to do was stop making mistakes and causing problems. I decided to avoid any further humiliating episodes by giving my companions some space and keeping my big mouth shut. Maybe if I didn't do anything stupid or say anything awful for a few days they might begin to forget why they didn't like me.

Chapter 112

When we stopped to water the horses Esperanza seemed to be in better spirits. She smiled when our eyes met and I felt like less of an asshole. Then she watched Matt with the animals and said to him—

"You ride like a cowboy."

So I wasn't the only one who had been surprised. Matt grinned back at her when he answered—

"That's because I learned from one."

"They have cowboys in Pennsylvania?"

"The guy who taught me was from Oklahoma."

Then he told us about a summer spent helping a cowboy mend fences on a farm near where he lived. In exchange for which he learned how to ride. By the end of the summer he felt like he was born to it.

"And then what?" Esperanza said.

Matt frowned.

"What do you mean?"

"What happened to the cowboy?"

Matt frowned.

"He disappeared. The farm was put up for sale."

"And that was it?"

"Yeah. That was it."

"How old were you?"

Matt thought for a moment.

"Twelve."

"Have you ridden since?"

"Nope."

"But you still remember what you learned."

Matt grinned again.

"Yeah. I do."

Then his face clouded over.

"Two weeks before school started I went out there and he was gone. A few days later there was a For Sale sign next to the mailbox."

Matt stood up straight and stuck his hands in the back pockets of his crisp new blue jeans and peered off into the distance out from under his spanking white cowboy hat. The young Pennsylvanian looked every inch a raw recruit fresh on the trail. But not one who would have any trouble holding his own.

"I told myself when I grew up I would buy that place. And then I would go find Luke."

Watching him stare off toward the horizon I remembered how the first time I encountered Matt Walker I had been determined not to think well of him. He was young when I was already feeling old. And he was handsome and he was Anglo and he had the girl. None of which made me want to like him. But now here I was liking him very much.

Matt frowned at his memories.

"Luke Norland. That's what he said his name was. But I think he was lying. Sometimes I had to say his name three or four times before he answered. And I caught him in some other lies. I think maybe he was hiding from something. An ex-wife. Maybe from the law."

Matt shook his head.

"And now here I am hiding from the law myself. Riding away from it on a horse just like he showed me."

He turned and smiled at Esperanza. She smiled back at him.

"You don't seem too upset about it," Esperanza said.

Matt's smile grew wider.

"No. I guess I'm not."

The look they exchanged was like a fluttering of harps and a swelling of violins. Unabashedly announcing these two young fools were madly in love. Right smack in the middle of this horrible wrong turn in their lives

576

❖   ❖   ❖

The day and the trail disappeared behind us. When we stopped for the night, at first, I was too busy to notice where we were. But once the horses were fed and our bedrolls were set out and we had something to eat cooking on McElvy's little gas stove I stopped and looked around. As twilight began to fall. Despite the gathering shadows, the landscape became familiar.

Then a cold shiver went all over me. When I knew we were camped near the canyon where my father died.

Years later bent over a detailed topographical map I determined we couldn't have been more than a quarter mile away. Which still strikes me as odd and disturbing. That fate brought me so close again.

I startled when Esperanza said—

"Didn't you find Elden out here?"

The second shiver was worse than the first one.

"Are you okay?" Esperanza said.

The third wasn't so bad. But three in a row like that made me wonder if I was okay. Maybe not. Maybe something was wrong with me.

"I'm fine," I said.

When I was under better control I answered her first question.

"I think you're right."

I pointed to the west.

"It was in a canyon over that way."

Esperanza smiled at me. A warm and kind and grateful smile that made my heart ache.

"He was my best friend," she said. "And you saved him."

Those shivers felt better than how I felt now.

Saved him for what? I wanted to ask her.

"Now you have saved me too," Esperanza said. "All these years later."

577

She stepped over to where I stood and squeezed my hand.

"You are a good man," she said. "Thank you."

I could not speak. Which prevented me from saying anything stupid. Like asking Esperanza if she knew what became of her good friend. And if she knew what it was that I saved him for. Since that remained a mystery to me. Given how things worked out for him.

I stood there in our little camp site beside the hiss of the gas jet on the little stove with the horses a short distance off slowly munching and occasionally stomping as night began to take claim of the high desert. And hoped things would work out better for Esperanza than they had for her friend.

I did not want to keep saving people so they could suffer and die.

We thought it best to sleep in shifts. But I don't believe any sleeping happened. I know we were all awake at midnight. Because we all sat up and took notice when the sound of a small engine appeared off to the south. Like a lawn mower or a go kart. Not the kind of engine you would expect to hear out in the middle of nowhere in the middle of the night. If you expected to hear any kind of engine at all.

As the sound drew nearer and grew louder we noticed another odd thing about it. Something our ears told us that we couldn't believe. But eventually there was no denying what we heard—

That little engine was up off the ground. Something small and motorized was flying toward us through the dark. Going low over the open desert. With no lights to guide its way.

"What the hell is that?" Matt said.

Then Esperanza pointed.

"I saw something. Like a shadow."

A moment later I saw it too. A dark shape passed before a cluster of stars. I saw it again as the sound of its engine reached its greatest volume. Which happened when the craft passed about two hundred yards to the east and maybe fifty yards off the ground.

"What the hell is that?" Matt said again.

This time I answered him. With something I remembered from my reading about the cartels—

"Ultralight aircraft. They use them to smuggle drugs."

We listened to the sound recede.

"Someone is actually flying that thing," Matt said.

"Yes."

"In the dark. And the cold. Over this uneven terrain. All the way from Mexico."

"That's right."

"Jesus."

"So who's out there?" Esperanza said. "El Frente?"

They both looked at me.

"I don't know. I guess either that or someone is freelancing."

"But they're down in Mexico," Esperanza said. "Whoever is behind that thing."

I looked at where the sound was going. And then at where it came from.

"They must have ground crews at each end of the flight. One crew to get them launched. Another to receive the drugs."

"Okay," she said. "But not anywhere nearby."

"I doubt it. I mean otherwise what's the point? If you're going to follow after them on the ground you might as well just drive the drugs across the border instead."

Esperanza nodded. Then shook her head.

"Still. We don't need any company. Even up in the air."

"You think there'll be more?" Matt said.

He looked at Esperanza when he asked. Then they both looked at me again.

I shook my head.

"I have no idea."

We listened and waited. Watching the sky off to the south even though we heard the first one long before we saw it.

About fifteen minutes passed.

"I guess that's it," Matt said. "Just the one."

We all turned back to the north. Waiting for our visitor's return. I was about to say they were probably freelancers. That with only one ultralight it was a small operation. I had read that the cartels flew multiple craft at one time to make sure at least some of them completed their deliveries.

What stopped me from speaking was seeing Matt turn back toward the south. He raised his hand and we listened. A moment later I heard it. A second slow approach commenced. That crazy lawn mower noise crawling toward us up in the air.

This one passed by maybe three hundred yards off to the east. Further away than its predecessor.

Another fifteen minutes brought the third craft. This one was closer. And lower to the ground. And a little higher pitched. With a slight stutter.

"Shit," Matt said. "That's not good."

It passed by about seventy-five yards away. I thought I caught a glimpse of the pilot's dangling legs against the sky. I pointed and said—

"There."

But no one else saw.

When number three was heading off into the distance Esperanza said—

"When do you think they'll come back?"

Matt answered—

"*If* they come back."

"They have to get home somehow."

"True. Poor bastards."

Esperanza turned to me.

"You think they'll come back tonight?"

"I would guess so."

She nodded.

"Yeah. Me too."

We watched the northern sky. And listened to the buzz of number three fade away into the night.

"Now he sounds like a little bug," Esperanza said.

"Can you imagine doing that," Matt said.

"No. But if you have people to feed I guess you do it."

"Yeah. I guess so."

A moment later Matt added—

"But damn. That's rough."

Chapter 113

When Esperanza got her rifle Matt and I did the same. It felt better to be holding a gun.

Two hours passed. We made no attempt to sleep.

On the way home they flew closer together. Less than ten minutes apart. The first two went past about three or four hundred yards off to the east. We couldn't see them.

Number three sounded markedly worse. Now it was erratic. Revving up and then threatening to stall. As if the pilot was drunk. Which would not be surprising. Given what he had to do.

He came almost straight at us. Flew past about thirty feet to the east and maybe fifty feet up. Like a giant motorized bat against the night sky. The horses were badly spooked. Luckily we had Matt to calm them down.

There was no sign that he saw us. No change in his direction or angle. And over the sound of that engine mounted right behind him I doubt he could hear the commotion of the horses.

Then his motor whined even higher. And sputtered. And whined again. And then stopped. The black bat shape glided out of sight behind a low hill. For a moment everything was silent. Then the sound of the crash came crackling and hissing through the scrub and across the sand and the dirt. Like a heavy wave against a beach beyond a row of dunes.

We heard no cries of anguish. No screaming for help.

The night was silent. It ate the crash and rested.

We kept our eyes on that low hill.

"He could be armed," I said. "And someone could come for him."

"So we don't see if he needs help," Matt said.

I shook my head.

"Probably not a good idea."

Matt pointed at the hill.

"The trail heads that direction. We need to go around him."

There was no need to say when that would happen. We all knew we would leave as soon as we were packed up. Which took maybe five minutes.

We went off the trail and on foot, passing to the east of that low hill. We assumed any newcomers would arrive from the west. That being the shortest approach from the nearest road.

Traveling quietly by foot through the dark, leading horses across open desert, makes for slow progress. Dawn lit up the eastern sky when we finally rejoined the trail. Back on our horses we made better time.

An hour later we heard a single gunshot. Cracking through the cold morning.

From back behind us in the same direction as that low hill.

A day and a half spent in the saddle. When we weren't used to the saddle. Two nights without sleep. Due to the stress of the past two days. We were a shambling wreck when we climbed up into the hills and arrived at the cabin.

Over lunch we agreed on two hour shifts. I volunteered to take the first one. In part to give Essie and Matt some time alone. But they were already asleep when I stepped out onto the porch. Where I passed the longest two hours of my life. Scanning the trail with binoculars. Clutching my rifle when alarmed. Which was often.

The worst part was a waking nightmare of being the doomed pilot. In my mind I was up there in the dark and cold. Dangling beneath that bat wing. I watched the moonlit desert pass beneath me and considered why a man did a thing like that. Like Esperanza said, it could be to provide for his family. The only other reason was for the thrill. But daredevils weren't what the cartel would want. A man who did such a thing for selfless reasons would be much more predictable.

And more importantly controllable. I wondered if the men up in those tiny crafts flying across the night all had someone they cared for being held by the cartel. Just to make sure they did as they were told.

When the ultralights flew away it was the gunshot that wouldn't leave me alone. I heard it a hundred times cracking across the morning as we rode away from that hill. And when I wasn't hearing gunfire I hallucinated men on horseback coming up the trail.

Fortunately everything bad that happened remained inside my head.

At the end of my watch I felt a hundred years older. When Matt came out to take over I almost kissed him.

The four hours that I slept went past in an instant.

After dinner we played cards. A kind of upside-down poker game I learned in the prison woodshop. The loser of each hand has to tell a story. That first night at the cabin Matt couldn't win a hand to save his life. But the next night he did better. And Esperanza did worse. I was a winner every time we played. Some of us are just lucky at cards. In our time at the cabin I became acquainted with much of what you already know about my two friends. And a few things you have yet to learn.

One thing I learned at the cabin was that Essie and Matt had been planning a trip when fate interrupted. Can you guess where to? Yes. That's right. The Grand Canyon. And they explained that was where it all began between them. I was struck a little dumb by learning that their connection went back that far. And began so mysteriously. Not to mention romantically. I am old enough now to admit I was jealous of what they shared. And awed by it.

You get the idea. Between the stories told during our card games, and the general conversation, I became familiar with my companions and the details of their lives. Less information flowed the other way. I did not lose when we played cards. And I was more reluctant to discuss my past. Age can make us less forthcoming. As will time spent in prison.

On the second night one of the things I learned about Esperanza was that before Matt entered her life the only close relationship she had was with her uncle. With Matt's support she began to question what kind of man her Uncle Joe really was. Which led to her contacting me. So if Matt had not entered her life I would most likely never have met her.

And none of us would have been at that cabin. Since apparently Armijo seeing her boyfriend as competition was what made her uncle attack Esperanza. And if she did not know me already when she ran outside afterwards my invitation to escape might well have been declined. An invitation I may not have extended to someone I had never met before. So Esperanza most likely would have still been there when Ortega arrived.

We tried to make light of it. A little gallows humor to dispel the tension. But it was a sobering turn of conversation.

We had many of those.

Every night we heard the ultralights. We were always awake at midnight when they started north. For no good reason. We should have been asleep.

On our second night at the cabin the moon was full. We stood on the porch and peered off to the west and from our vantage point up in the hills we saw a bat-shaped shadow skim across the desert. And then found the craft itself. And saw black dangling legs silhouetted against the sky.

We had been warm the moment before. Now we were cold. We shuffled back inside and went to bed. Where sleep was far away. When Esperanza broke the silence she said what I was thinking—

"Three nights in a row. You think freelancers could get away with that?"

"No," I said.

"Neither do I."

"So that's El Frente," Matt said. "Flying right past us."

I ran over it again and only saw one answer.

"I think it has to be. That's a real operation. People who know what they're doing. And have the resources to do it."

A moment later we heard the second ultralight in that night's triad. For there were always three. Never any other amount. We listened intently to the craft's entire transit. From when it first became audible. Then while the sound of that little motor swelled through the night, until when the buzz disappeared and everything was silent.

Everything stayed silent for a few moments longer. Then Matt spoke for all us when he said—

"I can't wait to get out of here."

Part XXXIII: Gracias Señor Beam

Chapter 114

McElvy left his truck at the airport where he rented an SUV. Tranquilino drove a car that belonged to one of my shadow enterprises. They went north in tandem then parted company in Colorado. From there the old man playing the part of Matthew continued north into Wyoming. While Tranquilino as Esperanza went east into Nebraska.

The plan was for Matt's trail to go cold in Montana. While Tranq continued to drop bread crumbs for Esperanza all across the Midwest. She was the bigger prize so he would keep her charade up and running. While McElvy flew back and retrieved his truck and got his horse trailer from the ranch and picked us up at a trailhead southwest of the cabin. From there he would take us to that place in Texas owned by the smuggler.

We arrived early. As the hour drew near we remained alone and our anxiety mounted. When the time arrived there was no sign of the old man.

Instead my cell phone rang. One of the reasons McElvy selected this spot was because he knew it had coverage. Giving us the ability to adjust our plans if that was required.

Which apparently it was.

"Tell me you're on your way," I said.

"Sorry to disappoint. Snow is coming down like God is trying to smother hell. Everything out of here is closed. Roads, airports, you name it."

"For how long?"

"A couple days at least."

"Okay. Could be worse I guess."

"You might want to reserve judgment on that. I haven't got hold of that friend of mine."

"So we don't have anywhere to go."

"Not at the moment."

I licked my lips and squinted and my head ached.

"Anything else you need to tell me?"

"Why? You want more bad news?"

❖   ❖   ❖

More time to kill back at the cabin. More days of anxiety and tedium. More nights marked by the passing of the ultralights.

When four days had passed we returned to the same trailhead. Where we replayed the same scene as before. Except this time the call did not come from McElvy. The number on the display belonged to Tranquilino.

"This cannot be good news," I said.

"No, brother. Wish I could say different."

"What happened?"

"The old man is indisposed."

"What does that mean?"

"He didn't say. And about that place? It's not there anymore."

"What?"

"The place he wanted to take you? Burned to the ground. Last summer. Remember all those wildfires?"

"He just found that out?"

"He said it didn't occur to him to wonder if it still existed."

I couldn't argue with that.

"Fuck."

"Yeah. I hear you."

"So where do we go?"

"The only idea he had was head back to the ranch. He says if they haven't shown up there yet chances are they never will."

"Yeah. Maybe. And they could be there waiting for us."

"He said that too."

❖   ❖   ❖

Technically it wasn't winter yet. But in a land where the rain comes in two flavors, one named for summer and the other for winter, if there is a chill to the air when the rain comes it is called winter rain. Which is supposed to gently soak the high desert. Not wash it away.

After my discouraging phone call with Tranquilino we spent the night back at the cabin. Where despite our planned departure for the ranch at dawn once again we were awake at midnight. Listening to our bat-winged friends. When they had come and gone and we had slept for a couple of hours the rain woke us. A tin roof makes a deluge hard to sleep through.

The rain was still pouring down when dawn came. We waited another hour before setting out into it. Our progress was slow and cold and hazardous and needless to say entirely wet.

And finally halted by a flooded arroyo. Which despite our pleas not to, an enraged Esperanza almost attempted to cross. She started down into it before coming to her senses. Then vented her frustration screaming like a banshee against the tempest.

Back to the cabin. The rain came and went as the day passed into night. And finally tapered off and then ended as midnight came on.

And at midnight the buzzing came out of the south.

Chapter 115

The next morning we tried again. Under clear skies in a biting chill. I can't say for certain we got any farther than we did in the rain. I believe we did. But the conditions were so changed we seemed to be riding a different trail.

And now instead of slogging and slipping through sopping mud, the crust of the earth was frozen. The horses' hooves sometimes broke through this crust into slick mud below. Sending a leg sliding out quick and giving you a nasty jerk in the saddle. I almost went down twice. Once Matt had to execute a quick dismount to avoid sending his horse and himself tumbling down an embankment.

We were passing behind some boulders approaching the edge of a bluff. As usual Matt was in the lead. He moved past the rocks blocking our view to the north and out onto open ground. Then wheeled around and started back. Waving furiously for us to do the same. As we hurried to comply Esperanza and I caught a glimpse of what had turned Matt back toward us.

There was a column of smoke rising in the north. Curling black and inky against the pale morning sky.

We gathered out of sight behind the boulders. Watching each other. Minds grinding away. Willing the panic to cease and coherent thought to return.

"So that's the ranch house," Esperanza said.

Matt and I nodded.

"We have to assume it is," I said.

"And that they're heading toward us right now," Matt said.

Esperanza gestured at me.

"Give me your phone. Let's see if it works out here."

I pulled off a glove.

"Who're you going to call?"

She didn't answer. I unzipped my jacket and reached for my phone. Realizing as I did that El Frente might have McElvy. If that column of smoke meant they had his house. So the phone I had used to talk with the old man could now tell them where we were.

I brought that phone out and starting taking it apart.

"What're you doing?" Esperanza said. "Stop that!"

"Sorry."

I pulled out another phone and handed that one to her.

"There are more where that came from," I said.

"Who are you calling?" Matt said.

Esperanza stabbed numbers into the keypad. Then held the phone to her ear while she answered—

"Somebody who owes me."

❖   ❖   ❖

You meet someone for the first time. This particular meeting occurs during the frenzy and stress of eluding a drug cartel. You smile and shake her hand and remind yourself not to forget her name. Which you have already drilled into your head. But reminding yourself once more cannot hurt.

Next you make yourself busy getting underway. Loading the horses that you rode there into the trailer pulled by the old Dodge pickup driven by the elderly Spanish gentleman whose name you have already forgotten. Juan? Jose? Jorge? Waving goodbye to him as he drives away. Waiting until he is out of sight. Then packing your accomplices and your weapons into the back of the SUV. Hidden under a stash of supplies and equipment.

You take a seat beside your new acquaintance. Riding shotgun in her SUV. And drive off to commit

591

an indeterminate number of crimes. You and she being the public faces of a hastily planned operation smuggling fugitives and firearms across an international border.

At the border you will present a false identity that should be airtight. Having been constructed with care for insurance back when your life included the leisure of making detailed preparations. But this identity was not tailored to the present circumstances. And therefore does nothing to explain how you know the woman seated beside you. If providing an explanation becomes necessary you will claim to have met though a rideshare ad on Craigslist. There is a cybertrail supporting this claim. This story is not likely to satisfy any determined interrogators. But hopefully would be sufficiently difficult to disprove. In any case it's the best you could concoct given the circumstances.

The woman you just met will be the main perpetrator. She owns the vehicle and is behind the wheel. Making her doubly accountable for the contents. And the primary actor in this operation. Your fate is in her hands. Either she does her job well or you all wind up in jail. And even if she does her job flawlessly you could still all wind up in jail.

So here you are. Just the two of you. With miles of road ahead before you do anything illegal. Either you break the ice and start talking. To pass the drive time that precedes the actual crimes. Or you both hold your tongues. At least until the main event is over.

We held our tongues. We did not talk on the drive to the border. Or while we waited for our turn to pass through the crossing. Or when our turn came. During which my new acquaintance did not appear unduly distressed. Although I did notice she did some deep breathing.

The man who handled our passage glanced at our paperwork and at our faces and waved us through. Then turned and complained to someone I couldn't see that his head was killing him. Our asses may have been saved by the border guard suffering a migraine.

So now our crimes had been committed. And still we did not speak. For a good ten miles into Mexico. Then the woman I had met a little more than an hour ago smiled at me and said in a chipper voice like she was making the smallest possible kind of small talk—

"So how do you know Esperanza?"

I pasted a smile on my own face and pointed it right back at her.

"I was going to ask you the same thing."

"She was a student of mine."

"Do you commit felonies for all your students?"

Score. She had not seen that coming. She glared at me and into her mirrors. Then put that smile back on again.

"Only those who maintain an A average."

"Tell me why you would do that. Why is she special to you?"

Her eyes cycled back through the mirrors. Then stole a glance my direction. They darted forward again when she saw I was watching.

"She's the best student I ever had."

"You taught her at the university."

"I did."

"And went on a dig together. Correct?"

"Yes."

"And yet things between you seem awkward. Strange that should be so."

She frowned and swallowed.

"I don't like your tone."

"Neither do I. It's a nasty tone."

"I don't want to discuss this any further."

"How odd. Neither did she."

593

Our conversation lapsed for the next three or four miles. During which my companion studiously ignored my presence. I indulged myself in frequent and lingering glances in her direction. Which she tolerated with apparent difficulty.

"So what's the prognosis?" I said. "Couple of months? Maybe a year? Thought you might as well go out with a bang? Have you started chemo?"

She had already glared at me twice by the time I finished. She glared at me again when I was done.

"I don't have cancer. And that's not funny."

"So you're not dying."

"No. Sorry to disappoint you."

I grunted and looked out my window. Then spent some time pretending to think. She glanced my way a couple of times while I put on my show. Her glare became just a frown. The last time she looked my way I could tell she was curious. I waited another few beats before I said—

"So you're in love with her."

Her hands jerked the steering wheel.

And I had my answer.

Chapter 116

I did not harass Leslie Davidson merely for my own amusement. Although I was amused by doing so. It provided a welcome diversion. While half-expecting the Mexican police to come swarming along the road and pull us over. Then shoot us first and later not even bother to ask questions. Because I did not like Mexico. And maybe they could tell.

I gave Leslie a hard time because I wanted to know why she was doing this. The moment we got in her car we became dependent on her. I wanted to gauge how reliable I could expect her to be. And her reliability depended on her motivations.

I knew why the old man helped us. Because he got off on it. That was how McElvy was wired. And I knew why Tranquilino helped us. Because we were friends and I was in a jam and he was that kind of guy.

But mostly I was in a jam because of the kids. So why was I helping them? Because I liked them. And I liked being part of something. Even if I would have been better off on my own. And maybe I was a little like the old man. Maybe I got off on playing hero like he did.

When McElvy's plan fell apart, it would have been the logical point for me to part company from the young fugitives. Stay behind in the States where I had plenty of money and I owned property and I had excellent false identities that I could use to hide from the bad guys. Going to Mexico was a stupid move for me.

I did not like Esperanza's plan any more than I had liked McElvy's. Less so even. But with the collapse of his plan hers was the only plan we had. Once again we were bereft of alternatives in regards to plans. Apparently Matt and I were useless at coming up with them. At least in that particular set of circumstances. And as has been better said by others—

Lead, follow, or get out of the way.

— Thomas Paine

And also—

Desperate times call for desperate measures.

— So damn old nobody knows who said it first

So I went along with Esperanza's plan. With less griping than when we got started with McElvy's. Which may have been due mostly to fatigue. And perhaps because she was a young woman while he was an old man.

A young woman I found myself increasingly taken with.

But I only allowed myself to express a single objection—

"Does it have to be Mexico?"

"Yes. Of course it does. What other country could it be?"

"Canada?"

"I don't have anywhere to go in Canada. Do you?"

"No. But I was hoping to avoid Mexico."

"What do you have against Mexico? Have you ever been there?"

"No."

"You should give it a chance."

"I have my reason. For disliking it."

"Which is?"

"Manuel Ortiz."

"Sorry. I don't know who that is. And to dislike an entire country because of one person is crazy."

"But you *do* know Manuel. You're looking at him."

"So you have a multiple personality disorder?"

"Oh ha ha! That's quite hilarious. Manuel Ortiz is the man your uncle said I was when he put me in jail. I didn't like being Mexican."

"You weren't Mexican. That's just stupid."

"You know what I mean."

"No. I really don't."

"Mexico has not been good to me."

"Mexico has done nothing to you. My uncle did that. He is the one you should be mad at."

"And I am. Most certainly. But I'm also mad at Mexico."

"You're making my brain hurt. This is absurd."

"I know. And yet still I hold Mexico accountable."

"You blame the entire nation of Mexico for something one person did to you."

"Yes. And he was an American."

"Well that's just nuts. You're nuts about Mexico."

"You spend ten years in jail as a Mexican and we'll see how rational you are about Mexico."

Esperanza put her head back and laughed. Then she pointed at me—

"You sounded very Mexican when you said that."

And then she laughed again.

I cannot imagine how I could have possibly sounded Mexican. Certainly not my accent. My tone of voice? My choice of words? I really have no idea. But Esperanza was beautiful when she laughed and when she said it. So I did not care. If she had said I sounded like a braying donkey and that amused her it would have been fine by me.

As you may have inferred from that exchange we had been drinking. McElvy had a fresh bottle of Jim Beam stashed under the sink in the cabin. Where since we had nowhere else to go we returned after seeing the ranch house was on fire. That bottle was brought out and cracked open and passed around while Esperanza told us her plan.

Matt and I did not interrupt her. When she was done I gave Matt a chance to respond first. He smiled and said—

"I always wanted to travel abroad."

When we were done laughing at that I took a slug of the whiskey, which happened to be in my hand at that moment, then gestured with the bottle at Esperanza when I said—

"So you want to hide in El Viento's vest pocket."

La Soldadita looked at me with defiance. She even tossed her head when she spoke—

"Why not," she said. "It's the last place he'll look."

I didn't know if that was true. I thought maybe it wasn't. But I also could not say for sure that it was false. So instead of saying anything I took another hit and passed the bottle to Esperanza. Then she and Matt watched while I assessed our accommodations with a disapproving eye.

"Why not," I said. "I could use a change of scenery."

We laughed as if that was uproarious. Then made more bad jokes while we made the bottle empty. That was when Esperanza and I had our little conversation about Mexico and Manuel Ortiz and why I did not want to go there. When the whiskey was gone we said curses that we did not have more. But in the morning, of course, we were glad for it.

When I think of it now, that was the only night we spent in the cabin when we were not awake to hear the ultralights. *¡Gracias Señor Beam!*

So we got drunk in the face of impending doom. And laughed like idiots and like fools. The next day we put our plan into action. Before you could say *¡Vaya con Dios!* we were in Mexico.

❖ ❖ ❖

Even now it makes me anxious to think about how stupid our plan was.

But apparently the members of El Frente who were sent to catch us were even stupider. If they had half a brain between them they should have found Leslie Davidson. Who was not an insignificant figure in the life of young Esperanza Armijo. Any investigator with his cerebral cortex mostly intact should have had her name in a matter of hours. And followed her straight to us. Then El Viento could have reached right into his vest pocket and plucked us out. I cannot imagine how we could have made things any easier for them without actually trying.

Not to imply that Esperanza was stupid. Just because her plan was. Stupid or not at least she had a plan. All Matt and I had were headaches from the whiskey.

And her plan did beat staying at the cabin. Where the well was running low trying to supply three people and four horses. And the human food was dwindling and the horse food was all but gone. And where they would have found us if we stuck around. Maybe even the next day after we left they made the cabin match the ranch house and burnt it to the ground. Either that or there was an arsonist wandering the backcountry of Doña Pero who just happened to torch those two places.

Two places where we had hidden out. Both burnt to the ground. And a third place where we were supposed to hide out, that smuggler's joint in Texas. Also burnt to the ground. That one by the hand of God and not the hand of El Frente but still—that was just too much burning to the ground. Not to mention that they also torched Armijo's place. I don't know that it was burnt all the way to the ground but I also don't know that it wasn't.

Either way it was getting ridiculous. We needed a place where getting burnt to the ground was out of the question. And that place was across the border down in Mexico. Because it wasn't on the ground.

Whether I liked it or not Mexico was necessary. Something I could sense even as my conscious mind rejected it. Logic and reason saw only danger. But intuition groping around in the dark for the true path emphatically insisted that this unwanted step had to be taken.

So I embraced our stupid plan. *¡Viva Mexico!*

Part XXXIV:
Automatic

Chapter 117

Other than the unfortunate nationality of our new digs, like my companions, I greatly preferred them to our old ones. And "digs" they were quite literally. Leslie Davidson brought us to an archeological site in the Sierra Madre. Where to pass the time and justify our presence we would work the digs. An isolated encampment with an excellent cover story. If not for the obvious connection to Essie's past it would have been perfect.

The site was in a small box canyon on the side of a remote valley. Access by four wheel drive stopped at a flat expanse of packed dirt just inside the canyon mouth. Beyond that you went on foot. A path climbed through the scrub and cacti on the canyon floor then ascended a series of rock ledges to the back wall. From there you went by ladder up to the cliff dwellings.

I was told it wasn't on the ground. And therefore could not be burnt down to it.

The main encampment was where the vehicle access ended. There was a metal storage container for equipment and supplies that was kept locked up when the site was not occupied. Next to it was a water tank trailer. And set off by itself a tan plastic portable toilet.

Beyond the canyon the valley floor was flat and gently sloped. A small stream wandered through the pines and oaks and scattered boulders. Unfortunately once or twice El Frente had been known to wander through here as well. Tracking down and eliminating freelancers. Although neither they nor those they hunted had been seen in this vicinity for some time.

601

But just in case they received any unwanted visitors the archeologists who worked this site kept among the equipment and supplies locked in that storage container four pistols with gun belts. Which they wore at all times. When Leslie Davidson showed us the guns Matt said—

"Where's the bullwhip?"

We all looked at him. He pointed at the pistols.

"Kind of Indiana Jones, don't you think?"

Now we all got his joke. But none of us laughed. Matt stuck his hands in his pockets and shrugged.

The pistols were Colt 45s. Just like the one I found at Sorenson's place and the one McElvy pointed at me in the graveyard. I kept seeing that damn pistol everywhere I went.

Esperanza picked up one of the guns and one of the belts. We followed her outside. She draped the belt over her shoulder and snapped open the cylinder of the Colt. When she snapped it shut again she handed the pistol to Matt.

"Careful. It's loaded."

"I saw that."

We watched her strap on the belt. When she had it set how she wanted she took the gun back and slipped it into the holster. She adjusted the belt again.

"I never liked how these things feel."

Matt smiled at her.

"Sounds like you wore one pretty often."

"When I was out in the hills. My aunt didn't like me off by myself. When I wore a gun she didn't worry so much."

"That's kinda sweet. In a badass western kinda way."

"One night my uncle put me to work. Guarding the bingo game."

A cloud passed over her face. When we realized why, we lowered our heads.

"My life is all screwed up," Esperanza said.

We looked at her. She was looking up at the cliff dwellings. When she turned and saw us watching her she shrugged.

"What are you going to do? No use crying over spilt milk."

Matt snorted and shook his head.

"That's one way of looking at it."

"What about you, cowboy? How're you with guns?"

"Twenty-two rifle. Plinking at cans. That's about it."

"You better practice with one of these things."

"I guess I better."

Esperanza turned to me.

"And you?"

"The belt will take getting used to. I can handle a pistol."

I turned to Leslie.

"So are there items in your budget for firearms and ammo?"

"What do you think?"

"I think you bought those out of your own pocket. South of the border. From some guy whispering in an alley."

"He said they belonged to Pancho Villa."

Esperanza laughed.

"Good thing we brought our rifles. Do these things even work?"

Leslie nodded.

"They get the job done."

"So where is everybody?" I said.

Everyone frowned at me.

"What do you mean?" Leslie said.

"The people who are supposed to be working here."

"Gone until we get more funding."

"When will that be?"

"A few months at least. Plenty of time."

❖　　❖　　❖

Whether or not Leslie was right depended on what our next plan proved to be. And whether a few months would be enough time to put that plan into action. Because the only plan we had concluded when we arrived at the cliff dwellings. Beyond that we had nothing. All we could hope for when we jumped the border was that we could buy enough time to come up with something else.

As it turned out that something else came from me. About five minutes after we finished our conversation over the guns I knew what we had to do. Or more exactly what I had to do. Since I was the only one who could do it. And I was more than a little ashamed I hadn't thought of it before. But our circumstances before we got there had forced me to think in the short term. Sometimes you have to complete step one before you can even contemplate step two. Now step one was finished and step two became obvious.

I started by borrowing Leslie's digital camera and taking some images of Matt and Essie standing against the side of the storage container. Which provided the flattest background and would best allow the images to be manipulated. Next I arranged for Leslie to return me to civilization or the nearest best approximate. Somewhere I wouldn't attract too much attention. And could have some privacy while I got on the Internet.

The next day she drove me to Nuevo Casas Grandes. Which is located in a wide high valley on the Mesa del Norte. Adjacent to the Paquimé Archaeological Zone, home of the Casas Grandes. Considered the most important archaeological site in northern Mexico. Also nearby are Mennonite and Mormon communities. Not quite what I expected of Mexico in my prejudicial state. *¡Ay Chihuahua!*

And not that I saw any of that. Since I was not there to play tourist.

I holed up in a motel room and got busy. The first order of business was to assess our present risk. I checked the news for Doña Pero County and found nothing. No mention that the sheriff was dead or that he was missing or even that his house had caught fire. Whoever had assumed Armijo's power still kept a tight lid on their little mess. Which could mean they were still looking for us. And wanted to keep control of the department while they used its resources to hunt us down. Or those same resources were being put to some other purpose. Like keeping those ultralights in the air undetected. With no way to know, we had to assume we were still on their to-do list.

Next I checked up on the ones left behind.

"So you live," Tranquilino said.

"So it seems."

"And your friends?"

"Them too."

"Well that's something."

"You hear from the old man?"

"Yeah. Do you know about his place?"

"I saw it happening."

"Close call for you then."

"That would be my guess."

"He said he's alright. He has somewhere to go."

"You believe that?"

"I believe he can take care of himself. How about you?"

"We're not in the best situation at the moment. But I'm working on that."

"Anything I can do?"

"No. Thanks. Any word out on the fat man?"

"Just that no one has seen him since his place burned down. But apparently they didn't find him there."

"I was expecting something by now."

"I hear you."

"So it's just business as usual. With him gone."

605

"Yeah. That's what we got."

Which wasn't anything to work with. Our pressing matters settled, I had to move on. I promised to stay in touch and said goodbye to my friend.

Old business dealt with, it was onto the new. Which began with verifying my funds. Since you can't do a damn thing in the world of men without money. And since McElvy had me worried about how safe my money was. With his little speech about how they would wait until I needed it most before they took it away. So far I still had plenty of funds.

Next I began reconnecting with my criminal network. Since only criminals can help you when you need to break the law. Even those who assist you that were not lawbreakers before become so the moment they come to your aid. If not in actuality than in spirit.

By that I mean you Leslie Davidson. And God bless your soul.

My object was new identification for Matthew and Esperanza. Passports and driver's licenses and birth certificates that would allow us to come out of hiding and start over somewhere far away from El Frente. I had millions after all. What else was I going to do with it? Why not help these good kids? Who had the crazy audacity to be in love?

Unfortunately I was unable to reach the forger I had worked with in the past. The one who did all my personal fake paperwork. As insurance I put out some feelers while I waited to hear back. If my go-to guy proved to be out of commission I wanted someone else already lined up.

The next day I bought a truck and some food and drove myself back to the digs. Where I was greeted by three drawn pistols. When they saw it was me, the guns were re-holstered and went unmentioned. Just a fact of life in the land of the narcotrafficantes. When you heard someone coming you got out your gun.

I put the food away and strapped on my Colt and joined the others. Leslie gave me an overview of what was being done at the site. Then explained in more detail what Essie and Matt were busy with. Then provided a tutorial in basic archeological field craft. When she was satisfied I wouldn't mess things up too much she was ready to leave.

Before she drove away Leslie said—

"Be careful out here."

We nodded at that. Then we waved and she was gone.

I wondered if that would be the last we saw of Leslie Davidson. Which I believe the others wondered too. Although of course it went unmentioned. Not being something anyone cared to discuss.

Instead we got back to work. Being eager to do something that wasn't only about evading bad guys. With Leslie gone Esperanza was in charge. We were excavating a debris pile on the canyon floor. Taking advantage of the cooler winter months to do the work that was out in the open. When the heat returned the research would move up into the shade within the dwellings. Where the midday sun only penetrated as a single shaft in the topmost room.

The actual archeologists and other workers who legitimately staffed this site all camped down below outside the canyon on the valley floor. For us that would not do. Although they had sufficient cause to be vigilant the others who stayed here were not being explicitly hunted by El Frente. We required more impregnable accommodations.

The cliff dwellings consisted of two tiers. The lowest had seen sufficient traffic over the centuries for its value in the present research to be badly comprised.

While other items had been deposited. Such as fecal matter from a variety of animals, mostly notably a jaguar in the fifteenth century. An arrow shaft of indeterminate origin from the late eighteenth century. Tin cans and a broken Bowie knife from the 1870s. And evidence of occupation by a man and a woman from across the border in 1910 or shortly thereafter— newspapers from Tucson; an extensive assortment of tin cans for a variety of foodstuffs, including smoked oysters; five spent cartridges from a .38 revolver; a six inch square scrap of red velvet; and one cracked porcelain button.

We would only be the latest in a long series of interlopers. Leaving our stains and footprints behind like all the others. I made my residence in the first room. Esperanza and Matt took one a little higher up. In each room two rifles and a supply of ammunition were positioned beside the single small window. At night when we prepared to sleep we would pull up the ladder behind us. Anyone coming in would have to climb the stone wall.

Another ladder led up to the second tier. Then a third led to a hole in the ceiling of the topmost room. From there a combination of scrambles and handholds ascended to the top of the cliff.

Which on our third or fourth day there Esperanza insisted Matt and I climb with her. She said we needed to know all about our environment if we were to defend ourselves. But mostly I think she just wanted to climb up there. At the top she was all smiles and satisfaction.

I hated that climb the first few times I did it. My bad leg didn't help and at one point there was a lateral transition that I could not see well because of the lost peripheral vision in my right eye. I had to grope my way through it. But if not perfect, practice does at least make us better. And it was good to get up there and feel the air and have a look around.

Chapter 118

We were aware that the year was running out. But did not really pay attention to the date. Then one day we were surprised to notice that tomorrow would be Christmas.

The Aztecs had their dead in great multiples. The Christians have their solitary god-man worshipped for his life after death. Death is the constant and what varies is the amount; but in Mexico death is what glues Catholicism onto the Aztec past. Which is neither here nor there. I digress to postpone.

That year the Eve of the great Christian celebration of the birth of their Lord was concluded for me with an awkward serenade. A painful one too. I lay awake in the still dark winter night listening to the undeniable sounds of Matthew and Esperanza making love. Something they usually did at some remove and out of earshot. They would wander off together holding hands and return looking blissful.

On this occasion I suppose they assumed I was asleep. And I should have been. The hour was late. I was tired. But even though I had spent most of my adult holidays wrongly imprisoned and should have been thoroughly desensitized to any longings the return of Christmas could conjure up, I found myself oddly disturbed. And lay awake in my sleeping bag with the chill of the night on my face staring up at the ceiling of my cliff room. When rustles and moans began to emanate from my neighbors I experienced each and every sound like a hot stabbing knife wound.

I could not help wishing I was the one with the girl. And the one with that girl in particular. I was struggling every moment of every day not to be completely besotted with her.

That was the second loneliest experience of my life.

A few days later I was back in town trying with limited success to follow up on those IDs for my friends. But at the first opportunity I cast this business aside and wandered away from my forlorn motel room in search of a willing señorita. Of course I had to be parted from some of my pesos before the señorita I found became willing. But a man in need is a man in need.

Afterwards I lay beside the woman I had bought and could not stop myself from weeping. Which disgusted her. The pretty young whore called me a few choice names as she kicked me out.

Back to my motel I went. Where I was the most lonesome I have ever been.

The next morning I returned to the digs feeling enormously sorry for myself. Simply dripping with self-pity. And was not at all in the mood to hear what Matthew had to say. Or what anyone had to say. About any conceivable topic other than my own wretchedness.

Matt waited until he found a moment alone with me. He watched Esperanza walk away from us then turned to say in a lowered voice—

"Remember when we were riding to the cabin and you asked if you were the only one enjoying yourself?"

Of course I remembered. And I felt like a piece of shit remembering. But probably anything I could have remembered at that moment would have made me feel the same. Such was the filter I viewed the world through.

I nodded. Being unable to muster actual speech. Matt nodded back at me.

"Well I was too," he said. "I was enjoying the hell out of it. I felt bad because Essie was so miserable. But now I'm enjoying myself even more. The truth is this is the happiest I've ever been."

He paused and smiled and his smile became a wide grin.

"I've never felt more alive."

I stared at Matt's exuberant expression. And managed another weary nod.

Oh woe is me, I thought. There is no expressing the grief I endure.

Or at least that was what I wanted to think. I was entirely reveling in my misery and very much wanted to wallow in my self-absorbed bathos.

But despite my intentions, some positive inclinations began to stir. Maybe it was just that I have always been susceptible to the moods of others. Or maybe what Matt said gave me a jolt I couldn't ignore. And pushed me out of my own pathetic bullshit. Forcing me to admit that I was taking some not inconsiderable pleasure in this adventure of ours. The way we were living was certainly not dull and ordinary.

And I wasn't in prison. Every day on the outside was a day to be celebrated. Even when fleeing from a drug cartel. And sick with jealousy over a young woman and the young man that she loved. Who loved her right back. While sitting beside him as he grinned at me.

Before I knew it I was smiling back at him.

"Yeah," I said. "I know what you mean."

Matt nodded at my answer. And then he laughed.

He had an excellent laugh.

Esperanza was right when she said El Viento would not look for us in his vest pocket. Although given more time maybe he would have thought to pat himself down. But as events transpired when El Frente came for us they did not come for us.

They came for the water tank. Matt had the misfortune of catching them in the act. I wonder now if he recognized any of them. From the pictures he and I studied with Esperanza. Trying to memorize the faces McElvy had photographed. In case we encountered any of them anywhere.

But that seems entirely unlikely. El Frente was a sizable organization. With specialized roles. The men in McElvy's photos were moving product across the border. The men who came for the water tank were policing their territory south of the border. Different jobs mean different men.

But I want those to be the men who came for the water tank. So I can have faces to hate. And men to wish dead. Although given what followed many of them could be dead anyway. Such is the way of the narcotrafficante. Not a trade that comes with an extended life expectancy.

One defect of our location was the acoustics of the valley and the entrance to the box canyon channeled away the sound of approaching vehicles. And there was wind that afternoon. And maybe we had our guard down. We had been out there for weeks and seen no one. Not a soul that went on two legs.

We had stopped work and were getting ready for dinner. Matt had gone down for water. Essie and I were up in the cliff rooms. She was saying something when the moment came. I don't remember what.

Three shots in rapid succession. Which I assumed were fired by Matt killing a rattlesnake that had taken up residence in the vicinity of the portable toilet. We had given up trying to convince our unwanted guest to move along and had agreed that the snake must die.

Essie stopped midsentence and stared at me. I remember how her entire being was frozen at that moment. Like a statue of herself. No more animated than the rock wall we were living in.

Chapter 119

There was a brief silence after those first shots. Two seconds at the most. Just enough time for the echo of the last shot to return from the valley outside. A respite during which I believed the greatest challenge we would face in the aftermath of that gunfire would be having to decide who would do the skinning and filleting. So we could carry through on our pledge to eat the remains. *Tastes like chicken*, we had taken turns saying. When we joked about the rattler's demise.

But then that brief silence ended.

Why is "machine gun" no longer the preferred term? Why instead do we say "automatic weapons"? We refer to automatic gunfire. Why is the source not called an automatic gun? All guns being machines I can understand the switch to "automatic". But why instead of "gun" do we use the far less specific "weapon"?

I suspect the nomenclature we have adopted is an attempt to distance ourselves from the carnage. An automatic weapon is not necessarily fatal. Unlike an automatic gun—or let's get back to it—a machine gun. Since "machine gun" sounds brutally malevolent.

You never point a gun at someone without death being a distinct possibility. Since guns are built to kill. Weapons can fall short of that finality. They can stun or wound or maim but not bring death. A gun doesn't mess around like that. And a machine gun sounds about as fatal as any weapon ever devised. More fatal than one that is merely automatic.

Essie and I never saw Matt torn open by all those bullets. From where we sat at that moment he was hidden from our view. And taking a look would have meant exposing ourselves to the same treatment.

Instead we began our ascent. Climbing up away from the threat down below. We went into motion without saying a word. Acting on the training that La Soldadita had imposed. We were pulling the ladder up behind us from the roof of the top room when the gunfire halted.

Then came four distinct shots spaced about a second apart. When the last one echoed back at us Esperanza said—

"There goes your truck."

I had no idea what she meant. Which must have shown on my face. Because she explained it for me—

"They shot out the tires."

I almost lost it when Essie explained those last four shots. I almost tumbled through that hole in the roof back down into the room below. Why I can't say. I hadn't thought of how useful my truck would be if we managed to survive. I was occupied with trying to believe that Matt was not necessarily dead and hoping I would not become so myself. How Esperanza had the presence of mind to know what those shots meant still astounds me.

Now I wonder why they bothered to shoot all four. Two flats would have been sufficient. I only had one spare. Three viable tires were not enough to carry that truck out of there.

I guess they were making a statement.

We left Matt behind and climbed out. Away from the men with the guns who had just killed our friend. We did what we had to do.

As we climbed they started shooting again. Blasting away in every direction. I wonder if any of those bullets they shot all over the place punctured that water tank. I sure as hell hope they did.

Luckily we were mostly hidden from their line of fire. But during that lateral transition I mentioned earlier, the one I had trouble with, a ricochet caught me in the leg. At least it had the decency to pick my bad leg. Leaving my good one intact to keep me mobile.

Although not mobile enough to prevent me from falling down and knocking myself cold. Which happened a little while after I was shot. I am told the head injury is the cause of my memory loss. I don't remember being hit or the gunfire or even being up on the cliff. Essie told me what happened later.

Part XXXV:
Godforsaken Mexico

Chapter 120

I am seated uncomfortably on a boulder beside a precipitous mountain road. My wounded leg throbs and my throat burns. I hear an engine approaching and turn toward it. An open jeep is descending toward us. I see the driver is a woman and that she is alone. I hope that means we will not be killed.

She pulls to a stop and speaks with Esperanza. She has a broad stern Indios face. Wide and rugged and indomitable like the country we are lost in. She shakes her head and I think we are done for. That now she will drive on and leave us there to die. Maybe of thirst. Maybe at the hand of whomever might come along next.

But then the woman gestures for us to get in. At least for now we will live.

The ride down the mountain is lost to me. Bouncing around in that jeep with a bullet in my leg must have put me out.

I wake up flat on my back in an actual bed with clean white sheets. And even more implausibly there is an IV in my arm. Beside my bed is a short old Spanish man in a battered black cowboy hat. He stares down at me. He nods once and says—

"Es mejor saber."

It's better to know.

I try to say "what?".

"Whhh," is what comes out.

The woman who drove the jeep appears on the other side of my bed. That stern face of hers frowns at the old man. He turns away and shuffles off. The jeep woman peers down at me.

"So you live," she says. "How does that suit you?"

"Whhh," I say again.

But this time I mean "water." The jeep woman turns and leaves. I do not like being alone. I am afraid the old man in the black hat might come back and speak more nonsense. That prospect frightens me.

The jeep woman returns with a glass of ice water. I am dumbfounded that she knows what I want. It occurs to me that maybe she didn't and this is just a coincidence. Bringing sick people water is a common thing to do.

Whatever the case she delivers the most delicious glass of ice water I have ever tasted. And most certainly ever will. There is room in life for only one such glass of ice water. That glass of ice water was as close to a divine experience as I have ever known.

When I turn to thank her the jeep woman is gone. In her place is Esperanza. I have never been more glad to see anyone.

"Thank God," I croak out.

"Yes. You should. You almost died."

I cannot imagine it was as bad as all that. Here I am in this nice comfy bed with these lovely clean sheets. Having just enjoyed the best glass of ice water in all of human history. How could I possibly have almost died?

"Are you sure?"

Esperanza laughs. Just a chuckle at first. But slowly it grows and then she is laughing so hard she is crying. When she recovers enough to speak she points at me and says—

"That is *so* you."

I find myself with no answer for this. I just sit in my bed and shrug.

When the jeep woman returned for the second time I realized she was a nurse. This was revealed by the presence of the doctor that came with her. A tall lean stoop-shouldered Anglo. I could tell he was the doctor because he was the one wearing the stethoscope.

The doctor told me my body did not like having a bullet in it. That carrying the slug around in my leg had put me into some sort of shock. And the shock almost shut down my system.

Or at least that's how I remember it. My confidence in the accuracy of that recollection is slim. He might have told me something completely different and I forgot what he said and filled in the blanks later with something I remember from a TV show. Somehow I fear that is what actually happened.

Which is especially embarrassing considering that I almost died. You would think I would remember exactly why. So I could take pains to make sure it never happened again. Like maybe I'm allergic to bullets and really should avoid having them enter my body.

But I do remember one thing clearly from that exchange. I asked them about the old man in the black hat and they told me he was nuts and could be a pest but was entirely harmless. And that if he became a nuisance I should ask him to go get me something. Like a blanket or a book. Because then he would wander off and forget what he was sent after and become occupied with something else.

That part of our conversation I remember clearly all these years later. What to do if the old man came back again.

But not the details of my medical condition.

And there you have my priorities.

Let us not be too horrified by the Mormons. Although they give us many reasons to experience horror. Magical underwear. The Angel Moroni. Mitt Romney's smile.

Kirtland Fenimore Sorenson. Who was so damned Mormon. I can picture him clearly as a clean-cut young man going door-to-door proselytizing. And staring at young boys that he saw along the way.

But one rotten apple does not spoil the entire barrel. Or apples in another barrel. Because the Mormon I am thinking of now lived away from the main body of his kind, down south in the Sierra Madre. He was descended from the ones who moved there at the end of the nineteenth century to escape the newly-enacted laws north of the border criminalizing polygamy.

Among whom were Mitt Romney's great-grandparents. Which seems very un-American to me. Leaving the U. S. of A. because of what conservatives would now call a lifestyle choice. And then fleeing back again when you feel threatened by a little local revolution. So what if the Red Flaggers were coming for them? If polygamy was important enough to leave home for, they should have dug in and fought for their way of life. Since their way of life is what people like them are always going on about.

Instead they folded their tents and ran away. With their tails between their legs. Bunch of no-good quitters if you ask me.

But enough of those damn Romneys. Let's get back to that other Mormon. The one currently relative to our narrative. The doctor who fixed me up after I was shot by El Frente. To him I remain indebted and grateful.

Although there is one medical decision he made that I still question. The morning after I woke up again he deemed me well enough to travel. Which to my mind seemed hasty. Having just the day before awoken from unconsciousness only to be promptly told I had almost died.

Chapter 121

The next time we were alone Esperanza told me that Matt killed two men and wounded a third before they gunned him down. One man he killed on the spot and the other died on the way here. This small clinic being the only place within hundreds of miles where a man could be patched back together.

And therefore a place where El Frente made frequent visits.

"So we're not safe here," I said.

Esperanza nodded.

"As soon as you can we should leave."

I considered what our presence could mean for the doctor and his staff.

"Do our hosts want us gone?"

"Yes."

We were quiet for a moment over that.

Then Esperanza told me that El Frente came after the water tank. That they weren't sent there after us. It had not yet occurred to me that they could have been. I hadn't given the matter any thought. It wasn't something I wanted to think about.

"Did they figure out who Matt was?" I said. "That he was someone they were after?"

"I don't know. But I don't see why they would. We had a good reason to be there. So they won't think to ask who he was."

She frowned at me.

"Do you agree?" she said.

I did. So I nodded.

Then I asked her a stupid question that was bugging me—

"What did they want with the water tank?"

She had wondered the same thing. The men never said and the doctor and nurse never asked. It was best for them to know as little as they could about cartel business. I assume it was part of El Viento chomping down on the hand that fed him. Which was revealed to us later. But beyond wanting that water tank I will never know what sent those men to the cliff dwellings where they killed my friend.

Maybe they were just thirsty. It could be as stupid as that.

The nurse drove us out of there in that same open jeep. This time I remained conscious. Although at moments just barely. My leg complained bitterly the whole length of those terrible roads.

Atop a ridge we found ourselves facing a long line of approaching vehicles. The nurse pulled over so the oncoming SUVs and trucks and something that looked like a homemade tank could go rolling past.

There were no women. Only men and all heavily armed.

Here was El Frente on the move. And here we were watching them. The very same ones they wanted dead. But didn't expect to find down here on their side. Where they had unknowingly already killed one of us.

In the middle of this caravan was an open jeep. And in the back seat was El Viento himself. Not a big man but his presence was formidable. This was clearly his command. He sat looking forward with his eyes hidden behind aviator sunglasses. If he saw us we did not register on his stony face.

I recognized him from photographs I had seen online. And even if I hadn't the nurse told us who he was. And then she told us something else—

"Things got better after he came along. When the cartels stopped fighting through here. But now he's decided this isn't enough for him. He wants all of it. So he's moving against Juárez. Which means the fighting will start up here again. Because if he gets what he wants then he will leave and this will return to being a battleground. And if he doesn't get what he

621

wants the same thing will happen. Because they will kill him and no one will control this place anymore."

❖   ❖   ❖

Esperanza stared at me when the nurse was done talking. I waited for her to say something but she just kept staring. I stared back. That still didn't get her talking. Finally I couldn't take it—

"Why are you staring at me?"

"You said he would do this. How did you know?"

I had no idea what she was talking about.

"I did?"

"Back at McElvy's. You said he would bite the hand that feeds him."

And then I remembered. Beginning with my vision of the fire-starter. With his nickel-plated lighter and his cigarettes. Lighting up the gasoline he had splashed on Armijo's living room floor.

"It was a lucky guess. I said he might. Not that he would."

"If you say so."

"You don't believe me?"

She shrugged.

"I don't know what to believe about any of this."

On that point we could agree. I was relieved she didn't press it any further. The painkillers weren't doing much good. My leg hurt horribly.

And I was spooked by having called what would happen. Because now I really did not want it to happen. El Frente crawling all over the country we needed to cross was not good news. All I wanted was to get the hell out of Mexico. And I hated anything and everything that could make that any more difficult than it already was.

Chapter 122

First Leslie noticed the flat tires on my truck. Next she saw that the water tank was gone. These things told her that something bad had happened. And she knew out there in that bad country bad things tended to be *very* bad.

So she was not surprised when she saw what was left of Matt. Although she didn't know that was him yet. But she did guess it was one of us by the gun belt around the middle. Then she saw the boots and knew they were too big for Esperanza. As she drew closer she recognized his jacket. She had seen Matt put it around Essie's shoulders one morning while we had coffee.

Coyotes had fed on him. Their tracks were all around.

Being an archeologist she knew about bones. And what could happen to them when a person was killed. She said her guess from what she could see was that the bullets shattered his right forearm and his bottom ribs on that side. And may have severed his spine just below his ribcage. Judging by how torn apart he was the man who shot him was standing very close.

But he moved closer still. When Matt was on the ground the man stood over him and blasted his victim's head into mush.

Leslie was a rational woman. A scientist by both training and inclination. And also brave. She did not panic. She kept her head and took some time to gather her thoughts. To assess the situation. To establish the facts so she could best determine her options and the risks.

She knew Matt wasn't carrying any ID when she last saw him. And any he might have obtained since would be fake. His dentistry had been blown into oblivion. Making dental records useless in identifying his remains. If anyone knew that he was missing and might be looking for him, they would have access to his dental records. From what she knew of his history that seemed unlikely. There was no family to come searching after their lost boy.

She didn't find any ID among the things we left behind in the cliff dwelling. And nothing else that could indicate who had been there. Just anonymous items that could have belonged to anyone. The only thing she found that could connect us to her was the key for the storage container. Which she gave to us when she brought us there. Now that she had it back again no one could prove it was ever out of her possession. To be on the safe side she wiped it clean of our prints. Just in case the law didn't like her story.

The only other problem was the pistols. Our two Colts had gone with us only to be abandoned somewhere between the top of the cliff and that road where the nurse found us. When Esperanza decided they were too heavy to keep lugging along. Since she had half-crippled me to contend with.

Leaving Leslie with just the one on the ground next to Matt. So she couldn't put the guns away and lock up. She couldn't make it look like we were never there. She considered breaking into the storage container. Making it appear that was how we got the guns. But instead she just left it unlocked. That seemed simpler and cleaner. No one could prove it was locked when we showed up. Maybe we picked the locks.

She returned to Matt's remains. Should she dispose of them? A challenge in that rough country. Digging a grave would take too long. The best she could do was to haul him away somewhere and cover him with rocks. But the less she did to disturb this scene the less that gave the law to tie her to it.

But she was tied to this place more than anyone. This was her dig. Her name was on the paperwork. She entered Mexico for no other reason than coming here. If someone stumbled on the body and told the police who then decided to investigate they could date the remains and check the customs records and determine when she should have arrived here. Then her failure to report a corpse at her own dig would not sit well. Which could lead to her sitting in a Mexican jail cell.

Before she left she stood beside Matt with her hands folded together and her head bowed. She gave him his moment of silence. And commended his soul to whatever higher power might guide the affairs of man. Which as a scientist she very much doubted was anything more than the laws of physics.

Then she drove to the police station in Nuevo Casas Grandes. And arrived the day after it had been firebombed by El Frente. Leslie approached an officer standing guard before the wreckage. He demanded to know her business. When she told him she wanted to report a dead body out in the desert he laughed at her.

And then he told her how it was and what she should do—

"We're busy trying to keep our own bodies from getting dead. Bodies that are already dead we can't do anything about. Listen to me. Señora. Take my advice. Get the hell out of here. Go home and never come back. Why would you be here if you don't have to?"

Chapter 123

The nurse took us to a motel in Nuevo Casas Grandes. Then said good luck and goodbye and drove away. She saved our lives and for a few days she was part of our lives. And then we never saw her again.

I eventually sent the clinic a check. Enough to cover what they spent caring for us and then some more to put a few other people back on their feet. Unfortunately the others they helped with my money may have been narcotrafficantes. But when you give a gift it should come without strings. You have no business telling the recipient how they can use it.

When we had checked into the motel Esperanza wanted to call Leslie. I was worried El Frente might be watching the archeologist and any contact with her could be dangerous.

"What if she goes out there and gets herself killed," Essie said.

"But they're not there. They got what they wanted. Why would they go back?"

"We have to warn her. Just in case."

I was too tired to argue. Instead I went to sleep. When I woke up Esperanza was gone. She left a note saying she couldn't reach Leslie and went out for food. She came back just before I feel asleep again.

I slept through the rest of that day and most of the next one. But I was awake long enough to make arrangements for a delivery. On our third day a package arrived containing the fake IDs I had commissioned.

The last time I saw a counterfeit Mexican driver's license was that blown-up one presented at my trial. With my own photo on it. In which I had been about the same age as the individual whose image I was looking at now.

Esperanza took it from me and stared at Matt's picture.

"You must think I'm some kind of monster," she said.

I was stunned by this. I stared at her. She glanced at me as she said—

"That I haven't cried for him."

I wasn't aware that she hadn't. Not that I had thought about it. But for all I knew she had wept over her lost love the entire time I was unconscious back at the clinic. And maybe even while we scrambled over that rough country during our escape from El Frente.

She handed his fake license back to me.

"But I can't right now," she said. "I'll do that later."

The next day her morning sickness began. She said nothing of it. But I had been around enough pregnant women to know what was going on. When I was young there was always an expectant mother nearby. I remember vividly being very small watching a neighbor vomit at the side of the road while my aunt held her hair.

A few days passed. I spent it recuperating and when I was awake enough making plans. Essie spent it throwing up. Then one morning after once again refusing any solid food, then becoming ravenous after the nausea had passed, she held her coffee cup in both hands and stared at me over it.

I knew what that look meant. I put down my fork.

"I'm pregnant," she said.

I nodded once.

"Yes. You are."

She blinked a few times. She put her coffee down.

"You knew?"

"Yes."

"Why didn't you say anything?"

"Why didn't you?"

627

Her mouth came open. She put a hand up in the air and pointed off to her side. I looked to see where she was pointing and saw nothing I could connect to our conversation. I turned back to her and learned she was pointing at the past when she said—

"I just realized about an hour ago."

She put her hand down.

"How long have you known?" she said.

"Since you started being sick."

She stared at me again.

"I thought it was the flu or something."

"Have you taken one of those tests?"

She shook her head.

"You should," I said. "Just to be sure. And we should get you to a doctor. When we get settled."

She nodded. We resumed eating. I wanted to ask if she was going to keep her baby. And hoped I already knew the answer was yes. And definitely knew she would tell me when she was ready.

On our walk back to the motel I told her what I had been up to. When I was awake to do anything.

"Why Costa Rica?" she said.

"Why not? I hear it's beautiful."

"We can't go home?"

I had wondered if this would be her response. And what that could mean.

"You want to go back to Doña Pero."

She didn't answer.

"Is there anything there for you?"

After a moment she shook her head. Watching her then and imagining what she must be going through and what her desire to "go home" meant I saw how very young my companion was. And how this child in her belly had in some ways made her younger. And I knew that while we got ourselves away from the threat that chased after us and started over somewhere new, she would put herself entirely in my care. Because for now all she could do was hold herself together.

My misgivings about El Viento acting on his ambitions proved justified. Not that it was particularly perceptive of me to realize his war would expose us to danger. His war exposed the entire region to danger. That's how war is. And how it is with men like El Viento. Hell follows in their wake.

We had a brush with that hell a few days later after our usual breakfast. We were out in the street when the gunfire began. A spray of bullets struck a sedan parked beside us as we dove around the corner of a building.

We never learned who they killed or why. Some said there were three left dead and others said five. Some claimed the dead men were from the Juárez Cartel but others insisted they were just normal civilians. Even that one of them was a relief worker employed by the Catholic Church. All anyone agreed on was that the killers were from El Frente. Because the killers made sure everyone knew who they were.

We walked past the bloodstains every day for the rest of our stay there. Which of course we made as brief as our conditions would allow. We were a pair. Me gimping about and Essie always barfing. It's a miracle we moved fast enough to avoid being shot.

Chapter 124

Before we move on perhaps now would be a good time to finally explain what the fat man did for El Frente.

As previously mentioned the agreement El Viento had with Juárez limited his operation to human traffic. Controlling the flow of illegal immigrants across their desolate empire. Armijo meanwhile made his stock-in-trade at election time demonizing none other than those very same undocumented migrants. Starting with the fictional Mexican he selected me to portray.

Whenever there was an immigration bust in Doña Pero the fat man was nearby to hog credit. Even if the Border Patrol or the INS made the arrest Armijo would claim he was indispensable to their success. And apparently often enough this boast was valid. For the sheriff of a sparsely populated desert county with a limited budget and staff, he had an amazing track record of knowing when and where illegals could be nabbed.

Which tells us at least part of what was being communicated by Danny Ortega. On his trips back and forth between the smugglers and the sheriff.

The DEA had limited resources covering Doña Pero County. They weren't aware of enough drug traffic to justify a bigger commitment. And since it was a backwater office the agents assigned there were not the best. They had their hands full with what they could catch of the occasional freelancer. And had more success ferreting out local meth cooks than stopping anything coming across the border.

Which meant the only relevant federal law was the Border Patrol. To whom Armijo fed disinformation. He sent them chasing after illegals in one corner of the county while El Frente was smuggling heroin in another. Or moving guns the other direction. Since that was the second of my wild guesses that proved to be true. El Viento was arming himself for his uprising with a pipeline through Doña Pero.

Often enough to keep them compliant the Border Patrol was provided with actual illegals to round up. El Frente handed over a share of their human product to keep the law happy. And the drugs and guns flowing.

"Like a shell game," McElvy said when he learned about it. "Three-Card Monte. Draw away the eyes of the mark."

Later I would learn that with his attention focused on the war he had started, El Viento's other concerns became lower priorities. And in his organization every priority began with him. By all accounts it was entirely top-down. So policing the death of Armijo and punishing that loss fell off the radar. Which is ironic given that he started his war when he did because the fat man died.

Because the death of his puppet sheriff meant his smuggling operations were over. They could continue only until the Armijo scandal unfolded. To resume them after order was reestablished he would have to acquire new influence in Doña Pero. If he could find any to get his hands on. Which was not a given. This time an honest man might take office. In which case he would have to rethink things.

And there was also the possibility that the disappearance of Armijo could become big enough news that Juárez would wonder what was going on up there. And stick their noses in. Which could be very troublesome indeed.

So although he was still short of weapons and money El Viento decided to strike now. To move against Juárez while he still retained the element of surprise.

Now let us answer one last question about Armijo—whatever became of the fat man's corpse? It was never recovered. Not in the charred ruins of his house or anywhere else.

Officially he remains another disappearance in the borderlands.

We traveled by bus. And took a meandering route. Acting like tourists as we made our way south. Esperanza was often zombie-like. Staring straight ahead and wide-eyed as she jostled in her seat.

Old women looked at her with a deep and knowing sympathy. I bet more than a few of them could have told you she was pregnant and her man was gone. They had seen the symptoms before. Or even suffered with them. And maybe one or two could have told you her man was not just gone from her side but gone to the other side. They had seen those symptoms before too. If not in this life then in one of their many other ones.

What I remember most clearly about our journey down the length of Mexico was something that happened near the end. Most of the other days were too much alike and too wearying to recall. So let us just revisit this one day and be done with the rest.

We had shared a bus ride into the Yucatán with a striking couple that even Esperanza had noticed. Despite her semi-comatose condition. The woman was blond and German, and the man was dark and looked Arab. They communicated in English.

We saw them at dinner and afterwards followed them along the streets only to discover they were staying not just at the same hotel but in an adjoining room. That proved to have paper-thin walls. Which we learned as we sat reading. As was our custom in the evenings. We realized how thin those walls were when our neighbors began having very animated sexual relations.

Our eyes came up from our books and we stared at each other. A smile crept onto Esperanza's face. Not the morose smile I had become used to. The old one that was full of mischief.

Then the German woman said very distinctly—

"I vant to zee yewr eyez ven yew fahk me."

Esperanza burst out laughing.

That was when I knew she would be all right.

❖   ❖   ❖

I wish I could say that my proposal was extremely romantic. But that would have been inappropriate to say the least. So instead what I said to Esperanza was entirely pragmatic—

"You are a young, pregnant, and a fugitive. As your friend I can do only so much to help you. As your husband I could do much more. I have money. More than I know what to do with. And who else do either of us have in this world? We're in this mess together. Let's do everything we can to protect ourselves."

She said nothing. Her only reaction was to blink. Then she resumed staring. So I soldiered on—

"I don't want to bring up anything unpleasant. But if something happens to me, as my wife you'll be better taken care of. As my friend, no matter how we set things up, maybe not. Things could get ugly. They often do. And on the other hand, if anything happens to you, as your husband I can care for your child. If I'm just a friend—"

"What would you expect from me?"

I spent a few moments sifting through her possible meanings. All the ways she could want me to understand those few words. Then concluded there was only one thing she could mean and decided to tackle it head on—

"Nothing sexual."

I couldn't help being hurt that her relief was evident. I hid myself behind more pragmatism—

"But the same way that as your husband I could help you, as my wife you could help me. We become united under the law. Whatever law that is. Wherever we choose to live."

She frowned. Then shook her head a little.

"I thought it was Costa Rica."

"Sure. It still can be. If that's all right with you."

She said that it was. Even though neither of us had been there. In retrospect I find it odd that we were so certain about where we would live. Given the uncertain state of everything else about our lives.

Three days later we were married. Which is easy enough to do in Mexico. A little paperwork and a brief ceremony at the local Oficina del Registro Civil. With that accomplished we continued on our way.

There was nothing more we needed from that godforsaken country.

Part XXXVI:
Obituaries

Chapter 125

Esperanza cried for Matthew the day after their child was born. She held their son in her arms and wept all over him. She did not have to tell me why she was crying. I remembered clearly that she told me she would do this when she could. And now she could. Now it was time.

When she was done she told me how they had planned their future. A few days after being reunited they had the big picture all worked out. She would return to school and he would find a job in the city. When he had been in-state long to qualify for reduced tuition Matt would start college. Meanwhile Esperanza would continue on toward her doctorate. Somewhere in there—as soon as they felt the time was right, probably no more than a year or two—they would get married.

We were quiet for a moment. The baby was asleep.

"And children?" I said. "Did you plan for them too?"

She nodded and the tears returned. One dropped smack into the middle of their son's forehead. He frowned but didn't wake up. Esperanza gently wiped her tear away.

"When we were both done with school," she said.

She laughed softly.

"If we could wait that long."

Then she told me that when Matt shared his plans with his employer, Señor Martínez suggested he open a location of El Gallo Bonito near the university. Not just as the manager but as one of the owners.

"My wedding gift to my miracle worker," Señor Martínez said.

Matt had scouted locations and was close to selecting one when everything went to hell and we wound up on the run.

We were quiet again. No more tears now. The baby slept soundly.

Esperanza sighed deeply before she broached what was next on her mind. She wanted to return to the Sierra Madre for Matt's remains. To find his bones and bury them. As you can probably guess, as I have already made my sentiments abundantly clear, I had no desire to ever set foot in Mexico again. No matter how badly I wanted to give Matt his proper due. But I made no attempt to dissuade Esperanza. It was not the time to challenge anything she thought or felt.

Instead I told her about my father. How he died and how I went looking for him. In that remote canyon near where she and I and Matt had camped and first heard El Frente's ultralights doing their midnight work. The story of my father's death and his lost remains came flowing out as a natural thing to share at that moment.

Esperanza hung on every word. And when I was done she had changed her mind.

"You're right," she said.

Although I spoke with no intention of being right about anything.

"That's where Matt should be," she said. "He was happy there. I can't think of anywhere better."

She smiled at me.

"Thank you."

I could only manage to nod my head.

Matt died defending the woman he loved. Maybe somehow he knew that he also defended their unborn child. I want to believe that is true.

And if the cliff dwellings were built to defend against raiders, as many have suggested and as seems entirely self-evident, then he died like many of their inhabitants must have before him. Fighting off superior forces while his loved ones scrambled to safety. Acting quickly and valiantly while his own death came straight at him.

The centuries go clicking past and in many ways nothing changes. There are still good deaths and bad deaths. And those deaths are still good and bad in the same ways.

Matt may not have had the best life. But he had a good death.

Esperanza wanted to name her son after his father. But if anyone out there was still hunting us down we might as well have hired skywriters and set off fireworks. She considered Mateo for Matthew but that did not feel right. The little boy did not seem like a Mateo to her.

But she wanted something that told of their past. That kept their families alive. Maybe having lost her parents when she was so young made that sense of continuity especially important to her. What she settled on was Francisco Hermán. Francisco for Matt's father and Hermán after her own.

And the last name? Not Delmorales. Although legally he was my son. I didn't marry Esperanza so that she could give birth to a bastard. But I wasn't using that name anymore.

It doesn't really matter what surname we were using. Say it was Garcia.

Chapter 126

About a week after the birth I told Esperanza another story from my past. This one concerned her more directly. And it was one I had wanted to tell her for a long time.

I shared with her the details of how I spent my time in Denver. When I was done she told me what else I must do. To complete that unfinished business. Something I already knew should be done.

A few days later the FBI office in Denver received an anonymous package. A month or so after that I found a story online. From a local newspaper in Idaho. The FBI had not wanted to go public with what I sent them. But they had shared what they knew with the families connected to the cases they had closed. And there was a grieving mother in Mountain Home who damn well wanted the whole word to know about the evil that was Fenimore Sorenson.

I can't say it felt good exactly to have taken that step. There is no good to be had in such matters. But I did feel relief. I can't speak for the families of those lost boys. I hope it brought them some measure of peace. But I can say it brought some peace to myself.

❖   ❖   ❖

One more piece of the past to be done with. Before we can quit looking back and resume moving forward. I had managed to find my little sister.

She had joined the United States Marines. Which was a great shock to me. The idea of her in uniform. The truth was I found it unthinkable. Nothing about her seemed right for the military.

Since I did not know who else might have found her and could be watching and listening in the hope I would eventually reveal myself I was cautious in making contact. She was stationed at Twentynine Palms. I called her from a burner phone while standing on a street corner in Los Angeles. No reason to let anyone know I had left the United States. And getting back in by myself was no problem. I had enough ID to go anywhere in the world.

Magdalena was not glad to hear from me.

"You're a disgrace," she said. "A monster."

I tried to explain. She did not listen. Instead she quoted the Bible. My little sister had become a hardcore fundamentalist fanatic. Nothing I said could convince her I spoke the truth. When I told her she could go online and find accounts of my conviction being overturned she accused me of faking them. When I tried to explain that was impossible she offered this as her summary dismissal—

"The Internet belongs to Satan."

After that what could I say? Her mind was closed. Shut so tight it was like a black hole. Any facts you sent in there disappeared.

Which made it official. The only family I had were my wife and son.

Neither of which were really mine.

Enough of the past. Let's get moving again. But to do so we need to step back just one more time—

Thanks to the seeds of doubt planted by McElvy, I began our flight from El Frente uncertain if my wealth would be intact if I was ever again in position to make use of it. When that came to pass I discovered that one of my investments had proven outstandingly successful. My personal fortune now approached thirty million dollars.

A truly staggering sum. And especially unlikely to have been obtained by one such as myself. Of minority heritage. Born and raised in poverty. Second-rate education that ended in the tenth grade.

Imprisoned while still young. Without a career of any kind let alone one that produces riches.

And without ever having made the acquisition of further wealth one of my objectives. I had managed my financial windfall in support of my primary goal— achieving what I hoped could be called justice. Now both the men I had gone stalking after were dead. And my money had only multiplied. Instead of expending capital I had acquired it.

Unless it was a trap. Back at that motel in Nuevo Casas Grandes when I was recovering from the bullet wound in my leg and Esperanza was suffering through her nausea it occurred to me that if El Frente had cracked open my corporate empire instead of robbing me of my money they might use my accounts to launder some of their own. Maybe my spectacular returns were a fraud. And if I touched the accounts they would find me.

So I moved it all at once. I sent my money around the world. Moving it in and out of accounts scattered across the globe. Opening accounts one day and closing them the next. Buying with one hand what I sold with the other. Creating a web so elaborate that sorting it out would require the cooperation of two dozen national governments. Most of whom were by long practice disinclined to cooperate on anything.

After that I felt safe enough to use some of it. I acquired a hotel a few blocks from the ocean in a quiet beach town in Costa Rica. And I also purchased a building across the street. Which had a fully equipped restaurant sitting idle on the ground floor.

I owned and operated the hotel. Esperanza did the same with the restaurant. Together we raised Matthew's son.

Chapter 127

In the special election held following the still unresolved disappearance of Doña Pero County Sheriff Josef Armijo, guess who was swept into office? Or I should say back into office. Which gives away the answer—Clarence McElvy once again had a star pinned to his chest. And could not have been happier wearing it.

Unfortunately he was not to enjoy his revived career for very long. A little more than a year after taking office he returned home one night, in the midst of contentious budget negotiations with the county commissioners, to the double-wide he had just installed next to where his ranch house had burned to the ground, sat down in his recliner, turned on his television, and died of cardiac arrest.

He was buried beside his wife in the same cemetery where he confronted me with his Colt 45. On one of my surreptitious returns to the country of my birth I put a stone atop his marker. Because shortly before his death McElvy had a DNA test done and was surprised to learn of his Jewish ancestry.

"Coulda knocked me down with a feather," he said.

And then he laughed until he started coughing.

While he waited for his insurance settlements from the torching of his house and his cabin the old man stayed at the house I had in town. He told me the man I found to clean up Ortega's remains did an excellent job. But McElvy still had nightmares sleeping there. He helped me sell the house and the office building across from the Sheriff's Department and the place out by Armijo's house that I never used. I tried to pay him a commission but he refused. Maybe he wanted to prove that he was on the straight and narrow. After our little tiff about his sugar smuggling.

During that time I belatedly connected two things I knew about the old man. That he had once been a smuggler. And then later had worked as a private investigator who specialized in stopping smugglers. When I finally put those two things together I gave him no end of grief about it. I yanked that chain at the slightest excuse.

To this day I wonder why El Frente didn't torch my house. They torched everyone else's. And mine had a dead body in it just like Armijo's. My house seems to have been an excellent candidate for torching. I'm almost offended they didn't burn it down.

Before we let the old man go there was an interesting piece of information he shared with me. This conversation came just after he took office. He told me that Tomás Martínez, the restaurateur who was a partner in El Leñador, had reported Matt missing to the Sheriff's Department. This call was placed two days after Armijo was killed and we went into hiding. Two days after that Señor Martínez called again, this time to offer a reward for information on Matt's whereabouts. He suggested the amount of ten thousand dollars but was willing to provide more.

These calls were dutifully logged by the clerk on duty. Who was the same middle-aged Hispanic woman both times. But since the department was a corrupt shell hollowed out by the fat man's death no action was taken. And if any action had been taken, if the reward had been posted and it yielded any results, that only would have served to deliver us to El Frente.

The clerk brought these calls to McElvy's attention when he took office. And although she did not say so, the old man got the distinct impression she had connected the dots and guessed that the disappearance of this Anglo kid was related to the disappearance of her boss and his niece. Maybe she knew through the grapevine that Matt and Essie were seeing each other.

McElvy put on an act of wishing the trail on this Walker kid hadn't gone cold. But he wasn't sure the clerk bought it. He didn't think she would push it any further and that proved to be correct. She needed the job. So she punched the clock and kept her mouth shut. McElvy was glad she did because he needed her. She was the only one who knew all the nuts-and-bolts of running the place. Not to mention where the bodies were buried.

McElvy and I discussed how we might inform Señor Martínez about the death of his protégé. But no way of going about it could be certain not to bring trouble. So we decided to leave it alone.

They did a nice obituary of Sheriff Clarence McElvy in the local paper. A few choice quotes from his interviews over the years captured the tenor of him. Although I couldn't help thinking how much more colorful it would have been if they put in even half of what was omitted.

A few years later another obituary came to my attention. This time I was unaware that the subject had passed. And I felt like a heel when I read about her death. At first I didn't know why. Then I remembered during our ride down into Mexico making a tasteless joke about her having cancer.

And now Leslie Davidson had died of it. Pancreatic cancer that took her just five months after the diagnosis. Before her illness became too much of an impediment she was able to wed her partner, a lawyer and activist that she met at a gay pride event, in a civil ceremony on Cape Cod.

One of her colleagues recently published a paper on the work Dr. Davidson had pursued at that dig in the Sierra Madre. Which was unfortunately cut short by violence in the region before she was able to substantiate her theory that the cliff dwellings were built in response to raids conducted as part of a human sacrifice chattel trade network spreading up out of Mesoamerica into Northern Mexico and the American Southwest. She had initiated that dig on a hunch that closer to the source of any such trade she might unearth some proof that it existed. A theory that may yet prove to be her enduring legacy.

And whatever came of the dig itself? The one where El Frente stumbled into us? I am sorry to say that site remains abandoned. Another victim of the drug wars. A few weeks after her last trip down there Leslie filed paperwork relinquishing the permits from the Mexican government and shutting down the funding she had applied for. The tools and equipment at the site were left behind and written off.

To be watched over by the remains of Matthew Walker.

❖　　❖　　❖

Those who have reason to know say he was way off the mark. That the site of the 1895 stagecoach robbery he was searching for was a good three miles away. But it doesn't matter if he was in the wrong place. All we care about is what the retired postal worker and amateur treasure hunter found when he went out into the backcountry with his metal detector.

According to the report issued by the Doña Pero County Coroner's Office, the deceased had a freshly broken leg when he was killed by a gunshot to the head fired at close range. The weapon used was a large-bore rifle. The nature of his broken leg was consistent with a fall. What exactly he could have fallen from was not obvious. Since he was found near the top of a low hill. Where he had lain undisturbed for approximately eight years.

Perhaps El Frente recovered the crashed ultralight. To be rebuilt and flown again or converted into spare parts or just to cover their tracks and obscure their purpose in being there. But maybe they left it and someone else came along and took the wreck away prior to our treasure hunter stumbling on the scene. There was plenty of time for others to find it. But in either case the wreck was taken and the dead pilot left behind. Which illustrates that in the borderlands his remains were less important than the battered machinery that dropped him there.

Part XXXVII:
A Handsomer Man

Chapter 128

Being married to Esperanza made me drink. Here I was still a young man with a wife who thought of me like an older brother. When I most definitely did not see her as a younger sister. And since my wife did not want me I went with women who did. Most any woman I found pleasing who would have me. But since these women were not Esperanza I smoothed our way by blurring the distinctions. Alcohol was my partner in these exploits. When the time came for me to be with a woman a good bottle always joined us.

And there were plenty of women to be had. American women mostly. With some of their Canadian cousins. The others came principally from Europe. English and German and Dutch and French. The occasional Belgian. Portuguese. Italian. Beyond that there was the infrequent South African. The occasional Japanese. The rare Korean.

But these women did not come to our small beach town expecting to bed a hotelier. They were always a little surprised and yes a bit disappointed that I was the one they wound up with. Their fantasies had to have involved other more dashing types. Ruggedly handsome boat captains. Brilliant and daring archaeologists. Impeccably dressed and groomed and impossibly handsome international playboys. Men with a bold air of adventure and mystery. Not the fellow who rented them a room and was happy to provide extra towels.

But I am a presentable man. Not too old and not bad looking. I keep myself fit. I am polite. Articulate. Observant and reflective and good for an amusing story or two. Owning a successful business may not carry the scent of danger but it does make me respectable. If they can't have one they want the other. So when the boat captains proved to be gnarled and smelly drunks; and the scientists were all academics on vacation who had only set foot in the jungle as part of a tour group; and the impeccably well-dressed and well-groomed impossibly handsome men were all looking at each other—there was me.

And when a few too many days of their escape from the lives they must return to had slipped past, these women decided I would do. And recast their leading man as a Hispanic gentleman of subdued charm and insufficient ambition. Being willing to while away his middle years in this sleepy beach town. But maybe that fault made me a bit more romantic. Even a little poetic in my nature.

And dare I say it?—more Spanish. It being no coincidence that none of these women were Spanish themselves. When you purposefully travel far away from your own kind you do not seek your own kind to sleep with. You want the Other.

And in my welcoming establishment they found him at the front desk. With a smile on his face and a good bottle at his hand.

More than a few times I sat with one of these women and wondered how she would react if she knew the truth about the man across the table. That he was once falsely convicted of sexually assaulting a child. Because even when they learned that conviction had been overturned and ten million dollars put in his pocket to make things right the stink could well remain on him. The same stink he wanted to believe he had long ago rubbed off on the world. Maybe that smell would be too much and the evening would come to an abrupt end. Or maybe instead that aroma would not be a stink at all. But an aphrodisiac perfume. That would make her want this man so much more.

And what would they think about this mild-mannered hotelkeeper if they knew he once hunted down a pedophile and persuaded that monster to commit suicide. Would they admire his resolve and his resourcefulness? Or fear what similar tricks he might be pull? This time upon them?

And how would they react if they learned he had once on the spur of the moment and at the scene of the crime joined forces with a young woman who had just taken the life of the man who raised her. A murder committed in self-defense but still a murder nonetheless. One for which she was wanted dead by evil forces that operated on both sides of the law. And that they had escaped across an international border. To hide out in the remote desert. Where they left their closest friend dead after he was murdered by narcotrafficantes. Would that send the woman smiling at me now moaning into my arms? Or running down the street calling for the police?

And perhaps most surprising of all—what would they think if they learned that this man they believed was native to this exotic locale was in fact really an American? Although I am certain some of them must have known. My accent had to give me away. It did at least once. There was a woman who said to me across the front desk that I sounded just like her brother-in-law's family. We then discussed where they were from. Which was of course none other than Doña Pero County. Which made the oddest thing happen.

For a moment I felt homesick.

I will not pretend I was not happy to satisfy the appetites of these hungry women. I did after all spend the most ardent years of my life locked away from female company and still feel to this day that I have been greatly cheated and have a vast amount of lost time to make up for. Such is the vanity of the male beast.

And I will not pretend all of the women I have conjoined with have been unmarried. That I have not cuckolded other men and even taken satisfaction in it. The ring itself may have been hidden away but the band around the finger was still clear to be seen. Either literally or metaphorically.

As was the case of one woman who stands out from among the rest. First because she did not seem the type. She did not advertise that she was alone. Her behavior was much more circumspect and demure than that exhibited by women who are off in search of a holiday fling. After watching her come and go for a few days I began to suspect she had gone traveling to recover from a divorce. Or perhaps even that she had been recently widowed.

She was also remarkable for being more attractive than the others. Not just the other women who found their way to my side. But most other women in the world. She possessed a great and delicate beauty.

I could tell that she found me not unattractive. But I was still surprised when one day she sought me out. We dined together that night. The evening was a success. Afterwards she made it clear in her ladylike and respectful manner that there would be nothing physical between us just yet. But somehow held out the promise that perhaps there would be in the future. Then we dined together a few more times and that promise seemed to become just a bit stronger on each encounter.

And finally the moment arrived when I was invited to her room.

Which was where and when the promise ended. Because alone in her room that ladylike calm broke. She became rattled. She began to babble inanities. At first I thought she was having a simple case of nerves. I tried to calm her down by being calm myself and letting her steer the conversation wherever she needed for it to go. And finally she found her nerve again and conjured up the resolve to ask for what she wanted.

Which was to be impregnated.

Once the request was made she began to babble again. About how she was a woman of independent means and there would be no obligation on my part to our shared offspring. How as awkward as this was she found the clinical alternatives too exactly that. Meaning too clinical. That she believed in good old-fashioned sexual copulation as the correct means of reproduction. That she only lacked one thing needed to become a mother. She looked very prim when she said what that was—

"Sperm."

I flinched when she spoke that word. She gasped a little at my reaction and then a stream of apologies followed. Then a brief pause.

After which she said—

"I'm ovulating."

Which is the most distressing thing anyone has ever said to me. Even in prison no words sent my direction had such a disturbing effect.

I smiled in what I hoped was a reassuring manner. While I took a moment to collect myself. And to let some of the awkwardness pass. Then said I would be happy to comply with her request if we could spend some more time together first.

Her response was immediate—

"How much more time?"

I took another moment to gather my thoughts.

"Enough time to decide if we are willing to be married."

That was when she flinched. Her right hand went for the absent ring on her left. I took leave to excuse myself.

Checkout was painful for us both. But there was no else on duty who could do it. I was short staffed that day.

And to this day I wonder if she succeeded. When she left my hotel I don't know that she went home. She may have only relocated. And with her window of opportunity rapidly closing my replacement would have to be acquired with considerably more haste than she had expended in selecting me. The deed had to be done soon. While the egg was in place. I had thrown a real wrench into her plans by not complying.

Perhaps in the days since, while going about my business here in our sleepy beach town, I have wandered past the man who was willing to do what I refused. Maybe one evening while sharing another bottle with another woman who had decided I was the one she would take into her rented bed, this other man had sat at a table nearby with another woman of his own. Perhaps instead of being a dull hotelier like myself that man was something even more boring. Maybe he was an accountant.

Chapter 129

With the birth of her son the old Esperanza returned. The caution with which she approached life vanished. La Soldadita was again on the march.

And this time it was her restaurant that got cracking. It became a sensation. Before most her business came from feeding the patrons of my hotel. But now traffic went both directions. My guests still dined with her just as frequently, if not more so. But everyone who went there waited longer for a table. Which meant her customers had more time to take in their surroundings. Some who were staying elsewhere noted the quaint hotel across the street and decided to have a closer look. I learned to recognize them when they ducked into our lobby for a glance around. And maybe to inquire if we had any rooms open. Some decided to switch to our place from the more generic one they were booked into. Or stayed with us when they returned for another holiday.

Essie's restaurant and my hotel were now featured in guidebooks. At first the higher profile concerned me. I was still paranoid that someone was after us. Even though without a body there was no murder case against Armijo. And his disappearance was retreating into the past. Eventually no one would care. And El Frente seemed unlikely to remain a threat. As I will explain shortly.

Esperanza did not share my concerns. She was certain all that was done with. She had rebuilt herself around her son and her business and was entirely focused on their future. Sometimes late at night after a few glasses of wine she still cried for Matthew. I know because occasionally I caught her at it. She made no attempt to keep from me what grieved her. I was the one and only person she could share that with. She was always glad to take my hand and tell me how much she missed him.

And maybe to shed a few tears on my obliging shoulder. The shoulder that would always be there. The one that would never refuse her.

❖   ❖   ❖

So El Frente. What became of them? Why were they no longer a threat?

Because they had become something completely different. And of course the story of that transition is also a story of El Viento. He and his organization having been practically one and the same.

His war with Juárez lasted two and a half years. Far longer than could reasonably have been predicted. He was outmanned and outgunned and outspent. His war was rashly begun. And had always been a lost cause.

And it ended in betrayal. When El Viento was assassinated by a group of his own officers. Who cut off his head and sent it to Juárez. Along with a letter offering their surrender and swearing their fealty.

In reward for which they were invited to meet with their new masters. Where they were the guests of honor at a great banquet. In the middle of which they all had their throats slit. And then their own heads were removed and sent back to what remained of El Frente. I believe if the Juárez Cartel had men who knew how to cut out a still-beating heart that would have been done instead. But such knowledge died with their Aztec forefathers.

Everyone in El Frente who might possibly remain loyal to the memory of El Viento was located and dispatched. The main body of the organization was then absorbed into the Juárez cartel and transformed into their death squad. The enforcers for an organization that was already infamous for being forceful. When Juárez really wanted to send a message it was El Frente who now delivered it.

653

You may be wondering why this means El Frente no longer posed a threat to us. Shouldn't we be more fearful than ever? Given that death was now their only line of business?

But we were no longer their concern. El Frente now lacked any institutional memory of our transgressions against their interests. And those interests had been completely transformed. Now they did nothing that Juárez did not explicitly tell them to do. And Juárez had nothing against us. Even the opposite. We had been enemies of their enemy. Which made us something like their friends.

Of course this was a friendship we were eager to keep purely theoretical.

Among those loyal officers that were killed was Benecio Vallejo. In case you don't recall he was the one Tranquilino identified in McElvy's photographs. The one who stood beside the man who was in charge that night. Vallejo rose within the ranks during the war with Juárez. By the time the end came he was speaking directly to El Viento. His assassins found Vallejo seated at his cousin's kitchen table. Having coffee and dessert at what was supposed to be his last stop before he fled North America for Brazil.

He should have known better than to say any goodbyes.

❖   ❖   ❖

Before we leave El Viento to molder headless in his grave, I will share with you one last murderous act performed during his reign of terror. Which his men executed the same day they firebombed the police station in Nuevo Casas Grandes. That night six musicians were gunned down leaving a wedding in Cananea. El Viento left them alive long enough to play this one last gig. Out of respect for the bride and groom and their families.

Then had them killed because he didn't care for a narcocorrido he believed one of them had written. Those are the drug ballads from the norteño folk music tradition that extol the exploits of narcotrafficantes. It is doubtful he had heard the song. Since it had yet to be recorded or performed publicly. But somehow a rumor of it had reached his ears. And that was enough for him to order the death of the man who wrote it. Which he did while also having just started a war. Apparently this song was that offensive to him. The strutting cock will always stop to preen.

Word has it that although the song praised El Viento it failed to do so with real conviction. It rang hollow. And some say it even included a lyric that could be interpreted as likening his name (The Wind) to passing gas. Unfortunately the song has not survived in any form I have been able to locate. So we cannot judge for ourselves if those offenses were true.

But back to the dead musicians. Their only association with the song in question was that one of them was a cousin of the man who wrote it. The one El Viento actually wanted dead. The others who died that night were only guilty of being in the same band.

Maybe the song never existed in the first place. There is no real evidence that it did. Maybe it was just a rumor started by someone with a grudge against the songwriter. Maybe another norteño who wasn't as good. And the green-eyed monster got innocent people killed.

Which would be so very typical of life in today's Mexico. Because life there has never been cheaper or stupider or meaner. Why doesn't everyone in the entire country who isn't a narcotrafficante just leave already? How could that be worse than staying?

Chapter 130

Enough of Mexico and its horrors. For the moment at least. Since it has more horrors in store for us. But for now let us return to sweet Costa Rica. And our lovely town on its beautiful beach.

One day when Francisco was still a toddler and I was still drinking my way through trysts with women who were not Esperanza, a handsome Spanish man appeared at my front desk. Having called him good-looking you might want to mock me when I say that in appearance he could have been my own brother. He was taller and better built and his features were more defined and more striking. In every aspect his appearance was superior to my own. If I had a handsomer brother he could have looked like this man.

I enjoyed our conversation while I checked him in. During which I learned that he was a physician with Doctors Without Borders. He came to San Jose for a conference and managed to tack on a few extra days so he could relax on our beach before he was sent off to address another humanitarian crisis. Such a man could be forgiven for being sanctimonious and self-important. Instead this one was modest and personable.

Fifteen minutes later I saw him again on his way out. His destination was across the street and his objective was to fill his empty stomach. Having read about this wonderful restaurant in a guidebook he had postponed eating until he could dine there. And now he was famished.

But once across the street he was unable to satisfy his hunger. Even though his timing was fortunate and the place was not too busy and he was seated almost right away. Because when he saw Esperanza his appetite vanished. He could only pick at the delicious plate set before him.

For Santiago Avilés it was love at first sight.

❖   ❖   ❖

For Esperanza it took a little longer. Three years give or take a few months. And in the end I do not believe she ever loved Santiago with the same great passion she felt for Matthew. Who remained too strong a presence in her heart for any other man to completely win her affections.

Not that my opinion on the matter should be trusted. I can't say that I trust it myself. Watching this dashing handsomer globe-trotting doctor version of myself romance the woman I loved was pure torture. At times I would have preferred to be back in prison being beaten senseless. But then a pretty woman would stop by my desk with a smile and I would purchase a nice zinfandel and for that night at least I could block out the pain.

Don't get me wrong. Santiago was a great guy. Like everyone else I was very taken with him. He was a hard man not to like. And he wasn't constantly hanging around getting in my face. His work kept him away. He was only present when the latest crisis allowed him some time off.

But he was Mexican. And by now you will not be in the least surprised to learn that was something I very much did not like. Did I ever mention this dislike to Esperanza? No. Of course not. Do you think I am that stupid?

In fact he was even born in the same town in the Yucatán where Esperanza and I were married. How crazy is that? And he had been married himself. When he was a young medical student he met a pretty administrator at the teaching hospital and somehow while interning he found time to wed. And to make his wife pregnant. She now lived in Mexico City with their daughter.

But it was not his daughter or the good doctor's ex-wife that shaped our narrative. So we can

657

forget about them. It was his mother. Who fell ill and was facing death. Before she left this world she wanted to meet the woman who had won her son's heart. And she was not well enough to travel.

So Esperanza would return to Mexico. A plan I absolutely hated.

❖   ❖   ❖

We had a pact that if either of us ever wanted a divorce the other would agree without objection. I had hoped if that ever came to pass the request would come from me. Since she wouldn't be injured by it. While I would feel my heart being torn out.

Which is precisely what happened. Making it impossible to hide my feelings. She asked before they left to go see his mother. I had to suffer both the request itself and the humiliation of involuntarily making explicit what we both knew and had never acknowledged. Because she was aware of how I felt. She did not have to be told. She was far too astute not to have realized long before we came to that moment.

The truth is that I took advantage of Esperanza when she was vulnerable. I never should have asked her to marry me. There were other ways I could have protected and provided for her and her child. The way I chose to do that was selfish. Ultimately hurtful to all three of us.

When she was gone I fantasized about running away. Walking out the door of my hotel and starting over on another beach. Maybe one in Tahiti. I was alone at the front desk imagining myself rolling around in the surf with an exotic Samoan beauty when the telephone rang. I lifted the handset to my ear with my fantasy girl's supple body still pressed against mine.

Do I have to tell you what devastating news that call brought to me? They were in Mexico. That should provide a clue. And the police were on the line. Which should be enough for you to know.

Half an hour before it happened they were at a gas station. Where they spoke with another couple. Who then followed them on their way. From across a gorge these two chance acquaintances witnessed a mountainside coming down and obliterating the road ahead of them. Into this tumult disappeared the car carrying the striking couple they had just met.

So instead of being killed by a fall from a mountain—which as you will recall is how her parents lost their lives—Esperanza died when a mountain fell on her. Crushing the car she was in.

And also like her parents there was drinking involved. Not the human kind. No one involved was drunk that I know of when the avalanche began. Instead it was the mountain itself that had too much. Heavy rains over the preceding two weeks had made the slope. Sending it sliding down, taking trees and boulders with it.

Along with one little car that was in the wrong place at the wrong time. A few minutes, maybe even a few seconds, sooner or later in making their way along that road and they would have been spared. Just as was true for her parents when she was still an infant.

Esperanza remains entombed down in that gorge. Santiago too but I don't care about him. Call me heartless but there it is. I will own it. Once or twice when my hurt was still raw and my mood especially sour I was even glad that he died. Not because I blame him for her death. I do not. But because his being dead spared me from having to commiserate with him.

As you may have guessed I blame Mexico. By now that should not surprise you. I heap the majority of my abuse into its borders. And why not? In my life Mexico has been a wellhead of wretchedness.

Part XXXVIII:
To Hell With San Diego

Chapter 131

Esperanza had been dead for three years. During which I behaved like a man hit in the head too many times. I just kept stumbling around. Maybe this newest loss was piled atop too many old ones. Whatever the cause I had lost my equilibrium.

There was a small group of Korean engineers staying at my hotel. Five or six, I can't remember the exact number. The gentleman standing before me was their leader. Maybe not in rank. There was another man who was older and probably senior in their organization. But this one clearly had the unanimous respect of his peers.

He was tall. Over six feet. Lean and catlike. Handsome but not too pretty. Nothing girlish about him. He was very much a man. And very affable. Disarmingly charismatic. You met him and you wanted to be his friend. And you felt that he wanted to be your friend too.

He complimented my hotel. With perceptive observations about the building and what we had done with it and the service we provided. I answered with practiced graciousness clothed in stock phrases. Speaking so to a man such as himself made what I said tasted bad before I got it out of my mouth. But I didn't have the presence of mind to halt my habitual response.

Next he praised our idyllic tropical location. I did better with that one. It was easy to join in when someone wanted to celebrate the incredible place where we found ourselves. I could take neither blame nor credit for God's work.

Then he posed a few personal questions. Was I from here? Had I always been in the hotel business?

That sort of thing. Perfectly innocuous and presented with a warm smile and flawless politesse. I smiled back and answered with lies polished smooth by many years of repetition. Reciting the autobiography fabricated to protect me from my past.

Now I wish I had told him the truth. Knowing what would follow makes it feel wrong to have lied. Of course to have known in advance was impossible. But still it bothers me. I can't shake it.

After we spoke the man left with one of his companions. They were off for a walk on the beach. I wished them well and forgot about them. My bruised mind was only able to handle one thing at a time. And I had other things that kept me busy at my station.

A little more than half an hour later his companion returned.

"May I help you?" I said.

A phrase my occupation has me repeat often and reflexively. Never before or since has saying it seemed more inadequate to the situation. Once this man's condition fully registered.

He was wide-eyed and overwhelmed. Staring with his mouth open. There were drops of water on one lens of his eyeglasses.

"My friend," he said.

Then he left his mouth hanging open again.

I came out from behind the desk. That simple change of dynamic can make all the difference. Now he could tell me.

His fractured English painted the scene in disjointed pieces. There was a boy and a dog. The dog was in the surf. The boy went in after the dog got into trouble. Then the man's friend went in after the boy got into trouble.

In the end only the dog survived.

My first thought was of Francisco. But then I remembered he was doing homework in my office behind the front desk. I turned that direction when his presence there occurred to me. Then turned back again when the man before me said—

"He best of us."

This from the one who did not go into the water. The one who stood on the beach and watched in horror as the man he admired most of anyone he had ever met plunged into the waves to save a boy neither of them had ever seen before. And gave his life in the attempt.

I stood where I was and let him stare at me. That seemed to be what he needed. And as he stared I observed that while evil may be a permanent presence in our existence it wears a transient aspect. While virtue appears eternal and immutable. It is easy for me to imagine those who are evil being permanently extinguished and utterly destroyed. But not the good. It seems that they should go on forever.

"The good dead," the man before me said. "Always good die."

That first phrase fit so neatly into my own thoughts I had to repeat it—

"The good dead."

"Excuse?"

I swallowed and shook my head.

"Nothing, sir. Forgive me."

I extended my hands toward him.

"What can I do to help?"

A moment later I was back behind the desk locating the other members of their group. All of whom were distraught. Several wept openly. When the time came to make the arrangements to return their deceased friend to their distant homeland they turned to me for help. And while I did what they needed done but could not do themselves, the scattered remains of my father and of Matthew and of Esperanza all crowded into my awareness.

❖　　❖　　❖

The next day I made an appointment to see my doctor. I had been having stomach pains that I pretended to ignore. But you can't really disregard what makes you grimace and double-over. The abrupt death of that remarkable Korean man made me end this little farce.

Maybe if you have a long memory you know what is coming.

At my appointment in the middle of the following week the doctor told me he would need to conduct some tests. And when the results of those tests came back in the week after that they confirmed I had the same stomach cancer that killed my uncle.

I had come back to life just to learn that I might be dying.

While the doctor stood before me with respectful patience allowing me a moment to absorb this dreadful news, my thoughts returned to that brief conversation with the Korean engineer who had watched his friend drown. And that phrase he uttered and then passed over in his attempt to say in a language which was not his own that his friend deserved reverence.

Would I soon go forward to join the good dead? Was I good enough? And what can we the living who aspire to goodness do but proceed through this life we are given and in our turn hope to join the good who have died and gone before? Since that is all, as best we can determine, this life has ever had to offer anyone.

I thanked the doctor and excused myself. There was a spot on the beach where I wanted to sit and stare and think. Before he let me go the doctor said we could discuss my treatment when I felt up to it.

"But don't take too long," he said. "Time is of the essence."

Chapter 132

Before the surgery I bought my first pair of real eyeglasses. My diagnosis had forced many things into perspective, one of which being that it was past time to admit my eyes were not what they used to be. And in San Jose I couldn't expect many visitors. So books and my computer and television would have to fill the hours. I would need my eyes to keep me distracted.

I also grew a beard. An acquaintance had mentioned that after he had similar surgery shaving had become too ambitious; but the itch of his new beard had been an irritant he didn't need while he was forced to be idle and was already so uncomfortable. So I took his advice and got the itching over with.

The day before my departure I happened to look in the bathroom mirror with my new glasses on. And saw a face that took me back to Denver. Which was the last time I had a beard and glasses.

I remembered seeing myself in the mirrored door on Sorenson's medicine cabinet. Where I found the Vicodin I would persuade him to consume. And now if this surgery before me was a failure, soon it would be my turn to die. And maybe I would overdose like him. When the pain became too much. If not by my own hand then by those who cared for me. Whether by accident or on purpose. When I was too far gone to know what was going on.

The years had written themselves all over this face that looked back at me. The last time I looked like this I was trying to look older. Now no effort was necessary. I didn't need any hair dye to get silver at my temples. There it was all by itself. And those lines on my face. Who painted those on?

❖ ❖ ❖

What had I done with the years that were gone? What was the point of this life I was living? The only reason I knew of for my continued existence was to raise the son of my deceased friends. And the entire point of their lives seemed to be having him. They struggled and they suffered and they met and they fled and they conceived and he died and she gave birth and then she died and other than what I could see of them living on in the child they left behind, they were both gone.

And I took up where they left off. Caring for the boy they made. What did that make us? Only necessary in the creation of this one boy? Ancillary to his existence? Especially myself. Since I had not even contributed DNA. I was merely support staff. None of the organic me would live on in him. Only any ideas and concepts and values I managed to impart and that fate chose he should retain.

Even though I loved Francisco deeply that did not seem like much of a life. To serve in his parents' stead. To have gone through what I went through with prison and all that just to play nursemaid. True my life was a good one by most any measure. I had money to spend and lived in a paradise and there were women who would be with me. There was abundant pleasure to be had. But such a life could only sustain a devout hedonist. Which I was not.

If this surgery did not save my life, soon I would be dead and would leave no legacy. No children and no meaningful accomplishments. Standing before that mirror disapproving of my reflection I recalled that in one of the Don Juan books I read in prison the old *brujo* said that while he did not know that it was impossible to acquire knowledge without having children, everyone he knew who had knowledge also had children. Which made me wonder if I should have obliged that nice Anglo woman and made her pregnant. So I could have knowledge and understand what the hell I had done with my life.

Which was of course absurd. There is certainly no cause and effect between procreation and wisdom. Many if not most people who have children also continue to live their lives like children themselves. Some even regress. Gaining knowledge from being a parent is far from given.

And then I vaguely recollected Don Juan saying something about the state of parenthood being a powerful connection and that other states of similarly strong connection could also lead to knowledge. Or some such blather. So all this shit about having kids was only that. Yet more shit smeared around inside my head. And I remembered some quote from Jesus to the effect that the written word was dead and the only place to find truth was out in the world around you. Not a quote you'll find in the bible I suspect. Probably one of those alternate gospels that the original editors of the New Testament decided did not fit with their vision of the Savior.

When those worthless thoughts had come and gone, I looked at that aging joker staring back at me from that unflattering mirror and asked him what he had learned since he last looked this way. What had he absorbed from his days since he walked out of prison and was set free on this world? All the crazy unexpected things that had happened and that he had done.

I was surprised by the answer. Not the least because there was one. I was bullying myself and like a bully I expected and wanted stunned silence.

But that wasn't what I got.

Here then is my treatise on my intellectual development during my life lived post-prison. My accounting of what wisdom I gained during the inexplicable second act of my inexplicable life. The answer I gave to that haunted time-bending reflection that stared back at me.

I have come to believe that human life is beyond human comprehension. That understanding how and why consciousness exists will always defeat all of our intelligence. I salute the scientists and philosophers and other seekers who labor to prove me wrong. But my wager is firmly placed on our ultimate ignorance.

And even if anyone manages to unravel the meaning of our existence I doubt that will serve to enlighten the great masses of humanity. Among which I include myself. Because apparently the rules of the universe are written in higher mathematics. That is the code existence is programmed in. And only a select few can read that code. So in darkness the rest of us will remain.

I believe our universe is complete and utter chaos. And at the same time that it ticks away like a well-oiled clock. Once I believed only one or the other could be true. Now I believe both at once and it no longer troubles me.

I believe in free will. And also I do not. Because when I examine this life of mine I am forced to admit that at every significant turn there has never been any sense of being free in the choices I have made. At each junction where my life could have diverged along different paths there was only one path I could actually advance upon. Only one that the universe would permit me to enter. The other choices may as well have not existed. They seemed put there only to confuse and demoralize.

Let me make this more concrete with an example. At the supermarket I am always free to purchase whatever toothpaste I desire. There is no sense of being confined to a single option. But when we had to abandon McElvy's cabin the only way to go was down to Mexico. Even though I knew that would be the ruin of us. Apparently we had to be ruined. Because while my head was screaming *no!* my heart said *you must.*

667

And if we had not gone to Mexico then Francisco would not exist. His entrance into this world could only have commenced in that location and at that moment. At any other place and time, the conditions would not have existed that sent the particular sperm and egg required to make him to their fateful rendezvous. As much as I despise the nation of his conception these facts must be acknowledged. To deny them is insanity.

I believe destiny is the thing you cannot escape.

And there was something else I knew as I stood before that mirror not liking what I saw. I knew that soon I would face my destiny once again. I sensed that my life was about to take its most significant turn since I found myself outside Armijo's house on the night he assaulted Esperanza. And that this change was not the surgery that would look for death lurking in my belly. Or anything directly related to my illness. But some other thing that would happen to me while I was at the hospital.

Of course I did my best to dismiss this presentiment. I like to believe that I am a rational man. But the feeling persisted. Long after I turned away from that mirror. Like a low level hum at the root of my consciousness. Returning now and then in paralyzing bursts. To have a vague sense of events to come can be both a great stress upon your sanity and enormously reassuring. The rational mind suffers with its insistence that the future cannot be known. While the soul rejoices at being told there is something more than just this string of passing moments.

Chapter 133

My roommate at the hospital was an old man who slept soundly. And not just at night. He slept straight through my first day there. Leaving me alone with my thoughts in our little room, only disturbed when the nurses came through on their rounds.

I spent that day trying not to worry. Half about the operation and half about my mental health. My little episode before the mirror as I was preparing to leave had left me feeling shaken. That night I only managed to sleep for a few hours that came well past midnight.

I had been told to expect an early summons. But the appointed hour came and went and no one appeared. When another hour had passed a nurse came and told me my procedure had been postponed for a day. There was an emergency keeping the surgeon occupied. Then she left again. In the other bed my roommate continued to slumber and snore.

I filled the morning with my books and my computer. Trying to fill my mind with thoughts other than my own mortality. And attempting to deny that part of me welcomed the idea that I might die under the knife. That when they put me under that could be the end of my consciousness. Which would solve the problem of my continued existence seeming to lack any significant purpose. If I were gone Francisco would be well provided for. Being my sole heir. And without his glum father figure hovering dolefully over him maybe his life could proceed more productively.

I detested those thoughts and the weakness that produced them. It pains me to mention them. But I want to be frank in my reckoning of those dark hours. As this long saga of ours finally winds down.

So it is the morning of the day when I should have been headed into surgery. But the knife has been halted on its way to my belly. Another day must pass before they will cut me open. To distract myself from the stress of this delay, I have filled my mind with things beyond myself and my concerns. Now I have taken a break from my reading. And have turned to look at my roommate slumbering away in the other bed. While I wish he would wake up. And talk with me or at me I don't really care. Just as long as distracting myself becomes a shared task instead of a solitary one. Even if he turned out to be someone I couldn't stand, that would be preferable to being alone.

Then a presence filled our little room. A warm glow that pushed into every corner and banished all shadows. While in my head it consumed my awareness and disallowed any other thoughts. I turned and saw this radiance came from a woman who had appeared in the doorway. Where she stood in a pillar of light. Then she moved into the room and the light moved with her. I could not see her features distinctly because of the brilliance that enveloped her.

She crossed the room and stood beside my roommate's bed. For a moment I thought she was the angel of death come to take him. But then the blinding light departed leaving only an aura around her. Allowing me to see her in all her serene loveliness. She was entirely human and completely real. With her head bowed looking down at the old man sleeping before her.

And then I knew she was the cause of my premonition. The one that stunned me at the mirror when I was preparing to leave for the hospital. And told me my life was about to change in ways I could not imagine. Now here was that change standing before me. In human and feminine form. I knew that if this woman did not agree to join her life with mine then I would spend the rest of my life after she was gone out of it wanting only to be dead.

I have never felt so much hope or so much fear.

And then this vision of a woman raised her head. To look directly at me. Our eyes met and my heart stopped. Every iota of my being resonated with her voice when she spoke—

"Excuse me. I'm sorry to bother you. But would you happen to know how long my father has been asleep?"

When I met her, Filomena Saucedo was an Assistant Professor of Spanish at the University of San Diego. The intellectual daughter of her intellectual father. She had just arrived from an academic conference in Madrid. The first family member to appear at his bedside since he took ill.

And almost as much as his illness, that was what vexed her. That her brother and sister had not come to see their father. Even though they both lacked any pressing commitments that could delay them.

Not that she told me so right away. Those issues were revealed later.

First she told me about the man in the bed next to mine. When he retired Hugo Saucedo was a professor of history at the Universitat de Barcelona. He had studied at Oxford and Columbia and had lectured at the University of Toronto and the University of California in San Diego. A long row of books in both English and Spanish bear his name upon their spines.

Filomena was proud of her father and close to him. She regretted how their lives kept them apart. And worried how he would care for himself now that age was catching up with him.

Common concerns of an adult child separated from an aging parent. She apologized for unburdening herself. I told her I didn't mind. She smiled but suspected I was only being polite. I could see that behind her smile.

"Really," I insisted. "I don't mind at all."

And then she was convinced.

Which felt like a door had opened between us.

Talking with Filomena while she waited for her father to wake up made the day I was supposed to be cut open vanish.

And broke my life in two. Cracked it right down the middle. With the force of old truths about life and love and the meaning of human existence. Our purpose in being here on this earth. How knowing and loving a woman like this one could transform a poor used-up wreck like the man who sat smiling at her from his hospital bed, worshipping her every word and movement.

What I experienced in those few hours could fill volumes.

But you've had volumes enough already.

Her wait was not completely in vain. Three or four times while we filled the hours with conversation Hugo Saucedo raised his gray head and added a few words of his own. But even his joy and relief at having his adored daughter beside him could not keep the old man awake for very long. Soon he was gently snoring again. And his inability to remain conscious seemed to me the tender hand of God working to bring Filomena and me together.

Then suddenly it was night and she was yawning. I became aware that the hospital was still and quiet. A nurse appeared at the door and reminded us that visiting hours had long been over.

Our farewell came and went in an instant. Filomena rose to her feet and smiled and thanked me for being good company. I stammered out that the pleasure was entirely mine. Then she said—

"I will see you tomorrow."

"Yes. Tomorrow."

And then she was gone. The instant after she disappeared I realized that tomorrow when she returned I might not be here in this bed. And if I was I would most likely be unconscious. Because tomorrow they would come for me early. And put me on a gurney and wheel me into surgery. Where they would slice into my stomach looking for the cancer that haunts my genetics.

One moment she sat beside me. This woman who changed everything. The next moment she was gone. And ahead of me loomed a long dark night. Which I would spend more alone than I had ever felt before. While dreading a day I wished would never come. A day in which while I was incapacitated this woman who already meant everything to me would come and go again. And maybe keep on going and be gone for good.

She had a husband and a career. Colleagues and friends. An entire life in San Diego. A place easy to live in and hard to leave. These things would conspire to keep her away from me. And her absence would create a vacuum that would suck my life empty. A black hole that would consume me piece-by-piece. First they would take some fleshy bits out of my belly. Then next in small installments my heart and soul would soon follow.

I mentioned earlier that upon meeting her I had never felt so much hope or so much fear. Well now my hope had all gone with her out that door. And down those corridors and into the elevator and out onto the street. And I was left all alone with just the fear.

While Hugo snored beside me.

Chapter 134

I did not sleep until just before dawn. And only briefly. Then awoke to find my roommate looking at me in a way he had not before. With a new expression on his old face. One of cold and considered assessment. I knew what was going on inside that learned head. A stern evaluation of this interloper fate had placed beside him.

"You know she's a married woman," Hugo said to me.

I assured him that I did. I could have told him that was something I knew in a way I had never known anything before. But I doubt he would have wanted to hear such talk.

I also could have told him that his daughter was not happy in her marriage. Which she had not said directly but had been abundantly clear. Perhaps most significantly they had no children. Because her husband had decided he did not want them. But chances are her father already knew those things.

After I answered Hugo scrutinized me for another moment. Then nodded once and turned away. We did not speak to each other again that morning. If there had been more time perhaps we would have. Maybe we would have opened our hearts on this subject of unexpected mutual interest.

But a few seconds later they came for me. Two nurses and behind them an orderly pushing a gurney. I remember being wheeled down the corridor and into an elevator. Then my memory goes blank. Next I remember the anesthesiologist asking me to count backwards. Apparently during the part I can't recall they rolled me into an operating room and thrust a needle into my vein and began adding drugs to my blood.

And then I woke up back in my room. After I remembered where I was and understood that I felt almost destroyed because they had knocked me out and cut me open I determined that something was different. That something had changed from that morning when I was last here in this same spot. After much squinting and blinking to clear my reluctant eyes I determined it was the lack of light in the room. And especially over at the window. While I was under, the day had come and gone. Now it was night. And judging by the quiet all around me it was late.

Which meant Filomena had come and gone also. And then I felt sick fearing she would not return. Maybe that prone form in the next bed was not even her father. Maybe Hugo had been discharged or relocated and some other man was sleeping there.

But his light snore had already become familiar.

There was an empty chair placed between my bed and his. A chair that belonged over on the far side of Hugo's bed. Yesterday Filomena had moved it so we could talk more readily. Without calling across the room to each other. And then the orderly had moved it back in the morning. To clear a path for the gurney that rolled me away. Now here the chair was back again. So while I was drugged and unconscious someone had replaced it there. And who could have done that but her?

I wondered if the seat was still warm. I told myself maybe she was just down the hall stretching her legs. Or went off to find something to eat or drink. Even though I knew it was too late for that and she was back at her hotel.

And then I felt his eyes on me. And looked over to see Hugo peering intently through the dark. We stared at each other for a moment before he said—

"What have you done to my daughter?"

His hand came up and a crooked old finger pointed at the chair positioned between us.

"She wouldn't leave your side," Hugo said.

His hand went back down again.

"Next to you I was nothing."

And with those words came rushing back all that intoxicating hope.

❖   ❖   ❖

But my hope was soon to be crushed. In the morning when Filomena returned everything was different. Now her unaccountable behavior had to be atoned for. When she was worried about me instead of worried about her father. A sin that hung his bad health like a funeral wreath around her neck. She was a married woman visiting her ailing father. And I was a stranger in the next bed. What had she been thinking?

I could see all that on her face. A woman by any rational standard that I barely knew. But I was certain of what was going on inside of her.

All I could do was wait and watch for my chance. Which I saw coming as noon approached and Hugo grew weary. When he complained of a headache, Filomena found a nurse who gave him something for his discomfort. And then he was asleep. And I offered thanks up to God.

Then not wanting to disturb the old man I whispered to Filomena—

"How long will you be in San Jose?"

She gave me a look like that was half delight and half shame. Before she could speak her phone rang. She let it ring again before she took the call. Which of course was from her husband. Who else could disturb us more thoroughly at that moment?

Meanwhile out on the street a taxi had arrived. From which stepped a man and a woman who had encountered each other unexpectedly at the airport. Forcing them to share this ride here together. To do otherwise would have been too foolish even for them.

While Filomena endured her husband droning on predictably about himself and his work, the two from the airport made their way to the elevators and rode up to our floor. Where they were disgorged and

676

came chattering along the corridors both speaking at once and each ignoring what the other said. They swept noisily into the room just as their sister finished her call.

Joachim and Dorotea immediately commenced a clownish competition to prove who was more concerned about their father. Filomena and I were never alone again during my stay in the hospital. The next day she left her father in the clutches of her siblings and flew back to San Diego. I did not blame her. There was nothing she could do to improve the situation.

❖   ❖   ❖

Back to our little beach town. Where I recuperated impatiently. When I had done enough of that I returned to San Jose. But not to the hospital. This time I went to the airport and caught a flight to San Diego. Where I rented a car and checked into a hotel and showered to freshen up. Then drove to the university and located the Spanish department. Where I waited in a hallway outside a closed door. Having arrived ten minutes early for her posted hours of availability.

And where I had the most irritating experience of my life. Because soon I was not alone. An ugly shambling Anglo boy in torn dirty clothing with his hair cut so it hung in his pimpled face came and stood on the other side of her office door. I tried to convince myself that he had more right to be here than I did. Being an actual student seeing his professor during her office hours. But having come all this way to profess myself, the last thing I wanted was to compete with this disheveled mess for my beloved's attention. Even if all he wanted was to turn in his homework. If I had to be interrupted did the one doing the interrupting have to look so utterly disgusting?

And why at this of all times did I have to feel so judgmental? That was not a good frame of mind for this endeavor. Which should be approached with an open heart full of good will. Not rankled by this atrocity slouching against the wall. On which he would probably leave stains.

Since this attitude could prove to become a problem I resolved to change it. And admonished myself not to be superficial in my assessments. Repeating internally the old saw that you can't judge a book by its cover. Perhaps this young man was brilliant. The very best of her students.

At that moment he proceeded to pick his nose.

And in the next moment there she was. Turning a corner down the hall on the far side of the lounging horror. I did not care anymore about that vile thing who was still digging away at his boogers. Although I did note his lack of embarrassment at being caught in the act when she appeared beside him. And registered the look of disgust that flashed across her face.

Along with conventional decorum the nose-picker also proved oblivious to the electricity that crackled between me and his professor. He still did not even seem aware of my presence. Or maybe it never occurred to him that this old guy was here to see an instructor let alone the same one as him. Or maybe he felt that by ignoring me he could stake first claim to her time. Which he did. And to which she and I both acquiesced. Wanting very much to be rid of him.

I listened to their voices murmuring through the door. And for an instant I fought an urge to leave. To just get out of there and let her live this life she had made. What right did I have to intrude?

But like all instants that one passed. And my second thoughts went with it. Leaving me profoundly resolved to achieve the goal that brought me there.

When her office door reopened the nose-picker finally looked at me. At least I assume that was what he did behind that veil of greasy hair when he turned toward me. Maybe on his face was written petty spiteful triumph at having cut me out to get the first word with Filomena. Who knows and who cares? Whatever he thought or felt, his time there was done and his odiousness was soon gone. Which is all that matters.

She watched him move away down the hall. As if a certain distance between us and the abhorrent one had to be established before she could admit I was standing there. Waiting for myself and my purpose to be acknowledged.

And then her full attention slammed against me. In a look that brought all my delirium-inducing hope crashing back again. And then she turned that look away and I followed her inside.

Where she gently pushed the door closed behind us.

Chapter 135

Filomena must have needed to do a very great amount of thinking. Because a considerable amount of time passed in which she could ponder what I asked of her and what I offered. Days and weeks and months kept going by and I did not hear from her. The phone never brought her voice to my ear. No messages with her name attached ever appeared in my email inbox. No envelopes bearing her handwriting ever arrived in the day's post.

So she never said yes and she never said no. Instead she said nothing at all.

More than once I checked on her. Verified that she was still employed by the university. That she was still teaching classes and still seeing students. I even almost hired a detective to make sure she was all right. That she hadn't suffered a thump on the head and gotten amnesia and forgotten I existed.

This was the lowest point in my life. Even lower than after Esperanza died. In part because it was the next major misfortune. The blow that followed the one that almost destroyed me. And also because of a disturbing similarity. Now two women that I loved had been taken from me without my ever having had either one of them. Leaving my male vanity pretty much obliterated. Apparently I could not get the girl.

But what gave this one an extra jolt was the pointlessness. It seemed so unnecessarily cruel to have even met Filomena in the first place. The chain of events that had to happen, how the stars had to align—and then nothing? Did Fate have to grin and twist its knife?

The party of Korean engineers had to stay at my hotel. There were many others they could have chosen. And they had to stay for the correct period of time. So that the remarkable one among them could drown as he did. In a most tragic manner. Making the end of his life ricochet into the middle of mine. So that I was inspired to call my doctor when I did. At the right time in order to obtain the correct appointment.

If I had gone to see the doctor earlier or later, and then found the surgeon he recommended available in another week or another month, or even just a few days off in either direction, my roommate at the hospital would not have been Hugo Saucedo. Who had to wind his way along his own path to arrive in the bed beside mine when he did. And if the surgeon had not then had an emergency to deal with that led to my procedure being postponed for a day, and Filomena had not been delayed in seeing her father by being in Madrid at that conference, and Hugo had not been unable to wake up long enough to claim his daughter's attention, then she and I would not have found ourselves tossed together for an entire day with nothing to do but talk.

All of this was required to bring us together. And mountains more that I am not aware of and cannot recount. Innumerable lives had to pass exactly as they did for their aftershocks and reverberations to toss against each other. The stars and planets all had to line up just so.

And for what? And after all that she was gone.

Forcing me to conclude that God can be one mean bastard.

If not for Francisco I might have gone to the beach and walked into the surf and let the ocean take my life away. At my worst moments I went there and contemplated the appeal of those actions. To have the waters wash me clean of my pain. Which seemed endless. And death the only escape.

Knowing that I had not made the kind of impression on others that would have me mourned like the Korean engineer made it all that much harder to resist. Who would grieve for me?

Only my son. Who wasn't really mine.

Every day I thank God for that boy.

❖ ❖ ❖

This went on for so long I came to expect that was how the rest of my life would pass. A long dark tunnel to nowhere. Mornings were the worst. On many of them I wanted to climb up to the roof of my hotel and jump.

Then a morning came that was even more trying than all the others. I awoke with an enormous weight on my chest. If it had been a real weight it would have crushed me. And that would have been welcome. But instead it was just the worthless spiritual kind. That sat there pressurizing my misery, making it more focused and intense. And therefore even more debilitating.

I spent an hour struggling against it before I could climb out of bed. Coffee still retained some of its magical power to lift my mood. So after consuming a sizable quantity I could passably imitate a functioning human being. Which got me through the morning and into the afternoon.

When I found myself in my office staring at nothing. There was work to do spread out on my desk and loaded up on my computer. But the letters and numbers all swam together and became nonsense. The only thing I could see clearly was that if this kept on much longer my business would stop limping along under my inattentive stewardship and start to crumble. And eventually would come the fall. Instead of leaving this hotel to Francisco I would have to sell it. Maybe it was time to hire someone to replace me. Who could clean up this mess before I made it any worse.

Then a head and shoulders appeared thrust through the doorway. A face I knew was speaking at me. Who was this man? Right. One of the front desk clerks. The one who was on duty. What was he saying? I hadn't caught any of it. I asked him to say it again. His wife had gone into labor a month early. He was married? And they were expecting? Yes. I knew these things. Here in this world made of tissue and gauze all ready to be torn into shreds.

Before he could ask I put on a smile that I hoped was avuncular. I raised a hand and waved it toward the main entrance. Slogging through the motions of the compassionate employer. I had a reputation to maintain.

Then you better get out of here, I said. We'll see you in two weeks.

What? Yes. You'll get paid. I promise.

He thanked me and was gone. I sat there staring at the empty doorway. The words I had just spoken seemed to echo at a great distance. I knew there was something I was supposed to do next. After telling what's-his-name he could leave. Right. I had to find someone to take the rest of his shift.

Or finish it myself.

Well I wasn't getting anything done here.

I put my computer to sleep and wished I could join it. Then struggled to my feet and shuffled out to the front desk. Where I looked at the bookings and tried to form a mental record of who might soon arrive wanting their lodgings. But none of it would stick. When I looked away from the computer screen my mind went blank. I sighed and looked back at the screen again. And lost everything when I looked away. This went on for ten or fifteen minutes. Which felt like several hours.

Then that weight returned to my chest. The one that had pinned me to my bed when I woke up. Which was puzzling since it crushed my chest while I stood upright. Apparently this weight had its own frame of reference within which gravity behaved accordingly.

Then a warm glow poured through the front door. Or maybe I should say a different warm glow. Since the afternoon sun was already turning the lobby golden. Now there was something otherworldly about

683

the beautiful light. I became slack-jawed behind the desk staring at it.

I should have known that glow. I had seen it before. When it proceeded her into my hospital room. Just before she crossed that room within a pillar of it. Now she did the same crossing my lobby.

I managed to close my mouth when she stood across the desk from me. A dry ache went from my tongue down my throat into my belly. I swallowed and the ache became worse. How would I speak to her?

I couldn't. She would have to speak first.

I might never be able to speak again.

She spoke—

"Am I too late?"

All I could do was weep.

❖   ❖   ❖

I managed to book our guest into a room. Not an easy task when you keep tearing up. And of course I gave her the very best room we had available. Then explained my present situation. That I was on duty because the clerk who began this shift was now off becoming a father. And that while she was upstairs settling in I would try to find someone who could replace me.

But I didn't have any luck with that. None of my other clerks were available. So instead Filomena joined me behind the desk. And we spent the rest of the afternoon talking. Not about anything too significant. We would save that for later. Instead we kept it light. She told me about an elderly woman she met on her flight. A retired doctor who had once worked in the Amazon. I told her about some of our more colorful lodgers.

When about two centuries had passed, the night clerk finally arrived. Actually she came in about fifteen minutes early. As was and still is her usual habit. A good woman we're lucky to have.

Filomena and I went across the street for dinner. While we were waiting to be seated I told her this restaurant that had become and remained such a success was founded by the deceased mother of the boy that I was raising as my son. Although I was not his father.

And after we were seated I told her the rest of it. All jammed together. And seemingly in one breath. As it began to pour out I admired her lovely face as she worked to absorb what I was throwing at her and decided if she was going to take a chance on me. She had a right to know what she was getting into. If she was going to decide coming here was a mistake best get that over and done with. While the words came flowing out I waved goodbye to my other options. Telling her gradually over time. Getting my hooks into her before she knew of my questionable past. Not telling her anything. Just being cagey whenever she probed at my history. Or cooking up a fake one that was nice and safe and nonthreatening.

But here it was already too late. The cat was being tossed from the bag.

I kept talking all through dinner and through coffee and dessert and while we strolled down the street and out onto the sand. We were standing at the edge of a gentle surf looking out over the water as the sun set behind a bank of orange and pink clouds draped across the horizon when my account of myself arrived at the present moment.

For a few moments after that we were both silent. Then Filomena sighed and took my hand. The electricity from her touch still runs through me. I had to look down and confirm that her fingers were indeed woven into mine. My eyes wanted their own proof.

And my ears wanted to hear some reaction.

"What I just told you can't be welcome news."

"I wouldn't say that. Not that I know what to say."

"So you aren't ready to get back on a plane?"

She laughed and shook her head.

"No. Not at all."

She turned to me.

"What do you think of that?"

"I think that's wonderful."

She smiled and raised her chin. Then she laughed again.

"I came all this way worried that you might be—"

She stopped and frowned.

"What?" I said.

"A boring hotelier."

I laughed and she joined me.

And then we resumed strolling along the sand while she told me how her marriage had ended.

Don't ask what we did with the rest of our night. I do not kiss and tell. All I'll say is that we didn't wait until we got back to the hotel. And when we did we resumed what we had begun on the beach.

The next morning we enjoyed a leisurely breakfast followed by a long walk and then a swim. The day was glorious and the woman I loved was truly the crown of all creation.

Halfway through lunch she beamed at me and said—

"To hell with San Diego. Who needs it."

"You could live like this? Nothing much ever happens here."

"Perfect. I don't like it when things happen."

"Then you will be very happy."

She threw her head back and laughed like a madwoman.

Epilogue

If at this moment I stood before you I would bow. And perhaps that small gesture would end with another. This second being a rolling flourish of my extended hand. As if in the midst of these final moments spent together I had been transformed into a flamenco dancer. Although I have never learned the steps. And as I did these things I would tell myself this is how they must be done. At such a moment. In such a situation. Executed with a precise sense of style. Accompanied by a delicate and delicious hint of irony. The slightest trace implying other shades and deeper meanings. All to be derived from our briefest words and smallest actions. That to my mind is the essence of the classic Spanish manner. Not so heavy handed as things are done by those vulgar Mexicans. With a big grin showing their bean-eating teeth.

Your humble narrator Andreas Delmorales bids you a most fond farewell. If to do so now seems premature, given that many more words follow below, please accept that I must before I share what those words say. Let me not depart without offering my goodbyes. Even if there is more to be said before we finally part.

And now I will attempt to belatedly bring my belabored narrative to its end. If the beast breathed any longer I would have to put a bullet in its head. Whether it is finished or not I am done with it. For reasons which will soon become obvious. Please forgive any loose ends left behind that nag at you. Further proof that my meager skills have been inadequate to the task.

I arrived at my decision to force this to a conclusion while at the beach. Lounging in a folding chair with Filomena and Hugo beside me. They were discussing what they would make for dinner when we could drag Francisco out of the water. The old man has his appetite back and is making the most of it. We feast day and night. I will grow fat in his good company.

Having him here has been a godsend. Filomena hasn't seen this much of her father since she was a child. I have found his counsel to be indispensable. But Francisco prizes his presence more than anyone. The boy finally has a grandfather. And what an *abuelo* the old man makes. Attentive and wise and frequently hilarious. Sometimes when the two of them are giggling together Hugo seems like a boy again himself.

Right now Francisco is running through the surf directly in front of us. And as always with the neighbor's dog. But now three other boys run beside him. This is a new development. His nature has before kept him mostly solitary. Closer to the animals than other children. But in the last few weeks he has become a leader among his peers. An outgoing side of him has emerged.

He looks and sounds so much like his father. And thinks and acts so much like his mother. The past is alive in him. Which he seems to be aware of. He is comfortable with what sets him apart. And others admire him for it. When he is older I hope this chronicle of mine can help him to understand where he comes from. All the forces that were at work when he was pushed into this world. And continued to shape him after.

Today Francisco is eager to meet an outsized character from my long-ago past. Someone I told him about only recently. An old friend who will arrive here tomorrow to be my best man.

The internationally renowned *santero* Tranquilino Rojas.

Dear God how I look forward to seeing good old Tranq.

While he is here I will ask my friend to make me a carving. The subject I have in mind is Saint Jude. The patron of desperate cases and lost causes.

Not that my situation is entirely desperate or hopelessly lost. But I will take all the help I can get.

In five weeks I will return to the doctor. A specialist at the hospital in San Jose. For my one year post-operative evaluation. The doctor will perform tests that will tell us the probability of my survival. If the results come back clean the cancer is most likely gone for good. The chance of the disease proving fatal in the next three years is only seven percent and entirely negligible beyond that time span. But if the results are not in my favor there is an eighty-four percent probability that the cancer will kill me in the same next three years.

My amazing woman still wants to marry me. Even though I might die on her. She wants the marriage for her own sake. But also for the sake of our child. Who could conceivably be born after I am dead. If the cancer comes roaring back as it sometimes is known to do.

And if that happens like Matthew with Francisco I will leave behind another child who never knew her biological father. Unlike Francisco she may never know any father at all. Filomena says after me she is done with marriage and with men. That she will become a brittle haughty widow who scares people away from staying at our hotel. I tell her that is bad business. Think of the children. And we both manage to laugh.

We will be married right here on the beach. Then my bride and I will depart for a month-long honeymoon to Spain and France and Italy. Places she has already been but I have visited only in my dreams.

We don't know for sure yet that the baby is a girl. But in our hearts we are both already certain. Between the wedding and the honeymoon will come an ultrasound that may let us know. So perhaps I will have that to take with me. Both to Europe and my grave. The gender of my only child.

And when she is old enough like Francisco my daughter will have this to read. If she wants to know what kind of man her father was. Assuming we are right and she is a she. (Please forgive me my son if we were wrong.)

I may not be good. I have tried but maybe I failed. Maybe I crossed a line back in Denver. Or somewhere else without noticing.

But I am happy. And a happy man wants to live.

So whether or not this disease kills me as promised above I am done with providing this account of my life. You will not hear from me again. A few more words and I will be gone.

For if I am to die soon what is the point of documenting the last few steps in the long march? Just to leave you hanging at the end when I become too feeble to record what goes on. And why waste my final days chronicling what happens when I could cram my final hours full of actual life?

And if I am allowed to live then I am determined to avoid further drama. There will be no more child molesters or corrupt sheriffs or prison sentences or drug cartels or stomach cancer and especially no more deaths of those I love in remote locations. I am resolved that my new life will be one of peace and harmony and the most complete domestic bliss.

And what kind of ending does that make?

A boring one. That's what kind.

So I ask of you one last favor. A final request before we part company. Indulge me in how I want this narrative to end. If the ending were up to me. If I could write my future as well as my past.

When you are done reading this please imagine I defeat this stupid disease. And my remaining days prove both numerous and serene. Give me that new life which is dull and uneventful.

But please pass by that tedium I would personally find so welcome. You don't need to labor through that. Jump over my prolonged bliss straight to the end. Which I ask that you make gentle and humane. When you have me step from this world into the next please put a smile on my gray-bearded face. Placed there in my final moments by the presence of those I love. Have my family and my friends all around me. The good ones who will remain behind among the living.

Then go ahead and push me forward. A little shove is all it takes.

You will be God in that instant.

And as God you can forgive. I beg that as God you will wash me of my sins. Whatever sins that could keep me from where I hope to spend eternity.

Cleanse my soul so that I may join the good dead.

www.ingramcontent.com/pod-product-compliance
Lightning Source LLC
Chambersburg PA
CBHW071328020726
47502CB00001B/10